FIRE BECOMES HER

ROSIEE THOR

SCHOLASTIC

Published in the UK by Scholastic, 2022
Euston House, 24 Eversholt Street, London, NW1 1DB
Scholastic Ireland, 89E Lagan Road, Dublin Industrial Estate,
Glasnevin, Dublin, D11 HP5F

SCHOLASTIC and associated logos are trademarks and/or
registered trademarks of Scholastic Inc.

First published in the US by Scholastic Inc, 2022

Text © Rosiee Thor, 2022
Jacket art © 2022 by Jacey
Jacket design by Yaffa Jaskoll

The right of Rosiee Thor to be identified as the author of this work
has been asserted by her under the Copyright, Designs and Patents Act 1988.

ISBN 978 0702 31607 4

A CIP catalogue record for this book is available from the British Library.

Printed by CPI Group (UK) Ltd, Croydon, CR0 4YY
Paper made from wood grown in sustainable forests and other controlled sources.

1 3 5 7 9 10 8 6 4 2

Book design by Yaffa Jaskoll

www.scholastic.co.uk

FOR CLAIRE:

YOU ARE MY MAGIC.

CHAPTER ONE

It shouldn't be legal to feel like this.

Strictly speaking, it wasn't, but the law couldn't touch Ingrid Ellis as long as Linden Holt did. There on the dimly lit dance floor, holding her glass in one hand and Linden's shoulder in the other, she was safe. She could drown herself in flicker, knowing the Holt name would serve as an adequate shield if the night turned.

Ingrid touched the crystal flute to her lips. Magic tasted like sour pears and possibility; power surged against her skin, speckling her tongue with electric bite. It spread down her arms, warming her fingers and toes, until she felt as though she could burn the whole speakeasy down with a single flourish.

Here, magic was alive in every corner. Speckles of flicker burst in bronze and gold from dancers' toes as they triple-stepped across the floor. A man at the bar exhaled sparklets. By the door, a smiling woman made tiaras of illusive silver for her friends before they rushed toward the dance floor, a medley of giggles and nerves.

Ingrid curled against Linden's practiced frame, letting him lead her through the lazy steps of a tired Balboa. She couldn't even hear the sharp brass of the band over the roar of magic, her toes brushing the ground like guesswork.

1

"Ingrid, are you awake?"

Ingrid lifted heavy lashes and a heavier head. The band had transitioned to a melancholy blues tune, the lagging rhythm shaking sprinkles of silvery magic from her fingertips with each note of the wavering bass.

At well past midnight, this song was more her speed, and she longed to press her face into the curve of Linden's neck, bury herself in his closeness until the sun rose over Candesce's city skyline. Instead, Ingrid pushed herself upright, taking command of her limbs once more as Linden led her off the dance floor. Curious eyes followed them.

She and Linden were an unusual sight in this part of town. Linden reeked of money, with his three-piece suit, polished wingtips, and slicked-back hair the color of a worn gold coin. Besides, he'd drunk not a drop of flicker all night. To a casual eye, he might look like an outright prohibitionist, but if any of their observers watched more closely, they'd see a vial engraved with a bold letter *H* peeking out from his pocket. He didn't need their bootleg flicker when he had a pocketful of flare.

Ingrid set her glass down on one of the wooden tables lining the dance floor and slid into a high-backed chair, taking care to cross her legs and lean her chin on her hand, ever so carefully casual. Had they been at Ainsley Academy, she never would have let herself go like this. There, every word and every whisper mattered. But here, no one knew her. It didn't matter what they saw, because it wouldn't matter what they'd say.

"What is the point of having the most talented dance partner in the room if she's only going to fall asleep on me?" Linden asked with an exaggerated pout.

"When everyone knows you're good, there's no need to prove it."

2

Linden threaded his fingers through the wooden dowels of the chair back, brushing fingertips against the sequins of her blue-green dress, and leaned forward until they were only inches apart. "But how will everyone know I've got the best girl?" He said it like it mattered, like he meant it.

Ingrid suppressed a shiver, unfurling a smile on her lips instead. "As long as *you* know it."

"Ingrid Ellis, I'll never forget as long as I live."

He pressed a kiss to her temple, and magic thundered to the place where skin met skin. Her cheeks warmed, a combination of his touch and the last sparks of flicker rushing through her, and then her stomach cinched. It was a familiar sensation, subtle at first, a gentle rocking of her insides like she was seasick. The unsettling nausea rose inside her like a wave each time he looked at her, each time he touched her, knowing it was temporary and dreading the day it had to end.

She'd wanted Linden Holt for years—his status, his money, his magic. She'd played him like the band played swing: too fast and hard for him to keep up. It was supposed to be about power, about her rising to the top no matter the cost. It was never supposed to be about love.

But that's what this was—love. Nothing else could poison her from the inside out. Nothing else, except maybe a glassful of magic.

Linden brushed back her hair, fingers tangling with her cropped chestnut waves, and Ingrid's stomach lurched again. When he'd invited her out that night, she'd known it for what it was: a last hurrah. She'd known it the moment she saw his signature calling card outside her dormitory—a plain rock, the size of a coin, wedged in the gap between door and floor with eight lines drawn in white chalk to denote their meeting time. It was quiet and unobtrusive, just like their love. Almost invisible. All through their school days, that little rock had brought her hope. Now she felt as though it was lodged in her throat, waiting for her to swallow and choke.

"I need another drink," she said. It was easier than the truth: *I need another day*. But she'd not get the latter, so the former would have to do.

Injecting her steps with her very best flounce, Ingrid let the sharp sequins of her dress scrape against her knees as she walked away. The bar was as good a place as any to let herself breathe.

"Give me enough to drown in." Ingrid shoved her empty glass toward the flicker chemist, a girl about her age with sharp eyes and sly curls peeking out from her cap. The flicker was particularly good that night—an ambitious brew that cut across the tongue at first but mellowed to a slow simmer in her stomach. It wasn't quite flare, but the speakeasy's bootleg was as fair a substitute as Ingrid had ever tasted.

"Careful," the girl said, snatching Ingrid's glass. "With the look on your face, people might take you at your word."

Ingrid massaged her cheeks, sliding onto an oak stool. "That bad?"

"I've seen your type before. Out on a Sunday night, dressed like a magazine ad, with your very own Rich Richerson footing the bill."

"I'm not a type," Ingrid snapped.

The girl shrugged. "Well, I've seen *you* before."

An uneasy silence built a wall between them. Ingrid's eyes snagged on the way the girl smiled with her whole jaw. She had a round face dusted with freckles and a bit of an underbite, but no trace of malice in her expression. She hadn't meant it as a threat, Ingrid felt sure of it.

"Louise," the girl said.

4

"What?"

"My name. Louise."

Ingrid scoffed. "I didn't ask."

The girl—Louise—shook her head. "And you say you're not a type."

Ingrid narrowed her eyes. When she'd first come to Ainsley Academy, vacating her life of poverty for a life of scholarly pursuits, Ingrid realized the quickest way to be treated as an equal was to mimic the vague dismissal her peers showed those they considered beneath them. But when had she started actually believing people like Louise were *beneath her*? Louise was no one to her, nothing. But still, Ingrid teetered on the edge of wanting to be better and needing Louise to know she wasn't.

I am just like you, she wanted to say without saying it. *I won't be for long.*

To Candesce's elite, names were power, names were history, names were currency. It was why she wanted to replace Ellis with Holt so badly. But here in this place, where snitches wore the same disguise as them all, names were dangerous. This girl had given Ingrid hers for no other reason than to prove a point. Ingrid could respect that enough to do the same.

"Ingrid," she said, surprised to find a note of regret in her own voice. "My name is Ingrid."

But Louise only gave her a quick nod before busying herself with Ingrid's drink. She poured pink lemonade into a short, wide glass and squeezed three drops of flicker from a pipette, silver tears sliding through the air until they crashed onto the surface. For a moment, Ingrid was filled with the absurd urge to reach across the bar and take the pipette and squeeze drops of flicker directly onto her tongue. But power was power, and flicker was not flare. She

5

could drink every drop of flicker in this club, but it would never be the same as the raw, rushing wildfire of real magic. Flicker was no more than a weak imitation.

Just like her.

"You're good at that," Ingrid said, the compliment slipping through a cage of teeth.

"I know." Louise didn't look up from her work.

"Have you always been interested in flicker?" Ingrid asked as she watched Louise slice a lemon and dip it in sugar. Flicker chemistry was an art, one Ingrid had little chance to learn about in her proudly proper school. From the scattered experience she had in flicker clubs like this, she understood each chemist had their own recipe, a magic all its own.

"I'm not interested in flicker," Louise said, sliding the lemon onto the rim of the glass. "Like everyone in here, I'm interested in flare, just can't afford it."

Ingrid glanced over her shoulder at Linden, his vial of flare tucked safely in his pocket. It was a marvel he didn't think to hide it better. Even in an establishment operating outside the law, Linden still felt protected by it. Any one of the patrons might spy his vial of liquid fire and think to steal it. They had him outnumbered, certainly. It wouldn't even occur to him to consider such things, so she'd have to do it for him.

"That boy . . ." Louise said, staring over Ingrid's shoulder. "You want me to scorch him?"

"No, no." Ingrid waved her away. "He's with me—though likely not for much longer."

Louise placed the glass in front of Ingrid, rosy delight with a silver magic finish on the surface. "That why he's so jumpy? Knows you're about to chuck him? He looks like he might bolt."

"He doesn't need to bolt. Everything always goes his way."

Louise snorted. "But not yours?"

Ingrid shot her a look. "That's different." *I'm different.*

"Sounds like you're a perfect match."

"You're the only one who thinks so." A harsh laugh escaped Ingrid's chest, the painful truth ricocheting against her lungs. *You're the only one who knows.*

Secrecy was how they made it work. It was how she justified a relationship that couldn't last beyond their school days. They loved only in the dark, behind closed doors, between towering bookshelves, in shadowy corners of illicit flicker clubs. They loved with an unspoken promise that no one else could know, no one else would understand.

Linden Holt was the kind of boy who'd grow up to be president, and Ingrid Ellis was the kind of girl who'd grow up to be trouble. It was a headline waiting to ruin him.

But it was a headline that could reinvent her. Linden's father was an eight-term senator with the largest parcel of magic-rich land in Alorden, the westernmost district of Candesce. Senator Holt practically had a lock on the upcoming presidential election, with President Morris stepping down. Ingrid was no one; she had nothing—nothing except this. Sometimes when she closed her eyes, she let herself imagine a life beside Linden—the flashing cameras, the fashionable clothes, the unlimited access to flare. But only in the moments between wake and sleep did Ingrid ever let herself feel so in control, so powerful against those who would never see her that way.

"Last day of school tomorrow," Ingrid said by way of explanation. "Got to make this night count."

"There will be other nights." Louise cocked her head, fixing Ingrid with dark eyes like polished stones. For a moment, the space between them sharpened. "You dance like you might catch fire if you stop." Her words settled over Ingrid like a new string of pearls around her neck.

"Best not to stop, then." Ingrid raised her glass as if to toast her misery and let the magic run down her throat.

When she rejoined Linden near the dance floor, Ingrid was roaring with magic. Louise's flicker wasn't flare, but it was surprisingly good quality. Silver shimmers curled away from her fingertips in wisps and spirals. One of the tendrils of magic caught on a loosely hung leaflet sporting a drawing of a flame and the phrase *Everybody burns.* What was once the mantra of a long-dead revolution was now a common saying in speakeasies like this, along with *Share the flare*, *All's flare in love and war*, and *Flicker? I hardly know her!* There in the speakeasy with flicker rushing through her, Ingrid felt like it was a little true. They could all burn, regardless of class, regardless of birth. Magic didn't discriminate.

Since coming to the capital, she'd seen all the things flare could be. Without the threat of poverty, magic could be so much more than utility. It could be art, it could be skill, it could be danger. She'd seen the way her classmates used it to light up their complexions with an ethereal glow, and the way Flare Force officers used it to burn their enemies from the inside out.

When Ingrid was small, flare seemed so much larger. In the corners of the world where a vial of flare was a small miracle, it was unthinkable to waste it on such frivolities. To her, flare was life. It was the warmth of the radiator, the light in their lamps. In the one-room house where she'd grown up, it was the difference between starving or freezing, living or dying. To put her lips to flare when it could be fuel, when it could be light—once, it would have been unthinkable.

Now it was all she could think about, how it would feel to have so much she didn't have to choose between light and warmth. To have so much, she could drink a whole glassful and still have more. Without the weight of worry on her shoulders, her only fear would be what might happen if she drank too much, the embers beneath her skin igniting to end in naught but ash.

Magic was more than a little like love—too much of it, and she'd burn right up.

With untrained focus, she sent a flurry of silver into the air, flicker bursting from her hands like confetti. The shimmers slowed and died, vanishing as they languished in midair.

A sigh rippled through her. "I wish they didn't disappear," she whispered.

"Why's that?" Linden asked. "We can always make more." He sent his own magic after hers, flare cutting through the hazy air in swooping golden spirals. The threads of magic danced double time before the power burned out, leaving an imprint on her vision like a sunspot.

"*You* can make more." Ingrid stared at her fingertips, feeling the power ebb and die against her skin. Linden would never run out of flare. Those at the top had enough to fill a reservoir, and the rest of them had to make do with the little they could earn in an honest day's work. Or not so honest, depending on how refined they liked their magic. Flicker would do in a pinch. The illicit, synthetic magic never made more than a temporary impression on the world. It couldn't light up a city or power a town car, but it could still burn inside her, a short fuse waiting to diminish or detonate.

Ingrid let her arm fall, the absence of magic in her bones crackling through her like dying embers.

9

Linden caught her hand, his wildfire smile spreading quickly across his lips and through his touch to warm the coldest parts of her. "Night's still young."

"And I intend to make the most of it." Ingrid tried to pull away, heading toward the dance floor, but Linden's grip tightened.

"Seriously, Ingrid. Are you all right? You're acting like it's your last night to live."

"Isn't it? Tomorrow, you start your new life." They would all go off into the world for their senior-year internships, applying what they knew and learning more than they could possibly dream. But it did not matter that she had top grades and a stellar application. She was still the daughter of a convict, with no meaningful connections. No one with any sense would hire her. Linden and their other classmates would rise, buoyed by their family names, their family money, their family magic; and Ingrid would sink, with no family worth calling her own. She lowered her voice to barely a whisper. "And just like magic, I'll fade away . . ."

"Now that I can't abide." Linden placed his palms on either side of her face. "You, my dear, are brighter than any magic, and I won't allow anyone to take away your shine."

He kissed her then. Ingrid thought she could taste flare on his lips, and her desire to feel power in her veins warred against the unsettled attachment churning in her stomach—that consuming love, a beast all its own.

"Linden." His name, a plea from her lips to his, passed between them. She hovered in the space between demanding more—knowing she was worth it—and accepting less—knowing she couldn't have it.

He pulled away, taking her chin in his hand. "Ingrid, listen. You know you're my girl. You *know* that, right?"

She'd prepared for the blow, rehearsed the moment in her mind. He would be gentle, but in the end, they'd both walk out alone. One way or another, their relationship wouldn't last the night. Now the moment Ingrid had been bracing for all evening had finally come, and she wasn't ready for it. In fact, she thought she might be sick—though that could have been the excess of flicker.

"Can we do this tomorrow?" she asked, barely hearing her own words.

"Do this? Do what?" Linden's freckled cheeks became a patchwork of red.

It almost made her want to apologize. This boy who was a legacy disguised as youth could blush like the rest of them.

"It's the last day before senior year. You'll be off to your father's campaign, and I'll be—well, I'll be off too. Can't we have this one night before it all ends?"

"Whoa, before it ends? Ingrid, slow down a second."

Ingrid sighed, straightening the shoulders of her frock—a luminous viridian thing adorned with peacock feathers at the hem and sequins that dug into her palms like shrapnel. She'd worn it precisely for this unfortunate occasion; if she was to be humiliated, at least she'd be humiliated in style. "It's all right. You're a Holt, and I'm . . . It's all right. But can we pretend for a little while longer?"

"Pretend? Ingrid, I don't—" Linden ran his hands through his hair, a nervous laugh escaping his lips. "Scorch it, I'm doing this all wrong, aren't I?"

"Honest truth, I've never been dumped before, so I wouldn't know the right way from wrong." If he was going to end their relationship in the middle of an underground speakeasy, music blaring

11

and flicker pulsing through the air, she would do her best to endure it. She would not be submerged by this, she would not sink, she would not drown. She was not just another fish in the sea—she would show him what a shark she could be. "If it's over, it's over. Just let me have this last night."

Linden reached for her hand. "It's not over—at least, I don't want it to be." He met her gaze with amber eyes that shone under the flicker lights. "I understand if you do, but I—I'm still doing this wrong." A nervous smile quaked across his face.

"Apparently." Ingrid pulled her hand from his, but a hesitant heat rose in her chest.

"I'm sorry. It's just I've never done this before, and I want to make sure I do it right." Linden put his hands in his pockets, shoulders shrugging closer to his ears.

Linden might play sheepish for the masses, charming them with his smile, but Ingrid knew the boy beneath the act. His tricks wouldn't work on her. Though from different ends, they were still cut from the same cloth—the kind that did not wrinkle.

"Ingrid," he said, his cheeks flushing again.

"Linden." If he could be obtuse and dramatic, so could she.

A frown creased his lips. "Come on, I'm trying here."

"Well, maybe you're not trying hard enough." *Try harder, try harder.*

"Iloveyouokay?"

"What?" Ingrid forgot to feign disinterest, her arms falling to her sides.

"I. Love. You. I love you, and I don't want to lose you."

Ingrid didn't move, his words a spell far stronger than any magic.

Linden removed his hands from his pockets and took a step toward her. The space between them narrowed and vanished until they were in close embrace—his hand against her spine, her fingers at the nape of his neck—a frame for a small dance. Neither of them moved to the music. They stood in perfect stillness, a perfect moment for a perfect minute.

He removed a sapphire-and-diamond ring from his pocket and leaned in, his breath a whisper against her ear. "Marry me?"

Ingrid's fingers closed around the weighty piece of jewelry, but before she could form a coherent response, a crash sounded from the opposite wall. The trapdoor on the ceiling swung open to admit a stampede of officers. Their boots drummed duty, their eyes flashed danger, and their hands blazed with roaring red flare.

CHAPTER TWO

The band was the first to go. Their instruments screeched to a halt in the middle of a peppy swing number as officers swarmed the stage. Gleaming fire and silver handcuffs flashed from every direction as the patrons turned to run. Glass shattered under dancers' feet, and sparks of flicker were engulfed by jets of flame.

A scream followed, then another.

Ingrid's insides seemed to shrivel, then burst, her heart beating too fast. She wanted to scream too, but her vocal cords felt frozen along with her feet.

Linden took her hand, his grip warm and secure. He was still with her. She would not be alone. She clung to him as he charged toward the stairs, a stampede of patrons following in their wake. "Stay close."

Stay close. She could do that. She *must* do that. Linden was her armor, and without him, she'd be swept away with the crowd toward officers who wouldn't know her from the rest. As long as she was with him, she'd be safe. But safe seemed a long way off as a jet of flare soared over their heads, a crackling spark of light. Gold shattered against the rafters, peeling off in dizzying spirals. A warning shot.

14

"What the——" Ingrid whipped around, but Linden pulled her into the shelter of his arms, shielding her from danger, shielding her from reality. She wrestled with his protective grip to get a better look.

"Ingrid," Linden hissed, tugging on her waist.

Part of her knew she ought to go with him, slip out while attention was pointed elsewhere. She relied on his status to insulate her on nights like these, so why not take advantage? But her eyes lingered on the crowd.

"Everyone remain calm." The booming voice of the officer in front rose above the chaos. "On suspicion of illegal and treasonous activity, you will all be detained and questioned. There's no need for this to get out of hand if you all cooperate." Magic flashed in his palm as he uncurled his fingers.

"Is that a threat?" asked an elderly man near the officers.

Others chimed in in a cacophony of dissent. Another ball of flare soared above them, knocking a string of flicker lights from the wall. One of the officers grabbed the old man and tore him from the crowd. He cried out, and a woman lunged for the officer, only to be met with fire. She screamed as an officer's fiery palms branded her skin and she fell to the floor.

Around them, there was stillness. And then there was everything else.

Charged anger released like a flood. Patrons hurled dainty stemmed glasses at the officers and used anything they could find to defend themselves against the overpowered Flare Force. Dancers pulled their shoes from their feet, brandishing them heel out like weapons. A musician tried to beat away an officer with his trombone, and another patron held a chair out like a shield.

Heat warmed Ingrid's face, and courage bloomed in her chest.

She lifted her foot, summoning the last vestiges of flicker in her blood to her hand. She eyed the Flare Force officers. She could hit one of them at least. The power in her veins spluttered and sparked, an anxious flurry of golden light pooling at her fingertips.

Another ball of flare careened over their heads, hot and blistering. Ingrid recoiled, cradling the weak magic against her chest.

Ingrid had used real flare only a handful of times. Once in class, when her teachers had needed to extract the magic from her before she was lost to its power, and then after, when Linden had offered to teach her properly. He'd given her only a sip, but there in the small, enclosed supply closet that became their meeting place, he'd taught her how to make light in the dark.

You can't save up magic like money, he'd said. *Spend it or it'll spend you.*

Flicker was not flare. Flicker was bright and bold, but flare was brighter and bolder. Flare was fire, and flicker was only a shadow of the flame. She would not win this fight.

"Don't." Linden closed his hand around hers, extinguishing the sparks.

Ingrid turned to see resigned quiet in Linden's eyes. There was no fury there, no righteous indignation as these people—*innocent* people—were treated like criminals. No, even worse, they were treated like enemies. Ingrid scanned the scene, looking for any sign of hope. Her eyes fell on the server, Louise, still behind the bar. Her hair had escaped its cap and a smudge lined her cheek, but her gaze was cold and determined, fixed over Ingrid's head at the top of the stairs. Something made Ingrid want to call out to her.

"I have to help them," she said.

Linden jerked her back. "They're trained officers, Ingrid. I think they can do without your help."

Ingrid's limbs went loose in Linden's grip. It was nights like this she had been taught to fear. Flare Force, the supposed protectors of Candesce, didn't really protect them all. She looked at the Flare Force officers and saw nothing but danger, but Linden, he saw them as allies. To Linden, they *were* allies. Linden was not pulling her away to escape the threat of Flare Force, but to escape whatever threat Flare Force had come to quell.

"Let's go." Linden led her through the crowd, shielding her against projectiles, and up the stairs. The officers standing there parted to let them through. Ingrid could hardly believe it until they reached the top of the steps and a cold voice spoke.

"I see you're studying hard at that school of yours, Linden."

Slowly, as though her eyes were stuck in heavy syrup, Ingrid shifted her gaze up to the man before them. Senator Walden Holt was a broad-shouldered man with thick silver hair combed back under a bowler hat. Even in the dim lighting of the speakeasy, he held an impressive command of the space.

Linden shrank under his father's scrutiny. "Wrong place, wrong time?" he asked sheepishly.

"Must be." The senator narrowed his eyes and moved his gaze to the scene beyond them. "Get her out of here." Then he brushed past them, knocking Ingrid's shoulder with his own as though she were nothing.

"Come on." Linden tightened his grip and pulled her up to the street.

They were met by clean night air, fresh and unburdened with the thick curl of dust and sweat and the heat of bodies packed together. For a moment, everything slowed, her heart rate leveled, and oxygen poured into her lungs.

Behind them, people expelled from the speakeasy, flanked by

17

officers on all sides. A parade of patrons whose crimes amounted to little more than a night of fun was outnumbered by Flare Force officers two to one. It was clearly overkill for such a small establishment, too many officers for too little threat.

Ingrid turned to say as much to Linden, but the words dissolved on her lips the moment she saw his expression. Pinched and sour, she followed his gaze to the front door, where his father stood silhouetted against the dark interior.

"That's the last of them," Senator Holt said, nodding to the remaining Flare Force officers to go on before turning his attention to Linden. "I thought I told you to get rid of her."

Linden stepped forward but wasn't given a chance to speak.

"No matter. Let's finish this, shall we?" Senator Holt closed the distance between them.

Standing together illuminated by street lamps, Linden and his father were like dual shadows in a spotlight. But for their disparate energies, their silhouettes were nearly identical, mirror images of age and youth. Senator Holt's rumbling presence towered over Linden, even if his stature did not.

From Linden's front pocket, Senator Holt plucked the vial of flare Linden had been nursing all night. The silver *H* glinted in the lamplight.

Linden shook his head.

The senator raised the vial higher.

Linden frowned.

The senator arched an aggressive eyebrow.

Ingrid held her breath. She knew the wounds of unspoken words only too well, the silence between family so loud it could shatter the world.

Finally the senator spoke: "Do it."

He was the spark, and his son was the match.

Linden took the vial and raised it to his lips. Flare streamed from his fingers, strong and singing with energy. This wasn't the innocuous sparkle of flicker served in the club. This was flare. Bright gold tendrils of power snaked their way around the building like chains, spiderwebbing up into the air to connect in a dome at the top.

A flash of movement inside the speakeasy drew Ingrid's eye. The hazy outline of a person crossed in front of the window, but then Linden lowered his hand and golden light dropped with sudden force.

"No!" Ingrid reached out, but her cry was swallowed by a thunderous roar.

Fire rained from the sky, illuminating the street with an eerie glow. One moment, the speakeasy had stood dark like the night around them; the next, it lit the sky on fire. It was there, a haven, a respite, a place where no one knew their names, and then with a whisper of magic, it was gone.

CHAPTER THREE

Smoke stung Ingrid's eyes. It was invisible against the night sky, but she could taste it on the air as it settled over them.

Beside her, Senator Holt clapped a hand on his son's shoulder, and the motion rippled through Linden's frame.

"That's my boy," Senator Holt said, tone hollow and laced with malice. It was not praise; it was pride, twisted and barbed.

Linden stiffened at the endearment, and Ingrid clenched her jaw against a flurry of words she knew she couldn't say. Her fingers itched to lace through Linden's, to hold him, to ground him.

Then a light that was not fire snapped across the square.

Ingrid shrank back toward flame. She knew the flash of cameras all too well. It was a thrilling white, blinding and brilliant. With the orange fire climbing higher and higher behind them, it would make a chilling photograph in tomorrow's paper. The people of Candesce would look at the black-and-white image and see only the flames and the boy who'd put them there. They would see only the moment captured by a single shutter of a camera lens.

It was powerful, to tell a story so simply. It was powerful, and it was dangerous. What would they do to her when Linden's proposal put her before their lenses? Her heartbeat quickened at the thought. No one could ignore her then. No one could dismiss her or cast her aside. Immortalized on film, she would be untouchable. But just as she'd known fire would be hot without ever burning herself, she knew instinctively to fold herself into the shadows, away from the press, away from Linden and his father, away from the spotlight.

"What can you tell us about the arrests made tonight, Senator?" a reporter called through the night.

Senator Holt turned, flying his bright smile like a flag. "I expect you can get a full report on the charges from official channels in the morning," he began. "But I'll tell you now, it's a win for all of Candesce when establishments like this are shut down so seamlessly. When we heard rumors of a rebel plot to attack this place tonight, well . . . What an opportunity. Two torches, one flame."

"Can you tell us more about the rebel plot?"

"I'm sorry," Senator Holt said, not an ounce of contrition in his voice. "I really can't be sharing those details until everything is wrapped up. Rest assured, we're confident any plans for aggression were successfully deterred tonight by our raid."

"What do you have to say to your political opponents who say it's a waste of resources to fight this kind of victimless crime?"

A shadow crossed over the senator's face for a split second before he recovered his bland confidence. "There can be no victimless crime where unstable magic is concerned. These flicker clubs may seem innocuous, but there's no telling how their different concoctions might react to the human body. Even with no ill intent, a flicker chemist might mix a deadly cocktail by mistake. Regulation is the only way to ensure the safety of all citizens, and anyone who

21

patronizes these establishments is in direct conflict with that endeavor."

"Even your own son?"

The question was flung with the same ferocious velocity as flare. An attack.

Linden's bottom lip trembled ever so slightly as he opened his mouth to reply, but Senator Holt wrapped an arm around his son's shoulders and spoke for him.

"Tonight, Linden took part in an intricate, planned operation from the inside. His role in this success cannot be overstated."

Ingrid's stomach dropped. They'd used the speakeasy like a getaway, danced to their music, and drunk their flicker. Had Linden known all along it would end this way? Cold spread out from her core like ice fracturing against an empty glass. Linden couldn't have known, could he?

"Very dedicated, my son," the senator was saying. "He's always had a strong sense of civic duty—like me, I suppose."

"Do you plan to follow in your father's footsteps?" The reporter turned their attention to Linden, who opened his mouth to reply only to be spoken over by his father once more.

"You know, as a matter of fact, there might be a certain Senate seat opening up I think he'd be perfect for." He laughed, the sound ricocheting through the quiet.

"I'm only eighteen," Linden said, a note of levity in his voice that didn't match his body language. His fingers curled tight around the vial of flare. "I still have to finish school."

"You've grown up with a senator father, though. Isn't that essentially a crash course in the political landscape of Candesce?"

Ingrid's stomach dipped as Linden flexed his fingers. He'd often brushed aside the privilege of his father's position, refusing to talk with her about capital politics or answer questions about his father. She understood, of course, not wanting to write papers about his own father for their civics and government courses, and when it was only the two of them, he still never wanted to share what he knew with her. Even with a reporter in his face and his father to his left, he resisted. If she'd had a politician for a father, she'd never have been so selfish.

"Linden's always been thorough." Senator Holt grinned, but his hold on Linden tightened. "Even when it comes to his education, he's not the sort to leave a job half done."

Linden threw on a smile to match, but his eyes were daggers. Ingrid had been brushed aside just like that herself on a hundred occasions, and she'd learned to bear it. To see Linden, who usually commanded attention by merit of his name, grapple with the same injustice was a sight indeed. Was it only a passing frustration, or was that true anger Ingrid spied in the tightness of his jaw?

The senator ignored him and leaned forward, as though to let the small crowd of reporters in on a secret. Before he could reveal it, however, a monstrous scream hit the air.

Ingrid whirled around. The sound had come from behind her, guttural and grotesque. It was the sound of desperation, the sound of death.

Rage incarnate rose from the still-burning speakeasy in the form of a girl. She was soot stained and badly burned, but she was alive. With a swoop of her stomach, Ingrid realized she must have been inside the building when it caught fire. The girl's skin shone under the light of cameras going off around them, her burns glassy in places. Her hair was singed off one side of her head, and ash climbed her chest and throat like a sweater.

"You!" she rasped, pointing a finger at Senator Holt. "I'll kill you!"

"There is absolutely no need for that." The cavalier expression dropped from his face when he saw the press had scattered, leaving camera flashes in their wake, and his tone turned like sour milk, no longer performing for the reporters. "Now, don't make a scene. That won't go well, I promise you that."

"A promise from a politician. That's rich." Her voice scratched and scraped, but her eyes were merciless. From the wreckage, she pulled a half-burned wooden plank with a nail protruding from the end and swung hard.

Senator Holt crumpled, bleeding from the head as he landed awkwardly on the street.

Linden fell to his knees beside him, dropping his vial of flare as he went. He pulled his father's body toward him, cradling the unconscious senator's head in his lap.

The silence was punctuated only by the flashes of cameras as the reporters regained their courage and circled the scene like vultures.

Get help was all Ingrid could think. What were they doing? Senator Holt was a giant of a man in Candesce. If they wouldn't intervene on his behalf, then . . .

"You burned me." The girl advanced on Linden next, slowly and steadily. Her hands, raw and bruised, reached for the vial as it rolled across the pavement toward her. "Now I burn you." She lifted the vial to her lips and drank.

Ingrid willed Linden to do *something*. Run, fight, anything but stand still and wait for the worst to happen to him. But Linden had never been the proactive sort.

With a rush in her ears, Ingrid launched herself out of the

darkness and into the girl, knocking her to the ground. Heat brushed Ingrid's skin as they collided, tumbling closer to the still-raging fire. Ingrid wrestled the vial from the girl's fingers, but then their gazes met. Recognition sparked as eyes the color of chaos and a rocky riverbed bored into hers.

She wasn't just the girl swallowed by Linden's flames. She was a person, and to Ingrid's regret, she had a name. Oh, how Ingrid wished she didn't.

"Louise?" she whispered against the cool glass of Linden's bottle of flare.

Louise sneered. "Not a type, huh?" she whispered, fire curling from her lips.

Ingrid shook her head to clear it. They'd joked together in the dim flicker light earlier; they'd exchanged names. Louise had trusted her, and Ingrid hadn't deserved it in the slightest. "I didn't know. I didn't—please." Ingrid didn't know how to find the words to express how bad she felt for Louise, how if wishing made it so, the speakeasy would still be standing, Louise would be unharmed. But if Louise went after Linden, Ingrid would not fail to act. She would protect him, whatever it took. The senator, unconscious as he was, wouldn't be wrong: This would not end well. "You don't want to do this."

"You don't know what I want," Louise said.

Ingrid tightened her grip around the vial, readying herself. "Just walk away now. He's the senator's son. You can't attack him."

"I can, and I will," Louise said with a twisted smile just for Ingrid. "Everybody burns."

The words, so casually penned on the speakeasy walls, fell like embers coming from Louise's lips. Ingrid could do nothing but match her, so she emptied the rest of the flare into her mouth.

Flare carved its way down Ingrid's tongue. It wound in spirals through her veins, languid and desperate all at once. Inside her, magic multiplied, and when it hit her bloodstream, flare wasn't just a suggestion like flicker. It did not flirt with danger; it *was* danger. Magic curled around her heart, and inside her, it roared.

Louise lowered herself into a crouch, tongues of flame twisting up her already-burned arms.

With no warning, Louise hurled a ball of orange-gold fire at her. Ingrid ducked, and the flame soared over her shoulder into the wreckage of the speakeasy.

"Your sort did this to me!" Louise spat. "You all have everything, and still you take and take and take."

"I don't want to take anything from you," Ingrid said, sending back her own shot of magic, unsteady and unpracticed. The magic felt too light in her hands, like she hadn't grabbed enough of it or she was holding it wrong. Light soared through the air, but Louise darted out of the way, and it missed her by inches.

"You have everything you could ever want," Louise growled. "Why take what little the rest of us have?"

Ingrid stopped short, a weak flame in the palm of her hand. An unfathomable need surged through her, more powerful than any magic. She wanted Louise to know they were the same. Just as it had struck her before when they spoke at the bar, it felt important now.

Louise lunged for her, burning hands grazing Ingrid's bare arm. "You come into our world, you drink our flicker, and you pretend you understand. But you risk nothing, you lose nothing. And we lose it all. How is that justice?"

Ingrid wrenched herself from Louise's grip and shot a ball of flame directly into her stomach, knocking her back several steps.

"What you're doing isn't justice either," Ingrid said, panting now from the effort of holding on to so much magic. Ingrid cheated a glance at Linden on the ground beside his father. He looked unharmed, or at least unburned for now.

"Feels like justice to me." Louise growled, steam expelling from her nostrils.

Ingrid summoned more magic to her hand but paused on the cusp of letting it loose. They were playing little more than a fiery game of tennis. Besides, she didn't want to fight Louise. She wanted them all to walk away from this alive, but at this rate, they'd both burn up from their own magic before they did any damage to each other.

That's when Ingrid felt the fever spreading from her fingers, through her arms, to root in her chest. Warmth cascaded over her, and her vision wobbled. For a moment, she felt like she was floating. Then the pressure began to build.

Already, Louise's face was damp with perspiration. Ingrid wasn't far behind. She knew what came next. Soon, sweat would drip from her brow and her breath would turn to steam. By the time her skin began to crack, hot magma moving beneath her flesh, it would be too late; she would be wholly consumed by magic. As heat climbed up Ingrid's spine, realization built with it. She might know how to wield flicker, but flare was different. She couldn't keep treating the power inside her like the knockoff. She had to treat it like the real magic it was.

Spend it or it'll spend you.

Guided only by the ghost of words long passed, Ingrid dove inside herself, searching for the source of her power. Flare crackled and spit, flames hissing almost in song. She pictured herself reaching toward the sound, following the rising heat of magic with her fingertips. Her skin burned, but she plunged her fist deep into the fire, withdrawing a cord of tightly wound magic, threading it through her insides like a maze, until it burst forth from her fingers.

She opened her eyes to a bright golden world. Power shimmered in her hands, hot and horrible. She let the raw power stream from her fingers, bright flame against her skin.

Louise stumbled toward Linden and the unconscious Senator Holt.

"Ingrid! Do something!" Linden shouted as she drew closer. He looked to her with pleading eyes, his father's head still resting in his lap, and for a moment, Ingrid forgot he was the same boy who'd burned down the speakeasy with no more than a snap of his fingers mere minutes ago. Perhaps a ruthlessness lived somewhere inside him, but it would not show itself again today. Ingrid would have to be ruthless enough for the both of them.

Ingrid poured magic from her hands, fashioning it into a long rope of fire. Sending intention into her fingers, she compelled the rope to lengthen and slither across the street. If she could only keep Louise's attention on her, she could bind the flaming cord around Louise's limbs and tie her down until more Flare Force officers arrived.

If they were coming at all.

"Murder's a serious crime," Ingrid said, trying to keep the edge out of her voice. "They give you a permanent jail cell for that sort of thing." Her chest tightened. Ingrid, who'd spent the majority of her adolescence visiting her own father in jail, couldn't wish the fate on even her enemies.

"Oh, I won't be going to jail," Louise said, closing the gap between her and an ashen-faced Linden.

"Not if you stop now. You don't have to do this." Something

like pity twisted her stomach as she advanced, reaching her magic as far as she could. Louise wasn't an enemy, just a girl who'd lost everything. Ingrid knew what it was to be so desperate, so angry. She just had to get a little closer, and this would all be over.

"Oh yes, I do."

Ingrid and Louise locked eyes; then Louise lunged. Ingrid flung the cord up and around Louise's hand. She snapped the rope taut and Louise crashed forward, but she didn't fall alone. With her other hand, Louise clamped her fingers around Linden's wrist, pulling him with her.

"No!" Ingrid yelled.

Linden howled in pain as his knees hit stone. Louise's skin had to be iron-hot by now, branding his forearm with her handprint.

"Let him go!" Ingrid cried.

Louise only grinned, a wide, wild smile full of mirth and magic. She wouldn't last much longer. "This is what you deserve."

Ingrid wanted to scream that it wasn't, that she deserved more than what she'd been given. She wanted to show Louise that she'd come from a cold hearth and empty coffers, and she'd earned the life she'd built herself. She wanted to take Louise by the collar and, she was surprised to discover, not throttle her, but show her instead how she could do so much better than this half-baked justice, that she could win if only she'd play the game.

"Ingrid!" Linden's cry brought her back to the present. "She's going to burst! You have to end this."

But what could she do? She'd immobilized Louise as best she could with the magic she had. She didn't have it in her to do what Linden wanted. She wouldn't burn this girl who'd already felt too much fire for a lifetime. But if she did nothing, Louise would die anyway.

29

"You have to use it," Ingrid said in barely more than a whisper. "If you don't, you'll die. The magic will tear you apart."

Ingrid pooled the rest of her magic in her palms, trying to imagine the wave of fire required to take Louise's life. The thought alone made Ingrid's skin crawl.

"Maybe that's for the best." Louise's breath turned ragged.

Ingrid's heart plummeted. In another life, Louise could have been Ingrid; in another life, Ingrid could have been Louise. Killing her would be like killing a piece of herself, and though she'd tried to disguise it with silk and sequins and status, she wasn't ready to let it go. The anger in Louise's heart was all too familiar. Ingrid had felt it in her bones for years after her father had been sent to prison. That anger was what kept her warm on the coldest of nights when she slept on a stone slab with only the moon for a blanket. It filled her belly when hunger threatened to rip her open from the inside. And after a few years, it settled into fierce determination, taking the shape of a well-mannered girl with a string of fake pearls around her neck.

Ingrid pulled her fire back, tightening her grip on the magic cord instead. She wasn't sure if it would work, but she'd never know if she didn't try. Closing her eyes, she took a breath and listened, trying to remember how the instructors had done it. Magic hummed in her hand, a gentle note, electric and elegant all at once. She followed the sound, carrying her consciousness across it like a tightrope, a careful balancing act until she reached the other side.

Louise's magic was loud and hot, a roaring fire. Flare devoured her from the inside. It was almost too much to bear, like thunder echoing in rapid succession. Unlike with her own magic, Ingrid didn't have to reach very far to latch on to Louise's. It was there at the surface, waiting to spill over.

Ingrid took a shaky breath and pulled.

Her eyes snapped open, and magic flooded into her, hot and unbridled. It shot through her body, activating every muscle. She couldn't breathe; she couldn't move. She could only burn.

As fire closed in on her vision, she saw Louise crumple, the whip between them disintegrating into the night air. Linden tore away from her and charged toward Ingrid, but it was too late. She held too much magic, and it all had to go somewhere. She tilted her head toward the sky and opened her mouth to scream, but no sound came out, only a violent, vibrant column of flame before darkness claimed her.

CHAPTER FOUR

Death was a cold and fitful place. All the poetry Ingrid had read promised it would be peaceful and warm. Liars, every one. She curled her body around her knees, tucking her toes beneath her. If she were to be alone for all eternity, she would at least hold herself.

But she wasn't alone. Something moved beside her. Something was breathing. *She* was breathing.

She was alive.

"Ingrid Caroline Ellis, if you carry on feigning sleep, I shall have to empty this water pitcher directly over that pretty face of yours."

Ingrid blinked, her vision foggy and her head pounding. She lay in a hospital bed, surrounded by white linens. A vase of pink roses sat at her bedside, a wrinkled newspaper was folded beside her knees, and a stern-faced Charlotte Terry hovered in the space above her, swimming in and out of focus.

"What . . . ?" Ingrid didn't quite know what she wanted to ask. She imagined most people would ask where they were (*in the hospital, obviously*) or what had happened (*she'd engaged in an ill-advised flare fight*). She knew the answers to the pressing questions, but a hazy inkling that she was missing something—like perhaps all the bones in her neck—thundered against her temples. "What day is it?" she asked finally.

"You've been asleep a full three days, my friend."

"Then why don't I feel well rested?" Ingrid rubbed her eyes. They watered against her touch, still burning from the memory of fire. The lights were too bright, the blankets were too warm. She tried to sit up—to what end, she didn't know—but the motion caught her directly in the throat as though she might throw up if she fought gravity.

Charlotte placed a hand behind Ingrid's head and helped her lean back against the headrest. "Because you never feel well rested," she said with a heavy air of exasperation.

"It's almost like you know me." Ingrid tried to narrow her eyes, but it made her forehead hurt, so she stopped.

Charlotte mimicked the expression. *"Almost."*

If not for the quiet resignation in the word, Ingrid might have thought Charlotte was only teasing. The two had been suite mates at Ainsley Academy since their first year. Ingrid had never expected to enter the world of the rich and mannered and actually make any real friends, but Charlotte was a small girl with a big heart. Ingrid had been powerless to resist Charlotte's wit and warmth, and she was the only person besides Linden who really knew her.

On another day, Ingrid might have let Charlotte's comment go, playing passive-aggressive for days before one of them finally let the matter drop, unaddressed and unattended. But Ingrid had left her patience back in the speakeasy along with her best coat. Both were nothing but ashes now, so she said, "What do you mean, *almost?*"

Charlotte sighed with her whole body—all five feet of it. She

33

was short with dark brown skin and black hair carefully styled into exquisite finger waves. She ran a thumb below her perfectly painted lipstick line as she surveyed Ingrid; then, with a flourish, she picked up the newspaper and deposited it on Ingrid's lap.

"I'm an invalid, Charlotte. You can't expect me to read this myself. I might get rheumatism or a spontaneous hemorrhage," Ingrid groaned.

Charlotte didn't even crack a smile. Instead, she cocked her head and said in a deadpan, *"Holt Colt's Secret Flame."*

"What?" Ingrid tried to sound bewildered more than bombarded, but her heart sped into a gallop.

"It's a bad headline. Don't let it confuse you." Charlotte snatched up the paper and began to read. "'Linden Holt, rising star at Ainsley Academy and son of Alorden's senior senator, found himself in hot water last night when a speakeasy raid went sideways. What would have been a triumph ended in flames when an unnamed patron attacked reporters and both senator and son.'"

"I know what happened, Charlotte. I was there." Ingrid pressed the heels of her hands against her eyes, trying to blot out the flood of images returning in a deluge of fire.

"I'll skip down a bit, shall I?" Charlotte folded the paper with a snap and continued. "'A classmate Holt identified as an Ainsley Academy scholarship recipient came to his aid, subduing the attacker through presumably dangerous flare techniques that rendered both girls unconscious. Holt was seen cradling his classmate's form in an intimate fashion after the attack, leading this reporter to ask if Holt, who has never been romantically attached, might be participating in more charity work than his father knows.'"

Ingrid blanched. *"Charity work?"*

"And there's a picture." Charlotte shook out the paper for Ingrid to see.

There at the top of the page was the photo Ingrid had envisioned: Linden and Senator Holt standing resolute before a bright flame. And below it . . .

"That's me!" Ingrid exclaimed. Not that the paper had bothered to name her. She was simply *an Ainsley Academy scholarship recipient*. She was not even worthy of her own name.

"I know, you walnut."

Ingrid's eyes swept over her own limp body, held upright in Linden's arms. A twist of her stomach threatened to undo her, but Ingrid gripped the blankets in her hands to steady herself. It unnerved her more than she could have imagined to see herself so defenseless like that, so absent. The reporter had been right about one thing, though. Linden hadn't hidden even a single one of his emotions for the camera's benefit. He leaned over her, lips pressed against her forehead, with what looked to be a tear rolling down his cheek. Perhaps it was only a defect in the photograph.

"Well?" Charlotte demanded, shaking the paper again.

"Well, what?"

"Oh, come on." Charlotte let the paper drop between them. "You didn't just forget to tell me you were dating *the* most eligible bachelor at school. That's not the sort of thing that simply slips your mind, Ingrid. You lied to me."

Ingrid fell back against her pillows, a dull ache in her ribs the only sensation in her entire body. She'd known this day would come eventually. She'd wanted Linden and everything that came with loving him, but now it was out, the pressure on her chest had doubled, the weight on her shoulders tripled. She'd never wanted to tell anyone, but she'd wanted everyone to know. The dichotomy split her down the middle until her breath came like a stray dog's—ragged and desperate.

"I wanted—I wanted to tell you. I did. I just—" Her words suffocated as she struggled to breathe.

"You just?" Charlotte folded her arms.

"I didn't tell anyone," Ingrid continued. "I didn't really think anything would come of it. I thought I wasn't good enough for him."

Charlotte scoffed. "No, you didn't."

Ingrid smiled at that. "No, I didn't."

"You thought *he* thought you weren't good enough for him." She leaned in almost conspiratorially. "And you were embarrassed you might be right, so you kept it a secret?"

Ingrid slouched—a gesture she'd not allowed herself in years—and muttered into her hands, "His father."

Charlotte made a face.

"I only don't like him because I assume he won't like me. I know I must overcome it."

"I can think of a few other reasons to dislike him," Charlotte said. "His voting record, for a start."

Ingrid's ear found her shoulder in a shrug. "He's very well respected."

"Then he doesn't need you."

"Please don't be cross with me, Charlotte. I wish you'd heard all this from me."

But it was more than Charlotte, more than wishing she could have been the one to tell her friend. It was wishing she could be the one to choose what and when and how much people knew. It was wishing she could take it all back. But the words were in print; the

36

speculation was circulating. Gossip was like a derailed train—too fast and uncontrollable to stop without a few fatalities in the mess. It was too late for anything but to let this run its course.

"I promise to forgive you," Charlotte said. "If—*if*—you tell me and only me all the gory details. I want to know about you and the *Holt Colt*."

Ingrid wrinkled her nose. "Never call him that again."

"You mean you don't like the *Candesce Courant*'s headlines? Shocker! The good news is their new intern will bring a bit more panache to their paper. With me on their staff, they'll never have another subpar headline again."

Ingrid reached for Charlotte's hand and squeezed. "They'll be lucky to have you."

Charlotte gasped and clutched Ingrid's hand tighter. "What sorcery is this?" She pointed violently to the sapphire ring on Ingrid's finger.

Truth be told, Ingrid had nearly forgotten Linden's proposal. The ring, presumably too valuable for the hospital staff to consider removing, had been hidden beneath the bedsheets but now glittered under the harsh hospital lighting. A massive sapphire with clusters of diamonds unfurling from its sides like rose petals sat on her finger, delicate and domineering all at once.

"That's Portia Holt's ring!" Charlotte examined the stones with wide eyes. "It's probably worth as much as my parents' house!"

It wasn't an overstatement. Portia Holt, Linden's grandmother, had been a woman of exceeding taste, a fashion icon, the Gwendolyn Meyers of her day. Portia Holt's wedding ring on Ingrid's finger would send the rumor mill at Ainsley Academy into a frenzy. Pauline Ackerman would have a conniption at the very sight. But her classmates would never see her as a peer, no matter how large a rock Linden gave her. All she could do was collect their vitriol like pennies—eventually she'd have enough to buy their respect.

Ingrid snatched back her hand. "It's nothing."

"What a thing to say!" Charlotte stood up, sat down, then stood up again. "Why is there a ring on your finger? Did Linden give it to you? Are you two engaged?"

Ingrid chewed her bottom lip. "He did ask," she said hesitantly.

"And?" Charlotte leaned over her, a combination of mirth and murder dancing in her eyes.

"And I didn't have a chance to give my answer."

"But you'll say yes, of course."

"Of . . . course," Ingrid repeated. "Of course."

Linden had proposed. He'd given her his grandmother's ring. It was all she'd ever wanted. She should have been happy. But Ingrid didn't trust happiness. It was only a feeling, and she couldn't buy anything with it. Happiness never came without a cost, and just like with magic, she'd brace herself for the inevitable crash to come.

"Ingrid Catherine Ellis!" Charlotte snapped her fingers to return Ingrid to the present.

Ingrid wrinkled her nose. "It's not Catherine either."

"Cate?"

"If you want to know my middle name so badly, why not simply look it up? You're a journalist! Act like it!"

"That would be cheating, and I intend to make my way through the entire alphabet before employing such underhanded methods—and don't change the subject! How long has this even been going on?"

Under Charlotte's scrutiny, Ingrid wanted more and more to

simply slip beneath the covers of her bed and drift back to that place between living and dead, where no one wanted anything of her. No one had any questions for her there. No one cared who she loved. No one cared who she was. It was her worst nightmare of them all—to depart the earth an unknown—but in that moment, she thought it might be preferable to the alternative.

"Are you two in love? Please say you're in love—you know how I love a love story!"

Ingrid did know. Charlotte had always loved romance. She read novels hidden inside the jacket of her schoolbooks and played matchmaker with all their classmates. She loved the dramatics, the story of it all, but when Ingrid had asked her why she'd never sought out a beau of her own, Charlotte had explained she preferred friends to lovers. She planned to never marry but instead surround herself with platonic love.

It sounded like a dream, one Ingrid couldn't afford. Romantic love was altogether too much and not enough for Ingrid. She felt as though she might drown in the pursuit of enough love. If only she knew with as much conviction as Charlotte the precise kind of love she wanted, perhaps she wouldn't feel like she'd die without Linden's and like it would also be the death of her.

"A wealthy bachelor, a clever girl, and a terrifically horrid father-in-law. It's all so romantic, and— Oh!" She gripped both Ingrid's shoulders and faced her squarely with a serious note to her voice. "You'll be the next Gwendolyn Meyers."

"Except Gwendolyn Meyers isn't married," Ingrid countered, but pride swelled inside her at the comparison. "She got there all on her own."

Gwendolyn Meyers was the woman of a generation. From her humble beginnings as a lounge singer to her thunderous present as a philanthropist and adviser to the president, not a single word from the lips of Gwendolyn Meyers went unreported by the papers. Her every move was a road map for young ladies—whether the destination was triumph or trouble, no one could quite agree. When the papers said she was only new money, she turned around and showed them how much. When the radio called her washed up, she'd held an outdoor concert in the rain, just to prove she still had talent soaking wet. She did not so much shatter expectations as she did reshape them in her image.

And now she was running for president.

Charlotte bit her lip. "And I suppose she is quite a bit taller than you."

"Precisely. In the most literal and figurative senses, I will never measure up to Gwendolyn Meyers."

The words made her ache, but in Ingrid's experience, truth was never painless. Ingrid had tacked a photo of Gwendolyn Meyers—clipped from a magazine some-odd years ago—to her vanity. She left her idol there, in place of a mother or sister, to watch over her beauty routine. Ingrid had always found comfort in the half-forgotten tale of a girl from nothing growing up to be everything.

"You're still going to be *someone*." Charlotte stood up and placed the newspaper carefully on Ingrid's bedside table. "Imagine, the papers will someday print your name—Ingrid *Holt*."

Despite herself, Ingrid smiled. Anyone who said a name was only a name had never been an Ellis wishing she were a Holt.

A twinkle in her eye, Charlotte linked their fingers. "Ingrid . . . Colleen Holt?"

"Not even close. I'd let you keep guessing, but that could take all day."

"Lucky for you, I'm your only visitor. We've got all the time in the world."

And though Ingrid laughed along with her friend, she couldn't help but glance at the empty doorway, wondering why the boy who loved her best was nowhere to be seen.

CHAPTER FIVE

Ingrid was not built for rest. The medical professionals who'd saved her life insisted she remain in bed until the end of the week. No protestation on her part could change their minds, though it was not for lack of trying. There was much going on outside her hospital walls—as reported by the equally informative and inflammatory Candesce newspapers—and Ingrid couldn't stand that she wasn't a part of it.

Linden visited the day after Charlotte, setting another bouquet of roses on her bedside table to match the first.

"You were here before," Ingrid said, nodding to the twin bouquets.

Linden swallowed with difficulty. "You were so still." His voice came from far away, and his eyes were cloudy. "I stayed for hours—until the nurses made me go home."

"Linden, I'm fine." She grabbed his hand, forcing him to look up. She wished she could knock the melancholy from his face. She was the one who'd been unconscious for three days, and somehow he'd made that his own personal tragedy. "Are you all right?"

He still looked past her instead of at her, as though afraid she

42

might be a ghost and not a girl. "They discharged my father this morning."

"I asked if *you* were all right, not your father," she said, but a chill struck her. His father . . . his father who surely opposed their marriage, who had rejected her internship application. What would he do to them now that he knew? Without thinking, Ingrid gripped the ring on her finger. "Linden, are we—"

He cut her off, as though she had never spoken. "I didn't know, Ingrid. You have to believe me, I didn't know my father would— I didn't want to, but . . ." The desperation in his tone gripped her tighter than his hand around hers.

"Didn't know what?" she asked, squeezing his hand in turn. His voice shook with a tremor she'd not often heard before, and an aching, heavy dread filled her up. His father would not approve of their engagement. Had he woken to discover what Linden had done and told him to undo it? Was this the end of them?

"The speakeasy." The word fell haunted from his lips. "I had no idea my father was going to raid it. He's telling everyone I was part of it, but I wasn't. I didn't want to burn it down. I didn't want to hurt that girl."

Ingrid's chest constricted. She wanted to reach out and comfort this boy who was heartbroken and bruised, but then she remembered the way his magic had roared, the way it had devoured the speakeasy like a hungry beast. "Then why did you?" It wasn't the question she should have asked, but it was the one she wanted answered.

"My father—he thought it would look better if I did it. No one would question my presence if I took part in the raid. He said it would make everything easier."

43

"Your father wanted you to do it." Ingrid tried to hold back the waver in her voice.

Linden nodded gravely.

"And so you did."

"Yes, but I didn't want to—"

"And if he tells you I'm no good for you, that the path forward will be easier without me, will you let me burn too?" Ingrid recoiled, pulling her hand from his grasp.

"Ingrid, no—I wouldn't."

"Wouldn't you? If your father tells you I'll be bad for his campaign—"

"It's his campaign, not mine." Linden scrambled forward onto the bed to catch her face between his hands. "I won't cast you aside. I don't want to."

"You didn't want to burn down the speakeasy either."

"My father was right about this. Pretending I was part of the raid protects me—it protects us. It *is* actually better this way."

"And if it's better that you pretend we never met?"

"Ingrid." Linden tucked her hair behind her ear with careful fingers. "Nothing about that could ever be better. I would never leave you. I love you, and I still want to marry you, if you'll have me."

If she'd have him. It was almost funny, the way he said it, as if there were truly any decision to be made, as if it wasn't what she'd been too afraid to hope for all this time.

Ingrid's fingertips unwittingly found the ring she still wore. "Your father won't like it."

Linden's smile faltered. "My father doesn't have to like it."

"It matters, Linden." Though she took heart at his confidence, that Linden would marry her no matter if his father liked his chosen bride-to-be, it left Ingrid to carry the brunt of the burden, and she cared infinitely more than he'd ever know. "It matters to *me*, and it matters to your father. Don't offer me marriage if you're not at liberty to follow through."

Linden bit his lip. "Perhaps it's best we don't tell Father just yet."

"Maybe you should have asked him first." Ingrid began to wriggle the ring from her finger. "I know what happens to girls like me when boys like you make promises you can't keep."

"Ingrid, stop." Linden stilled her hands and straightened the ring on her finger. "My father might get to decide who I grow up to be, but he doesn't get to tell me who to love."

Ingrid frowned. "I'm sure he'll still try."

Linden raised his hand to tick off the criteria. "She must be beautiful, the kind of girl who will look the part of a senator's wife; she must be clever, a political mind we can use; she must be well spoken and able to give speeches; and she must be from a good family with connections."

"Well, it sounds like he's found you a perfect girl. Why aren't you marrying her?"

"Don't you see? You *are* her." Linden reached out to smooth a lock of her cropped brown hair down. "You're the loveliest girl at school, you're far smarter than me, and you could rally a room full of sloths to your cause if you tried. You're perfect."

Linden's flattery was that of a skilled politician, and Ingrid was not immune. Her father had filled her childhood with imaginings of a future full of grandeur and triumph. He'd told her bedtime stories of the money he'd earn and the magic he'd give her, painting a picture she'd spent the last five years chasing.

But fortune had not smiled on them in the hollows of West

Cendium. No matter how hard her father worked, there was never enough food or flare to go around. And so he set out to steal it. A rich man, Oscar Ellis had taught his daughter, wouldn't notice a few pennies missing from his purse. But the magic he stole was worth a lot more.

His hubris lost him his freedom. It lost Ingrid her father.

And eventually it would lose her Linden too.

"I'm not from a good family." *I'm not from any family at all.*

"I've got enough of a family name for the both of us." Linden reached for her with hesitant fingers. "I see how perfect you are, so we'll just have to make my father see it too." A twinkle in his eye lit like a spark of magic.

"Easier said than done," Ingrid muttered, thinking of the impersonal rejection of her internship application, returned to her with the word *inadequate* scrawled across it. But before Ingrid could press Linden into more specifics, their conversation was cut short by the arrival of her nurse.

"Miss Ellis, you have a visitor."

The nurse was flanked by none other than the very subject of their conversation.

"Senator Holt!" she exclaimed, and quickly shoved her ringed hand beneath the blankets.

"Miss Ellis," he said, her name like cold tea in his mouth. He leaned against the doorframe, a lazy irritation in his stance. "We've not been properly introduced, but I hope you'll forgive my intrusion, considering the circumstances."

He did not give her time to protest, not that she would have. She knew the word *hope* for the lie it was, and she knew the word *circumstances* as blame.

Then he shifted his eyes to Linden, whose hand was still

outstretched in a motion of intimacy. "Linden," Senator Holt said, the syllables layered with meaning.

"I was just . . ." Linden flexed his hand. "Offering our gratitude to Ingrid."

"I am capable of expressing thanks myself." He cocked his head. "If you please . . ."

Linden stared at his father for a motionless moment. Then he stood, gaze lowered, and slowly left the room without another glance back at her.

I would never leave you, indeed.

Once they were alone, Senator Holt returned his gaze to hers and carried on as though Linden had never been there at all. "I am grateful, you know. Your intervention may very well have saved both our lives."

Ingrid opened her mouth to brush away his thanks. She'd done nothing extraordinary. She'd done what anyone would do for the person they loved. But then Ingrid remembered herself. She had earned Senator Holt's thanks—she'd earned much more—and she would not let something as silly as humility stop her from accepting it. She was so much more than her love for a boy, and she would not diminish herself for him.

"Should you be up and about?" she asked instead, indicating his head, which still sported a bandage peeking out from beneath his black porkpie hat.

"The doctors assure me I will make a full recovery with some rest," he snapped.

Ingrid tucked her chin and cleared her throat.

"So shouldn't I be resting?" he asked, daring her to agree.

"It's an election year. Rest can wait."

47

Senator Holt took off his hat. "That girl owes you her life too, you know."

Ingrid sat up straighter. She had combed the papers each day looking for Louise's name, but not a single publication she could procure in the hospital had mentioned her condition. "She's alive?"

"More's the pity."

Ingrid frowned. Perhaps Senator Holt lacked the creativity to imagine the desperation of a girl who had lost everything. Or perhaps he could and simply did not care. "If not a single life was lost, I'll count that as a victory."

"I suppose. She would have been a powerful martyr."

Ingrid did her best to remain expressionless, though his flippancy unnerved her. He had almost died that night. Linden had almost died. If he could not manage an appropriate tone on her or Louise's account, he ought to at least take his own mortality seriously. What, Ingrid wondered, must it be like to feel so untouchable?

Senator Holt surveyed her with narrowed eyes. "Have you heard of the anarchist group fashioning itself the Shadow of the Flame?" he asked.

"It rings a bell."

"I imagine you've seen their propaganda in those flicker clubs you and my son apparently frequent."

With sudden clarity, Ingrid knew precisely what he meant. The posters on every flicker club wall were different, some sporting thick-lined art, others simple calligraphy. "Do you mean those silly slogans like *Truth or flare?*"

"Life isn't flare," Senator Holt said with derision.

Ingrid couldn't help but smile. *"Tender loving flare."*

"Everybody burns."

A shiver shot through Ingrid's body, an ominous weight to his tone. Louise had said exactly those words.

"Everybody burns," Ingrid repeated in a whisper.

"The Shadow of the Flame was a revolutionary group some decades ago. They were at their height of power when I was young." He swallowed with controlled effort. "They care not for the law. They don't stop until they get what they want, and what they want is the end of order."

"But if they've not been operational since you were young—"

"Movements do not die. They simply rest until someone new comes along to resume their work. Do not underestimate the power of a strong leader. As long as their message still spreads among the populace, the Shadow of the Flame lives on."

"So that's why you raided the speakeasy?"

Senator Holt nodded. "I received a tip there might be some members in attendance that night."

"And were you correct?"

"I've been debriefed on what occurred after I was incapacitated, and I think it's safe to say the speakeasy posed a significant threat." He glanced up to where the bandage still covered his wounds. "The girl knew their slogan—*Everybody burns.*"

Ingrid chewed her lip, not caring for once how she appeared before this man who held her fate in his hands. "Perhaps it is a good thing she lives. She can provide information."

"Law enforcement is refusing to release any news to the public, but they've informed me privately they believe she may indeed know something. For now, she's refusing to talk, as you might expect. Denies all affiliation. If she truly has nothing to do with them, she has an odd way of showing it."

Ingrid balled her fists. "She may prove useful once she's recovered. Give her time." *And a modicum of respect.*

"A few days in a holding cell ought to do the trick. Once she's been weaned off the fluffy hospital pillows, she'll be more talkative." Senator Holt's tone turned sour. "She didn't suffer a single injury related to her overdose of flare, thanks to your quick thinking. The medics say she will recover from her burns eventually. The irony is, of course, had she not attacked us, she never would have been given the medical attention her injuries required. Degenerates like her blame us for all their problems, but without our medical care, she'd be dead."

Ingrid was too tired to stop herself from arguing. "The true irony is that if not for us—if not for the raid—she never would have needed medical treatment in the first place."

"A peculiar perspective." Senator Holt frowned. "You confound me, I must admit. Most would not have bothered to save a classmate."

Ingrid's fingernails bit into her palms beneath her blankets at the word *classmate*. He didn't know about the engagement, but surely he knew they were not merely classmates. The papers had noted their obvious attachment, so the senator could not be so completely ignorant.

"A smarter girl, perhaps, might have indulged in self-preservation," he continued.

A smarter girl he would not find inside the walls of Ainsley Academy, Ingrid was sure, but she would not waste her words telling him so. Instead, she said, "There is no end of the things I would do for what I care about."

He surveyed her, and she saw the exact moment when his eyes changed from open to closed, from considering to considered.

She'd given him an opportunity to address it, and he would not take it.

"For an untrained novice, you handled yourself well. I've been told your use of flare was . . . inventive, to say the least. I wish I could have seen it." The compliment stumbled from his lips, clumsy and uncomfortable, followed by a more natural slight. "I did not expect such skill from someone with your . . . origins. But I suppose you must have had lots of practice with your father's line of work."

Ingrid's fingers went to her wrist instinctively. She pulled at the skin, imagining invisible cuffs there. She'd borne all the snide comments her classmates could think to levy against her, against her parentage. She'd never taken the bait, never challenged them, but now that it was Senator Holt, a man so far above her he seemed a giant, she felt the itch to defend herself.

She ought to defend her father too, but her loyalty to family had been slowly squashed beneath the boot of isolation; every year, she got a little stronger on her own, and a little sadder.

It had been a night like any other seven years ago when Ingrid's life had been ripped out from under her. Every night, she waited up by the radiator—whether they could afford to keep it on or not—for her father's morning return. She'd inevitably fall asleep before the sun rose, but she'd wake to his singsong voice calling her his morning dewdrop and planting a scratchy kiss on her forehead. But that morning, she'd woken late, roused not by a loving father returned from his work, but by the bright sun and chirping birds, untroubled by the disturbance in her world.

She'd known immediately something was wrong, but she didn't find out what for another cycle of the sun, left to fend for herself until the sun came down, and still she was alone. At ten years old, Ingrid was a resourceful child. She'd learned to take care of herself well enough. Her father worked odd hours as a bootlegger, leaving her to be her own parent for most of the day. She didn't need her father to feed her, bathe her, or teach her. She didn't need her father to take care of her; she needed her father to love her. She needed him to come home each day and remind her she was not alone.

It wasn't until the following morning that a Flare Force officer and a stern-looking woman Ingrid would grow to hate came to fetch her. They said her father was a bad man who'd broken the law. Ingrid said he was a good man who'd broken the law. It didn't matter either way. They'd taken her from the one-room home she'd known and deposited her in an orphanage. There, she wasn't alone, but somehow it felt lonelier.

That loneliness never truly left, but to admit it would be to admit vulnerability, and Senator Holt was too important to see her any weaker than she already was.

"I am not my father," Ingrid whispered. She would be better. She would accomplish what he could not.

Senator Holt regarded her with a contemplative stare. "Indeed, you are not. We are none of us our fathers, only ever a shadow. Few of us are lucky to shine brighter, but perhaps I have misjudged you."

Ingrid felt so infinitely small in the truth of his words. Senator Holt was not an easy political act to follow. She knew Linden had qualities his father would never see as valuable—things like patience and kindness. They were weaknesses, she knew, but so too were they strengths. Perhaps the senator could not see beyond the shadow he cast. When he was gone, then Linden would have a chance to shine.

The senator dropped her gaze and sighed. "You saved our lives at great risk to your own, and that cannot be discounted. I've been told you imbibed an inadvisable amount of flare but managed to harness not only your own power but your opponent's as well. A risky maneuver. Not many would be foolish enough to try it."

This time, Ingrid failed to stay silent. "Foolish or creative?"

Senator Holt's lips thinned. "Either way, it cannot be denied you managed a difficult feat. Some might call it impressive."

"And you?"

"It takes a lot to impress me."

Ingrid's heart sank. She'd done all but die for Linden, through no fault of her own, and still his father didn't respect her. The word *inadequate* flashed before her eyes.

But then Senator Holt took several more steps into the room and sat in the armchair near the foot of her bed. He crossed his legs and said, a humorous lilt to his voice, "So, Miss Ellis. Impress me."

Ingrid tried to sit up and failed. "Pardon?"

"Linden tells me you're the brightest student at Ainsley Academy, the most dedicated. He tells me quite a lot of things." He narrowed his eyes. "But I've always preferred to make up my own mind. So I'll give you one chance to prove him right. Consider it my thanks."

"What chance is that?"

"I leave for Alorden a week from today to campaign before the first debate."

"What exactly does that mean?" Ingrid barely managed the words, afraid if she said the wrong thing he'd take it all back again.

Senator Holt stood slowly, returning his hat to his head. "The train leaves the station at nine a.m. sharp. Best make sure you're on it."

CHAPTER SIX

Ingrid hated the sound of her heels on tile. The click-clack reverberating through the prison's high entryway was a veritable death march. It was the day before her departure, and she had little time to spare after begging to be discharged from the hospital early, but Ingrid couldn't leave the capital without first making her way across town to inquire about a prisoner.

"You're early, Miss Ellis." The jovial voice did not match the somber nature of jail. "We weren't expecting you for another week by my count."

"Are you questioning my punctuality, Officer Scott?"

"I wouldn't dare. It is always a delight to see you, scheduled or no, but I'm afraid I can't sign you in to see him." Officer Scott, a man with round cheeks and a kind smile, had been stationed at the capital prison for as long as Ingrid had been a visitor. He had welcomed her once a month to the quiet, eerie halls of the capital prison, for once a month was the frequency the state had deemed appropriate for a child to visit her incarcerated father. Once a month, and not a day sooner. It was enough, they said, to keep her from adopting his bad behavior, enough to make it seem as though they cared for her well-being, enough to say they'd done something without doing anything at all.

It was never *enough*.

And it was too much.

The routine of it made it seem like a chore, one day each month she had to slip away from school without arousing suspicion. She didn't want to remind anyone of her shame. What was worse than the shame itself was the way it only inspired more shame. He was her father, and he'd done nothing but try to take care of his family. She ought to honor that, but instead she oscillated wildly between guilt that he'd done it for her and anger that he'd done it at all.

"That's okay," she said, knowing she sounded like a liar. "I didn't come here to see him."

The wounds left behind by her father's crimes still stung. She'd bandaged them with silk and smiles, but underneath it all, she was still bruised and bloody. Officer Scott had seen that piece of her more than anyone, watching her grow up on a diet of pain. Even so, she wanted him to see her strong. She wanted him to see her in control.

Leaning forward on the counter with an air of nonchalance, she tipped her chin up and continued. "I've heard you have a new resident. A girl." Ever since Senator Holt had mentioned Louise's fate, Ingrid couldn't seem to get it out of her head. Maybe it was guilt, maybe it was curiosity. Either way, she needed to see for herself that Louise was all right.

Officer Scott's brow furrowed. "How'd you hear—"

"I've come to see her." Though Senator Holt had assured her of Louise's survival, Ingrid didn't fully trust his account. And, of course, there were the allegations about her connection to the Shadow of the Flame. As in all things, information was power. The more Ingrid could get Louise to tell her, the more she'd have at her disposal with which to impress her future father-in-law. "So are you going to let me?" Ingrid asked, plying her words with sweetness.

For a moment, Officer Scott looked like he might refuse, but he sighed and fumbled with his key ring. "Come on."

He led her to the visiting room, a small, enclosed space that somehow still felt drafty. A wooden table that had been warped beyond any natural beauty of the original tree with a metal bar running horizontally across it sat in the middle of the room. She made a beeline for it, but Officer Scott cleared his throat rather too loudly and she looked up.

"She's in a cell that's a tad far away, so . . ." He trailed off as he kicked a small cinder block into the doorframe with his foot. "I might be a bit longer than usual."

Ingrid nodded once and watched as his eyes flicked to the cinder block once more before he retreated.

Ingrid reversed course and followed him at a careful pace toward the cell where she knew her father spent his days.

"Papa?" she called in a soft voice as she approached.

"Dewdrop?"

Ingrid found the husk of a man who was her father leaning against the bars of his cell. Caged and tired, Oscar Ellis was as far from the man who'd raised her as she could imagine. The father of her childhood had been large and joyous, perhaps in part because she'd been so small. But as she'd grown up, he'd seemed to grow inward, collapsing in on himself under the weight of his sentence. It made her want to hold him close. It made her want to leave and never come back.

"Papa—I don't have very long." She rushed forward, stopping just short of the bars.

"How are you? Are you all right? The guards—they showed me your picture in the paper. I feared the worst, but you're here." He gestured up and down at her, taking in her very-much-so living form.

"I'm alive—that's what's important." Ingrid shook herself of the desire to reach out and touch his fingers. It had been so long since they'd embraced. She hadn't known all those years ago it would be the last time; otherwise maybe she would've held on tighter. But after so many years of heeding the rules, Ingrid couldn't bring herself to break them. What if he didn't feel like her papa anymore? What if he didn't feel like anything at all, ghostly and faded as he was? And what if he was exactly the same, and it was she who'd been irrevocably changed by his prison sentence? It was easier not to know, so she flattened her hands against her sides and shook her head to clear it.

"I didn't ask if you were alive."

"We don't have time," Ingrid hissed. Usually their visits began with a series of questions, a checklist as it were. *Are the guards treating you well? Are they feeding you? Are they letting you exercise? Are you safe?* But he only ever had one question for her: *Are you happy?*

She never had a good answer, so instead she spoke of other things, like her classes and the news. She had stopped confiding in him years before she'd stopped wanting to, too afraid he'd see how well she'd scrubbed away the girl he'd known. She became something different from what he'd raised her to be. She'd become something better. She knew her father wouldn't like it.

"I'm going away for a little while," she said. "I've earned an internship, and—"

"That's wonderful news! Of course, I knew you would. You've always been smart."

Ingrid's face fell. He wouldn't say such things if he knew who she was working for. He wouldn't say such things if he knew *why*. Slowly, she shifted so the hand bearing Linden's ring was hidden behind her back. "It's just, I won't be here for a while. I don't know how long I'll be away, but I didn't want to leave without saying goodbye."

Her father smiled, too wide for his too-narrow face. "I'll be here when you get back. You go make me proud, Dewdrop." He kissed his fingers, then brought them to his cheek.

She mirrored him, a shorthand for affection they'd fallen into when he'd first come to prison. They couldn't touch, but they could hold their own hands, pinch their own cheeks, ruffle their own hair. It was a poor substitute for a thing she'd forgotten how to miss.

Each second that passed was an itch against her skin. She wanted to tell him everything, confess all her secrets to this man who'd once been her whole world. But now he was only a sliver of her life. Once a month, and no more. They didn't have the time for Ingrid to explain. Officer Scott would be back any moment. So instead, Ingrid took a small step forward and lowered her voice to barely a whisper.

"What do you know about the Shadow of the Flame?"

Ingrid's father pinched his brow. "The rebel group? They were active when I was your age. I never had any run-ins with them, though. Why?"

"They're saying the girl who attacked us was one of their agents. I just wasn't sure if . . ." Ingrid averted her eyes, letting them follow a crack in the stone floor down the hall. "If you knew anything else."

"I'm sorry, Dewdrop. All I know is they were anarchists, and not very successful ones. They were fairly loud and violent, but being a member went out of fashion quickly. I'm surprised there's any kind of resurgence."

Ingrid wanted to press him further, but the sound of footsteps echoed from down the hall, and Ingrid knew she'd overstayed her welcome.

"I have to go," she hissed, before scuttling back down the hall and through the door to the visiting room. She cast a single regretful glance over her shoulder, but her father's cell was out of sight. It was just as well. She didn't need a witness as she composed herself, nothing amiss except her heart.

A moment later, the heavy door creaked open to admit Officer Scott and Louise.

Ingrid almost didn't recognize her in the light as she entered the room. Prison had not treated her well, or perhaps more accurately, nearly burning to death twice had not treated her well. Her burns were covered in a thick salve, and her hair was gone, though burned away or shaved, Ingrid couldn't tell. Her cheeks were sunken and sallow, and her eyes looked far away, as though they'd not come with her to jail.

"Thank you for seeing me," Ingrid said, folding her hands atop the table as Officer Scott shackled Louise to the bar running down the center before backing away to stand by the door.

Louise stared at her hands in silence.

Ingrid cleared her throat. "I wanted to check if you were all right."

"I'm in jail," Louise said distantly, her eyes unfocused.

"Yes, I know. It's just—after everything, I wanted to make sure you were . . ." Ingrid gestured vaguely, as if hoping the right word would fall from the sky. Instead, she landed weakly back on "All right."

"I'm in jail," Louise said again. This time, she looked up to meet Ingrid's eyes. "It won't ever be all right when someone like me ends up behind bars because someone like you put me here."

"Someone like me?" Ingrid leaned back, her voice acidic. "We're the same, you and I, in case you didn't notice. I'm from West Cendium—far west West Cendium, *where the flare doesn't flow and the good girls don't go*."

The old nursery rhyme seemed to awaken something in Louise, whose hands became fists within her shackles. "You're just like the rest of them now, though, dripping with magic and an ego the size of that big fancy school of yours."

"I didn't grow up like them, coddled and bottle-fed pride."

"Then you learned it all on your own. How impressive." Louise sneered. "Tell me, if you're nothing like them, how come you look like them, talk like them, and act like them?"

Ingrid took it for a compliment. "Has any one of them ever treated you with respect—besides me?"

Louise raised an eyebrow.

Ingrid ignored her. "Because they respect me now. They didn't before—when I was less like them and more like you. I've worked very hard to earn that respect, and someday, it won't matter that I grew up in the wrong part of Candesce, it won't matter that my father's in this very jail, and it won't matter that I wasn't born into money. I'll have everything I never had when I was young, and more of it than I could have ever dreamed."

Louise leaned back in her chair, a crease of a frown across her face. "I can't believe I feel sorry for you."

"Sorry for me?"

"That's not respect, or any respect worth having. They don't respect *you*; they respect that you know they're better than you. They're making you be just like them to be worthy, when really you were worthy all along." She shook her head, burns shining under the flare lights. "You say you're just like me and in the same breath you denounce that girl. Which is it, Ingrid? Who do you want to be?"

"Who do *you* want to be?" Ingrid shot back. "Don't pretend you aren't playing the game too. At least my way to the top is legal and won't get anyone killed."

"I'm not aiming for the top." Louise let out a long, slow breath. "The rich aren't any better than the poor, just a little more ruthless and a lot more lucky. You think becoming one of them will make up for who you were born, but giving in to their impossible model of righteous richness will just nail the lid on the rest of our coffins. To be like them means killing people like us, and if you don't know that by now, I doubt you'll learn. I'll beg, borrow, or steal—scorch it, I'll even make it from scratch—but you won't catch me with more than my fair share of money or magic. So no, I don't ever want to reach the top. I'm just looking for my scrap of middle."

"What's the point of climbing if you don't reach the summit?" Ingrid hadn't meant to say it out loud, but the thought burned a hole in her tongue. She'd never understood the idea of satisfaction. Why bother being mediocre when she could be great? Why stop before she was finished? Why settle for happy when she could be . . . something bigger than happy, whatever that was? There was no end to Ingrid's race, only a moving goalpost that would keep her running until she dropped.

Louise scrunched her nose, wincing at the pain as her skin wrinkled and twisted. "No one at the top ever got there without throwing someone or other onto the tracks. I'm your sacrifice—I get that."

"I saved your life." If anything, it would have been easier to let her die. Or maybe it would only have been easier if Ingrid were someone like Linden and Senator Holt, who could so easily do what was easy instead of what was right.

"How convenient for your self-righteous little ego." Louise shrugged. "Don't pretend like your way's better than mine just because it's legal."

"Legal . . ." Ingrid remembered the way Senator Holt had so assuredly accused Louise of rebel activity. It had seemed preposterous then, but now Louise had insinuated it too. "So you admit you're one of them."

"One of who?"

Ingrid leaned in, danger in her voice. "The Shadow of the Flame."

Louise cocked her head. "The what?"

Ingrid couldn't tell if Louise's confusion was genuine. "The terror group rebelling against the government."

"I'm just a flicker chemist who dared to fight back. Maybe that makes me a rebel."

Ingrid jutted out her chin. "So you don't deny it?"

"Not everyone who disagrees with the government is wrong, and not everyone who supports them is right." Louise shook her head in resignation. "I won't say much else without a lawyer present—or unless you've come to pay my bail."

Ingrid sighed. "Suppose I came all this way for nothing."

"I don't know why you came here at all."

Ingrid rapped her knuckles on the table, and Officer Scott stepped forward to unhook Louise's shackles.

Ingrid stood and gave Louise one last look, taking in the edge to her jaw, the flare of her nostrils, the wound along the side of her head. This was a girl who wore rage like a badge of honor, and there was the difference between them. Ingrid's fire was buried deep inside, where no one else could see it. She kept it safe, waiting for a day when she had enough power to use it.

As if Louise could see into her heart, she said, "You can't fight the power if you *are* the power."

"You're wrong." Ingrid made for the door, the click of her shoes punctuating her exit.

"I hope so." Louise laughed as though Ingrid had told the funniest joke in the world. "I hope you change the world."

CHAPTER SEVEN

Ingrid found a small stone wedged in the corner of her doorframe the following morning when she emerged from her dormitory. It was almost eight o'clock already, and with the train station a fair walk uptown, they wouldn't have much time to spare. She pocketed the stone, and an uninhibited smile spread across her face. It would be good, at least, to see Linden alone before their departure.

Ainsley Academy was as stately on the inside as it was on the outside. Her dormitory was situated on the sixth floor in the south wing. It was dark and warm, with maroon carpet and oak paneling along the walls. Every part of the academy funneled to a central staircase that led up twelve stories to an arched ceiling. The acoustics were excellent, so Ingrid had to tiptoe as she descended to avoid attracting any notice as she made her way down two flights of stairs and toward the supply closet they'd made their own.

"Linden?" she whispered, rapping her knuckles on the door.

The door opened, and she was pulled into an embrace.

"Ingrid." He said her name against her hair as she sighed into his frame.

There in the small space, tucked against Linden's shoulder, Ingrid felt at home. With no means of privacy at school, they'd had to carve out their own form of intimacy. This room gave them somewhere to be themselves, hidden away. The halls of Ainsley Academy carried so much history, so much expectation. But the supply closet didn't ask them to be anything more than they were, letting their romance breathe in a world that had twisted it into the shape of their school days.

Over the years, they had turned it from a dusty supply closet into a small but sublime refuge from the world. In their first year, they'd hidden notes in a filing cabinet for each other, and in their second year, Linden had stolen the janitorial staff's key to the room—he'd paid them handsomely not to replace the locks—and in their third year, at the advent of their official relationship, they'd moved furniture into the space: an armchair big enough for them both if she sat on his lap, and a cheap flare lamp to see by. In their fourth year, she'd bought a wall hanging, and in their fifth year, he'd replaced the flare lamp with twinkle lights. It wasn't much, but it was theirs.

When last they'd met there, the night of the speakeasy raid, her heart had been dreadfully weighted down. Now it wasn't so much lighter as it was steady, braced for the work ahead.

"We don't have much time," Ingrid said against the lapels of his coat. "Train leaves at nine."

Linden pulled back a little and waved a hand to dismiss her concern. "I've got a car waiting, don't you fret."

"Everything all right?" she asked, eyeing him carefully. Something was different in his demeanor. Back at the hospital, she'd seen him beginning to unravel, his frayed edges showing in the wake of crisis. But now he seemed almost too sturdy. His smile was too bright, his shoulders too straight.

"I'm swell!" he said too loudly. "You're safe, my father's safe, I couldn't be better, honestly."

"Linden, are you sure?" Doubt sprang up in her chest. "It's not the engagement, is it? Your father didn't—"

"No, no, nothing like that." Linden waved her concerns away. "I got you something—two somethings, in fact." Linden reached into his pocket and withdrew a long silver chain. "I thought you could wear the ring on this—at least until things are settled and we can announce the engagement."

Ingrid produced the weighty ring, numb as she let Linden string it onto the chain. She'd endured worse things than waiting for better things than love.

"And the second thing?" she asked in a small voice.

Linden frowned, a darkness crossing behind his eyes for no more than a second. "I don't like how the other night went at the flicker club."

You and me both, she wanted to say but didn't.

"I'm so grateful you were there. You're always so quick thinking, and the way you jumped in to defend me . . ." He trailed off. "I should have done that. I was right there, and I could have fought her. I was the one with the flare, but I just froze!"

Ingrid's lungs constricted. "If you're about to scold me for saving your life—"

Linden looked stricken. "Not at all! It's just that I realized how dangerous the world can be, and it doesn't make any sense for us to wait until we're married for you to wield the same weapons I do." He uncurled his fingers and plucked from his pocket a small tear-shaped vial filled with cloudy golden liquid. "Keep this close for emergencies, just in case."

It was cool to the touch. She didn't know why she expected it to be warm. Flare was just like any other liquid before consumed or activated, but it was also so much more. It was unimaginable power, it was a shining status symbol, and it was the hopeful confidence of a boy who'd only just begun to understand the way the world might devour them if given the chance.

The train met them at the platform with a loud roar, shaking the ground beneath their feet. The air filled with steam and the metal-on-metal screech of a train coming to rest. She felt its cry in her very bones. The sleek flare engine train came into view as the steam cleared, revealing shimmering steel plate all around the outside. A crew was already at work wiping down the front of the train, making it shine and reflect the capital skyline like a mirror.

The Candesce Express traveled all around the border, carrying passengers counterclockwise through the surrounding mountain ranges from the central capital to the five districts: Alorden to the northwest, West Cendium to the southwest, through East Cendium, then to Excandridge, back up to Cintilmore, and then returning to the capital at the center. It was, in a word, inefficient. In another, roundabout. A third, typical.

Those rich enough to use the train would rather spend a whole day traveling around the border than bear the sight of the city proper, where they might catch a glimpse of a poor person. Ingrid had never traveled by train before, and the luxury of it choked her like the cloud of steam descending on them as the train came to a halt.

"This way." Linden ushered her through the crowd.

"Why are there so many people?" she asked, glancing around at the various senators and their staffs milling about.

"The first debate is only a week away. Everyone from the

two campaigns is headed to Alorden. Reporters too. Not to mention, there are a fair number of senators up for reelection. They'll all be going home to campaign." Linden pulled her forward and boosted her up the steps. "But you knew that already. Didn't you apply for just about every campaign staff? Won't they all feel silly for rejecting you when they find out who you're working for."

Ingrid hadn't told Linden his father's campaign was the only one she'd applied for. Her pride had only paid off through the most remote of chances. She wouldn't make that mistake again.

A tall man with salt-and-pepper hair and a polished mustache gestured them onto the train. As they passed, Linden muttered under his breath to Ingrid, "Father's valet."

Linden led her down the narrow halls of the train, passed the coach compartments, toward the back of the train, where the larger compartments would be located. Other passengers milled about in the halls, chattering animatedly without a care for anyone else. Illuminated by the bright flare lights running along the floor and domed ceilings, Ingrid saw more than a few campaign buttons proudly pinned to the coats of other aides sporting phrases like *Holt for President* or *Gwendolyn Meyers puts Flair over Flare*.

"Here we are," Linden said, sliding open a door on the left to reveal what looked to be more like a small sitting room than a train compartment. The entire length of the train car, the compartment was well lit, with an enormous window looking out at the mountains. A large table with clawed legs and a shimmering almost-liquid surface centered the room, which, upon closer inspection, appeared to be flare suspended in glass.

"What if the train crashes?" Ingrid whispered under her breath as the train began to move. It would have been far more economical, not to mention safer, to cast the flare in resin instead of glass. But then, there was nothing economical about the way the rich lived. She glanced about, embarrassed to have let such a thought escape her lips, but no one was looking at her. No one had even noticed her entrance at all.

To her relief, Linden waved her forward.

Senator Holt sat in a plushy seat by the window, newspaper unfolded and obscuring most of his face. Beside him, a copper-haired man spoke rapidly, shuffling through papers and balancing another stack on his knee. His suit was rumpled, shadow carved deep valleys in pale skin beneath his eyes, and even his mustache seemed askew.

"Gerald Cork," Linden muttered under his breath.

"Campaign manager." Ingrid didn't need to ask. No one but the campaign manager could look quite so disheveled and so controlled at once. Ingrid had read about him in the papers, and she'd even heard him give an interview on the radio a few times on behalf of a Senate campaign.

Senator Holt glanced up at them and beckoned, folding his newspaper and tucking it between himself and the armrest.

"We've hours yet before Alorden, but we'd best go over the schedule," he said without preamble.

Cork riffled through the papers on his knee and handed one to the senator and one to Linden.

Ingrid waited, but he did not offer her one, so she leaned over Linden's shoulder to get a better look.

"I'm sorry, have we met?" Cork stared at her, his expression as blank as his tone.

"Ingrid Ellis," she said, holding out a hand for him to shake.

Cork didn't take it.

"She's my—" Linden began, but the senator cut him off.

"She's an intern." He snapped his fingers. "Give me the polling on Halverson too."

"Governor Halverson, of Alorden?" Ingrid said in a rush. "Didn't you work on his reelection campaign last year, Mr. Cork?"

Cork nodded, eyes still vaguely trained on her.

"Then why would he have polling numbers? He's not up for reelection."

Linden bent his head toward her and said quietly, "He's offered Father his endorsement—after the debate, of course. We need to know how he's polling to know how it will benefit us."

Ingrid's stomach plummeted. She'd barely opened her mouth, and already she'd made a poor showing for herself. She cleared her throat and tried again. "That's prudent. Am I right in saying you worked for the late President Wallace as well? I remember reading somewhere—"

Cork coughed and looked up, meeting her eyes. "I did, but even I cannot procure the endorsement of a dead man. Now, if you're done reciting my résumé back to me . . ."

"We ought to discuss the rebellion as well," the senator interrupted from behind his newspaper. "Did you do any polling on that?"

"The rebellion?" The word shot through Ingrid like lightning. "Has that been confirmed? I thought it was still under investigation."

"I see you read the papers," Gerald Cork said evenly. "Congratulations on your literacy."

Linden's lips formed a thin line, but he turned to his father and said, "You polled on it just in case, right?"

"Yes, Linden," Senator Holt said, still unmoving. "We have to know how it will affect our favorables before the news breaks."

"Positively," Cork grumbled. "Rebels will motivate our base to keep things under control."

"Do we have a plan for that? Keeping them under control?" Ingrid asked.

Cork sent a sidelong glance at the senator, whose face remained hidden behind the paper. A beat of silence passed. And then another.

Ingrid's chest was practically vibrating from her pounding heart. "You do, don't you? You must."

"Do you?" Senator Holt folded his paper in half at long last, peering at her over the top with a deadened gaze. "Didn't think so."

Ingrid's blood churned as the senator looked back at his paper, but he'd dismissed her too soon. "I do, sir," she said.

"You do, what?"

"Have a plan."

Senator Holt looked to Linden a moment, as though inviting him to intervene. To his credit, Linden remained still, giving Ingrid the floor.

"And what would a girl like you know about subduing a rebellion?" Senator Holt set his paper down on the arm of his chair with the air of a challenge.

"I fought a rebel, if you'll remember. I'd say I know a fair bit." Ingrid chewed the inside of her lip. She'd fought and she'd won, which was more than the senator could say, but it was hardly the time to remind him of that. She knew how powerful men like him so often took the truth as an attack.

Senator Holt sat forward with a scowl. "All right, then. What's your brilliant plan?"

Ingrid took a deep breath and said, "Talk to them."

"Talk to them," the senator repeated in a deadpan.

"Yes. Most conflicts can be resolved by simply discussing the disagreement and coming to a compromise. If there is rebellion in Candesce, it must be because some people don't feel properly listened to. If you approach them with an opportunity to actually talk about what's making them rebel, I'd wager you'd have no rebellion at all anymore."

"Talk . . . to . . . them." Senator Holt rose to his full height. "You would talk to them."

Ingrid met his eyes. "Yes, sir."

"If I wanted advice from a nanny, I would have asked one. Those tactics might work on squabbling children, Miss Ellis, but they do not work on revolutionaries."

"I think they might, sir. Most fights can be settled before they truly begin in that way." Ingrid had more to say—about how she'd spoken to Louise, about what Louise had said of the inequality she felt in the world—but the senator cut her off.

"Compromise is a weak man's weapon. Why would I want to settle this fight when I could win it?"

"I—" Ingrid began, but Linden's hand tightened around her wrist for the briefest of moments. A warning. She lowered her head, but her blood boiled beneath the surface. Senator Holt would never listen to rebels. He would not even listen to her.

"Instead of spouting off ill-informed opinions, why don't you make yourself useful and fetch me another cup of tea?" He held out his empty cup and saucer.

She took the gold-leaf teacup and pointed around the compartment. "Where's the kettle?"

Gerald Cork snorted. "Just heat it up with flare like the rest of us."

Ingrid pressed a hand to her chest, feeling the small bump of

72

the vial beneath her dress. *For emergencies*, Linden had said, *just in case*. Surely this didn't count as an emergency, though the heat in her cheeks and the tears threatening to spill spoke otherwise.

The valet stepped forward and stooped so he was at Ingrid's level. "Kitchen trolley's at the back of the train. Smells like butter. You can't miss it." And he prodded her toward the door.

Ingrid looked to Linden for a rescue, but none came. He didn't see her. He didn't *want* to see her. Neither did Senator Holt.

So she'd find a way to make them.

CHAPTER EIGHT

Luxury filled the air as Ingrid made her way toward the back of the train. It was a richness altogether different from the polished jewels and luxe fabrics adorning the passengers. Tables were heaped with pastries and fruit and little glass bowls of parfait. It was enough food to feed a small army, which was roughly the size of the crowd of staffers lining up to eat.

Near the back of the trolley, Ingrid found the kettle, flare-powered, of course. Steam rose from its spout, gently curling up toward jars of tea leaves and herbal blends, infinite shades of green and brown. She'd not thought to ask how Senator Holt preferred the beverage, assuming the train would have limited amenities. Back at Ainsley, the serving staff all knew the students' drink orders from memory, so there was no need for Ingrid to learn about different varieties. She knew all she needed: she preferred hers black with a splash of cream, while Linden preferred his herbal with a splash of flare.

It was all the fashion at Ainsley for students to take flare with every meal—nothing like a little magic to enrich the learning process. Most of the other girls wore flare glamours across their faces, making their skin glow, or used it to brighten up their uniform.

Only Ingrid's blazer was the dull navy blue of the dress code. Everyone else took turns emblazoning slogans or images on the backs of theirs, burning through the fabric almost daily for the sake of fashion. But the staff didn't seem to mind. When students passed sparks of energy under desks or lit one another's hair on fire, teachers excused the behavior, saying it was good practice. What she could do with a fraction of the magic her peers threw away on silly pranks and spectacle . . .

"Don't even bother with that stuff. What you really need is a good jolt of caffeine to keep you going on these long campaigns."

Ingrid turned, coming face-to-face with a stranger dressed in a dark suit, with smooth golden-brown skin and a warm smile.

"I'm not here for coffee," Ingrid said coolly.

"Yes, but you really should be. Alex Castille." He held out his hand.

Ingrid took it. "Ingrid Ellis."

"First campaign?" he asked, inclining his head so his short brown curls bounced.

"How could you tell?"

"Well, the beverage choice for a start. No one seasoned drinks that stuff. There aren't enough hours in the day to sleep properly, you know, so we're all terribly reliant on the good stuff." He pointed toward the nearly empty pots of coffee.

"Noted," Ingrid replied, closing her eyes. "But I'm really not here for the coffee."

"Yes, you're falling asleep in the dining car because it's comfortable, I presume."

Ingrid wrinkled her nose. "I'm not sleeping. I'm trying to remember what kind of tea the senator takes so I don't get fired on my first day. If you could simply be quiet for a moment, I know I can just . . ." She trailed off, feeling his sharp gaze on her. Warmth singed her cheeks. She opened her eyes again and turned on him. "What?"

"Nothing!" Alex raised his hands in surrender. "I was being quiet."

"You were not."

He drew back, blinking furiously. "Didn't say a word!"

"Didn't have to. You were being plenty loud with your—" She gestured vaguely at him.

"With my what?"

"Your presence." Ingrid had rolled her eyes at plenty of rich ladies acting half as absurd as she was now. "Never mind. I can't concentrate anyway. What do you want?"

"Want? Why, nothing at all. I simply saw you acting impressively foolish and thought I'd intervene."

"No need, as I was acting entirely normal."

"You keep telling yourself that." Alex cracked a grin. "So Holt's treating you like this already?"

"How do you know I'm working for Senator Holt?" Ingrid asked, hand paused on the way to the kettle.

"He's the only one who treats his aides like servants instead of staffers."

Ingrid gritted her teeth. If there wasn't so much truth to the jab, she might have been able to stand it. Instead, she squared her shoulders and said, "It's an honor to work for Senator Holt, no matter what the task."

"Ah, yes. A very important task. For an important intern. Such importance."

Ingrid glared at him. Sarcasm would not be met with kindness this side of noon. But Alex's eyes weren't laughing anymore. They were flat, devoid of their prior mirth. If she hadn't known better, Ingrid might have said he looked sad.

"What do you want from me?" Ingrid asked, an edge to her voice.

"Look," he said, his voice low, his presence soft. "You make whatever choice you have to, but I heard him yelling at you back there."

"You heard?" Ingrid flushed from head to toe.

"Yes, well, you see, the compartment walls are a mite thin, and—"

"You were spying!" Ingrid pointed a finger at him, knocking him ever so lightly on the shoulder. "Who are you, a reporter?"

Alex raised his hands in surrender. "I was passing by on my way to obtain the world's superior beverage, when I happened to hear someone saying something very smart. And I learned early on that when something smart is being said, you listen."

"You were *spying*!"

"I was spying," Alex conceded. "But that doesn't mean what I said wasn't true. You're right, you know, about the rebels. If they're really out there organizing against the government, the best thing we can do is talk to them. We can't very well address their concerns without first hearing them."

"You really think that's smart?" she asked.

"Course I do. And, as a matter of fact, so do you. Wouldn't have said it in front of your boss if you didn't, right?" He shook his head and tutted. "What are you doing with them anyway? You hardly strike me as Holt material."

The audacity of this stranger, telling her she wasn't Holt material when that's exactly what she was. She had a ring to prove it, hidden though it was on the chain around her neck. But as she looked up at him, ready to tell him exactly that, she saw no attack in his eyes, only concern.

"I am," she said, though her voice wobbled.

"You know they're—well—*the Holts*, right?" He winced. "I don't mean to pry, but if you're back here fetching tea, I hardly think you're drowning in flare like the rest of them. Plus, your ideas aren't exactly their usual fare. Seems a strange choice, for someone like you to align yourself with people like them."

"I'm sure I don't know what you mean," she said. "Senator Holt is an obvious front-runner for the presidency, and an internship on his staff practically guarantees me a quality placement after graduation. Besides, the Holts have been kind to me. Why wouldn't I want to work for them?"

"If Senator Holt becomes president, it won't matter if he was kind to you. His policies won't be. He's only interested in keeping his lot at the top. Everyone else is expendable." Alex wrinkled his face. "Besides, if what I heard was the Holts' version of kindness, I'd say you can do a lot better."

Ingrid swallowed, trying to push away the feeling of truth to his words. She'd just experienced the senator's inflexible nature firsthand, and it wasn't as though her own personal politics aligned with his particularly well. If not for Linden, she certainly would not be supporting Senator Holt in the election.

"You're just free labor to them." Alex's jaw tightened. "They're using you, you know."

"I'm the one using them," she muttered under her breath.

"Look," Alex said, shifting his tone to a quiet, familiar level that far exceeded the threshold of appropriate for two relative strangers. "If you slip me your résumé, I can pass it on up to my boss. I'm a pretty good judge of character, and you're quick on your feet. I think you'd be a decent fit for our team—that is, if you want to do a little more than fetch tea." With a whip of his fingers, he slid his card into her hand.

Ingrid stiffened but took the card. "Who's your boss?"

Alex didn't need to say a word. He simply stepped aside, and there she was in all her glory. Six feet of perfection from head to toe with a purple wool suit and a white fur hat, an idol stood among them.

"Ingrid," he said, gesturing to the woman. "This is Gwendolyn Meyers."

Before Ingrid stood a woman of infinite presence. She was tall and blonde, with her hair curled in at the ends to frame soft features that glowed—not by merit of flare-infused beauty products, as were generally favored by the rich, but by the natural rosiness of her cheeks and the bright smile on her lips. Through her connections at Ainsley Academy, Ingrid had met senators and celebrities alike, her classmates children of societal giants, but not until today had she been truly starstruck.

Alex leaned in and bumped Ingrid's shoulder with his. "It's okay to blink."

Ingrid wasn't certain it was, but she couldn't let her meeting with Gwendolyn Meyers be all staring and no substance. That would be simultaneously wasteful and embarrassing.

"I—I'm Ingrid. Ingrid Ellis."

"So I hear," Gwendolyn Meyers said, nodding toward Alex.

Alex smirked. "Ingrid's working for the opposition."

"You don't have to say it like that." Ingrid scowled.

Gwendolyn Meyers raised her perfect eyebrows. "You're not satisfied with your position."

Ingrid waved her hand a little more frantically than was strictly necessary. "I wouldn't put it that way." After all, it was what she'd wanted. Never mind that her internship hadn't gotten off to the perfect start she'd planned. She'd simply have to try harder.

Gwendolyn nodded slowly, her blue-eyed gaze piercing Ingrid like a needle. "You didn't have to. It's written all over your face." Gwendolyn crossed to the counter and plucked a blueberry muffin from a tightly woven basket. "So, what is it you want, Ingrid Ellis?"

Ingrid, who had never cared much for baked goods, decided in that moment that blueberry muffins were her favorite food. "I suppose I'll have a muffin as well."

Gwendolyn laughed heartily and handed over the muffin, grabbing two more for her and Alex.

"She meant what do you *want*, like what are your aspirations? What do you want out of your internship?" Alex put the muffin in his mouth before he'd finished saying the last word, but she got the gist.

Gwendolyn nodded. "Clearly something's amiss. And so, I wonder if you've given any thought to what it is that you really want?"

Bright red and holding a muffin she had no intention of eating, Ingrid fought the urge to look at the floor. Instead, she raised her chin as high as she dared.

"N-nothing is amiss. The internship is what I want."

"And what is it about the internship? What is that going to earn you?"

Ingrid swallowed with difficulty, a lump in her throat forming over the excuses she tried to tell. Instead, she pulled the truth from the depths of her chest. "I want to prove myself. I want to be taken seriously, and I want to be listened to." Her voice got quieter as her words got truer. "I want to be given a real chance so no one can turn me away because they think I'm no one."

Gwendolyn nodded sagely. "Me too."

For the second time that day, Ingrid was struck silent. To think Gwendolyn Meyers still strove for recognition, for inclusion. She'd started out on the streets, just like Ingrid, singing for her supper until she was plucked from obscurity and deposited on a stage, her picture circulating in the papers and her name gracing thousands of records. Now she was a respected stateswoman. Gwendolyn Meyers had put her singing career on hold to pursue her law degree, and then again when President Wallace asked her to serve on his cabinet. She had more prestige than Ingrid could dream up, more power than Ingrid could touch. And still, she sought out more.

Ingrid's chest swelled with the sameness of them. She wanted more too. She didn't want to simply be someone. She wanted to be everyone. She wanted to be every*thing*.

"But you aren't no one anymore," Ingrid whispered.

"I never was." Gwendolyn leaned in as though they were two friends sharing secrets and whispered into Ingrid's ear, "And neither are you."

Then she was gone, leaving Ingrid alone with her unwanted muffin.

CHAPTER NINE

Upon Ingrid's return, she learned that the senator did, in fact, take flare in his tea. It was the only thing she learned from him that journey, as he didn't say another word to her, and his valet kept her from lurking too close.

The station deposited them high in the mountains, a blanket of snow covering each summit like a hat. Below, Ingrid could see the city's outermost edges, where tightly populated neighborhoods bled into tall evergreens, jagged rock, and frozen lakes.

Linden rejoined her as the other passengers began to disembark.

"Don't do that to me again," Ingrid said as he took her arm.

"Do what?"

"Don't let them shut me out. Don't leave me behind."

Linden smoothed a piece of her hair behind her ear, tracing his thumb along the curve of her cheek. "I never want to leave you."

"Then don't let your father send me away like that." She resented that she had to say it, that Linden had not understood after so many years together that this was important to her. "If this is going to work, your father has to know I'm capable of more than tea service."

Linden chewed his lip. "If only there were something you could do to really show him how smart you are. Obviously, I already know, but he's not going to just take my word for it."

"I know," Ingrid grumbled. "That's why I need to be included in the conversation. He'll never be impressed with me if I never speak."

"He'll listen if it's something really good. You'll just have to come up with something."

"Come up with something?" The muscles in Ingrid's jaw pulsed dangerously. If they weren't on a packed train surrounded by staffers from other campaigns, Ingrid might have given him a piece of her mind. But instead, she swallowed her pride and said as sweetly as possible, "Like what?"

"I don't know, like . . . find real evidence of the rebellion or . . . dig up some dirt on Gwendolyn Meyers. And if that fails, maybe protect him from another rebel attack?"

Ingrid raised her eyebrows.

"You're the smartest girl I know, Ingrid. You'll think of something. I'm sure of it." Linden's eyes dropped, and he turned his face a fraction. "I just wish you didn't have to worry about all this. I wish we weren't campaigning and you could get to know my father like normal."

"Yes, well. We all must make sacrifices for our careers." She resisted the urge to roll her eyes. What Linden would give up was so much smaller than everything she'd already lost.

He shifted back, holding her at arm's length. "We have so many opportunities to advance our careers and so few opportunities to advance our relationship. I want more than stolen kisses in speakeasies, more than secret moments in supply closets. I don't want to just see you every day; I want to spend time with you. I want to plan our future, I want to take you out on the town, I want to tell everyone I see on the street that you're my girl and I can't wait to marry you."

"There's an election going on, Linden. All those things can wait." She didn't tell him how most of those things made her queasy. She didn't want a night on the town; she wanted to be allowed to learn, to work. She wanted to be given the same opportunities Linden eschewed. She wanted what he had, but she would never get it without him.

"I want so much more of you and so much less of him," Linden said, penning their initials into her palm with his fingernail.

Her stomach churned uncomfortably at his honesty. What she wouldn't do to be the kind of girl who swooned at his romantic sentiment. It was a mercy he could not see how his words truly made her feel. Or maybe it was a curse.

She would endure whatever came, contorting herself to fit as the requirements changed. She already had.

"Let me do something for you," Linden said. "Let me show you how I feel."

He wanted to romance her so badly. How could she tell him not to?

"Show me by including me. Stand up for me when others dismiss me. Don't act ashamed of me whenever your father's in the room."

"I would never!"

"You would—you *did*." Ingrid gave him a withering look. "Don't hide me away. I shouldn't have to fight to be seen."

Linden cracked a tentative grin. "I don't believe for a second you've ever had to fight to be seen. You're too beautiful not to look at. The spotlight follows you wherever you go."

Ingrid didn't know how to tell him it wasn't that kind of seen she wanted to be, so instead she said, "So come with me. Support me. Don't make me stand up there alone." No one would dare throw stones if they knew she was Linden Holt's fiancée. No one would send her to fetch tea or call her a nanny.

Linden nodded solemnly and hooked his elbow with hers. "I would do anything for you."

She couldn't bring herself to make the same promise.

The moment they stepped onto the train platform, they were met with a maelstrom of reporters.

"Linden! Over here! Are you fully recovered from your injuries?"

Linden waved to them with a bright smile to rival their flashing cameras.

"Do you believe the rumors about a dangerous rebellion?"

"Will your father campaign on a message of stricter flare control? Do you agree with his policies?"

"What do you have to say to the girl who protected you from the rebel?"

Linden inclined his head carefully, pausing to answer this last question. "I would say I'm incredibly grateful for her quick thinking. She saved my life, and that's no small thing. And I'd say I'm sorry that my actions led to her injuries. If I could wish anything undone, it would be that." He squeezed her hand.

"And do you think she would accept your apology?" asked the same reporter.

"Why don't you ask her yourself?" he said before leaning down to kiss Ingrid on the cheek.

The way the reporters silently watched made Ingrid's breath halt. They looked at her as though she'd been invisible until Linden touched her, until he claimed her. His lips were like a branding iron, telling the world she belonged to him. It was all she'd wanted for weeks, for months, perhaps even years. But in the moment between awe and action, while the reporters hung frozen, the want in Ingrid's stomach shriveled up and crumbled like ash.

"What's your name?" a reporter near the back of the pack shouted, followed by a flurry of questions Ingrid never wanted to answer.

"How long have you been an item?"

"Does the senator know?"

"Kiss her again—for the cameras!"

Ingrid tried to smile, tried to take comfort in Linden's hand still wrapped around hers. But all comfort was gone when Linden swept her into his arms, tipping her back in a dip to catch her lips in a graceful kiss.

Usually, Ingrid felt the world melt away when Linden kissed her. When she closed her eyes and let herself be enveloped by his warmth, she always felt so steady. In the middle of the tempestuous seas of romance, his touch grounded her. But here in front of all these people, he was a stranger and his kiss felt like a performance. It was a puppet show, and she was the puppet, limp and held up by invisible strings.

He brought her upright again after the flurry of camera flashes slowed, leading with his body as though they were on a dance floor, not a train platform. She nearly swept her arms wide and curtsied, the expectation of applause etched into his grin.

She'd known all along Linden had to live his life like a show. When he was in public, he was for other people. She would be too if she married him. *They* would be. Their *relationship* would be. She knew she had to play a part, fool the world into believing she was who they wanted her to be. But as Linden looked at her now with honeyed eyes, glazed over and sugar sweet, she wondered if she'd somehow fooled him too.

"Senator Holt!" a voice called in the distinct tenor of a reporter, drawing the spotlight away. "How does it feel to be back in your home district?"

"A little cold, I'll admit," Senator Holt said as he descended to the platform behind them.

A young reporter near the front of the crowd raised his hand enthusiastically to get the senator's attention. "Running for political office means you'll be away from your duties in the Senate for a considerable time. Do you consider politics more important than governance?"

"What is this, the debate?" The senator chuckled and elicited a few laughs from the other reporters. "The Senate isn't currently in session. Besides, I consider earning the vote of my fellow citizens of Candesce an important part of my job. Regardless of what office I'm running for, it would be more disrespectful to stay in the capital than to come out and meet with the people of Candesce, especially now when they have an important decision ahead of them."

A good answer, Ingrid thought. She glanced over to see Gerald Cork mouthing the last few words along with the candidate.

"And are you looking forward to the debate?"

The senator pivoted to face this new reporter. "Very much so. It is always a pleasure to exchange ideas with my constituents, especially those with such a lovely singing voice."

"It's not a concert, so I'm not sure what my singing voice has to do with anything, but I'm glad to know you're a fan."

From the train, a silver heel descended the stairs, followed by pale skin from ankle to knee, then a blush of purple wool. Ingrid watched Gwendolyn Meyers flutter and land on Senator Holt's stage.

"Gwinnie, how delightful." Senator Holt extended a hand, a smile bleeding off his face like a wound.

"Fancy seeing you here, Mr. Holt." She placed her hand in his, and before he could bend to kiss it, she shook it.

Ingrid barely dared to breathe, hesitant to move at all for fear she'd miss some subtlety or another. Already, Senator Holt had tried to infantilize his opponent, calling her by her old stage name, Gwinnie. Gwendolyn had rebuffed him, not only by dropping his title when she addressed him, but by forcing him to treat her as an equal. If she'd let him kiss her hand, she'd have solidified herself as the celebrity, worthy of his adoration. Instead, she made sure everyone watching knew she was worthy of his *respect*.

"Ms. Meyers! What can we expect from your debate performance?" a reporter called into the silence.

Gwendolyn turned to face the cameras, and they flashed their applause. "Well, I've always been a good performer. Why don't you all come by and see for yourselves?" She winked and crossed the platform toward the waiting town cars in the snow, pausing when she drew even with the reporters and leaning in as though to tell them all a clandestine secret. "Mr. Holt and I go way back, you know. I was born here in Alorden, so he's been my elected official for quite some time now. Funny how this is the first time he's cared to exchange ideas with me. Odd for someone who considers earning the votes of the public to be of such import." She let the moment land for half a beat before saying with finality, "He certainly never earned mine."

Questions ricocheted forcefully across the platform. Ingrid

couldn't hear a single one above the others as the press swarmed them, crowding them all ever closer to the town cars assembled to take them back into civilization.

"Ingrid," said a melodic voice with an air of pleasant surprise. "I hope you'll be coming to the debate."

Ingrid looked into the clear blue eyes of Gwendolyn Meyers. "I— Of course I'll be there."

"Good. I think it's important for young political minds to witness debate. It's how we all learn, after all." She reached out to shake Ingrid's hand before vanishing into a town car.

Ingrid searched for Linden in the crowd. The prospect of his stunned face buoyed in her chest, bobbing up and down with the current of her breaths. Senator Holt would see then just how much she was worth. His opponent knew her name—his opponent shook her hand. He could not keep ignoring her now.

But Linden wasn't there. Senator Holt had stowed him in his own car and closed the door on the snow, on the press, and on Ingrid herself. So much for Linden's promises.

CHAPTER TEN

The days that followed were a stampede of headlines. The papers were obsessed with the dramatics of Holt vs. Meyers. With the campaigns mostly fundraising in the capital, there hadn't been that much to report on, but with the debate approaching, election season was full speed ahead.

Ingrid too was the unlikely subject of the press. LINDEN IN LOVE, read one headline in the *Candesce Courant*.

> *Eligible bachelor Linden Holt has found love at last. Holt the*
> *younger arrived at Alorden Station with a girl on his arm*
> *and his heart on his sleeve. The two exchanged a steamy kiss*
> *on the train platform. Holt, who comes from a long line of*
> *political heavyweights, and his new lady, a scholarship*
> *student at his school, inhabit very different worlds. The pair*
> *were seen at a capital speakeasy days prior. Though Senator*
> *Holt assures reporters his son was there in an official capac-*
> *ity, it's unclear if the girl's presence was planned or if our*
> *mystery maiden has corrupted Candesce's golden boy. With*
> *her humble roots and such illicit behavior, might her views*
> *align more strongly with those of Senator Holt's opponent?*

Will this campaign romance last an election? Cast your vote below.

Ingrid made a face at the paper and muttered, "Steamy?" The train's smoke cloud was the only thing on the platform that fulfilled that descriptor. Ingrid had been kissed a great many times, but never had she felt colder than in Linden's arms before a dozen cameras. The photo beneath the article depicted them mid-kiss, eyes closed, most of her obscured by Linden's frame. She felt obscured by much more—their speculation, their examination, and, most of all, their erasure. She was only interesting to them as an extension of Linden, and even then they hadn't even bothered to print her name.

It was a new day, though. No use wasting it on a foul mood.

But to waste it went, through no fault of her own. Linden's efforts to involve Ingrid in the campaign began and ended with his false promise. While Linden was actually campaigning, learning at the side of his father and meeting important people, Ingrid was fetching tea, fetching documents, fetching really almost anything. One might have thought her a well-trained dog. As the debate approached and tensions grew higher among the staff, she expected to find comfort at least in the regularity of the work, but to the contrary, her superiors all seemed to forget she existed at all.

Ingrid took her herringbone overcoat and headed for the front door. No one saw her go, not even Senator Holt's valet, who stood just off to the side and seemed to find her invisible. Once outside, she made her way to the nearest phone box. She dropped in a coin and asked the operator for the *Candesce Courant*.

"Charlotte Terry, please," she said when the secretary answered.

"One moment."

There was a sharp click and then—

"Charlotte Terry speaking."

"Traitor," Ingrid spat.

"Ingrid? Is that you? It's so good to hear your voice."

"You've betrayed me. It's clear to me now," Ingrid said with a dramatic sigh.

"It's nice to hear your voice too, Charlotte. How have you been? Oh, just swell, thanks for asking." Charlotte mimicked Ingrid's sharp intonation to alarming perfection.

"What do you have to say for yourself?"

"Honestly, Ingrid, I don't have a clue what you're talking about."

"The article!" Ingrid nearly shouted into the receiver.

"You didn't like it? I thought you'd love the attention, and the photo's not half-bad either—though your face is a tad obscured."

"Charlotte," Ingrid growled. *"Steamy?"*

"I didn't write it, okay? What do you want from me?"

"A little loyalty might be nice. They practically insinuated I was a flare fancier." Ingrid groaned. "How could you let them write that about me?"

"I think you're overestimating my sphere of influence—which I *love*, by the way. Please, keep that energy coming. Manifest my promotion with your powerful brain!"

"Charlotte, I'm being serious," Ingrid whined.

"Don't be. It was a fluff piece. Besides, I thought this was what you wanted. How will people know to be green with envy if they don't know about you two?"

Charlotte had a point. Ingrid *had* wanted the attention. But now she had it, she wasn't sure she wanted it anymore. Ingrid felt like a house cat who longed for the outside, only to discover it was cold once she'd been let out.

"Now, as much as I'd love to be scolded by my very best friend, I do actually have to get off the line in case—"

"Are you waiting for another call?" Ingrid asked, voice full of false scandal. "Who is it? Come, tell me."

"Well, if you must know." Charlotte paused, Ingrid assumed for dramatic effect. "I'm waiting on a quote from Governor Halverson's office."

A twist of envy plagued Ingrid's stomach. "You are? That sounds big."

"It is! I'm not an official reporter or anything yet, just an assistant, but they're letting me work on the election."

"But Halverson isn't running for reelection."

"No, silly. The *presidential* election! You know what that means, don't you?"

"What does it mean?"

"That this was all on the record because you didn't say 'off the record' and I can quote you on all of it!"

Ingrid's throat went dry. Charlotte was already writing stories, working on a highly sought-after section of the paper. Thousands upon thousands of people would read her words, or at least the quotes she procured for other writers' articles. No one would read anything Ingrid wrote. No one was likely to see much of her in this election at all, unless it was as Linden Holt's arm candy.

"Ingrid? Are you still there? That's not actually what it means. Ingrid?"

"I'm here," Ingrid said, her voice smaller than she expected.

"Good, because what it really means is if I need a quote from the Holts, I can come to you. My story's on hold until after the debate, and I'll want the Holt campaign's take on things once I get my quote. I'm sure you'll get me something better than the usual media liaisons we talk to. You have an inside man after all."

Ingrid didn't have the heart to tell her how far from inside she was. "You're waiting on a quote from Halverson? About the election?"

"Mm-hmm!"

"Is it about his endorsement?"

"Something like that," Charlotte said, but her voice sounded distant and a little uncertain.

"Charlotte! This can't be a one-way situation. If I'm going to tell you anything about the Holts, you'd best tell me what you know."

"Listen, Ingrid. I've got to run. Afraid if I stay on any longer, I'll ruin my journalistic integrity by telling you Halverson is endorsing Meyers after the debate. Bye!"

The line died, and for a moment, Ingrid thought she might simply keel over as well. If Charlotte was to be believed, the Holts had bigger problems than she thought.

The Holt estate was rather impressive in the late-afternoon light. Pristine white shingles made it look like a snow-topped mountain, and the sun's golden glow ricocheted off the fresh powder blanketing the extensive gardens. On the outside, all was light and welcoming, but the inside was dark. Even well lit with flare lamps throughout the hallways, the oak trim and dark-green-velvet-upholstered furniture contrasted starkly with the exterior. Ingrid rather liked the decor, and though she had never been one to count her chickens, she'd begun making mental notes of all the things she might some-day change about the house—when it was rightfully hers.

To Ingrid's surprise, she found Linden waiting for her, eyebrows knitted in worry, a line wrinkling his forehead. She repressed the urge to fit her thumb to the crease.

"I've been looking for you everywhere!" he exclaimed as she entered.

"And you've found me." She straightened and tried not to look at him. So many days of minimal interaction had made her clumsy at their love. Linden drew closer, the back of his hand pressing against hers in an all-too-casual way.

"I've missed you," he said.

"Yeah, me too." It didn't taste like a lie, so she let it sit.

His fingers found her chin and lifted it until her eyes met his. For a breathless moment, she thought he was going to kiss her. She wanted him to. A kiss to clean the slate. A kiss to reroute their path. But his lips only parted into a smile, and he said, "I have a surprise for you."

Ingrid had experienced her fair share of surprises and enjoyed not a one. Of course, those surprises had all been at the hands of authority—Flare Force raids, her father's arrest, pop quizzes. Even Linden's proposal had been more shock than awe. As Linden led her down the hall, her hand wrapped protectively in his, she endeavored to like his surprise, no matter what it was. But Linden did not lead her to the parlor or even to his bedroom. He guided her down the main hall to the other end of the house, to his father's study.

He came to a halt in front of the door and turned to face her. "No. I can't just leave it unspoken."

Her heart bloomed in her chest. "Linden, I—"

"I feel bad about our time in Alorden." He shook his head. "I haven't done much to make you feel at home here, I know. I've neglected you, even after you asked me to be more conscious of how my father treats you."

Ingrid's insides settled into familiar tension, perfectly taut like strings on a harp. He'd listened, and more than that, he'd heard what she said. Her eyes darted to the door, but she stayed her ground, trying her best to be patient.

"I've been at a loss for how to rectify it, I'll be honest. It's why I've been so distant." He smoothed his thumb over her knuckles. "I wanted to find the perfect way to make it up to you, and I think I've found just the thing."

Ingrid tightened her grip on his hand, unable to verbalize her thanks. This was the Linden she knew existed, if only she could coax him out from hiding, the one who was unafraid to ask his father for what he wanted—for what *she* wanted—and, when that didn't work, demand it.

"I asked some of the staff to help me out, and, well . . . why don't you see for yourself?" He grinned, inclining his head toward the door.

Ingrid took a step, then another and another. Her hand found the handle, and she pushed. "Good eve—" she began, eyes scanning the room for Senator Holt.

He wasn't there.

Instead, the room had been made over as a cozy nook for two. The coffee table had been draped in white linen with gold stitching, two place settings on opposite sides. An arrangement of candles and a bushel of red roses served as a centerpiece.

Ingrid's stomach dropped out from under her.

"Father's out making appearances at some last-minute soirees tonight before the debate tomorrow, so we have this all to ourselves." Linden's arm found her waist, and he leaned his cheek against her head.

Ingrid's shoulders went rigid. "So your father *won't* be joining us?"

Linden crossed to the table and deposited himself on an arrangement of pillows. "That would make this a bit awkward." He took a drop of flare on his tongue and lit the candles before beckoning for her to join him.

She wanted to join him all right, to upend the neatly decorated table, to snuff out the candles, to tear the petals from his flowers and toss them in his face. Her whole body boiled. She wanted to make him feel every bit of disappointment and betrayal she felt.

But anger would only ruin her. She would have to bide her time and bite her tongue, just as she'd always done. She took a deep breath and sat opposite Linden, wearing her smile like an apron, her control like a uniform. For though she was not the staff, she was still there to cater to him.

"How thoughtful of you, Linden. I knew I could count on you to cheer me up."

"I just want to make you smile," he said.

And so she sewed a smile onto her face and let it bleed her dry. It was all she had to give.

Later that night as she readied herself for bed, Ingrid stood before the washbasin and examined her lips in the mirror, dry with a ghost of red paint. She'd used the last of her flare-infused lipstick that morning. Linden would buy her more if she asked.

She didn't want to ask.

Ingrid draped the washcloth across her face and let the cool water drip onto her collarbone. Eyes closed against the fluffy towel, she submerged herself in darkness, in cold, in solitude. What a windfall silence could be. After a moment, she scrubbed her face of makeup, taking care to wipe away the speckles of lingering magic until she was clean.

A bare-faced girl frowned at her from the mirror, no magic, no makeup. No smile.

The girl Linden loved was nowhere to be seen. This girl would not smile for him simply because he asked. This girl would not smile at all. Not until she got what she wanted. And she would. Because this girl had known hunger and loneliness, cold and darkness. This girl had known what it was to have nothing but a heart full of flame. And when this girl was left all alone to do the work herself, that was when she burned her brightest.

CHAPTER ELEVEN

Magic flowed freely at the governor's home. Everyone who was anyone in Alorden's elite society swarmed the ballroom and adjoining halls, sipping on flare and scrutinizing one another's political views like a sport. The press flitted in and out of social circles, seeking loose-lipped socialites and senators who might give them a quote.

Linden had to attend his father before the debate. So Ingrid found her way to the ballroom alone. She'd taken an offered glass of flare-infused something or other but couldn't bring herself to take a single sip. All around her, the richest Alorden society had to offer gathered in circles to gossip and grumble. Flare, passed among them in glittering crystal glasses, turned into fiery portraits above them, their fingers the brush, the ceiling their canvas. It made a pretty picture, but never before had Ingrid felt so painfully out of place.

"You don't strike me as a wallflower."

Ingrid tore her eyes from a senior Holt staffer spinning the same line she'd heard a dozen times to a reporter—*The senator's a big fan of Gwinnie's music. Yes, I expect he'll still ask her to sing at his inauguration. We let bygones be bygones here on Team Holt.*

99

There at her elbow was Alex Castille, wielding a mischievous grin. His warm brown eyes glittered with the prospect of a challenge. He was dangerous—not like fire, but like fun. He was a band without a metronome, and she the unsuspecting dancer whose feet wouldn't keep up. She couldn't take the bait.

"I'm full of surprises," she said, and took a long drink, letting flare charge through her veins. It had seemed so special before. Now it seemed cheap, something she could only earn by becoming someone less than herself. Here, she could not be bold. Senator Holt's message back on the train had been clear. He wanted her to be seen, not heard. He wanted her to melt into the scenery. Ingrid couldn't let him have his way, but neither could she fight him outright without abandoning her dreams. There had to be a way to have both: herself and her future.

Gwendolyn Meyers would never make you choose.

The thought hit her with the force of the Candesce Express, and as though he could read her thoughts, Alex grinned over his glass, dimples puckering and eyes bright.

"My candidate is going to scorch yours tonight," Alex said, a hint of amusement in his voice.

Ingrid looked up at the golden lights decorating the high ceiling above, watching as flare twinkled like stars, bursting with a light and levity she didn't currently possess.

"Hey." Alex nudged her. "No comeback?"

"No," Ingrid said, a few sparks of her own magic flying unbidden from her fingertips.

"Come now. It's no fun if you don't tease back. That just makes me the smug asshole who won't let it lie."

"At least you tell the truth about who you really are."

"That's the spirit!" He clinked his cup against hers.

The room hushed and stilled around them as Governor Halverson took the stage to introduce the candidates. As a courtesy to both parties, the governor had not declared a favorite in the race yet, making him at least appear impartial as he supplied them with questions. He'd announce his preference the following week, when it was more acceptable—though Ingrid wondered who was more informed about what that preference might be: the Holts or the *Candesce Courant*. Either way, it was all expected to be rather civil, according to the papers. Debates had historically been a casual affair where the two candidates would simply discuss the issues before an audience as though they were sitting in their own parlor chatting over a cheese plate.

There was nothing casual about the candidates before them tonight. Senator Holt stood rigid in a black suit and tie, looking uncomfortable and as out of place as Ingrid felt, while Gwendolyn Meyers looked at home on a stage, sporting nearly the same outfit as her opponent and wearing it twice as well.

"She looks amazing," Ingrid whispered under her breath.

Alex leaned in closer. "She *is* amazing."

Ingrid shushed him.

Alex made a face and mouthed, "You started it."

She nudged him, catching only the very tail end of the governor's question. "How would each of you propose to address these threats of rebellion as president? Senator, if you please."

"Thank you, Governor. And thank you to everyone in attendance, especially members of the press." Senator Holt gestured out into the crowd with a smile that didn't quite reach his eyes.

"He's bloviating," Alex murmured.

"Are you joking? The press would eviscerate him if he skipped the pleasantries," Ingrid whispered back.

"Have you ever met a pleasant member of the press?"

Ingrid ignored him, gluing her eyes to the stage as Senator Holt filled it with his substantial presence.

"This is not the first time our country has been faced with internal strife. I, myself, have lived through more threats from within than without. I know what it is to feel unsafe in my own home, to question whether I can trust the people around me. I will not stand idly by and watch the next generation see the same violence. We must meet it with overwhelming force, so as to end any thoughts of resurrecting these tactics. We have evolved with each passing decade, and such malcontents cannot expect to be heard this way. They will make their complaints peaceably, or I will ensure they cannot make them at all."

His answer was met with static applause, the unceasing rhythm crawling up Ingrid's spine like a spider. He'd articulated his answer well. He'd given the answer his audience wanted to hear. He'd given the answer she'd expected from him. Still, it made her feel leagues from the man, miles and miles of snow and ice between them, not the mere yards she stood from the stage.

Ingrid cheated a glance at Alex, but he wasn't looking at her anymore. Instead, his eyes were narrowed as he watched the stage, his breath held so tightly she thought it might break.

"My opponent speaks of a threat. He speaks of unfathomable violence and a future we cannot accept." Gwendolyn Meyers stepped forward into the light. "This is what will happen if he is elected. The threat is not so much in our streets as it is in our Senate. My opponent would have his constituents speak peacefully or not at all, but if he will not listen, how can they expect to be heard?"

A whisper began to spread through the crowd like a crisp winter wind, cold but bracing.

"What my opponent calls malcontent is actually discontent," she continued, unfazed by the unsettled audience. "If we do not treat it as such, we will see it fester and grow into what my opponent so desires it to be. For if he can convince us all that citizens asking for their due is dangerous, he can crush them under the word *rebellion*. Let us not forget that our autonomy as an independent state is predicated on the very idea of rebellion, the idea that change is good and necessary. Violence begets violence begets violence. A healthy governing body does not need to subdue its critics, because its critics are what help it change. My opponent would do well to remember he is a public servant. If he does not seek to serve the public, I suggest he look into another line of work."

Ingrid exhaled hard, like she'd been hit from behind.

"She's not wrong," Alex murmured as the crowd seemed to trip and fall into applause, unsure that they should clap but compelled to nonetheless.

"Is this really the venue for it?" Ingrid asked, though her heart wasn't in it. She'd expressed similar sentiments back on the train, though not half so eloquently as Gwendolyn Meyers. One might go so far as to say they agreed. "She practically aligned herself with the rebellion. I doubt this crowd will reward borderline treason." Even as she spoke, Ingrid wanted to argue with herself. It wasn't treason to do what was right for Candesce. To attack its citizens and call it protecting the innocent when all it protected was the wealthy—now *that* was treason, or at least it should have been.

"Treason is what the voters decide it is," Alex said as though he could read her mind. "She may not win this whole crowd, but I'll bet you my last silver she sweeps the papers tomorrow."

Ingrid snorted. "If I had a silver to spare, I'd take your bet."

Alex tilted his head, a smirk creasing his smooth brown

skin. "Let's keep money out of it, then—and the press, for that matter. Let's make this about you and me."

"What did you have in mind?" Ingrid asked against her better judgment.

"You listen with an open mind to what she says tonight, not as a Holt staffer, not as *Linden's new lady*, but as the independent thinker I know you must be. If she convinces you, I win."

"If she convinces me of what? That she'll beat the senator?"

Alex shook his head. "No—I don't care about that right now. I care about *you*." He stuck out his finger and prodded her in the shoulder like a petulant child. "If she convinces you that she's right, you quit working for that antiquated excuse for a politician."

Ingrid didn't ask what happened if she won. There would be no winning for Ingrid tonight.

"Let us speak to those concerns, then, shall we?" the governor said, nodding to each candidate in turn. "How would you, as president, seek to address complaints of flare shortages across Candesce, in particular for working-class citizens?"

Senator Holt cleared his throat. "It's a simple problem with a simple solution. Our government collects the majority of the nation's flare in illegal taxation—via the election itself. When we vote, we give the winning parties free rein to allocate our magic as they will. In the past, a great deal of our nation's most valuable commodity has been exported in trade to other countries that are not situated atop a well of magic. We, as a governing body, must reverse these taxes. The people know what to do with magic far better than the government does, after all."

"You raise an interesting point, Senator." Gwendolyn Meyers smiled at him, a stark contrast to Senator Holt's expression of shock at being addressed directly by his opponent. "I agree with you that the collection of electoral flare is an improper, if not illegal, taxation. Although I suspect your quarrel with it is different from mine. Requiring a payment of flare in order to vote prevents so many from partaking in this civic duty, and it weights the accessible influence heavily to one specific demographic. But I digress. I would like to ask how allowing those with the most magic to simply keep it would help to alleviate the flare shortages for those most in need?"

The audience rippled with restless energy. It was highly unusual for the candidates to address each other directly, though it was not strictly against the rules. Historically, candidates spoke *about* rather than *to* each other. Yet one more way Gwendolyn Meyers had upset the status quo. A smile twitched at the corners of Ingrid's mouth.

Senator Holt straightened to his full height, a meek gesture against the power of Gwendolyn's presence. "It is well documented that those with means generate economic growth far better than any government project. Why should we not put our trust in the people to do what is right and necessary? If we reverse the election tax and allow the flow of magic to return to its original owners, they will be in a position to compensate their employees with not only money but magic as well. If we flood the top, flare will trickle down to everyone."

As eager applause rang out around the ballroom, Ingrid kept her hands by her sides and put all her energy into not rolling her eyes. She wouldn't give Alex the satisfaction.

Gwendolyn Meyers said nothing for a long moment after the applause died down. The silence unsettled the crowd perhaps even more than her radical platform, and they began to shift and sway. She took a step forward. Then another and another until she was descending the stairs to walk among her audience. Whispers shot up like geysers, the hot steam of gossip following as she made her way across the room to the refreshments table.

She picked up a glass and made a show of filling it with perfectly square cubes of ice. From her pocket she withdrew a vial of flare and held it up for everyone to see. "Trickle-down magic." She let the words fill the room for far longer than was comfortable. "In theory, the magic will spread from person to person, generating wealth as it goes. It will touch every citizen, bringing fortune and favor to all." She tipped the vial into the glass, letting a small amount of flare travel from the top to the bottom, sliding off each ice cube in its journey. "But in order to work, trickle-down magic requires the utmost generosity of its most affluent. It requires that all of us divest ourselves of the idea of wealth, that when our government relinquishes its claim on our magic, we in turn redistribute it to our community. It requires us to be unselfish and unburdened by greed. It requires us to acknowledge that we are *not* those things as it stands and to become them requires we remove ourselves from this unbalanced system of rich and poor."

The room had gone eerily quiet, every eye drawn to the glass of ice and flare in her hand. Waiting. Watching. Worried.

"It is uncharitable of you to assume such things of these good citizens of Candesce, Ms. Meyers," Senator Holt began, ready with a rebuttal not a one of them would ever hear.

"Is it, Senator?" Gwendolyn gestured to the crowd around them. "I do not see a room of humbled individuals. I see women with flare glamours lighting up their cheekbones and gowns sparkling with flare light sewn into the stitching, I see men setting off explosions in the palms of their hands for the simple thrill of it, and I see barrel upon barrel of flare carted in as refreshments, to be used as a frivolity on a special occasion, for no other purpose than to show off to one another. When we do this, we are saying our own entertainment, our own pride, and our own continued wealth are more important than flare equity. We say we are more important than them."

Ingrid's fists tightened, and pinpricks of numbness tingled through her hands. The first time Ingrid had walked into the world of wealth, she'd felt awestruck and then she'd felt sick. The way people at the top of the world used flare so casually, so incautiously. It was an insult. She felt the indignity of it all like a flint against her tongue waiting to catch fire. Gwendolyn's words struck against her insides, igniting a slow-burning rage into a full-blown inferno.

Gwendolyn Meyers swept her eyes across the room, and Ingrid could have sworn she looked directly at her before tipping her head back to drink from her vial of flare. "When we allow trickle-down magic to fail, it's us—not the government—who are willing to let the rest of them burn while we revel in our riches."

Ingrid looked down at her own dress. It was nothing compared to the gowns glittering with magic around her, but still far more glamorous than anything she could have dreamed up as a child. Such a garment—gifted to her by Linden, as so many of her favorite possessions were—would have fed her and her father for a month. Her engagement ring would have warmed their home for longer. If her past self could see her now, Ingrid didn't know if she'd be proud or disappointed.

Gwendolyn Meyers took one, two, three echoing steps into the center of the ballroom, then exhaled a jet a flame into her glass.

Gasps and yelps filled the air as the crowd collectively recoiled, but when the sparks and steam had cleared, the ice and flare were gone, leaving only a sparkling glass devoid of any trace of what had been.

"When they are gone, who then will we burn if not each other?"

Ingrid could stand no more. Before she could think better of it, she turned on her heel and stalked from the room, chased by the receding voice of her idol speaking a truth Ingrid had always known but did not want to hear.

"Ingrid, wait!" Alex caught her by the arm as she expelled herself into the cool night air of the gardens below.

"Don't." Ingrid wrenched herself from his grip, raising her hands to pull at her perfectly styled hair until her scalp stung. She let out a groan of frustration and kicked a nearby bush, scratching the top of her foot. "I hate this."

"Then don't do it." He jogged to intercept her path. "You have other options. You don't have to work for him."

"But I do. That's the problem." She resisted the urge to hurl herself into the shrub, knowing that the satisfaction of her tantrum would result only in ruining her dress. "If I want to be anyone, I have to do this."

"Not *anyone*," Alex countered. "If you want to be that one version of yourself—that version that is more them than you."

"Yes, well, that version is obviously better," Ingrid snapped.

"I don't think so." Alex crossed his arms and fixed her with a cold stare. "If you think that sacrificing who you are to become what they are is going to make you somehow better, you're missing the entire point."

"No, you're missing the point. No one values me for who I am; they value me for who I might one day be. If I don't become her, if I don't earn Senator Holt's respect and marry Linden and prove to everyone I am more than my birthright, then . . ."

"Then *what*?" Alex said the last word with a hard *h*, imitating the elevated class. "You won't be exactly like them, ruining things for the rest of us? Scorch it, Ingrid! You can still be powerful without them. You can still be important without them. And even if you're not, at least you'll be yourself." He threw his hands in the air.

"No one will respect me if I'm just me," Ingrid said quietly.

"Well, I won't respect you if you're not." Alex frowned. "We both know this is ridiculous. You might have gone to their fancy school, and you might be kissing around with their monied boys, but you aren't one of them. You're a lot more like me than you are like them. What do you think is going to happen? Senator Holt will look at you one day and decide you're *not* scum of the earth because you make a decent cup of tea? He treats you like a servant because he thinks of you like one. Nothing will ever change that."

"I know what I'm doing," Ingrid growled through her teeth, but the truth of what he'd said stung. She knew what she was doing all right, and she knew it wasn't working.

For a moment, Alex looked almost sad. "You don't belong with them," he whispered before he turned and walked back inside.

"Maybe not," she said as she watched him leave. "But someday— someday I will." And she smiled, because she knew exactly how to get what she wanted. Playing by the senator's rules was a losing battle. He was power, and she a mere pawn. No matter what strategy she tried, he'd block her. He wouldn't teach her, he wouldn't welcome her, he wouldn't so much as even look at her. She'd never beat him at his own game, so it was high time she made him play hers.

CHAPTER TWELVE

Ingrid couldn't sleep that night, so she waited until the rest of the house had gone to bed before emerging from her room. Wearing her most dignified pajamas and armed with a tea tray, she made her way toward the little ray of magical light at the end of the hall.

The study was dark but for the flare-gilded frames on the wall, housing the senator's many achievements and accolades. He sat in the armchair with his feet up on the coffee table, letting little swirls of flare shoot into the air and fall like snowflakes.

"Good evening, Senator Holt," Ingrid said, entering without permission.

"What in the—" Senator Holt stood up as the door swung open. "Miss Ellis? What are you doing up?"

At least he remembered her name. She crossed over to him and placed the tea tray on the table. "I saw you were awake and thought you might like a cup of tea. After all, it seems that's to be my singular job on this campaign, and I'd hate to disappoint."

The senator didn't thank her as she passed him his cup, only sniffed the beverage. He pulled a vial of flare from his pocket and let a liberal amount splash into his drink. He did not offer to share.

Ingrid sat in the chair opposite him, taking care to cross her ankles. Perhaps she had not dressed the part for an encounter with her future father-in-law, but she was still a lady.

Senator Holt narrowed his eyes, blinking at her as though taking her in layer by layer. "To what do I owe the . . . pleasure?"

Ingrid poured herself a cup of tea as well. "I thought we might discuss my position here."

"You are an intern. Your *position*, as you put it is, is to do as you're told and not get in the way." He took a slow sip of his tea. "There is nothing to discuss."

"On the contrary." Ingrid set her cup on its saucer, letting the sound punctuate her sentence. "There is much."

"I'm afraid, Miss Ellis, you'll find I have nothing to say on the matter." A spark of magic collected at his fingertips, and with an aggressive jerk of his arm, he sent a burst of flame into the fireplace.

Ingrid's heart threatened to jump from her throat. She'd thought, for a moment, that he meant to aim at her. But as the firelight played across the senator's face, she found a weariness in his eyes that surely was not meant for her to see.

"That's just as well. Gives me more time to speak." She plowed on before Senator Holt's expression had time to darken. She could not let him intimidate her. She could not let him change her mind. "I came to this campaign for many reasons, as I'm sure you're aware. I've admired your political career for a long time, and the chance to contribute, no matter how small, to your presidential campaign is an honor. That being said, there are a few other considerations to be made."

The senator sipped his tea, but he didn't interrupt.

"I am a student, and I understand you have more experienced staffers than me to do the heavy lifting, but unfortunately I fail to see how me fetching tea and being barred from important political meetings is going to teach me anything save for the perfect ratio of tea to sugar."

"I'd say you have a fair amount to learn yet in that arena."

"Yes, well, I don't aspire to open a tea shop, do I?" she snapped. Softening her tone, she added, "Sir."

"No, indeed. You have much higher aspirations. Much too high, some might say." Senator Holt leaned forward. "I have seen the way you and my son conduct yourselves, both in private and public. It is a thrill, I'm sure, to have the attention of someone like him, but if I may offer you a piece of advice: Don't get used to it. You amuse my son, to be sure, but do not take liberties based on a temporary attachment. You are not part of this family."

Ingrid swallowed over the lump in her throat. So Linden had not told his father of their engagement after all. The fact of it fell flat against her heart, like a boulder, not a blade. Linden's procrastination was a weight to carry, not a wound to bear. In Ingrid's experience, no one of Linden's social caliber waited for the last minute to do anything they *wanted* to do. Where time and money were in abundance, procrastination seemed a foreign concept, as though it belonged to a different class altogether. That he'd chosen to keep this from his father spoke to his indecision. Or perhaps it spoke to his shame.

"I am not a Holt," she said, and from beneath her nightdress, Ingrid lifted the ring on its silver chain. The diamonds caught the firelight, shining with an iridescent glow of flare. "But someday I will be."

"My mother's ring," the senator said quietly, reaching with hesitant fingers for the large sapphire in her palm. Then he seemed to catch up to himself, and he cleared his throat. "That was not Linden's to promise, not without my consent."

Ingrid stowed the ring back beneath her collar and said roughly, "You cannot tell him who to love."

"My son doesn't know what love is." Senator Holt narrowed his eyes. "He is going to be a senator, and maybe president someday. He is going to rise so very high, and frankly, I don't want to see you weigh him down."

"I won't." She clenched her jaw. "I am more than you give me credit for."

"Oh, I give you credit. Your marks at school are impressive, certainly—a future valedictorian, perhaps. It is not as though you are without talent. You could have any number of career options far above your station. For a girl with no birthright, your prospects are brighter than any of us could have expected. And yet you have set your eyes on matrimony. Why—when you could be a lawyer, a teacher, a writer—would you want to be a wife?"

Ingrid suppressed the urge to fidget with the ring. "Wife is not an occupation, simply a state of being. Who is to say I cannot be both wife and lawyer?"

"I have no doubt you believe you can." He set his cup down, splashing some tea over the side to pool in the saucer. "But that doesn't make you right for Linden. That doesn't make you his equal. I will not stand by and watch you ruin him."

"I won't ruin him. You'll see—just give me a chance—I deserve a chance."

"You deserve nothing; you must earn it."

Ingrid had him now.

She gripped the arms of her chair and sat as tall as she dared. "Then let me."

The light from the fire bowed across the senator's face as his expression went steely. "I told you to impress me."

She nodded. "I think you'll find my proposition adequate."

"I doubt it."

She took a deep breath and exhaled long and slow. "Victory is never assured in such things as elections, but if anyone ever had a lock on the presidency, it should have been you. Tonight's debate was . . . unexpected."

"Any one of my staffers could tell me that," he said, a bored tone to his voice.

"I'm not finished." Ingrid laced her fingers together in her lap, more to keep them still than anything else. It would not do for the senator to see her hands shake. "In a straightforward election year, there's no reason why you wouldn't win. But Gwendolyn Meyers is anything but a straightforward opponent."

"I thought I said to impress me." The senator scoffed. "She's an excellent performer, I won't deny it, but few of the truly powerful electorate will be impressed by her theatrics."

Ingrid pursed her lips.

"Don't tell me you are. She's an entertainer! The voting elite doesn't want some silly girl running the country."

"She's not a silly girl," Ingrid said, her voice much more defensive than she'd intended. "She is fresh air to a political arena that's been locked down to the same dozen families for decades. She doesn't come from money, so the common people will relate to her, but she's rich and connected and incredibly well educated, so your society will like her plenty too. She is the perfect balance of old and new, rich and poor. It is almost as if she was tailor-made to beat you." She paused, uncrossing her legs and leaning forward. "But you already know that, sir."

Senator Holt's voice was steady, but his face went ashen. "I'll be fine."

"You might be." She had only one bullet, and it was time to take her shot. "Interesting that Governor Halverson agreed to moderate your debate after he told my friend at the *Candesce Courant* he's planning to endorse Meyers next week instead of you."

Senator Holt adjusted his grip on his teacup. "I'm sure your friend—"

"Got the quote directly from his office." She wouldn't let him swat her away like a fly. "Believe me or not, you'll lose more than Halverson. You'll lose more than today's debate. Don't you want to be ready when you do?"

Senator Holt rose to his feet. "Go to bed. It's high time I did the same."

"I may not be of your particular pedigree, but I'm right and you're wrong, and the sooner you realize it, the better off you'll be."

"I'd offer to make you a wager, but I know how your lot is with money."

That one stung. She brushed it off as best she could. "I don't want to wager with coin."

"Well, this just got interesting." He sounded almost amused.

"I've made some well-placed connections with the opposition," she said quickly. "I believe I could easily gain a place on Meyers's staff."

"I'll not deal with traitors."

"If I was a traitor, I'd be gone already." She stood slowly. He was taller, but she was right, and that was almost as good. "I propose I make the move. If I'm right about Gwendolyn Meyers, having a spy on the inside will serve you well down the road."

"And if you're wrong?"

Ingrid swallowed. "I won't be."

"If you're wrong," the senator said more firmly, "you'll be off my campaign. It will be as if this conversation never happened."

Ingrid nodded slowly, understanding his meaning perfectly. If she brought him nothing of value, she would lose Linden. "Fair. But if I'm right, you give me and Linden your blessing."

The senator examined her for a moment before standing and extending his arm. "It's a deal."

She shook his hand, warmth spreading through her from head to toe, and though it was the dead of night, it was the closest she'd ever felt to the sun.

CHAPTER THIRTEEN

"I don't like it," Linden said when Ingrid told him early the next morning.

"You don't have to like it; you just have to let me do it." Ingrid had packed her bags already. "It was your idea anyway!"

"It was my idea?" Linden crossed the room to lean against the doorframe, his body blocking her in. "I would never suggest something as foolish as spying on the opposition."

"You did—when we were on the train. You said I needed to do something to impress your father, and I should try to dig up dirt—"

"I was obviously joking!"

"Well, I'm obviously serious." Ingrid sighed and fumbled with the chain around her neck. "Help me, would you?" She turned to let Linden latch the clasp.

"You realize this means we can't see each other, right? We won't be able to talk at all in public." Linden brushed his thumb along the nape of her neck. "Not at all. We'll have to pretend to be broken up."

No one really knew we were ever together. That was what she wanted to say, but instead she reached back and interlaced her fingers with his over her shoulder. "It's only for a few months. The election will be over come spring, and everything can go back to normal—*and* with your father's approval."

"What about letters? Can we at least write letters?"

Ingrid suppressed a shudder. Letter writing was so intimate, so romantic—*too* romantic. But it was also too risky. "Someone might intercept them. Best not to put anything in writing, I think. We'll simply have to bide our time until the opportunity to speak privately arises."

He stepped closer and wrapped his arm around her, holding her tight. "That's not enough," he whispered against her hair.

"I know." His warmth made her want to stay, to forget all this and carry on without his father's approval. But that wasn't the plan. And nothing was more important than the plan. "You have to let me go."

And he did.

She didn't dare look back, fearing she'd see the doubt she felt reflected in his eyes. Courage was a commodity, and Ingrid would be damned if she didn't use it while she had it.

And that was how Ingrid found herself on the doorstep of Gwendolyn Meyers's Alorden residence at the crack of dawn. The cold was bone deep, even in her herringbone overcoat and maroon wool hat. She practically danced in her boots to stay warm as she let the large brass door knocker in the shape of a raven fall with a thud against the door.

"Ingrid?" A groggy Alex answered the door, dressing gown pulled over only one arm. "Am I having a fever dream?"

"Good morning," she said cheerily.

"It's the middle of the wretched night."

"It's seven thirty in the morning. But that's neither here nor there."

"I wish *you* were neither here nor there."

"First you want me to join your side; now you want me gone? Careful or you'll get a reputation for inconsistency." An involuntary shiver ran through her, and she set her shoulders against the cold. "Aren't you going to invite me in?"

Alex rumbled his assent and opened the door wider.

As Ingrid followed Alex into the sitting room, she saw the sofas were piled with blankets.

"You're sleeping here?" she asked.

"It's not economical for all of us on the staff to rent. The candidate has a large house, and she offered, so here we are."

"I meant *here*." She gestured to the sofa.

"It's large enough for most of us." Alex shrugged. "I drew the short straw."

"I'll say."

Alex pushed his arm through the other sleeve of his dressing gown before sitting opposite her in a plush armchair. "So, to what do I owe the interruption of my beauty sleep?"

Ingrid's mouth fell open in exasperation. "You said you wanted me."

He raised his eyebrows.

"For a job. Back on the train, you said you'd pass my résumé on," she added hurriedly. "So I'm here."

"You're here. For a job?" Alex blinked at her, sleep still clouding his eyes.

Ingrid huffed. "Last night you told me to leave the Holt campaign."

That made Alex sit up a little straighter. "And you left?"

"I'm here, aren't I?" She picked up one of the throw pillows and biffed him across the knees with it. "Don't make me beg. Do I have the job or not?"

"That depends." He leaned back, crossing his arms as he surveyed her. "What changed your mind?"

"Would you believe me if I said insomnia?"

Alex glanced pointedly out the window at the slowly brightening sky. "Yes."

"I couldn't stop thinking about what you said at the debate."

A grin split his face. "I like that I'm in your head."

"Don't get used to it."

"All joking aside, what was it I said? I know I was pushing a pretty hard agenda, but if you want my recommendation, I need to know why you even want it."

"Want to make sure I'm here for the right reasons?" she teased, playing for time. If she'd known he would make her jump through hoops for this, she might have prepared a little more. Perhaps she should have guessed it—if not because of his entirely obnoxious personality, then at least because any normal person would expect her to interview first. She'd been silly to think he might just hand her the job, no questions asked.

"There's no wrong reason exactly," Alex said.

Ingrid took a deep breath. This was her chance. "You said I didn't belong with them, and you were right. They don't understand me, and . . . they're not going to try. Listening to your candidate speak last night, I get the feeling that might not be the case here." Ingrid had practiced her cover story on the way over. It was convenient that Alex had laid it all out for her the night before. Of course, it was *inconvenient* that it was also true.

"So you want to belong."

She wanted it so badly, the words burned her tongue. She'd kept that particular want inside for years as though it was part of her anatomy, tucked against her ribs. It was why she'd set her sights on becoming a Holt. It was why she planned to marry Linden. It was why it hurt so badly when Alex had said *you don't belong with them*. It hurt because it was true.

"I want to belong, and I want it to matter."

"Don't we all?" He cocked his head, surveying her with soft brown eyes. He wasn't teasing this time. "Well, I think you're making the right choice, for whatever it's worth. Anyone could see you were miserable working for the Holts. You'll be much happier here."

Ingrid didn't doubt him. But Ingrid didn't want to be happy. She wanted to be powerful. And she wasn't sure she could be both.

"So you'll have me?" she asked tentatively. "I have the job?"

"Whoa there." Alex held out his hands. "I promised I'd recommend you, but I don't have hiring power. That's all the candidate. You'll need to meet with her officially for a real interview first, but I'm not sure where in the schedule we can fit that in. Maybe before we— No, there's no time. The train leaves early, so . . ." Alex carried on muttering to himself, eyes unfocused as he mentally juggled the calendar.

It was just as well. Nerves shot through Ingrid's every limb. Though she could say she'd officially met Gwendolyn Meyers, the prospect of a formal interview with the woman herself felt infinitely more impossible. Back on the train, she'd made a fool of herself quite enough for a lifetime. She didn't need to repeat the experience.

"Can you believe our Alex?" came a melodious voice from behind her.

Ingrid turned to see a woman with an olive complexion and a center-part bob. Beside her stood a man with dark brown skin and a crooked tie. They threaded through a large archway into the sitting room with matching wide grins.

"Who do you think she is?" asked the man, as though she were not in the room at all.

"No idea," said the woman, leaning forward onto a high table, resting her chin on her fist and sweeping vibrant green eyes over Ingrid. "Do you think Alex knows this is the parlor? People use it. He knows that, right?"

"He does," Alex said ominously. "He would also take it as a kindness if his colleagues would take their whisper session elsewhere so as not to interrupt his important conversation."

"No can do, buddy," the man said, crossing the room and shaking Alex's shoulder. "We've got a schedule to keep."

"More important," the woman added, sitting herself at the end of Ingrid's sofa, "we have a guest. Kindly introduce us to your lovely companion."

Alex groaned and leaned back against the armrest. "Can't we have a cup of coffee first?"

"Come now, Alex, you were raised with more manners than that."

The man grimaced. "Was he, though?"

"Kindly shut up, Clarence." Alex stood and gestured to Ingrid. "Ingrid Ellis."

Ingrid rose to her feet and shook the woman's offered hand.

"Charmed! Faye Dupris."

The man, Clarence, didn't look nearly so pleased. He shifted his gaze from Ingrid to Alex and back to Ingrid, befuddlement twisting his features.

"I thought I told you to shut it," Alex said, glaring at him.

Clarence raised his arms in submission. "Didn't say a thing, did I?"

"So you must be that Holt staffer Alex has been trying to land," Faye said, gesturing for them all to sit back down.

Ingrid turned to Alex and mouthed the word *land*, a question in her eyes.

"Not like that—for the campaign staff!" Alex waved his hands wildly.

"And assuming the candidate signs off, whose staff will she be on?" Clarence asked.

Faye clapped her hands together. "Oh, please say mine. I could use another brain."

"My staff." Alex glared. "She's for *my* staff."

Face pinched, Clarence surveyed him doubtfully. "Do you really need a staff? You're an assistant."

"I'm a *special* assistant, thank you very much."

"Ah yes, I forgot your promotion." Clarence mussed Alex's hair.

Alex swatted him away and turned to Ingrid. "I'm the direct assistant to our campaign manager, Birdie. That means I do what she doesn't have time for."

Ingrid nodded. "So, then, what will I be doing?"

"What *I* don't have time for."

Clarence clapped Alex on the back. "So in charge!"

"No tea duty?" Ingrid asked in a small voice, wincing at how pitiful her words sounded.

"Birdie would have our hides if we treated you like that," Faye said. "She doesn't believe in free labor without an equal exchange. So, sure, you'll do a fair amount of menial tasks, but you're also going to learn—that's where Alex comes in."

Alex nodded vigorously. "I was in the trenches like you just a couple years ago, so when Birdie decided she needed another assistant, she asked me to put together a training plan and recruit someone. You're not going to just learn how to do this one job, though. I've done about everything there is to do on a political campaign, working with Birdie, so let me know what your interests are and I'll make sure you learn about it."

"Birdie sounds like an interesting boss." Ingrid glanced between her three new acquaintances. Already the Meyers campaign was starkly different from the Holt campaign. For a start, at least three people knew her name and no one had yet asked her to make them a beverage.

"You'll see when you meet her." Alex rose to his feet. "She'll be your boss too, after all."

"I thought you were my boss," Ingrid said.

Faye and Clarence both laughed.

"If we hire you, you'll report to Birdie just like me." Alex shot his colleagues a look before turning back to Ingrid. "I'm nobody's boss."

"Someone should tell *you* that," said a gruff voice.

Faye and Clarence stood, and Ingrid followed suit, funneling toward the foyer, where the stairs spilled out into the entryway. There, Ingrid saw the antithesis of Gwendolyn Meyers. Short with square shoulders and a thin white face, she looked as haggard as Ingrid felt. Her red hair was wild and poofy around her shoulders, combed but not styled, and she wore a loose-fitting black suit a little too long in the arms and legs, as though she were a child wearing a parent's clothes for dress-up.

"Birdie, meet Ingrid Ellis. Ingrid, Bernadette Collins, our campaign manager." Alex gestured between them. "Ingrid is the girl I was telling you about."

"Do you mean to tell me the reason I couldn't find you last night is because you spent the evening courting some girl?" Birdie plopped a bowler hat over her hair with the precise opposite of a flourish.

"For the campaign! I did it for politics!" He shrank back, his hands held above his head.

"Fitting last words. What were you thinking, meddling with something like that? I told you to let her be." She loomed with an impressive presence, despite her stature, and Ingrid, who had never made a mess in her entire life, found she respected Birdie's air of organized chaos. It was a commonality among campaign managers, it seemed: a sleepless, relentless energy that transcended all basic needs in the service of perseverance. Ingrid felt the same energy in her very bones, though she'd yet to let it show in her appearance.

Birdie turned to survey Ingrid, looking her up and down. "What are the Holts going to say when they find out you poached her, Alex?"

Ingrid cleared her throat, ready to be spoken to instead of about. "You didn't poach me. I left. I don't want to be somewhere I'm not wanted. Believe me, they won't care I'm gone." Ingrid tried to swallow the hurt in her voice, knowing Senator Holt would barely notice her absence. Only Linden would miss her. She'd have to pretend that was enough. "I'm not with them anymore."

"You'd better be worth it, or I swear to—"

"I am." Ingrid stepped forward. "Top of the junior class at Ainsley Academy, my focus is on political studies, and I'm a three-time champion of debate and speech. I may not be from the kind of society you prefer, but I think I have something to offer."

Birdie leaned back on her heels and crossed her arms, looking

Ingrid up and down. "And if I disagree? What would you say to that?"

"I'm sure——" Alex began, but Ingrid stopped him with a gesture.

"I would say, with all due respect, ma'am . . ." Ingrid began, surveying her with a searching eye. Bernadette Collins wasn't cut from the same cloth as Senator Holt's political operatives. Cork, her counterpart, would have been appeased by deference, but something about her energy told Ingrid it would only serve to make her more irritated. If she caved now, none of them would ever respect her, least of all Bernadette Collins. Ingrid set her jaw. "I'd say *tough*."

Alex choked, but Birdie narrowed her eyes and gave Ingrid a small nod.

"Good," she said. "Society is worthless."

"A new campaign slogan?" said a familiar voice.

Gwendolyn Meyers joined them, descending the stairs in a royal-blue suit. Faye crossed over to her to straighten the satin neckerchief adorning the candidate's throat before ushering her forward.

"Alex mentioned he thought we might be seeing you again, Ingrid. I'm glad to see he was right." Gwendolyn flashed her a smile as she shrugged on her coat. "Why don't we get to know each other on the train? Alex, you can prep her on the way to the station." She gestured them all toward the door. "Clarence can ride with you too, but I need Faye to update me on the rebel situation."

Ingrid lifted her case and followed, her heart pounding a painful game of racquetball in her chest. "The rebel situation?" Ingrid asked under her breath. "Have there been some new developments?"

"There have been rumblings," Alex said carefully. "Nothing concrete, but the debate last night is certain to stir up more gossip."

"The discourse sure has been thick lately." Faye nodded toward the door, leading them out onto the snow-covered porch. "You see, there was this girl who attacked Senator Holt a few weeks back. No evidence of any organized violence, mind you, but they've been pushing this narrative of a resurgence of the old Shadow of the Flame. It's probably hogwash, which is why none of the papers have run a story about it since the attack on the Holt boy. Did you hear about that?"

Ingrid kept her head down until she realized Faye was addressing her directly, and she nodded. "I—I was the girl who fought her."

"Well, I'll be! We have more than one famous face on this campaign," Clarence chimed in, nudging Ingrid's shoulder.

"That could work in our favor actually." Faye frowned. "I'd hate to politicize it if we can avoid it, but if this becomes a bigger story, we can use all the help we can get."

Birdie nodded gravely. "It will—become a bigger story, I mean. If Gary's half the campaign manager he should be by now, he'll find a way to make this campaign about security even if the threat's nothing more than a couple of bored teenagers."

"Gary?" Ingrid asked.

"Gerald Cork," Birdie spat.

"Senator Holt's campaign manager?" Ingrid's head snapped up. "I met him—odd man."

"Birdie's known him for years," Gwendolyn said, placing a hand on Birdie's shoulder. "They were rivals in school."

"I want to squash him with my thumb." Birdie mimed squeezing her fingers together.

Gwendolyn chuckled. "And apparently she never got over it."

"No one uninteresting ever had a rival," Birdie retorted.

"No one would ever accuse you of being uninteresting."

"So you think the Holts are overreacting?" Ingrid asked.

"They always do," said Birdie. "But as long as they're doing it, someone's bound to be paying attention, and that's bad news for us. Security's the one topic they beat us on across all districts, so as long as we can keep this campaign about literally anything else, we've got a chance."

A fleet of town cars pulled up to the house, and Alex guided Ingrid down the steps, his dressing gown soaking up moisture from the snow.

"Are you really going to wear that?" Ingrid asked, glancing down at Alex's pajamas.

"I'll change on the train." He shrugged and ushered her into the car.

"No, you won't." Clarence climbed in behind them.

"No, I won't." Alex leaned back with his arms behind his head. "What can I say? I like to travel in comfort."

"So what do you think of the others?" Clarence asked.

Ingrid let out a long breath. "I think I'm in shock."

"That's to be expected. Gwendolyn has that effect on most people. I don't think I made eye contact with her the first two weeks I worked for her."

Alex cocked his head. "Really? I know she's a big star and everything, but she doesn't seem all that intimidating. Birdie, on the other hand . . ."

Clarence laughed. "Birdie? She doesn't exactly strike fear."

"Wait till she reads one of your speeches out loud back to you in a monotone," Alex said.

Ingrid nodded. "She definitely doesn't like me."

"She never holds a grudge for long," said Clarence.

"I think 'Gary' might disagree," Ingrid grumbled.

Alex shrugged. "She'll be cold for a while, but she'll get over it."

"Yeah, and after that, she'll just be lukewarm." Clarence chuckled and leaned in toward Ingrid. "Seriously, you'll be fine. She'll tell you off in a few days, and all will be well."

A burst of cold air rushed through the car as the passenger door opened. Birdie stood there wearing a frown that fit her much better than her suit.

"Or maybe she'll do it now," Clarence murmured.

Birdie glared at Ingrid with narrowed eyes. "Don't ever call me *ma'am* again." And she slammed the door.

CHAPTER FOURTEEN

The Meyers campaign rode coach. They took up the entire train car, and Gwendolyn and Birdie shut themselves in a small compartment with a sliding door, but there were no tables made of glass or superfluous flare lights decorating the space like Senator Holt's compartment.

"Sit down," Alex said, patting the seat beside him.

Ingrid hesitated.

"What, coach not good enough for you?" Alex asked, raising an eyebrow. "Don't tell me the Holts have you that spoiled."

Ingrid sat quickly to dispel him of the thought. "Not for me, but I thought the candidate might . . . She is a celebrity after all."

Alex frowned. "She might be famous, but she's a public servant first. You'll learn that as you get to know her."

"Yes, I just mean, well, the Holts—"

"The Holts waste money on things they don't need, like the gold suite on the Candesce Express. You heard the candidate at the debate. All that wasteful use of flare when there are people in West Cendium without any at all makes us sick. She's not about to shell out for something exorbitant when something practical will do."

Ingrid, who had never had enough to be anything but practical, bit the inside of her cheek as she nodded. "That makes sense."

"It would be kind of a slap in the face to our supporters, really," Clarence said as he took the seat opposite her. "Especially where we're headed."

"Yes! Off to West Cendium," Alex said cheerily.

Ingrid swallowed the lump in her throat. "West Cendium?" Though she'd never admit it to Alex or anyone else on the Meyers campaign, Ingrid hadn't returned to West Cendium since coming to Ainsley Academy. She'd built up a wall around the memories she'd made there—the good, like playing with her father in their one-room home, and the bad, like cold nights full of hunger and hurt in the orphanage—and she wasn't sure what seeing those familiar streets again would do to her.

Alex shot a puzzled look at her. "The next campaign stop. We'll be there for a week before moving on to East Cendium, then Cintilmore, then Excandridge before circling back to the capital. Surely you knew that—Holt's agenda is the same."

"Oh," Ingrid said, looking down at her shoes.

Alex lowered his voice. "How much did they *not* tell you?"

Ingrid straightened her shoulders. "I know plenty of things—"

Alex waved her off. "I'm sure you do, but that's pretty basic information. Seems like the kind of thing you'd actually need your interns to know if they're going to do anything useful."

"Ah, your mistake is assuming they wanted me to do anything useful." Ingrid groaned. "They were a lot more interested in my ability to pour boiling water over tea leaves than my brain."

"You do, er, know how elections work, don't you?" Faye asked, sitting up in her seat and leaning over the back to face them. "You really ought to check these things before issuing a job offer, Alex."

"It wasn't a job *offer* exactly," Alex grumbled.

Ingrid cleared her throat, eager to prove she wasn't the waste of space the Holts seemed to think. "Popular vote in each district using flare. Whichever candidate receives the most voting flare wins the district, equal to one point. The victor is the candidate with the most districts in the end."

"Well, that's a relief," Clarence muttered.

"I did go to school, you know." Ingrid settled back in her seat. "I'm not completely useless."

"Good. You've got one up on Alex, then."

"Hey!" Alex crossed his eyes and made a face at Clarence.

"Ingrid."

Ingrid looked up to see the towering frame of Gwendolyn Meyers standing over her.

"Why don't you join me in my compartment?"

Ingrid glanced around, as if there might be some other Ingrid she was referring to. Pointing to herself, Ingrid mouthed, *Me?* This was already quite the change of pace from working on the Holt campaign, where she'd been unceremoniously shut out of Senator Holt's entire periphery.

"Of course you." She turned to Birdie, who had gone from standing to sitting much like a suit that had suddenly lost its starch. "Come find me after?" she asked in a low voice, thumbing Birdie's chin.

Birdie nodded curtly, and Gwendolyn brushed a swift kiss against her cheek.

Ingrid did a double take, glancing back at Birdie as Gwendolyn led the way to her compartment. "No one told you we're a couple, did they?" Gwendolyn asked as they reached the sliding door.

"I just didn't know—" Ingrid began, but she didn't know how

to finish. She'd been about to say *I just didn't know you were like me*, but Ingrid had never told anyone before. She'd sealed herself off, picking Linden from the pack based more on logic than a lust she'd never really grown into. She was lucky she'd chosen so well for herself, but it didn't stop her from feeling a thrill at a glance or a touch from someone else. And that someone else did not need to be male. She'd committed herself to one person—she was *in love* no matter how the words made her want to crumble into insignificant dust—but even so, the occasional flirtation still made her stomach churn with something an inch shy of desire.

The long and short of it was, though Ingrid's patience for romance was thin on the best of days, she knew her capacity for it was not limited by gender. She'd thought it didn't matter. She was with Linden. There was no reason to ever acknowledge or indulge that part of herself. But now, as the realization of Gwendolyn Meyers's identity washed over her, she knew how very neglected she'd left it. No matter who she was with or what gender they were, it was still part of her.

"We're a strange couple, I know, but we make it work by keeping it quiet and away from the papers. You understand, I'm sure." Gwendolyn gestured to the seat across from her. "Please, sit."

Ingrid did understand—more than Gwendolyn Meyers could possibly know. She glanced over her shoulder, feeling the ghost of watchful eyes on her, but it was only the other staffers, not a camera in sight, so she followed Gwendolyn into the compartment and sat at the very edge of the seat with her feet folded beneath her. She became suddenly aware of the stray thread on her skirt hem and the hole in the ankle of her hose.

Such things would have been unacceptable while traveling with the Holts. Ingrid couldn't very well be caught with her clothes unraveling while on the arm of Linden Holt. But here on the Meyers campaign, no one had made her feel as though she had to be self-conscious about her appearance. Aside from the candidate herself, no one seemed to put much effort into their presentation at all. Faye and Clarence kept things simple, and Birdie was like a half-dead suit wearing a too-small human body. Even Alex, despite all his charm and good looks, had a general rumpled energy to him, as though his clothes, if not he himself, had simply rolled out of bed and landed in the world. Only Ingrid noticed those things. No one was judging her but herself.

"Welcome, Miss Ellis," Gwendolyn said, passing Ingrid a blue-and-gold-patterned teacup. "Alex tells me you're quite the talent, that we'd be lucky to snatch you up from the Holts."

Ingrid felt her cheeks turn pink as she accepted the cup, grateful that someone other than herself had procured it.

"Still, it is for me to determine if Alex is right." Her words felt dangerous, but she smiled nonetheless. "I know your background, of course. Alex was thorough, and I must say your school marks are impressive. You certainly fit the bill for the job, and Alex is quite enthusiastic about you."

Ingrid swallowed with difficulty. "But you're not so sure?"

"I have to be careful. We cannot simply hire just anyone, you know, especially . . ."

Ingrid sat under her scrutiny for a few moments of silence, then said, "Especially someone fresh off the Holt campaign?" It was no use dancing around it, so she'd tackle it head-on. Anything less would surely be suspect.

"That is my particular reservation, yes." She stared for a beat longer, then sat up. "We haven't all day, of course. Best get to it."

"Yes, ma'am— Oh, I'm sorry, I didn't mean to—"

Gwendolyn waved off her apology. "Birdie's more particular than me. I promise not to bite your head off if you call me *ma'am*, although you certainly don't have to. *Gwendolyn* will do just fine."

Ingrid nodded slowly, spilling a drop of tea on her skirt. "Yes, ma—Gwendolyn." It seemed an utter impossibility that Ingrid was alone with the woman who'd presided over Ingrid's school days from her vanity table, the woman she'd worshipped at the altar of her girlhood. Gwendolyn Meyers, an icon, was serving tea to her, Ingrid Ellis, an outcast.

With as much decorum as she could muster, Ingrid sipped her tea.

"Why don't you tell me why you're here?" Gwendolyn asked, a neutral expression on her face.

Ingrid froze. "Be-because you invited me? Did you not? Have I just—"

"Oh, no, you were invited." Gwendolyn waved her off. "I mean why you want to join our campaign."

"Why I want to join your campaign." Her shoulders had begun to creep up to her ears, though she could not muster the will-power to stop them. "I like political science, I suppose. I've always excelled in those classes, probably because it has so much to do with analyzing why those in power do what they do and, well, I couldn't very well survive Ainsley Academy without that skill."

"Because you are not powerful?" Gwendolyn asked, no hint of judgment in her tone.

Ingrid nodded.

"Why do you think that?"

"Think what?"

"That you are not powerful?"

Ingrid slowly lowered her cup to its saucer. "Because I don't have any money or any magic, and I don't have the kind of name that makes people sit up and listen."

Gwendolyn eyed her cautiously before leaning forward on her elbows. "And who made you feel that was the only way to be powerful?"

She meant to say it wasn't. She meant to say a lot of things, smart things, things that would impress Gwendolyn Meyers and make her want to hire her.

Instead, she said, "My father."

Guilt rose in her like a tide. She had never put voice to that feeling before, but there it was, bobbing near the surface. Her father had never told her magic was power. He'd never needed to. He'd risked his life, risked their family, for just a little, and that was all Ingrid needed to know about what power was worth. If she had more money, more magic, more power, no one could hurt her ever again. She would earn what he'd failed to steal, and it would make her invincible.

"Fathers can be difficult," Gwendolyn said, and then charitably changed the subject. "So why choose our campaign? Or rather, why choose our campaign after first choosing another? Alex tells me you took quite an effort to persuade—though now that I've mentioned it, it wouldn't be unlike him to exaggerate."

"Unfortunately, Alex has the right of it." Ingrid let her nails bite into her palms. "I wasn't prepared to leave when he first approached me, but after some consideration, I decided Alex was right."

"Alex is often right, though between you and me, we tend not to tell him. He can get rather smug." Gwendolyn leaned back in her chair, surveying Ingrid with dark blue eyes, analytical and searching. "What aren't you telling me?"

Ingrid's heart slammed into her chest.

She knows.

"Forgive me my questions, but I'm sure you understand. I do not believe a girl like yourself would leave such a prestigious internship for ours simply because—what? Alex convinced you? He's charming, but he's not *that* charming." Gwendolyn chuckled. "Don't misunderstand me, Ingrid. I'm pleased you changed your mind, but it helps me if I understand why. After all, I'm trying to change as many minds as I can before the election. It would be nice to know what's working."

"It was less Alex's charm and more the Holts' lack thereof." She'd meant it as a half-truth, but even so, it felt as real a reason as any. The Holts had treated her like she didn't matter. Even Linden needed reminding to include her. But Alex had treated her like she was . . . special. A blush spread unbidden across her cheeks, and she hurried to cover it with words. "They wouldn't let me do anything or teach me anything. What good is a prestigious internship on my résumé if I don't actually learn anything from it? I learned twice as much in a single minute listening to you at the debate than I did in my time with the Holts."

Gwendolyn inclined her head, light wisps of hair falling across her brow. "So you want to learn."

Ingrid gripped her hands tightly in her lap. "I do."

"And what did you learn from me last night?"

"I learned I'm a lot more like you than I am like them."

"In what ways?"

Ingrid averted her eyes. It was one thing to compare oneself to a celebrity; it was yet another to list the similarities as though they somehow made them the same. "You were not born to wealth, and yet here you are."

"I also chose this profession when I could have chosen any other—same as you." Gwendolyn traced her finger around the rim of her teacup. "I won't lie, I see echoes of myself in you. You're ambitious and logical. I'd wager we have a great deal more in common than that too."

Perhaps it was Gwendolyn Meyers's agreement with the comparison that made Ingrid so brave, or perhaps it was something in the tea—or the simple fact that she'd not had to brew it herself. Ingrid sat as tall as she could and put on her most confident face before asking, "And why are *you* here?"

Gwendolyn eyed her sharply before softening. "Because when I was young, I wanted more than I was allowed. Because they told me I could not rise. Because they wanted me to sing but not speak." She slid her hands along the table and gripped the edge with precise fingers. "Now I have much more than I want. I walk higher than them all. When I talk, people listen."

Ingrid's fingers echoed Gwendolyn's, curling around the table ledge like it was a lifeline.

"I have everything," Gwendolyn whispered, her eyes turning glassy. "And that did not make me happy."

"But you don't have *this*." Ingrid understood what it was to want. She understood how the wanting never stopped. It did not matter how much she got, how much she took. She always wanted more. What would it be like to be the most revered woman in Candesce and to still not be satisfied?

Gwendolyn narrowed her eyes. "No, Ingrid. That is not the way of it. I don't want to be president because that's what's next. I don't want to *have* power; I want to *use* power. There is a difference. One is simply greed; the other is purpose." She drummed her fingers on the table slowly. "There is no end to greed until you cannibalize your very person. Wealth is the enemy of peace, and I fear this nation will undo itself before the people get what they deserve. With power, I can change that." She stood slowly, and Ingrid followed suit. "I have everything I want, and if I don't use it to create the change I know is possible—the change I know is necessary—I'm no better than the rest of them."

"No better than the rest," Ingrid repeated hollowly. She'd thought all this time she was reaching for something, but *this* was something. Change—that was real. Ingrid had only ever wanted to climb as high as she could. She'd only ever thought about how to get there, not what to do once she arrived.

"We have to be better, Ingrid. Otherwise, what's the point?"

CHAPTER FIFTEEN

Ingrid's first week as an official intern for Gwendolyn Meyers saw a great deal less tea and a lot more paperwork. First order of business, she'd signed a nondisclosure agreement stipulating that she would not share anything she learned during the campaign with the press unless otherwise directed. The Holts hadn't asked her to promise anything of the kind, verbally or in writing, but she supposed it was because they hadn't planned to tell her anything important. The agreement didn't say a thing about sharing information with anyone else, however, so she signed it without a second thought.

Every morning, Alex and Ingrid combed through every major—and minor—newspaper in Candesce for mentions of the candidate, her opponent, or any major issue that might come up during the course of the campaign. Ingrid was pleased to see no more pictures of her had landed between the pages and equally put out that not one of the publications that had so gleefully written about Linden's mystery girl seemed to care about the story anymore. They'd pivoted entirely to focus on a new rumor about Linden and one of their other classmates, Pauline Ackerman. Ingrid supposed she couldn't have it both ways, and lying low was best for her undercover operation.

In the afternoons, Ingrid was set to assist Faye, whose primary role was to communicate with the press and prepare Birdie and Gwendolyn for their public appearances. Ingrid had balked at first, unsure that Birdie would let anyone near her with a hairbrush, but Faye had only laughed and clarified that the preparation was mostly reminding them of important donors they were likely to meet and going over any talking points that needed ironing out.

All in all, it was at least more fun than working for Senator Holt, if not more tiring. Alex, true to his word, did not let Ingrid retire to bed each night before first going over some new detail or other about election politics in Candesce. He was a teacher, indeed. An annoying one.

On their last day in West Cendium, Alex didn't wake her at the crack of dawn with his usual sharp rap of knuckles on her door. Instead, her eyes opened to sunlight spilling across her face, feeling suspiciously well rested. Never in her life had she dressed so quickly. She was many things, but late wasn't about to be one of them.

When she arrived in the boardroom of the West Cendium Suites the Meyers campaign had rented out for a headquarters, she found only Faye and Clarence with a few other staffers.

"Where's Alex?" Ingrid asked, not even bothering with the coffeepot. She didn't like the feeling that had crawled into her stomach at his absence.

"It's the kid's day off," Clarence said through a mouthful of pastry. "Should be yours too. Didn't he say so?"

Ingrid shook her head. "I don't need a day off."

"Well, you have one." Faye crossed the room to take her by the shoulders and turn her back toward the door. "Best find something to do."

141

"If you run, you can probably catch him—Alex, I mean," Clarence called after her as she stepped tentatively out into the hallway once more.

Filled with the unsettling feeling that she was meant to be doing *something*, Ingrid took Clarence's advice. Ingrid wasn't good with idle time, so whatever Alex had planned for his day, she would do too.

She found him in the lobby exiting through the large double doors leading to the portico, but before she could flag him down, she saw him glance around rather shiftily, then duck outside.

It took Ingrid all of two seconds to decide to follow him. If Alex had a secret, she wanted to learn it, and from the look of him, it had to be a good one. Perhaps even good enough for her to pass back to the Holt campaign.

The cold air nipped at her neck and ears. West Cendium was always chilly this time of year. She'd spent many a winter huddled against her friends for warmth, hay bales stacked against the walls for cheap insulation. She'd left that life behind, but she couldn't shake the cold. Not without an overcoat anyway. With an ounce of regret, Ingrid tucked her bare hands into her armpits and took off in the direction she'd seen Alex go.

As she rounded the corner, she caught sight of his sleek black cap heading left down another street. She followed at a distance, keeping to the edge of the buildings both for the benefit of their shadows and to escape the bite of wind. After a few more twists and turns, Ingrid found herself in a back alley behind an industrial building. She saw a few trucks parked along the side of the street, but there was no sign on Alex. She had lost him.

With a heavy heart, Ingrid turned to retrace her steps, but the roar of an engine held her back. One of the trucks pulled forward and slowly accelerated down the road. She hadn't lost Alex after all, though she certainly would if the truck drove any faster. Ingrid launched herself toward the truck, throwing caution to the wind.

She landed inexpertly, slicing open her hand on a rusty screw in the wall of the cargo bed, but she made it. Swinging her feet over the ledge, she dropped down into a crouch between what appeared to be wooden barrels.

"Where are you going?" she whispered against her knees as the truck peeled away from West Cendium's central streets. Alex didn't strike her as the covert operation type, so why all the secrecy? And why the run-down truck with a cargo bed full of barrels?

With alarming clarity, Ingrid realized what was in those barrels. It was either alcohol or flare. Her money—or lack thereof—was on the latter. Her chest constricted, and not at the cold. If Alex was a bootlegger, he'd go the same way as her father. Sooner or later, he'd be caught, and then Ingrid would lose him too.

The truck came to a stop in a neighborhood Ingrid knew. It certainly wasn't the best part of town, but it was an odd place for a speakeasy. If Alex was off-loading flare, it seemed a strange rendezvous point.

"Scorch it, Ingrid, you scared me!" The metal backing fell away to reveal Alex's face, eyebrows clear into his hairline, nose pink from the cold. "Did you follow me?"

Ingrid couldn't bring herself to uncurl her body or meet his eye. "Are you a smuggler?"

"A smuggler?" Alex gave her an appraising look. "You think I'm a smuggler?"

"So you're not a smuggler?" She looked up then, doing her best to calm her racing heart. "I thought with all this flare . . . if you're not a smuggler, then what are you doing?"

"Nothing so salacious." Alex rolled his eyes. "I'm meeting with a few people, is all. Some real residents of West Cendium."

Ingrid swallowed. She'd hoped her return to her home district would be quick and painless, spent mostly behind closed doors assisting the senior staffers with their work. She would have rather fetched them all tea for a week than take one step onto the streets from whence she came. She'd made herself a capital girl and coming back felt less like triumph and more like surrender. But if it meant Alex might share his secrets, she'd share hers too.

"I'm a real resident of West Cendium," Ingrid said quietly, her words muffled a little by the fabric of her tights. "Or I was when I was younger."

"I didn't know that." He rolled his lip between his teeth, then said hesitantly, "Maybe you should stick with me today, then. I could use someone who knows these streets."

Ingrid blinked away the tightness in her eyes. "Why? What are you up to?"

"Giving back." Alex pulled himself into the cargo bed and sat beside her. "The candidate has a lot of passion projects, but it's difficult for her to personally oversee all her charities and initiatives while she's running for president."

"So all this flare?" Ingrid couldn't help the frown creasing her face.

"We're going to give it away."

"We're going to give it away." Ingrid straightened a little and squared off with Alex. "We're going to give it away?"

Alex's brow knit together. "I really thought you'd be more enthusiastic about this."

And she might have been had something much less pleasant not tangled her insides. "We're just . . . giving away flare," she said, and the knot tightened. "We can do that? We have enough that it doesn't matter?"

"The candidate is very wealthy." Alex stood and gestured to the barrels—nearly a dozen in total. The barrels alone would be worth more than she'd ever had growing up, and the flare inside them a hundredfold. She itched with the desire to grab one and run—not that she had the strength to carry one on her own, nor the need. She was going to be a Holt. Charity was for other girls living other lives.

"She has more than enough for herself, so she does her best to share what she doesn't need with those who can't get access."

"But it's an election year," Ingrid blurted. "Doesn't she need it for voting?"

Alex shrugged. "Maybe, but they need it more. You see, the candidate believes in flare equity whether she wins the election or not."

Ingrid rose to her feet and brushed her skirt smooth. The cut on her hand smarted terribly. It was a good thing she'd worn black and the blood wouldn't stain. "So why is this such a secret mission? Why not make it a photo op with the candidate? A picture of her giving away magic she could otherwise use to help her win an election would be——"

"A train wreck," Alex finished. "The candidate can't go giving out flare to her constituents herself, not during an election. She can't be seen doing anything that even remotely resembles bribery. If she's giving away all this flare to people, there might be some unspoken understanding that they're to use it to vote for her here in the West Cendium election."

"She was going to use it to vote anyway, though, so why should that matter?" Ingrid asked.

Alex sat on the edge of the truck, his feet dangling. "She would've used it to vote in Alorden, where she's from. It wouldn't be ethical to give all that flare to people in another district and then ask them to use it to vote. Otherwise, Holt could simply give his flare to someone in a district he's less likely to win and fix the election."

Ingrid pinched her brow and shook her head. "Right, but this would be the opposite. Gwendolyn's polling well in West Cendium. She's likely to win here, so wouldn't moving flare from Alorden to West Cendium actually hurt her in the election?"

"Look, it's not really about the election. These people aren't going to use flare to vote anyway. They need it for other things." Alex maneuvered one of the barrels onto its side and rolled it toward the back of the truck. "There are people who have to survive the winter without turning on their furnaces. It's cold out there, and this is actually something they need. It's not just a fun party beverage or something to spread across your face to make your skin glow."

"I know that," Ingrid grumbled. That he thought her incapable of being so destitute would have seemed a compliment only a few weeks ago, but now Ingrid found herself fighting the urge to keep the realities of her past tucked away. She wanted to whip them out like a flag to show Alex. She was not so out of touch. She was not so different from him.

"Help me with this, will you?" Alex indicated the barrel.

Ingrid shut her mouth. Now was not the time.

The weight of the barrel and the weight of Alex's words hit her at the same time.

"Would it really be so bad if they voted?" Ingrid asked, staggering a little under the weight of the fortune in her arms as they worked it down from the ledge.

Together, they shuffled the barrel toward the sidewalk, but when they put it down, Alex said, "Look, if they want to vote, that's their prerogative, but we aren't telling them we're from the Meyers campaign, and we aren't asking them to vote for us. Those are the rules, and they're very important." He leaned forward and plucked the *Meyers for President* pin from her lapel. "I mean it."

"Okay, okay," Ingrid said, holding her hands up in defense as Alex turned to knock on the door. But Ingrid couldn't help but wonder how it would be if everyone could vote. She knew these streets, and she knew these people. They deserved it as much as anyone. She only wished it was hers to give.

They visited a dozen homes that day—mostly group homes or shelters. Ingrid didn't see a single ungrateful face as they delivered flare to the old and young alike, but still something in Ingrid's stomach clenched like a fist. Resentment climbed inside her, and she knew if she didn't snuff it out, it would catch fire and burn, burn, burn. It would not do to dwell on what a gift of flare would have done for her back when she lived in West Cendium. She didn't need anyone to give her charity anymore. But still, the what-ifs tumbled around her, sending flashes of what might have been through her mind.

"One more to go," Alex said after he climbed back into the driver's side of the truck.

"Almost done."

"I'm thinking dinner after all this." Alex started the engine. "I could do with something warm—maybe a roast?"

As Alex listed options, Ingrid sank back in her seat and closed her eyes. It felt uncouth to talk about a hot meal when so many of the people they'd met that day hadn't had one in weeks. It felt like betrayal. She was just like these people.

She'd *been* just like these people.

She wasn't like them anymore. The thought made Ingrid want to strip herself of her fine clothes, of her clean skin and hair, of all the richness of her new world. She'd built herself around the promise of a better life, but the life she'd had before was still there in the streets of West Cendium, living on without her.

"Are you coming?" Alex asked, nudging her with his elbow.

"Yeah, all right." Ingrid stepped out of the truck and her eyes opened on a familiar street. A wave of nausea overcame her as she turned to look upon a place she'd lived but never called home, and the woman standing in its shadow.

"It's good to see you again, Ingrid."

CHAPTER SIXTEEN

The orphanage crouched on the far corner of the street. Its roof still sagged, its paint still peeled, and the gate still creaked as Alex ushered Ingrid through it.

The woman at the door was short and hollow like the wind might blow her away. She said something and shook Alex's hand, but Ingrid couldn't hear them above her pulse pounding in her ears. This place had housed her darkest days. This place had seen her shrivel under the weight of grief and stumble over pieces of herself as they fell faster than she could gather them. It was here in this house that she'd first looked life and death in the eyes and wondered if they weren't the same. She didn't like to think about those days, washing her memory of them with a single stroke of bleakness and tucking it away to be safely forgotten. But she couldn't very well forget, now she was here.

"I think I'll go wait in the car," she heard herself saying, but she couldn't move her legs.

Alex's mouth moved to the rhythm of her name, then the woman's, but Ingrid couldn't hear them. She could only stand there and sway.

The woman reached out a hand to steady her, and Ingrid let

herself be guided inside to a chair. She had been broken so many times, she didn't think anything else could truly take her down. Falling wasn't an option; *failing* wasn't an option. She resented these people who'd witnessed her waver even a little.

The woman handed her a glass of water.

Ingrid took it and drank. The tang of rusted pipes was familiar and potent enough to center her, sharpening on her taste buds to pull the rest of her senses into the present moment. The woman across from her was not a stranger. She was only a couple years Ingrid's senior, and there was recognition in her gaze and a kindness hardened by resignation in her smile.

"Ingrid?" The woman leaned closer, peering at her with familiar murky brown eyes.

"Frances?" Ingrid croaked, the name returning to her with the force of a storm.

"Ah, so you do remember me." Frances lowered herself into the seat across from her, a sad smile on her lips.

Alex crouched beside Ingrid and looked up at her with concern. "You two know each other?"

"We used to share a bunk back before this one got whisked away to that academy of hers." Frances's face fell slightly. "Thought we would have heard from you at least once, but I suppose life in the capital is more exciting than home."

Ingrid's hand gripped the chair arm, the wood so brittle she thought it might snap. "This isn't my home."

Alex's fingers touched Ingrid's wrist ever so delicately, as though to say *I'm here*. "I'll go get the barrel so you two can catch up." Alex stood and the absence of his touch left her skin somewhere just short of cold.

Ingrid pressed the balls of her feet firmly against the floor, bracing herself as if to run. She didn't want Frances to catch up with her. Ingrid was leagues ahead, and she didn't have any intention of slowing down.

Ingrid stood up on shaky legs and surveyed the room. "Everything's the same." But even as she said it, she realized it wasn't true. Little touches of personalization were speckled through the house. A straw doll sat in the curve of the window, a fraying red bow was tied around the washroom door handle, and new marks had been etched all along the far wall to mark the height of each resident upon entry and exit. Ingrid ran her finger over the wall, letting her fingers catch on the splinters.

"Yours is over there," Frances said, pointing a few feet to Ingrid's left.

"I know." Ingrid lifted her chin and followed Frances's eyeline to a pair of marks only a few inches apart. "I wasn't here very long."

Frances crossed the room and leaned against the wall, facing Ingrid. "But you were still here."

Her gaze was soft against Ingrid's harshness. Even as Ingrid wished she could be ripped from this place like a tree uprooted during a storm, Frances was so still and strong, like a lightning rod, determined to keep her safe. That had always been the way of it when they were children too. Ingrid would cry herself to sleep some nights, and Frances would hold her shoulders as she did. When Ingrid was at her very worst, Frances was there.

Now Ingrid wished she wasn't.

"I don't like to think about it." Ingrid's eyes shuttered.

Frances made a sound halfway between a cough and a laugh. "I can tell."

There was no judgment in Frances's tone, but Ingrid felt it all the same. "That's why I didn't come back, you know. It's not because

I—I didn't use you and then leave you behind for better things. That wasn't what I was trying to do."

"You sure got those better things, though." Frances smiled a little sadly. "We get the papers here, you know. Saw your picture a few weeks back."

"That wasn't—I wasn't—"

"I got to tell all the girls that I knew you. That we grew up together." Frances crossed over the sparse bookshelf and withdrew a copy of the *Candesce Courant* sporting the picture of Linden kissing Ingrid. "You give them hope, you know, that they can get out of this place and be like you."

Ingrid blinked down at the picture. The longer she looked at it, the less she liked it. The way Linden's hand gripped her waist, the way her arms were limp, the way her face was almost totally obscured. It was only a snapshot, though, and Ingrid knew that moment wasn't the one that mattered. It would all still be worth it. She wished she could tell the young girls of the orphanage that.

Instead, when she looked up, she asked only, "How could you tell it was me?"

Frances reached for her, tucking a stray lock of hair behind Ingrid's ears. Her hands were rough, her fingernails unkempt, but Ingrid still wanted to melt into the older girl, let her take care of her as she always had done.

"Do you remember when you first came to the orphanage how you used to have insomnia? You couldn't sleep, and you would toss and turn. I used to climb in with you, and that seemed to help—I think you didn't want to be alone."

Ingrid's body tensed. She'd put all that behind her long ago, the loneliness, the longing for her father's return. She couldn't sleep because she knew he wouldn't be there in the morning when she woke. He would never again wake her as the sun rose with a gentle kiss to the forehead and a *Good morning, my Dewdrop*. After Frances began sleeping beside her, the insomnia had ebbed.

It was all too much. Frances knew her in ways she couldn't stomach, and in ways she would not have survived without. "What does that have to do with—"

"I used to watch your breathing to make sure you weren't awake before I went to sleep. I'd watch the rise and fall of your pulse here." Frances pressed her fingertips against Ingrid's neck. "You have a little triangle of freckles."

Ingrid's chest prickled painfully as she stared at Frances. This girl had been like a mother, like a sister, like a friend. And Ingrid had not given her a single thought since leaving for the capital. The same, obviously, could not be said of Frances.

"Why are you still here? Why didn't you leave too?"

"Because someone has to run this place. Someone has to be here to help these girls."

"But you're at least nineteen now, right? Why didn't you just—"

"Leave? Because if I left, who would protect them? You? Someone worse?" Frances sighed heavily. "Not everyone wants what you want, Ingrid. For me, these girls are my kin, this place is my home, and I won't leave either to be wrecked by a world that doesn't want us."

A world that doesn't want us. That was the world Senator Holt wanted to keep. It was the world Ingrid had tried to conquer. But her success, no matter how her picture in the paper might inspire them, would not pull the girls of this orphanage out of poverty. It would not change the world, only *her* world. It wasn't enough.

"Maybe we can make the world see us differently," Ingrid said quietly. "Maybe it doesn't have to be like this."

Frances's gaze fell to the floor. "It *is* like this. You can wish and dream all you want, but this is our reality."

"I'm in politics now, you know." She winced, remembering Alex's warning not to say anything about who they worked for. She plowed on anyway. "I work for Gwendolyn Meyers. She doesn't just say the right thing; she does the right thing too. She could really make a difference for you."

Frances sighed. "Politics is never about us. They squabble among themselves at the top while the rest of us get left out to spoil and rot."

"But the election—"

"People talk about elections like they're the end-all be-all for change, like it's the only way to make a difference, but most of us can't wait four years to get a few more coins in our purses or an ounce more flare in our flasks. Most of us are working just to cling to whatever scrap we can get, and the waiting's what'll kill us."

Ingrid opened her mouth to argue, but no rebuttal came to her lips, only the empty quiet that meant it was true.

"You know I'm right," Frances said quietly. "You know it because you're not stupid. And you know it because no matter how you dress yourself up, no matter what company you keep, you're still a West Cendium girl who grew up between these walls."

"I know." Ingrid swallowed, her voice coming out small and young, like she was still that girl, hungry and chilled to the bone, weighted down by loneliness. But she hadn't always been lonely. Frances had been there. Frances had shared her blanket and her grief. Ingrid had known only one type of warmth in those days, and it was with her head tucked against Frances's, their arms wrapped around each other, holding on for dear life.

Without meaning to, Ingrid reached for the familiarity of

Frances's hand, tangling their fingers together. She let silence pass between them as they stood opposite each other, Frances a perfect mirror of the life Ingrid had walked away from. A few different choices, and Ingrid could've been stuck there too, caught in the drain of West Cendium.

"Thanks," Ingrid said at last.

"For what?" Frances asked coldly, though she didn't pull her hand away.

"For always being there when we were younger, and for being here now." Ingrid looked down at their fingers, remembering a time when both their hands were so much smaller, when both their *worlds* were too. "And for reminding me what matters, what it is I should be working for." Gwendolyn Meyers's words from the train had followed her the last few days. She was right—Ingrid had spent so much time chasing power, she hadn't left time to figure out what she'd do with it. *What's the point?* Gwendolyn had asked. And now Ingrid had her answer.

"Wherever you go, whether you mean to or not, you leave a mark." Frances pointed to the etches made seven and five years ago, two lines representing two years Ingrid had tried her best to erase. But there they were, forever cut into the wood like a scar.

Then, in a flash of sunlight on metal, a knife appeared in Frances's hand. Before Ingrid could so much as flinch, the serrated blade sliced through wood a hair's breadth away from the top of her head.

"What the—" Ingrid ducked away, pulling her hand from Frances's.

But Frances just tugged the knife free, leaving another etching higher on the wall where Ingrid's head had been. "You got taller," she said, shrugging.

"You got scarier." Ingrid pinched her brow and leaned away from the knife.

"Impossible. I've always been terrifying." Humor danced in Frances's eyes as she closed the distance between them and smoothed a wrinkle in Ingrid's lapel. "Don't forget about us, okay?" she added quietly, meeting Ingrid's eyes with her own. "We didn't forget about you."

CHAPTER SEVENTEEN

They left for East Cendium the following morning, leaving the district behind in a cloud of steam. Ingrid watched the buildings grow smaller as the train gained speed, a little ripple in her heart like a stone tossed into a smooth pool of water.

Alex and Clarence bickered most of the way there about the merits of the exclamation point. Alex was in favor, Clarence not so much.

"It denotes tone!" Alex said, shaking his fist.

"It's unnecessary direction. They can listen to the candidate deliver the speech if they want to know how a certain line was delivered. They don't need it shoved down their throat with your extraneous punctuation. Make it a period and move on." Clarence's voice was devoid of the passion Alex so clearly felt about the subject.

"Does it really matter? You're writing a speech, not a law. No one else is going to care. It's not like there's a misleading comma that historians will argue over for decades to come." Faye joined them after exiting the candidate's compartment, sitting opposite Birdie.

"They might!" Alex's eyes were wide, feasting on the electricity of debate.

Ingrid couldn't help but join in. "Bold of you to assume historians will read this speech at all."

Faye chuckled and pointed to Ingrid. "I like her."

Birdie didn't look up as she tore a sheet of paper from the top of her stack and handed it to Clarence. "It matters," she said.

"Aha!" Alex and Clarence exclaimed in unison.

"Really?" Ingrid asked, unable to keep the disbelief from her tone.

"Really." Birdie shuffled her papers and pulled another for Faye. "It should be a semicolon."

Everyone but Ingrid groaned.

"I'm going to get breakfast," Alex declared in defeat. "I'm starving, and I think my legs are going to fall off. I need to walk around."

"If you'd sit like a normal person, your legs wouldn't hurt," Birdie replied, her own legs tucked haphazardly beneath her like they were made of springs, not bones.

"That would be so misleading about my character, though."

"I could go for a bite." Faye stood up again.

"To the kitchen trolley!" Alex announced, rolling off his seat to a standing position.

Birdie did not dignify them with a refusal. She simply carried on reading her notes.

The other cars weren't nearly as packed as they had been when they'd traveled to Alorden. When she voiced her observation, Alex laughed.

"Of course not. The Senate isn't in session, so everyone's gone home to kick up their feet for a while," Faye said. "Not that they do much of anything while they're in the capital anyway."

"Is it really that bad?" Ingrid asked, heat rising in her cheeks as she realized the naïveté in her question.

158

Alex groaned. "It's almost embarrassing at this point. They just squabble and grandstand and no one actually passes legislation."

"Imagine if they did their jobs." Faye shook her head.

"Imagine if we stopped doing our jobs," Ingrid grumbled. "We'd all be fired."

"We might be better off without most of them, honestly," Alex muttered under his breath. "At least the Shadow of the Flame's got *that* right."

"You can't say that sort of thing—not in public." Faye's demeanor, so recently jovial, had gone tight and dark. "Be careful, Alex." Then she peeled away to inspect a bowl of fruit.

Alex looked poised for a comeback, but he stopped in his tracks, mouth slightly agape as his eyes flicked to Ingrid.

Linden stood at the other end of the trolley, an apple in his hand. He was leaning casually against a table piled high with fruit, his head bent in conversation with a girl Ingrid recognized from school.

Pauline Ackerman was nice in the way having a pebble instead of a large rock in your shoe was nice, or how breaking your leg but not dying was nice. She was the kind of girl who smiled at you to your face but sank her teeth into your very name as you walked away. Ingrid couldn't stand her in the slightest. She thought Linden felt the same.

"Wow, scorch him." Alex exhaled as he eyed them. "You want to turn around?"

Ingrid shook her head inconclusively. Her stomach pitched at the note in Alex's voice—pitying but defensive. Linden wasn't doing anything improper. Everything was fine between Ingrid and Linden last she'd checked, and Pauline Ackerman wasn't about to change that. They were together, they were solid, they were in love. Ingrid knew it. But Alex didn't. Alex *couldn't*.

Ingrid set her shoulders back and tipped her head higher. "No, that's okay. I'm fine," she said, injecting a slight waver into her voice for good measure. "Good riddance, right?"

"Boy moves on quick," Alex grumbled.

Ingrid shrugged. "I moved on quicker. Got myself a new job, didn't I?"

Alex laughed heartily. "He did not deserve you whatsoever. Come on, some pie might cheer you up."

"Are you sure it isn't going to just cheer *you* up?" Ingrid replied.

"That's a very real possibility, but you'll never know until you try." He turned to the waiter and said, "Two slices, please." Glancing at Ingrid, he added, "Really, the best thing for a broken heart is a baked good. Restorative effects are frighteningly powerful, you'll see."

But before Ingrid could take a bite of the promised panacea, the train came to a sudden stop. She hit the floor, catching herself—but alas not the pie—on her palms as a cascade of apples rained down on her.

Other patrons hurried to right themselves, some clinging to the countertop, others in various states of on-the-floor like Ingrid. She let out a long breath as the screech of the train's brakes faded.

"What was that?"

"Up we go." Alex extended a hand to help her stand. "Probably something wrong with the tracks. Nothing to worry about."

"Could be an engine malfunction," Faye said, beckoning them forward.

The loudspeaker crackled and a voice spoke. "This is your conductor speaking. We're experiencing an unanticipated delay. All passengers should make their way to the nearest exit to wait until the issue is resolved."

There was a collective groan as everyone pushed forward to disembark. Ingrid pulled herself to her feet with Alex's aid and followed him toward the door. They spilled out into the snowy surroundings, the area already swarming with passengers. Ingrid shivered against the cold without her coat and craned her neck to look for the others.

"Still think it's just the tracks?" Faye asked under her breath.

"Can't be," Alex replied.

"Why's that?" Ingrid turned her attention back to her companions.

"If it was only a blockage in the road or an issue with the tracks, they wouldn't have had us evacuate." Faye stood on her tiptoes, scanning the crowd. "Where are they?"

Just then, a familiar voice from the other side of the crowd spoke. "Please, friends, let us all calm ourselves. There's no use in a frenzy when we don't even know what's happened."

"There she is!" Alex nudged Ingrid and pointed.

Gwendolyn had climbed atop a box or a bench of some kind, towering over the throng. Ingrid's heart rate slowed as she took in the candidate's composed expression. The rest of the crowd didn't seem to react the same way, however. Some yelled speculations in the air: "Damn trains!" "Bad flare!" "Maybe it's the rebels!"

"Please, join me in patience as we wait for the conductor's assessment. We don't yet know what is responsible for this delay."

"Ah, but we do know, Ms. Meyers." Senator Holt did not climb any sort of box—he did not need to. Though Gwendolyn's shoes gave her an edge on his height, the senator's voice did the work for him. He was commanding in a way Gwendolyn wasn't. She was engaging, capturing, entrancing . . . but not authoritative. When Gwendolyn Meyers spoke, people listened; when Senator Holt spoke, people obeyed. "Rebels did this; there is no doubt in my mind. This train has been sabotaged, and who but enemies of order would do such a thing?"

Ingrid pinched her brow. Surely the senator knew there was nothing to be gained by fearmongering. If it turned out to be only an issue with the engine, he would look foolish. It would undermine all his strength if he was wrong in the end.

"We should wait for the official report, Senator. It is prudent that we learn all the facts before jumping to conclusions. Be patient." Even as Gwendolyn spoke, Ingrid could hear the confidence waning from her voice.

"Scorch patience!" Senator Holt's fist shot into the air. "We cannot afford to be patient with matters like this. Patience means they get away. Patience means they strike again. Patience is dangerous, Ms. Meyers."

Ingrid studied his words like a tome. The way Senator Holt insisted on calling her *Ms. Meyers* set Ingrid on edge. Something about it felt disrespectful, though she couldn't put her finger on what. And the way he used repetition . . . it had a way of energizing the crowd. Perhaps patience was dangerous, but so was his speech. Ingrid couldn't decide if she was impressed or terrified, forgetting for a moment that, in actuality, she still worked for him.

"Come on," Alex murmured. "Let's join the others."

Ingrid made to follow, but before she could even take a step, someone grabbed her by the wrist and pulled. She toppled back, losing sight of Alex as she fought for balance.

"What the—"

"Shh! Follow me." It was Linden, his voice quiet and his face half obscured by a thick scarf. He led her back toward the stationary train, ducking out of view just as Senator Holt's valet passed

162

them by. Once on board the now-deserted train, Linden half dragged her into a tiny supply closet at the back of the train and let out a long sigh.

"Linden, what are you—*where* are you?" The supply closet had no light source, and her eyes were not adjusted to the darkness.

Clumsy at first, fumbling for her in the dark, Linden traced her jaw with a shaking finger. He took her chin in his hands and drew her close. She could feel his breath on her lips, warm and familiar, but as his lips found hers, they were desperate and aching.

Ingrid let his passion sweep over her, a consuming flame. Darkness was a welcome friend. Out in the world, she felt pressured only to give—to carve away the pieces of herself that did not fit expectations, to mold her body to the shape of Linden's hands, to be the image of a girl in love. But here in the dark, she did not have to be anything but her whole self. She could mold Linden's hands to the shape of *her* body instead. She could be a girl in love without having to look the part.

She could take. And take she did, until she had her fill.

"Ingrid," Linden whispered, a whine in his voice like an injured dog. "I missed you."

"I know." Ingrid pushed against his chest to get a better look at him, though his features were still too shadowed to see properly. "Though you looked a mite cozy with Pauline back there."

Linden nodded solemnly. "Father's idea. He says I ought to be seen socializing with someone a bit more appropriate."

The word *appropriate* lodged itself in her throat as she tried to repeat it.

"I don't like it any more than you do," Linden added in a hurry. "I hate pretending not to be completely in love with you. We had to keep things secret for so long, and now we're engaged, I just want the whole world to know. Anything less feels like we're moving backward."

Ingrid swallowed with difficulty, a lump in her throat blocking any words she might have said. It was for the best perhaps. Because Ingrid didn't hate it. It was comfortable. It was quiet. It was peaceful. Sometimes it felt like Linden was the only person she could be herself around, and sometimes it felt like Linden was the only person she was being someone else for. It was an exhausting game of masks, and in the dark, she didn't have to wear one.

Linden tucked her hair behind her ear, his fingers lingering at the apex of her neck and earlobe, stroking the skin in small circles. "It's not the same without you."

"Hmm?" Ingrid's eyes had adjusted enough to see the look on his face, just one degree short of stricken.

"Campaigning, I mean. I . . . I'm not sure I even care to do it unless you're with me." He let his hand fall to his side. "You're always so much more insightful than me, and I think I just don't enjoy it unless it's because you're enjoying it."

"I promise we'll campaign together again someday—for your campaign, certainly." But as she said the words, his face fell—more somber than ever.

"If I even run."

"Come now, of course you will. You're the son of a well-respected senator. When he becomes president, you'll take over his seat, and you'll be the youngest senator in our history. Isn't that the plan?"

"It's just . . . I'm not so sure I want all that. My father thinks he knows what's best for my future. He wants me to be the heir to his legacy, closing speakeasies and passing tighter flare restriction legislation. He's sure I can win, but—"

"You *can*."

A moment of silence passed between them, thick and agitated. "What if I don't want to?"

"Linden, I—"

"I wish we could simply run away and leave all this election nonsense behind us," Linden grumbled.

"Well, we can't." Ingrid brushed her lips against his cheek with finality.

He caught the back of her head with his hand and leaned into her. He smelled like snow and pine, like his frozen mountain home, but his touch was anything but cold as it traveled up her spine to the nape of her neck.

The door swung open, and they sprang apart.

"There you are, Mr. Holt. I thought I saw you wandering around here."

Ingrid blinked up at the large and imposing figure of the Holts' valet.

"You'd best go join your father. It's not safe here on the train." He turned to Ingrid then, staring at her for a beat. "You wouldn't want the wrong people to see you . . . lurking."

Linden glanced at Ingrid. "I'll see you soon, right?"

Ingrid nodded, letting Linden's hand slip from her fingers. She let him leave first, waiting a few seconds before following, the eyes of the valet following her exit.

When she stepped back into the light of the snowy mountain landscape, she scanned the crowd for familiar faces and found them on the opposite side. She'd taken barely a few steps toward them when a burst of sound and color came from the train car behind her. The metal tracks seemed to buckle, and fire and smoke burst from the train.

Ingrid hit the snowy ground on all fours, the wind knocked from her lungs as the explosion propelled her forward. Cold seeped into her stockings, but she barely noticed, rolling forward to get away. Her ears rang, and her nose filled with the smell of something burning.

The crowd before her rippled in a wave of panic. Ingrid got to her feet clumsily and ran with them, putting as much distance between herself and the train as she could. Snow slowed her gait, and her breath came sharp and ragged as though she'd forgotten how to use her lungs. She'd been inside that train car only moments earlier. If the valet hadn't come to shoo them away—well, she might not be alive at all.

"There you are!" Alex caught her by the arm as she hurtled toward the trees. He brought her into a one-armed hug. "You're okay." His voice sounded far away, as though through a tunnel.

"I'm okay," she repeated, barely believing the words herself. "What—what was that?"

Alex shook his head. "I don't know."

"Didn't realize those words were in your vocabulary." Clarence elbowed him.

"Oh, come on, man," Alex replied, his brow furrowing. "My vocabulary is bigger than yours."

"If you say that it's not the size that counts, I will fire you both on the spot," Birdie muttered.

"If you'd all quit joking around for two seconds," Faye said, and pointed back at the train, "you'd see we have something a lot more important than your fragile egos to deal with."

Ingrid whipped her head around. Before them was a landscape of hurried footprints in the snow marred by the warped metal of what was once a functioning passenger car. The smoke was clearing now, and in its wake was a message scrawled in white paint against the usually pristine silver steel.

"What does that say?" Birdie asked, squinting.

Gwendolyn took a step forward, her silhouette stark against the snowy scene. "Everybody burns."

CHAPTER EIGHTEEN

Ingrid was greeted the next morning by a grumpy Alex and a stack of newspapers. He sat at the large oblong table in the center of their makeshift workspace in the hotel suite adjoining Birdie and Gwendolyn's room, scowling at her over a bagel. He wore a bulky maroon sweater dusted with crumbs and a pair of minuscule gold spectacles.

"You look like an adorable grandfather," Ingrid said, falling into a chair beside him near the end of the table. She reached for the other half of his bagel but was unceremoniously swatted.

"I feel like one too." Alex let out a tired breath and shoved his work away. "How many years has it been since I woke up this morning?"

"Hard at work, I see." Ingrid took a paper from his stack. She knew the drill. From a cursory glance at the headlines Alex had already pulled, she could tell what the main topic in the papers was: CAMPAIGNS DERAILED, REBELLION ON TRACK, and EXPRESS EXPLODES.

"Alex thrives under pressure." Faye clapped him on the shoulder as she passed by. "If you decide to hold it against him, we'll understand."

"Please," Birdie grunted from across the room. "I take offense at your offense. You're one of us. Deal."

"The press is being obnoxious," Clarence explained as he swooped past, snatching Alex's paper. "They don't want to write about anything except the train situation, and since there's nothing *new* to say about it until Flare Force releases any real statement, I say we should be obnoxious right back."

"Ah, yes, your natural state," Ingrid said with a wry smile. "But really, how do you propose to do that?"

"I'm glad you asked." Clarence cleared his throat. "The Holt campaign is taking every advantage during this situation. The conversation around security and the rebellion favors him, so as long as the press stays focused on it, he'll gain support without doing much of anything. He can ride this train, so to speak, to a landslide. So how do we disrupt that?"

A few moments of silence passed before Ingrid realized the question wasn't rhetorical. "I suppose we have to change the subject."

"Righto!" Clarence clicked his tongue and snatched a bagel from the tray in the center of the table. "So we bombard the press with new policy initiatives. They'll have to write about something else tomorrow and the day after and the day after. We have to keep looking ahead if we're going to win this."

"Are we going to win this?" Ingrid asked, a waver in her voice. "I mean, even if we can convince the papers to write about the topics we want, will that really be enough to beat Holt?"

Clarence crossed his arms, a slight frown creasing his lips. "You've worked for the man. You tell me, how would you beat him?"

Ingrid had never given any thought to it. Senator Holt was to be her father-in-law, he was her boss, and he was, if all went according to plan, the future president of Candesce. She didn't want to beat him, she wanted to *be* him. "I suppose I would exploit his weaknesses?" she asked hesitantly.

"And what might those be?" Alex asked.

Ingrid tried not to fidget in her seat. "Well, he's charismatic, and he has a lot of centralized support among the wealthy. He'll be strong in Excandridge and Cintilmore. West Cendium and East Cendium should swing toward Meyers, assuming enough people vote, so it's down to Alorden and the capital."

"And so . . ." Clarence waved for her to continue.

Ingrid thought back to everything she knew of the senator, to all the times Charlotte had complained about him, to even Alex and Faye's discussion on the train. "Policy," she said finally. "Senator Holt is stately and commanding in terms of presence. He *feels* presidential without doing anything particularly worthy of the job. He spends more time in the Senate blocking legislation than writing it. So you hit him on the specifics. You force him into a corner and make him show his hand."

"Nailed it." Alex tipped his chair back, balancing with two of the legs off the ground. "We have to get him on a topic he can't win on—like flare equity. You saw him at the debate, stumbling over himself to try to defend being irresponsibly rich. We have to make him say something so irredeemable, even his fellow *millioflares* can't support him."

"If you say *millioflares* again, you're fired," Birdie said, not even looking up from her paper.

Alex crossed his eyes and screwed up his face, causing Faye to choke on her coffee.

"But really, we can't beat him at his game, so we have to make him play ours." Alex reached for another paper and thumbed through the pages.

"Wow, they are really reaching," Ingrid muttered as she turned her attention back to her own news clippings. "This one says the train was a stunt orchestrated by both campaigns in order to organize a meeting of the two candidates. They're saying Holt and Meyers are in cahoots, playing two sides of the rebel debate in order to distract the nation from a greater threat."

"Do they say what the greater threat is?" Alex asked.

Ingrid held up a hand as she scanned for any sort of clarity in the matter. "No, in fact. They do not."

"That's *Capital Tales* for you," Faye said, joining them at the table.

"*Capital Tales* . . . more like Capi*tall* Tales, am I right?" Alex scrunched his face. "Hardly anything they print is factual, and even if it is, it's so blown out of proportion it may as well be fiction."

"Why do they do that?" Ingrid asked.

Clarence shrugged and took the paper from her. "It doesn't really matter if it's true or not, does it? If the electorate reads it, so do we. If they think it's fact, it may as well be. It doesn't help our polling numbers to operate as though they actually know what's going on in their country if they, well, *don't*."

"It's just about misinformation," Faye added. "If it derails the conversation, they're happy."

Alex groaned. "What's next? Consult a doctor if the election lasts more than four hours?"

Clarence chuckled. "With jokes like that, you could write for them, if Birdie ever follows through on her threats to fire you."

"Everyone, pack up," said the melodic voice of Gwendolyn Meyers as she entered the suite.

"Are you *firing* us?" Clarence asked without blinking.

"What? No." Gwendolyn furrowed her brow. "What would make you—never mind. We're needed in the capital. The president has recalled me and Senator Holt for a debrief on the train attack. We need to be there this afternoon."

Birdie stood, her height barely reaching Gwendolyn's shoulder. "I'm coming too."

Gwendolyn's eyes fell on her campaign manager. "The campaign doesn't end just because I have to take the day off. You'll need to keep things running here. East Cendium still deserves all our efforts."

"If you think I'm letting you go without me—"

Gwendolyn touched her lightly on the arm. "Bird, I need you here. I need to know East Cendium is taken care of," she said quietly, then bent her head to murmur something in Birdie's ear.

Birdie's lips thinned, but she nodded. "Alex!" she barked. "You go with the candidate." She crossed the room and put a hand on his shoulder. "You don't let her out of your sight, you hear me?"

Ingrid watched as the room broke out into a frenzy of packing. The others bounced around the suite, collecting papers and throwing them into briefcases. Ingrid wanted to help, but she didn't know where to start. She didn't know where to go. No one had given her a direction.

So she decided to take her own. She strode across the room to where Alex was attempting to carry more than an armload of papers and took half the stack. "Can I come too?" she asked.

"Wouldn't you rather stay? You'll learn a lot more from Birdie here."

"It's only . . ." Ingrid chewed her lip, eyeing the others. It was true she might learn more about the campaign, about their weaknesses, about how to beat them if she stayed, but somehow none of that felt so important anymore. There was a lot more in the capital for her than there was on the campaign trail alone with Birdie.

Hopefully Alex would understand that. "My father's in the capital. I don't get to see him very much because, well, legally I'm barred from visiting him more than once a month, and—"

Alex held up a hand. "You don't have to explain. You should come with us. You should go see your father." He smiled wide. "I bet he'll be really proud to hear about what you're doing."

Ingrid's heart sank. Alex was right. Her father would be proud. He would be proud, and it was all a lie.

"Ingrid? Is that you?" Oscar Ellis entered the visitation room with a hopeful note to his voice.

As a child, his had been the only voice in the world that could lull her to sleep. Her father hadn't always had money, but he'd always had a song on his tongue and a poem in his heart. Now his voice grated, filled with the kind of soul-deep fatigue she'd not yet felt. She wanted to shed the pearls and poise she wore as camouflage and become a child once more, to lie on the floor with their heads touching. She'd ask him to tell her a story, and he'd give her a song instead.

"Papa," she said, rising to her feet.

The smile on his face clashed discordantly with the haunted circles beneath his eyes. He looked as though he'd been sleeping even less than when she'd last visited.

"They told me there was a train accident." His words came too quickly, running into one another. "There was no other news. I didn't know if you lived or died."

A sad smile twitched onto her lips. "I'm sorry you had to wait in suspense."

"My little girl, always getting into some sort of trouble."

If Ingrid didn't know better, she'd have thought he looked almost proud.

"Speaking of trouble." His tone darkened. "I saw your picture in the paper with that boy again."

"Papa, I don't—"

"The Holts aren't any kind of people for you to be messing about with," he said. "They don't understand people like us. They don't even want to try."

"We aren't the same," Ingrid grumbled.

"What's that? Speak up."

"We aren't the same. You and me, I mean." Ingrid met his gaze, steeling herself against the hurt in his cloudy green eyes.

"We are the same blood, the same home, the same . . . the same . . ." He shook his head as he muttered the words over again. "They will not understand you when what you come from is this. They are too rigid, too prejudiced. They will not accept you as you are."

"Then I will become something else!" She slammed her hand on the table, the sound ricocheting around the small room. "You tried and failed. That's why you're here. You tried to take what they have, and you couldn't. But I can, and I will."

Her father exhaled long and slow. "I have no doubt, my Dewdrop. Anything you set your mind to, you will accomplish. I only mean to ask, Is this really what you want? To sit on piles of money and magic and throw parties and do nothing to make it easier for the rest of us? Do you really want to live your life like them?"

"I'm not going to live my life like them. I'm going to live like Gwendolyn Meyers."

"That's a fantasy, Dewdrop," he said quietly. "She's one in a million."

"I work for her, you know." Ingrid drew herself up, setting her shoulders back and elongating her neck to project as tall as she could. For even now, with her father in shackles, with her feet in heels, she felt small in his presence. Here was this man who'd risked all they had, and here was she, a girl too strong to be brought down by his mistakes. She was living, she was *thriving*. Part of her wanted him to see it and be proud, and another part of her wanted him to see it and be hurt. "I'm an aide on her presidential campaign."

"Really?" A spark lit his eyes. "My little girl, working for Gwendolyn Meyers. And she's running for president." His gaze darkened then. "Be careful, Ingrid. Politicians can be dangerously callous. Too often they care more about power than people. Don't let them step on you to get it."

"Gwendolyn isn't like that," Ingrid said, matching his somber tone. "She really cares. She talks about flare equity and ending flare-controlled elections. She even gives her own flare away to people who need it. She may be a politician, but she's a good one."

As the words spilled from Ingrid's lips, a weight pushed down on her shoulders. It made her so proud to say the woman she worked for was different, the woman she worked for was important, and the woman she worked for was more than a little bit like her. But she didn't work for Gwendolyn Meyers. She worked for the man who wanted to beat her. The lie she told was a wound in her chest as she pretended to be better than she was. That her father was proud of her too only twisted the knife.

His lips thinned. "Just don't align yourself with people who would sooner destroy you than lose. Don't let them change who you are any more than they already have."

"Who I am?" she asked, incredulous. "Do you even know who I am anymore?" The words escaped her, raw and angry and sudden. It wasn't his fault she felt so empty, but she would blame him anyway. It was easier than the alternative. "You left me, Papa. You *left*."

Her words hung in the air between them, an accusation, a lament. There were wounds there she hadn't meant to uncover, but now that she had, it was too late to bandage them back up. The damage was done.

"I didn't mean to leave you, Dewdrop." His fingers bounced as though he wanted to touch her, but he was shackled to the table. "You know that, right? I didn't want to."

"But you did. You left me with nothing, with no one. You left me in that place, and I had to drag myself out." Ingrid shuddered, feeling suddenly ragged and helpless, the way she'd felt outside the orphanage again after all these years. It was as if, looking back at herself, the polish she'd cultivated had been buffed away, as though if she acknowledged the past, everyone would see her bare and bruised and broken. "If I've changed, it's because I had to. They didn't make me change. If anyone did, it was you."

"You're strong that way," he said softly. "You were always adaptable as a child, and you're still changing. You've grown so fast . . . sometimes I wish I could reach out to grab ahold of time, shake a little sense into it."

Ingrid's stomach lurched, and her anger shattered. The quiet desperation of her childhood took its place, aching to be seen, longing to reach out. She wanted to know if he recognized her when he looked at her, if she was still the girl who measured her feet against his and learned to count the minutes he was away. When she was only a girl, she'd wanted to grow up to be just like him. Now she feared it above all else. "Am I who you thought I'd grow up to be?" she asked, her voice small.

Silence pounded louder than her pulse. The seconds wound

around them like a knot, siphoning away the honesty in the air.

"Of course," he said.

Not at all, she heard.

"Any father would be proud."

I'm not.

"You've really made something of yourself."

You were happier when you were nothing.

"Dewdrop," he said softly. "I just want you to be happy."

Ingrid didn't want to be happy. She wanted to be important, and she wanted to be valued. But something in her father's piercing gaze, in Gwendolyn Meyers's inspiring words, and even in Alex's unwavering hope made her want to be something else.

They made her want to be good.

CHAPTER NINETEEN

The Meyers campaign was headquartered in the heart of the capital, only a few blocks from Ainsley Academy, and a few more from the capitol building itself. Ingrid followed the hastily scribbled instructions Alex had given her to a corner building with a wide front door at the top of a short staircase. She knocked, but there was no answer.

"Alex?" she asked, tentatively trying the door to find it was unlocked.

"Hi," Alex said from the floor, his legs thrown up onto a mauve chaise at the opposite wall.

The office was spacious, with a large central table made of solid wood. Desks lined the right side of the room, set against windows looking out onto the street, and on the left was a makeshift kitchen area with a kettle and stove. Notably, there wasn't a single flare decoration aside from the lamps.

"What are you doing down there?" Ingrid cocked her head sharply to the left. "Is it bad news? Should I join you?"

Alex heaved a sigh. "No. I should get up. I don't think there's any blood left in my legs." He rolled to the side and pushed himself up on his elbows. "How was your visit?"

Ingrid moved into the room, sitting in one of the many chairs surrounding the center table. "It was all right." She tried to say the words as casually as possible, but a heaviness settled over her at the reminder of how her father's pride had made her feel.

"All right?" Alex exhaled loudly as he returned to standing. "Doesn't seem all right to me. What happened?"

Ingrid pulled her shoulders back. "How did you— What makes you say that?"

"When I asked about him, you got two inches shorter and did that thing where your jaw sort of twitches and your lip goes all wonky." Alex pulled a face in what Ingrid hoped was an overly dramatic imitation.

"Please, I don't do that." Ingrid felt her lip twitch and clapped her hand over her face. "That was just a coincidence."

"Sure." Alex sat opposite her and steepled his fingers on the table. "So what's wrong with your father?"

"Nothing's wrong with him," Ingrid said automatically, a defensive note rising in her tone. "He's okay. I mean, he's in prison, but I guess he's okay."

She half expected Alex to interject with some quip or another to break the tension, something like *I'd ask what's wrong with you, but we both know the answer would take too long.* But he didn't. He just sat in silence, offering her the space to continue.

Ingrid didn't usually feel like talking about her father. But then, she was usually talking to people like Linden who wouldn't understand. She always said she was nothing like him, but in reality, her father was kind and loving and always there—until he wasn't—and she didn't want to be nothing like him.

Talking with Alex felt different, though. He wasn't like her classmates, valuing her based on where she came from. He'd

179

judged her by her ideas and her drive. He hadn't held her association with Linden against her—at least no more than she deserved—and she didn't think he'd judge her for this.

"Have you ever loved someone who hurt you?"

"Yes," Alex said solemnly.

"Like, really loved someone, and then they did something that maybe they shouldn't have. And worst of all, they did it for you, so you feel guilty, but you also feel angry because they didn't ask if you even wanted it and it ended up hurting you so much. And you don't know how to forgive them because you know they meant well, but it still hurts."

"Okay, well, not quite so specifically." He gestured for her to continue. "I assume you mean your father?"

"He stole flare when I was little." Ingrid had never actually told anyone in words so plain. "He went to prison for it when I was only ten years old. I know he was doing it for us, to give us more, but he was all I had and they took him away."

Alex nodded but didn't interrupt her.

"I just feel so angry, and I feel so guilty for feeling angry. I know I should blame the system that forced him to act illegally to survive, and I do, but I also blame him, and a part of me blames myself. I want to not care, you know. I want to put that feeling away and never look at it. But if I let it sit for too long, it starts to feel like something inside me is burning. It's like drinking too much flare—if I don't use it, it'll destroy me." She let out a long breath through her teeth. "It's hard to go visit him and try to put all that aside. I only get one visit per month, and I don't want to waste it on this feeling." Her chest tightened. "I just wish I could be mature about it and move on, but for some reason, I can't. I don't know why."

180

"You don't know why?" Alex asked, peering at her with unreadable eyes. "I know why."

"You do?" Her stomach tightened as fear inched up her spine. Now was when he would lecture her. He would tell her she was being unreasonable and uncharitable. Her father was only trying to do his best, and she should honor that sacrifice.

But he didn't say any of that. Instead, he stood up and rounded the table to stand before her. "Of course I do. Ingrid, you were ten years old. It doesn't matter how reasonable your father's actions were. It still happened, and you were hurt. That pain doesn't go away just because you understand why he did what he did. Trust doesn't just come back because you're old enough to understand now. Trust takes time to rebuild, and if you're only getting one visit every month, no wonder you still feel this way."

"You don't think I'm . . . wrong to feel like this?"

Alex smiled sadly. "You feel how you feel. The fact that you know how you feel and why you feel it is honestly far more impressive than you think. It takes a lot to be that aware." He sighed and let his head flop heavily to the right. "I don't talk to my parents anymore. Sometimes I think maybe I want to, but they still see me as the person I was, not the person I am. They're so stuck on that single vision of who I should be, and I'm not interested in that fight. Plus, I have a new family now. Birdie and Gwendolyn—they're more my parents than anyone related to me."

"I didn't know that—I'm sorry." Ingrid bit her lip. She hadn't even thought to ask Alex about himself like this. She'd learned all his strange habits—his favorite writing implement, the way he always forgot about his beverages and had to reheat them. She thought she knew so much. But she didn't really know anything at all.

"Don't be. They were lousy parents." He shrugged. "This family I have now? It's a thousand times better."

"Don't let Clarence hear you say that. You'll never live it down."

Alex winced. "Yeah, better keep that to yourself. He already has enough to tease me about." He held out his hand to her. "Now, if you want it, I am willing to put forward a one-time offer of a remedial hug."

With his arms open and the disarming smile on his face, Ingrid couldn't bring herself to refuse. Besides, she didn't want to. She stood and fell into his embrace.

"You're really confident about the power of your hugs," she said, her voice muffled against his frame. He wrapped his arms comfortably around her back, but they didn't travel the way Linden's always did. He held on, not too tight, not too loose. Steady.

"They are truly potent. I have to be careful with how I give them out, you know. They are only to be used as prescribed."

She laughed into his shoulder. "You are so full of yourself."

"Better than empty." He let go and grinned. "Also, I was right. It obviously worked."

"On you too, apparently." She gave him a pointed look.

"What do you mean?"

"You were miserable as can be when I walked in. Now you're smiling."

Alex winced. "Is miserable the word? I mean, how can you really tell—"

"You were on the floor, Alex."

"To be fair, I am on the floor a lot."

Ingrid returned to her seat. Now that Alex had let go, she didn't feel quite as sturdy anymore. "Your terrible sitting practices aside, what's the matter?"

Alex followed her lead, sighing with his whole body as he went. "Gwendolyn had her meeting with the president."

"It went poorly, I assume?"

"It was supposed to be some kind of debrief about the situation with the Shadow of the Flame. A security information meeting, I guess." Alex picked at his fingernails. "Apparently, he called for a cessation of all campaign activity until we know more. Said it wasn't safe for two prominent members of our government to be traveling around the country if the anarchists are targeting transportation. So, until further notice, we're stuck here in the capital."

"And that's bad?"

"Well, it's not great for the campaign if we can't campaign." Alex sank down in his seat, his sweater bunching up around his neck to make him look like a turtle. "The others are being recalled to the capital for the President's Ball next week, and then we'll all be stuck here, unable to campaign in the districts that matter."

"The President's Ball?" Ingrid asked.

"Should've known that's what you'd get out of what I said." Alex made a face. "The president traditionally hosts a ball for the candidates and their staffs. A night of apolitical nonsense. There will be dancing and pâté on little crackers."

"Oh, do you think they'll have the fancy olives?" Ingrid couldn't help herself. The annoyance on Alex's face was worth every ounce of excitement she could inject into her words.

"Stuffed with pretention, probably."

Ingrid nudged him. "Come on, a night of fun won't kill you."

"Maybe I'll kill the night of fun," Alex grumbled.

"All right, all right." Ingrid settled back into her chair. "So what's your plan to deal with this whole stuck-in-the-capital situation?"

"I don't have one."

Ingrid narrowed her eyes. "I know it's not ideal, but it's not over. We can still do the work and earn the votes, right? I would've thought you'd be energized by this kind of political challenge."

"I am. I was working on a plan when you so rudely interrupted my floor ponderings." He sighed more dramatically than was strictly called for. "I'm just so annoyed Holt's the one who suggested this freeze. He knows it will damage our campaign more than his, but he framed it like it's good for all of us."

Ingrid's spine went ramrod straight at the mention of her secret boss. If he was in the capital, then maybe . . . maybe Linden was too.

Alex carried on. "This isn't even what I'm upset about. I'm upset because it means my 'day off' in East Cendium is canceled."

"You mean your free-flare day?"

Alex nodded glumly.

"I didn't realize those meant so much to you." As she said it, though, she found the feeling mutual. The good they'd done that day felt real. It wasn't some intangible possibility, it was reality. It wasn't waiting to be elected, it was acting. "Can't you go once everything is back to normal? We could go together."

"That's the thing. We can't." Alex pulled his sweater up farther so it covered his mouth and nose too, making his voice muffled. "Gwendolyn said we have to wait until after the election is over. She might need the flare if it comes down to a tie, and we can't risk the election for something like this."

Ingrid's heart sank. "But . . . they can't afford to wait. You saw them, Alex. Even if we win, it will be months before any real change is enacted, and probably years before they start to see the effect of those changes. And all that's assuming the Senate cooperates with Gwendolyn's agenda."

"I know," Alex groaned. "But Gwendolyn's policies will make a bigger change, a better change."

"So you think she's right?" Ingrid asked, outrage peppering her voice. "I thought you cared about those people. I thought you—"

"Whoa, Ingrid. I do care. Why do you think I'm so frustrated?" Alex sat up and held out his hands. "Look, it's complicated. I know what Gwendolyn is doing makes sense. I know it might even be the right decision. But I'm still not happy about it. Maybe it's a little like things with your father, I don't know."

Ingrid leaned down and put her forehead on the table. "Sorry. I didn't mean to snap at you. I'm just tired."

"Me too," Alex said quietly. "We're all tired."

CHAPTER TWENTY

When Ingrid retired to her dormitory at Ainsley Academy, Charlotte was already sleeping peacefully, which was more than could be said of her friend the following morning. Charlotte woke her by unceremoniously launching herself onto the foot of Ingrid's bed and tackling her into an enthusiastic embrace.

"I thought you weren't coming!" she shrieked. "I didn't see you earlier with the Holt campaign staff, so I assumed you stayed behind."

"Oh. I suppose I need to catch you up." Ingrid untangled herself from Charlotte's limbs with difficulty and went to sit at the vanity. She explained as best she could her new set of circumstances—excluding, of course, her arrangement with Senator Holt. Charlotte was Ingrid's best friend, but she was also a reporter, and Ingrid had had her fair share of bad press lately to make her wary.

"Let me get this straight," Charlotte said, ticking off the facts on her fingers. "You left the Holt campaign, joined the Meyers campaign, and you almost got blown up on a train."

"That about sums it up, yes."

"What was it like?" Charlotte asked quietly, a poignant note to her voice. "The explosion, I mean."

Ingrid examined her eyebrows in the mirror, doing her best to seem nonchalant. "A little disarming. We were all a lot more shaken by the political ramifications of the rebel attack than the attack itself, if I'm being honest."

"It's strange." Charlotte gazed over Ingrid's head, deep in thought. "For an anarchist rebellion everyone seems to fear so much, they've done a rather remarkable job of *not* hurting anyone. It's almost like they're trying not to."

Ingrid gave her an incredulous look. "What are you saying, that the Shadow of the Flame is suddenly a peaceful organization?"

"No, it's not that. I'm working on a piece for the *Courant* about this for tomorrow's paper, actually. It seems to me that this version of the Shadow of the Flame is markedly different from its earlier iterations. In the past, they've always been extremely specific about their attacks—more like assassinations, really. They stir up some kind of frenzy to distract everyone, take out their targets, and get out. They don't blow up whole train cars, and they certainly don't blow them up with no one on them."

"So you think this isn't really the Shadow of the Flame?"

"I don't know what I think. It just doesn't sit right with me." Charlotte frowned and leafed through a stack of *Candesce Courants* at the foot of her bed. "It's like that speakeasy raid. Wasn't there supposed to be a rebel attack that night? That's why Flare Force bothered with it in the first place."

"Yes, but Holt got there before the rebels could attack. In the end, it was just the one girl."

"It just doesn't make sense." Charlotte pursed her lips in thought. "Why would rebels set on destroying the government attack a flicker club anyway?"

"Maybe they're just against fun." Ingrid pulled a face. "Honestly, they're doing more harm to the Meyers campaign by simply existing than they've managed to do to any actual property. At this rate, they're going to be the reason we end up with Holt for president."

"And then we'll all have to join them," Charlotte said, an over-abundance of drama in her voice. "Speaking of Holt, what about Linden?"

"What about Linden?"

"Are you still engaged? Are you still together?"

Ingrid swallowed hard. She'd hoped Charlotte wouldn't ask so she wouldn't have to lie. "I heard he might be seeing Pauline Ackerman now." Ingrid's skin flushed cold as the other girl's name passed her lips. She knew their entanglement was no more than a ruse, a distraction to keep the press from digging any further into Ingrid's new allegiance, and to keep her new allies from realizing how current her Holt ties still were. Even so, Pauline Ackerman was enjoying the attention—from the press and from Linden—that ought to have been Ingrid's. It all left her feeling halfway between jealousy and relief, and she found no comfort in either emotion.

"Could he have chosen a worse replacement for you?" Charlotte winced. "I won't pretend to be terribly disappointed—you know I can't stand his father—but are you okay?"

"I was the one who chose to leave." Ingrid picked up a tube of lipstick and popped the lid off and on, off and on, too afraid to look her friend directly in the eye.

"Stop that." Charlotte reached out and took the lipstick from her.

"Sorry, just a bit fidgety."

Charlotte waved her off. "No, not that—although it's terribly annoying—I mean stop trying to brush this off. You're allowed to be upset even if you're the one who ended it, you know."

"I know." Ingrid's stomach churned with the discomfort of the charade. "But I really am okay."

"Well, if you're sure." Charlotte sighed. "Makes this a mite awkward, though." With a light *clink*, she let a small stone fall onto the vanity, eight white hash marks on the smooth surface.

"How did you—" Ingrid began.

"Please." Charlotte waved her off. "I've lived with you for five years. I may not have known who your secret paramour was, but your code wasn't exactly hard to crack."

Ingrid glanced at the rock. Eight slashes meant he'd be waiting until eight o'clock. She still had time, if only she could slip away.

"What do you think he wants?" Charlotte asked.

"I don't know." Ingrid picked up the rock and squeezed it in her hand.

"Do you think he wants to get back together?" An ominous note hit Charlotte's voice.

"Only one way to find out." Ingrid stood and shrugged on her dressing gown. With fifteen minutes until the hour, she didn't have time for primping first. Linden would see her in all her unraveled glory or not at all.

"Linden, it's me," she whispered as she opened the door of the supply closet.

"Ingrid." He pulled her close and murmured against her hair. "I'm so happy to see you."

It had been only two days, but somehow the time between felt heavy.

"Nice rollers," Linden said as they parted.

Ingrid touched her hair, a blush he couldn't see creeping up her neck. She'd left them in rather than do only half the job. "I didn't have time to—"

"I like them. I like you." He kissed her swiftly. "I like seeing you like this. It feels real."

The word *real* ricocheted through her chest. This was only a fraction of her. This was her face without makeup, her hair without pins. If he could see her visiting her father in prison or in the orphanage with Frances, *that* would be real. If he could see her working side by side with Alex, *that* would be real. If he could see her heart and the holes she'd torn in it to make room for him, *that* would be real. She hoped he never did.

Instead, she backed away. "I have a message for your father."

Linden reached for her hand. "Do we have to talk about my father right now?"

"Isn't that why you wanted to meet?"

"This is why I wanted to meet."

He traced the outline of her face with his fingers, ran his touch down her jaw, along the side of her neck. His lips captured hers, a kiss too quiet and too tender against the thunder of her pulse. His touch crept lower until it grazed the top of the engagement ring beneath her robe.

She leapt back, hand fisted around the cloth. The ring's cool metal suddenly felt hot against her skin, heavy around her neck, like a boulder weighing her down, ensuring she'd drown.

"We shouldn't waste time—there's important business to discuss," Ingrid said hurriedly, too afraid to meet Linden's eyes for fear of seeing the hurt in his gaze.

"Ingrid, I—"

"The Meyers campaign is worried about a tie." It felt strange to refer to them as *the Meyers campaign* and not simply *we*.

"So are we." Linden sighed and let his arm fall away from her shoulder, resigned. "Father's worried Gwendolyn's economic plans will overshadow his."

Ingrid's head snapped up, and she stopped pacing. "He is?"

"Obviously he doesn't agree with them, but he knows how convincing she can be. Her whole stunt at the debate with the flare and the ice cubes, that's the kind of thing that wins votes. Brave to call them selfish and spoiled to their faces, but they might feel guilty enough to vote for her or at least donate some flare to charity. Not that it will make much difference, since people will just squander it anyhow."

Ingrid bit her lip. "What do you mean, squander it?"

Linden waved a hand. "Oh, you know. It'll be like those flicker clubs, or they'll use it to blow up more of our buildings and trains."

"I'll remind you it was *you* who burned down that speakeasy, and it's you and your sort who throw lavish flare parties. You want to know how the poor use flare? Maybe try asking someone who doesn't come from money."

"Ingrid, I didn't mean it like that." Linden stepped toward her, reaching a hand to brush back her hair.

She swatted him away. "Yes, you did. You think poor people are too stupid to get high-paying jobs, so they must be too stupid to use flare. Tell me, Linden, do you think I'm stupid?"

"You're the smartest girl I know."

"Do you think I deserve to run my furnace? To turn on the lights?"

"Of course I do——"

"What about voting? Do you think I should be able to vote?" Ingrid couldn't stop now that she'd started. She hadn't meant to come here and lecture Linden, but she'd learned too much from

Gwendolyn and Alex and the rest of the Meyers campaign to stay silent.

"Of course you should vote. Ingrid, I didn't mean *you*. You're different from the rest of them."

Once, she would have relished those words. She'd spent so long trying to prove she was different, that she was somehow *better*. Now it felt like an insult.

"I'm not," Ingrid murmured. "I'm one of them. I'm not special; I'm not different." She'd thought it would feel like surrender to admit, but instead it felt like victory, like triumph. She'd seen the way Frances looked at her with pity, not envy, and she knew she had not *shaken* her roots the way she'd thought; she'd *lost* them. She was lucky to have found them again, and this time she would not run away from who she was.

Linden held his hands to his chest, eyes wide and weak with affection. "Yes, you are. You're special. You're special to me. You shouldn't be ashamed of that."

"Ashamed?" Ingrid had to keep herself from shouting. "My father is a convict who stole flare because he couldn't earn it." She tightened her jaw against the emotion building in her throat. "But I'm not ashamed of what he did, I'm ashamed of what the government did to him as punishment. I'm ashamed that this country thinks I don't deserve a dignified existence simply because I was born to a family less fortunate than yours. And most of all, I'm ashamed that you think *I'm* worthy, but not other people like me."

Images flashed into her mind, of Alex, of Frances, of her father. And another face joined them: Louise. She'd seen herself reflected in that angry fire-filled girl the first night they'd met. Perhaps it was not only Linden who'd failed to understand. It was not enough for Ingrid to be the exception; she had to find a way to be the rule. She had to make things right.

Linden's head fell forward in defeat. "I never thought of it like that, but you're right."

Ingrid thought it would feel better to hear him admit it, but she just felt tired. She didn't want to fight like this. She wanted him to already understand. After her talk with Alex the night before, anything less felt disappointing.

With a sigh, Ingrid adopted a businesslike tone. "Look, I know this is complicated and your father's expecting some kind of news, but I don't have anything for him he doesn't already know. His tactic to stall the campaigns seems to have worked, and at the rate the rebellion is going, he won't need my help to win anyway. Maybe that's for the best."

"Or maybe not," Linden muttered under his breath.

"I should go. I'm expected at the office." Ingrid drifted toward the door.

"Will I see you at the President's Ball?" Linden asked, pulling at her sleeve.

"You will, if you're not too busy making eyes at Pauline Ackerman." Ingrid couldn't help the bite to her tone.

"You know it isn't like that." Linden tried to catch her gaze, but she looked away. "Pauline's a friend of the family, and her presence keeps my father at bay."

"Of course it does. She's exactly the sort of girl—"

"Stop." Linden drew her hand into his. "Stop that. You know I only have eyes for you. If I could look at you without causing trouble, I'd never even blink."

Ingrid's heartbeat slowed a little at that, his honeyed words doing their job all too well. "Okay. I believe you," she said. But she didn't. Part of her would always wonder if he only wanted her when she was like Pauline, when she was playing at perfect.

"Good. I can't wait to see you all dressed up." He kissed her hand before she pulled it from his grasp.

He would see her again at the President's Ball, looking her best, and that would have to be enough. Perhaps he didn't mind the rollers, but she knew he minded her honesty, her history. She had shown him just this small piece of herself as she was, not as she pretended to be, and still he preferred the other. She tucked her realness deep into her pockets to be forgotten. He didn't really want it.

And maybe he didn't deserve it anyway.

Ingrid was going to be late. However, when she left Ainsley Academy, sans rollers and properly dressed, she marched right on past the Meyers campaign headquarters and beat the familiar route across the capital to the little-visited prison district. She'd told Linden people like her deserved a chance, and it was time to do her part.

They'd given her a small fortune in exchange for Linden's ring at the pawnshop across the street from the prison. It was easily the most valuable thing she owned, an heirloom, a promise, a symbol of so much more than jewels. But as Ingrid had handed it over, a weight lifted, as though the ring was made of lead instead of precious gems. With pockets full of coins, Ingrid spent her money the best way she could: to right a wrong.

Louise looked different out of her prison clothes, somehow smaller and larger all at once. Her cheeks had filled in a little since Ingrid had last seen her, and her hair had grown back—still patchy in places. Overall, she looked healthier, but mostly she just looked ridiculous.

"What are you wearing?" Ingrid asked, unable to keep the grin off her face.

Louise was dressed in what could only be described as a plum-wine ocean of a dress and a matching hat.

"My clothes burned. This is what they had left over," Louise said, her voice even.

"Well, first order of business is we find you something else to wear." Ingrid grimaced. "Don't want to attract too much attention." She headed for the door without another glance.

"First order of business," Louise said, chasing her out to the street, "is you tell me what's going on."

"I'm bailing you out." Ingrid snatched the hat off Louise's head and stuffed it in a nearby trash bin. "Or to be more exact, I already bailed you out."

"But why?" Louise recovered the hat and tucked it under her arm. "I'm awaiting trial for attacking *you*. Why would you bail me out?"

Ingrid led Louise down the street back toward the center of town. "Because you were right."

"I'm right about a lot of things. You'll have to be more specific."

Ingrid spotted a store farther down the block that looked the right balance of affordable and clean, but Louise caught her by the arm before she could step inside.

"Look, if you paid my bail just to kill me, know that I can throw a punch with or without magic."

"I'm not going to kill you." Ingrid stopped in her tracks, suddenly very aware of the mostly deserted street in which they stood. "Are you going to kill me?"

"Are you still an elitist snob?" Louise sneered.

Ingrid exhaled through her teeth. She wanted to deny that she ever had been, but if seeing Frances again had shown her anything, it was that she could see herself one way, but there was no accounting for how anyone else did. She had the benefit of witnessing all her own moments, but the people she met only saw a snapshot.

"You wouldn't believe me if I said no, would you?"

Louise's lips turned up, the hint of a smile peeking through. "That's promising. Are you still with that boy?"

"No." It barely felt like a lie. The natural way it rolled off her tongue caught her in the solar plexus, and it was all she could do not to double over. "Things are different now."

Louise leaned back on her heels, surveying Ingrid with light interest. "So *things* are different, or *you're* different?"

"Isn't that the same?" Ingrid pinched her forehead and waited for Louise to respond, but the other girl only gave her a tired look and leaned against the rough brick wall with expectation in her eyes. "I'm working for the Meyers campaign now."

"Well, let me get you your award." Louise made a face.

"I don't know what you want me to say. I know flare inequity in this country is out of control. I know that raid on the speakeasy did a lot more to hurt people than it did to protect them. You were right about all of that, and I just got caught up in some of the other elements."

"You mean that boy."

Ingrid huffed. "Well, yes. If you want to be specific about it."

"Oh, let's be specific." A cruel smile lit Louise's face. "You have weird taste in men."

Even though Ingrid was pretending she had nothing to do with Linden, the jab still hurt. Linden wasn't bad—not like his father, at least. But their conversation this morning had more than clarified that while he wasn't *bad*, he wasn't exactly *good* either.

"Why, what's your taste like?" Ingrid crossed her arms.

"Not men, for a start." Louise didn't flinch. "And certainly not rich ones."

Ingrid sighed. "This isn't the point. I'm actually trying here, all right?"

"Yes, well, trying doesn't make you a good person, does it?"

Without thinking, Ingrid asked, "What would make me a good person?"

Louise barked out a laugh. "You really want to have this conversation?"

Ingrid nodded slowly.

Turning on her heel, Louise marched down the street, stomping in her ill-fitting shoes.

"Louise? Come back!" Ingrid chased after her. "Where are you going?"

Louise didn't stop or even slow. Instead, she simply said, "You actually want to *talk* talk, you're going to have to feed me first. I'm not doing this without something in it for me."

"I just bailed you out of jail! Isn't that something for you?"

Louise halted rather suddenly outside a run-down-looking café. "I thought you did that out of the goodness of your heart."

"Well, I——"

"Did you do it because it was the right thing to do, or did you do it because you wanted something from me?" Louise crossed her arms and cocked her head to the side. "I'll happily say you did a good job and send you on your merry way if that's what you want, but if you want me to process all this"——she waved a hand at Ingrid's face——"I need a hot meal provided by you first."

"Yes, fine, all right." Ingrid motioned her through the door.

Ingrid waited while Louise ate the hot stew she'd ordered. It was a large bowl, and Louise ate much slower than Ingrid could have imagined, leaving her plenty of time to think about what Louise had said.

Ingrid wasn't sure whether she'd paid Louise's bail because it was right or because she knew Louise would think it was right. She rolled her lip between her teeth, trying to think what it would be like to be a good person. What would it even look like? She couldn't imagine it. Instead, her mind circled around the heavy guilt in her chest that had lodged there ever since she'd first seen Louise behind bars. Now Louise was free—until her trial, at least—but the weight hadn't budged. Ingrid should have felt better. Why didn't she feel better?

She knew why. It was because Louise was just one of many, just like Frances, just like Ingrid's father, even a little like Ingrid herself. Doing one right thing didn't fix a world full of wrongs. Frances's words from that day at the orphanage followed her— about how the change Ingrid was chasing wouldn't happen fast enough to matter. She had to find a way to matter.

"So what do you want?" Louise asked after finally setting her spoon aside.

The idea burst into Ingrid's mind like a firework. It was absurd. It was risky. But there would be no reward without risk, and there would be no success without dreaming. "I think I have an idea. And, if you're willing, I'd like your help."

"I'm listening."

Ingrid explained about Alex's pet project—about the flare and the charity, about the way Frances had talked about the reality of their existence, and the way it had all reminded Ingrid of her past. She told her how she wanted to do more, how she *needed* to do more.

"That's a start, I guess," Louise said. "But what do you want my help with? It sounds like you've got a good operation going with Meyers supplying the flare and you and your friend distributing it."

"That's the thing—it works, but it doesn't work hard enough. There are still a lot of people who need flare and not enough flare to go around." She drummed her fingers against her elbow. "And the program's suspended until after the election. We just found out last night."

"Well, that's a real bummer," Louise said. "What are you going to do about it?"

Ingrid took a few steps closer and leaned against the wall too. Looking up into Louise's eyes, she tried to read the other girl. "Promise not to laugh?"

"Absolutely not."

"I should've expected that." Ingrid took a deep breath. "I've been thinking about flare. Just . . . the whole process of mining, distilling, distributing . . . there are so many hoops to jump through to even acquire it. I thought if we could figure out how to *make* it, people wouldn't have to rely on a broken system to keep the lights on. They could run their furnaces with homemade magic."

Louise frowned. "Don't get me wrong, artificial flare would change, well, everything. It would disrupt the entire economy based on keeping it from us, and I'd love nothing more than to watch all those rich folks realize their carefully hoarded magic is actually worthless. But, Ingrid, no one's ever made artificial flare before."

"You've made flicker." Ingrid shrugged a shoulder. "And you're good at it. The flicker you made is as close to flare as I've ever tasted. If someone could break down the chemical components of flare and re-create it, it's you."

"You know what flicker is, right?" Louise wrinkled her face. "It's every chemist's attempt at flare. We've already broken down the chemical components of flare and tried to re-create it. Doesn't work like that."

Ingrid's heart sank. "You think it's impossible?"

"I didn't say that." Louise traced a knot in the wood of the table with her finger, eyes carefully avoiding Ingrid's. "Just hasn't been done yet. The thing is, raw flare is totally inedible. You'd probably die if you consumed what they bring up from the mountain. Flare is made through a complicated distilling process, and I just don't know it."

Ingrid sat up straighter. "But what if you did know it? What if we could get you that information? My school has the second-largest library in Candesce. I bet there's something in there that could help us."

"Maybe, but that doesn't solve the other problem. Flare factories are huge. It's not like I can just build one in my house. Same will be true for all the people you want to help. They can't make homemade magic if the machine they need is twice the size of their home."

"Could you make a smaller one?" Ingrid asked.

Louise opened her mouth, mirth in her eyes; then she closed it again and chewed her lip. "I suppose I could."

A grin broke out across Ingrid's face.

"Don't get too excited just yet. I don't know if it'll work, and then I have to get the flare recipe right too."

Ingrid couldn't shake her smile. "I think you can do it. I've seen the way you handle flicker, Louise. You know your way around a pipette."

"If you're trying to flirt with me, you're doing a terrible job."

Ingrid rolled her eyes. "What I'm saying is, if someone can figure it out, it would be you. You're a damn good flicker chemist, so why not be the first flare chemist too?"

"It won't be easy, and it won't be cheap. I'll need a lab and equipment, not to mention some flare to start with." Louise narrowed her eyes. "You sure you're up for this? It's illegal. If the wrong people find out what we're up to, we could very well end up back in there with matching hers-and-hers jail cells."

Ingrid withdrew the bag of leftover coins from pawning Linden's ring—far more than she'd ever had in her lifetime—and pulled the chain holding the small vial of flare over her head. "I'm sure."

CHAPTER TWENTY-ONE

Between her campaign work by day and her secret meetings with Louise each evening to pore over library books, the President's Ball quite snuck up on Ingrid. She'd taken a half day to prepare, pinning each curl in place with meticulous precision, but even in her best dress, she paled in comparison to the ballroom, which was gussied up far beyond her means. Thick, triangle-shaped cut glass tiled the floor, reflecting fiery fractals across the room. Dark curtains fell across full-paneled windows leading out to a garden terrace, and through a wide set of double doors, a dining room set for more people than Ingrid could fathom awaited.

Inside, she spotted the rest of the campaign staff immediately. Shimmering from head to toe, Gwendolyn wore a fully beaded gown. Its crystals glittered without the addition of flare, shining blue and purple at different angles. Ingrid shrank under her splendor, glancing down at her own dress and wishing she'd chosen better. After all, this dress, a gift from Linden made of black silk with crystal beading and flare stitched into the seams, was just another costume in her ever-reaching quest to be something she wasn't. Gwendolyn Meyers walked a different plane of beauty. She didn't need magic to make her skin glow or make her clothes sparkle. She stood out all on her own.

"Well, aren't you a pretty picture!" Alex leaned out toward her from the periphery, a nervous energy in his posture. He wore a black suit with a maroon satin tie, a far cry from the knitted mustard tie she'd seen him wear around the campaign trail. Next to Birdie, who appeared to be frozen by the sheer effort of wearing a dress in public, Alex looked almost comfortable, but the tentative smile on his face betrayed him.

"You clean up nice yourself!" Ingrid joined him near the wall, a perfect vantage point from which to observe the room.

"I borrowed it from Clarence," Alex muttered, his shoulders inching dangerously close to his earlobes.

"Everything all right?"

He cleared his throat and adjusted his tie. "Yeah," he said unconvincingly.

"You don't like parties much, do you?"

"It's not the parties I mind, but the people and the spectacle and the expectation."

"Funny, that's exactly what I like about them," Ingrid said, but the words felt like they'd landed wrong, all twisted ankles and prickling pain.

Alex's eyes found the floor, and he scuffed his shoe against it. "Everything's so false. No one here likes one another—we're all trying our damnedest to knock each other down every other night of the week. But here, we have to pretend like we're playing for peanuts, not the moral compass of the country. And all this extravagance is such an insult! If I had this kind of money—well, I wouldn't go spending it on things like this. It feels impossibly crass."

"Come now, don't hide your true feelings."

His cheeks reddened. "I hate it. I hate how we have to dress ourselves up to be palatable to them. I hate that we're judged for the price of what we wear and how well we wear it, as if we're somehow more worthy because we have the ability to place coin on a counter and point at a suit." He slumped against the wall.

"You do, you know." Ingrid leaned back to join him.

"What's that, now?"

"Wear it well." She gestured to his suit.

Alex didn't look at her, instead letting his gaze rise to the ceiling. "Took a lot of practice," he said finally before blinking the moment away and snatching a couple glasses full of bubbly pink beverage from a passing tray.

"What are we toasting to?" She took the offered glass and lifted it to let the light filter through it.

"We don't have to pay for dinner."

"Cheers."

They clinked glasses, but before liquid touched her lips, Ingrid froze. Across the room, she caught sight of Linden in shallow conversation with Pauline Ackerman. He faced away, Ingrid's eyes drawn directly to the space between his shoulder blades. He was tall and tempting and *there*. She'd known he would be, and yet she felt like she was seeing him for the first time all over again.

It had been in a ballroom much like this one—smaller, to be sure, but still full of people she didn't know and magic she didn't own. He'd been shorter than her, with a lopsided smile and a center part in his hair. There was a lilt to his shoulders and a lift to his lips that remained even now, a gentleness she'd learned to love far more than the good looks he'd grown into over the years. But none of that had mattered. She'd seen the glint of silver at his belt, the vial with a large letter H, and she'd known it then as sure as she knew it now. He was her future. He was her freedom.

When they first met, she hadn't known the rules. She'd marched up to him as brazen and bold as could be and asked him to dance. Decorum was something she'd begrudgingly learned later, and for both their sakes, she had to remember her place, remember her plan. That didn't stop her from wishing he'd look her way. She'd been harsh with him before, and part of her wanted to tell him she was sorry. But she wasn't. Not really.

And behind him loomed the silhouette of Senator Holt. From across the room, he didn't look nearly as intimidating as Ingrid remembered him. He was absorbed in conversation with his campaign manager, Gerald Cork, who whispered furiously as Holt's frown lines deepened and twisted. Then he looked up and his gaze fell on Ingrid. It was only for a moment, but it felt like longer. His eyes were shadowed, his hair thinning. He looked worn and tired, but still he made her feel minuscule, like she didn't matter, like she was no one.

She wasn't no one.

"Dance with me," Ingrid said suddenly, knocking Alex's elbow with hers.

"I beg your pardon?"

She tore her gaze away from the Holts. "I said, dance with me."

The dance floor was sparse, with only a few couples enjoying the music—a band of string musicians playing a tune rather devoid of pep were lodged in the corner. It was a far cry from the loud, brassy tones of the music she usually danced to in flicker clubs, but it would have to do. She had too much restless energy, and if she didn't burn it off, she was afraid she might march across the room to start a fight with Pauline Ackerman.

"Are you all right?" Alex asked, peering at her through narrowed eyes.

Ingrid didn't meet his gaze, instead glancing back toward Linden. Senator Holt had disappeared, much to her relief, but then Pauline laughed at something Linden said, and a piece of Ingrid shattered.

"Dance with me right now. Please?"

Alex followed her line of sight and let out a groan. "Oh, Ingrid. No. Don't do that."

"Do what?" She tried to keep her voice airy.

"Show off to make him jealous."

"I don't know what you're talking about. Can't a girl simply want to dance?"

"Sure, but *you* don't. It's written all over your face."

"Why won't you dance with me? Are you a bad dancer?" Ingrid stuck out her chin, doing her best not to let her vision drift back toward Linden.

"No, I'm an excellent dancer, I'll have you know."

"Then why won't you dance with me?"

Alex paused for a moment, looking from her to the Holts to the dance floor and back. "I'll dance with you."

Ingrid grinned, her heartbeat doing a jig inside her chest.

"But not in here."

Her stomach sank. "What do you mean?"

"You want to dance that badly, I won't deny you, but I'm not about to enable your poor decision making. We dance outside in the garden alone, or not at all." Alex held out his elbow.

The party that had started inside her veins at the idea of dancing with someone else in front of Linden died as she let Alex lead her into the cool night air. Instead, something like embarrassment curled around her throat.

"I'm sorry," she breathed as they exited into the garden.

"For what?"

"For, you know, all of that. I just . . . saw them together, and it was like my brain ran off on its own. I shouldn't have tried to use you like that, especially not for something so petty."

"Petty, I don't mind so much." He led her off the path and toward the shadow of immaculately trimmed hedges. "But I couldn't just let you make a fool of yourself. You're better than that. You're better than *him*."

"What if I'm not?" Ingrid whispered.

Alex made a face. "Don't even pretend to ask that in earnest. Now, are we dancing or not?"

The music was much quieter outside, but they could still hear the rhythm, so Ingrid set down her drink and let Alex fit his frame to hers.

Alex hadn't lied; he was a good dancer. Not as practiced as Linden or the other boys at Ainsley Academy, perhaps, but Ingrid didn't mind. Linden's lead always felt like instructions, a strong guide through the movements, leaving Ingrid no question as to what to do or how to do it. Alex's was much less aggressive——a suggestion more than an order, with room to add her own embellishments. Alex didn't get frustrated when he executed a spin wrong or when he didn't quite catch on to the intricacy of her footwork. Instead, he let it go and tried something different, embracing the chaos of improvisation with a laugh.

It made her laugh too. When she added a new styling into the mix, he'd elaborate on it with his own and then invited her to do the same like they were having a conversation until they ran out of ways to change the movement.

As the song ended, he swung her into one last spin, holding out an arm to catch her, but Ingrid's heel caught on a loose stone and she careened toward the hedge. Unable to stop her momentum, Ingrid pulled her arms around her chest and closed her eyes, bracing for the prickly impact. Instead, she hit something warm and solid.

"Be careful," said a gruff voice.

Ingrid opened her eyes to see the tall man who'd broken her fall instead of the shrubbery. His face was cast in shadows, but the flare lights from her dress lit the hollows of a familiar face. It was Senator Holt's valet.

"Th-thank you," Ingrid stammered, regaining her balance. "And my apologies."

"Best get back inside. They'll be starting the meal soon."

"Ingrid, are you all right?" Alex shouted after her, jogging to catch up.

"I'm fine, thanks to——" But when Ingrid turned to indicate her rescuer, he was gone.

Alex took her by the shoulders and looked her up and down, trying to ascertain if she'd been hurt—or perhaps he was simply looking for any stray sticks or leaves caught in her dress.

"Come on, let's go back inside."

Alex took her arm, and they followed the other guests over to the dining area, where tables with identical place settings waited for them.

"Here we are." Alex brought her around to a circular table near the back of the room and frowned at the place settings. With a swift motion, he swapped two so he was seated next to her instead of Clarence. "And now *here* we are." He grinned at her.

She endeavored to grin back, but something still tugged at her mind from the garden. What was Senator Holt's valet doing at this sort of event? The senator didn't seem the type to invite members of his personal staff to such an important dinner. She certainly wouldn't have been invited if she'd still been his intern, though she supposed the valet had at least ranked higher than she had.

She was saved the agony of fixating on it further by the president making his entrance at long last.

President Morris was older than Senator Holt, his hair all salt and no pepper. Still, he walked with a spring in his step and a life in his eyes Ingrid had rarely seen from a seasoned politician who'd weathered the harrowing process of election more than once. He waved to the assembled crowd and mounted the stairs to a raised platform where he and the two candidates would dine.

When he reached his seat between Senator Holt and Gwendolyn, he gestured to the room, and said, "Thank you for coming tonight. It is my pleasure and my privilege to host such fine political minds for an evening off."

The last time Ingrid had truly had an evening off had been the night at the speakeasy, over a month ago. She'd not felt so unburdened since, full of flicker and the certainty she was about to have her heart broken. How oddly comforting it had been to know something was coming to an end, even though she hadn't wanted it to be over. How unsettling it had been to be wrong.

"You all work too hard for too little reward. So leave your ailments and agendas at the door with your coats and your hats."

She let the memory wash over her, the carefree feeling of walking into that flicker club and dancing the night away. She steeped herself in the dark, dusty world that made her. She swayed on a crowded dance floor, cheek tucked against the steady shoulder of a boy she was going to marry. But she felt anything but secure, wavering like melancholy notes of the music, waiting for the floor beneath her to collapse.

"Tonight," President Morris said with a snap of his fingers, "we dine with the finest our capital has to offer."

The capital's finest. Flare Force officers descended the speakeasy steps in her mind, rushing the crowd, pushing Ingrid and Linden toward the door. She couldn't breathe; she couldn't think. They were on them, and it was over.

"And we'll dance until the sun stops us."

Fire roared in a furious jive, crashing through layers of brick. Linden stood before it all, a dark shadow against the bright orange night he'd made.

Ingrid blinked rapidly, trying to shake the memory before it consumed her. She reached for Alex's hand as bright light bloomed across her eyes. She saw flare everywhere, magicked into the beads on dresses, smoothed across rosy cheeks, twinkling in every champagne flute. It rushed through the floor, crackled in the crystal chandelier on the ceiling, turning the clear stone yellow, then orange, then red.

The chandelier burst, shards falling in every direction.

It wasn't until her knees hit the ground, pulled below the table by Alex, that Ingrid realized it wasn't a fiction of her mind, but reality.

CHAPTER TWENTY-TWO

Pauline Ackerman was the first to die. Ingrid watched from beneath the table as Pauline fell. A shard of glass from the chandelier was stuck through her, reflective crystal protruding from either side of her throat. She didn't cry out. She didn't flinch. All she did was fall.

Ingrid didn't have time to feel anything for her, a girl who'd done nothing except be what Ingrid wasn't. The jealousy she'd felt before was washed away by an overwhelming wave of panic.

Magic lit the air, a furious cascade of heat tumbling down the walls as the world crashed in around them. Screaming and scrambling filled Ingrid's ears, and a rumble shook the floor, the ceiling, and the table under which she and Alex crouched. Ingrid touched a hand to the floor. It was warm.

"Come on." Alex tugged her forward.

They had to run. Pauline Ackerman was dead. More would follow.

"Everybody burns."

The murmur swept through the crowd like a fog rolling in.

Ingrid's heart thundered in her ears so loudly she could hardly hear the pounding of feet. She lost Alex in the crowd almost immediately as all around her heat bloomed up along the walls. Towering flame devoured the curtains and licked up to the ceiling like glittering golden waves. She saw the fire, she smelled the fire, but she did not feel it. A cold, clammy sweat broke out across her skin as the crowd jostled her forward.

White-masked rebels wove among them. It was the first time Ingrid had seen a rebel up close, but she didn't have time to ponder that reality. Too many elbows and shoulders shoved forward, burying Ingrid in a clamor of desperate people funneling through the only exit. Bodies pressed in around her, becoming a single stream of forward energy. If she tried to escape, she'd be trampled.

Pauline's body had already been trampled.

Several more lay underfoot.

Ingrid could not bring herself to look in case she saw a familiar face. She knew if she saw Clarence or Birdie or Faye below her heels she would lose her resolve. If she saw Alex or Gwendolyn, she would crumble. If she saw Linden, she would unravel.

Instead, she swiped two champagne flutes from a nearby table and downed them both. It was barely enough flare to make a spark—perhaps a single drop in each—but it was better than nothing. She silently cursed herself for giving the vial of emergency flare to Louise. She'd not imagined a scenario like this could *really* happen. She'd been a fool, and perhaps she'd die for it.

The rebels flooded the edges of the room, fire spooling out from their hands like rope. Those at the periphery did their best to fight, limbs flailing without magic. Others simply screamed. Where was Flare Force? She'd seen officers around the perimeter of the president's mansion on her way in, but how many? Perhaps too few to stand a chance against the Shadow of the Flame.

Ingrid scanned the room for a better exit strategy, and her eyes snagged on Gerald Cork, whose face had turned ashen as two men in white masks pinned him against the far wall and let fire climb him like vines. Flare ensnared his limbs, embracing his middle and then finally, longingly, lovingly devouring his face.

Bile surfaced in Ingrid's throat. These were the deaths they'd all been promised. This was the kind of attack worthy of the Shadow of the Flame. Ingrid remembered what Charlotte had said, what she'd written for the paper, that the other attacks weren't a credible threat, that they pointed to pacifists or pranksters, not an anarchist rebellion. Ingrid couldn't help but feel they had been warning shots, a prelude to this main event.

Ingrid turned away, unable to watch as Gerald Cork came to an end, but she found herself face-to-face with a white-masked man only a few feet away, staring her down with a familiar stone-gray gaze. Somewhere in a quiet recess of her mind, a memory fell like a coin into a wishing well.

She pulled the strings of magic lying in wait deep in her belly to the surface. The feeling rocked inside her, familiar and foreign all at once. It was the same as before, at the speakeasy, only it was rebels, not Flare Force, who held all the power.

Flare Force, rebels, a boy with a vial full of magic. All of them held fear in their hands, left fear in their wake, sent fear into the hearts of all. They were the same but for the uniform.

Magic made a mess of them, rich or no.

"Everybody burns," the rebel mouthed at her.

Ingrid closed her eyes, and magic purred against her ears, then burst from her fingertips. "Not if you burn first," she snarled.

The rebel lowered into a solid stance and circled her. She followed suit and readied her shaking hands. Fire climbed inside her.

The room pulsed with it. He wasn't going to strike; he was waiting for her to fight or burn.

She hurled a ball of fire forward, and it hit its mark. She let out a whoop, but it was premature. Through the flames, the masked man emerged, not even so much as singed. In his hands, he held her fire. He'd stolen it, just like she'd stolen Louise's at the speakeasy. Now he held all the power and she held none.

She closed her eyes and braced for impact, for death, for fire.

It never came. Instead, a scream rent the air as a body slammed into hers, knocking her to the ground. She opened her eyes on Linden, climbing back up to face the masked man, hands full of flame.

"Where'd he go?" Linden shouted. "I'll kill him!"

Ingrid scrambled to her feet. "Linden?" His name tore from her chest as she reached for him. "We have to run." She glanced around, but their attacker was nowhere in sight, melted back into the crowd to terrorize someone else.

"This way." Linden collected his fire in one hand and pulled her away from the crowd with the other, farther into the ballroom. Toward danger.

She saw a snapshot of the room in all its ruin, the curtains ablaze, the walls crawling with flame, faces stricken in disbelief, before a final jerk of his arm sent her out of danger and into the night.

She was met with a quiet terrace, two stories above the garden where she'd danced only minutes ago with Alex. Iron lattice webbed out around the perimeter of their hiding place, and a ceramic pot housed a cluster of dark purple flowers. Linden lit the flare lamps and sent a scurry of twinkle lights into the trees below them with his excess magic, creating a serene ambience that clashed horribly with Ingrid's panic-driven heartbeat.

"You're safe," Linden murmured against her hair, closing his arms around her from behind.

Ingrid stepped out of his embrace, and cold air snared her wrists. "We're trapped," she said flatly. "What are we supposed to do if they come out this way? There's hardly anywhere for us to go from here." She peered over the side of the fence. It was dark, but by the flare light, Ingrid estimated the fall wouldn't kill her.

With a loud scraping sound, Linden dragged a potted tree across the narrow terrace to block the door.

"Yes, that will stop them." Ingrid rolled her eyes. But there was no *them* to stop. No one had followed. "I don't even have any flare to fight them off with if they come through."

"Where's that vial I gave you?" Linden asked, his voice rough.

Ingrid tensed. "I didn't—I didn't think to wear it. It didn't really go with the ensemble." She gestured to her dress.

Linden reached for her throat, as if willing the vial to be there, hanging around her neck anyway. "I told you to wear it always. I told you to wear it in case of an attack like this." His jaw hardened; his brow dipped. She had seen this face before, but not on him. It was the look of his father.

"Linden," she said softly, reaching hesitant fingers for his arms. "I'm sorry. I should have worn it. I just didn't think something like this was possible."

Linden relaxed into her grip. "I watched her die, Ingrid. Right in front of me." He choked out the words. "Pauline was nothing to me. She was only there because I thought . . . because I wanted to bring her to . . . to make you . . ." He trailed off.

She knew what he'd been about to say. He'd brought her there to make Ingrid jealous. The mess of it reverberated like a gong inside her. They were two people in love, two people heartbroken.

They weren't even really broken up, but somehow that falsehood had wormed its way into the truth.

"It was so sudden, so random," he said against Ingrid's shoulder, his head bent low. "It could have been you."

"Or you."

"No," Linden said firmly. "No, don't think of that."

Ingrid felt small in the circle of his worry. She could not bring herself to move her arms, to return Linden's embrace. If not for the natural mechanism of her lungs, Ingrid wasn't sure she would have had it in her to breathe.

She could have died.

Linden could have died.

But even as he held her, Ingrid could think of nothing else but what had become of Alex, what had become of Gwendolyn. Would she return only to discover one of them had been burned along with the ballroom? Would she know how to bear it? Her chest constricted. An almost pain spread out through her core, an almost agony, almost affection. Her breath came in short bursts. Her arms shook. Her whole body shuddered.

Linden ran his hands up and down her back, making hushing sounds as he cradled her form. "I'm so sorry," he muttered against her hair. "I'm sorry. I'm sorry."

She tried to push herself up and away. He was sorry. He was *sorry*. He'd no idea what she was feeling or why or for whom.

"I have to get back." The words came before she thought them, but they were true. If everyone was all right, they wouldn't be giving way to emotion. Alex and Clarence were probably crafting a speech as she stood there in the cold. Birdie was probably shouting at the ceiling, and Faye was probably fixing everyone a cup of extra-strong coffee. Now was the time to act, to work, to make something from this terrible mess. Besides, this was no time to be trapped on the veranda with a boy she wasn't supposed to love.

"What?" Linden looked up, amber eyes watery.

"We can't be here together like this." Ingrid gestured at the courtyard. If she stripped the fabric of her dress into ribbons, she could tie it to the fencing, reduce the distance she had to drop. "Anyone could see us." The excuse was as feeble as they came, but it was all she had.

She couldn't very well say she *wanted* to return to Team Meyers, to help them craft their message, to do the work that would oppose Linden's father. She couldn't tell him she would rather be busy with them than idle with him. She couldn't tell him they were more home to her after only a few weeks than he had ever been after all these years.

She couldn't tell him everything. She never could.

So instead, she kissed him, a hope on her lips that it would feel like love. And maybe it did. And maybe it didn't. Somewhere, somehow, Ingrid had learned love was more than a secret, more than status. *More* felt heavy. It filled her up like nothing ever had, but at the same time, it cleaved the space between them.

"I have to go. They'll wonder where I am," Ingrid said when she broke away, turning toward the railing. She could climb down the trellis at least part of the way, and the drop from there looked manageable.

Linden grabbed her hand. "It's my fault."

"What?" Ingrid stopped shredding her dress.

"This." He gestured at the building they'd escaped. "The rebellion. I did this."

For a moment, Ingrid thought it was a confession, but even she couldn't logic her way through that. "Don't be ridiculous. Of course it isn't your fault."

"It *is*." His grip on her arm tightened. "If I hadn't attacked that speakeasy, that girl would never have——"

Ingrid tried to shake him off. "You're being silly. This rebellion didn't start because you burned down *one* speakeasy. Didn't your father say they were going to attack the speakeasy anyway?"

"Things are changing so fast. My father—the campaign." He pulled at his hair. "Would you still love me if I wasn't a senator's son?"

Ingrid wrinkled her brow. "Where did that come from?"

"Everyone's always saying I'll do great things in the Senate, that I'll be my father's son. But what if I don't want to do those things? What if I don't want to follow in his footsteps?" Linden stared at her shoes, stubbornly not looking her in the eye. "What if I want to run away with you and never look back? Leave all the politics and elections behind, just you and me, somewhere in the hills of Alorden living in the quiet where we can be whoever we want with no expectations."

If he'd not been a senator's son, would she have even looked at him twice? *No.* The answer bobbed its way to the surface. She'd set her sights on him because of who he was. He was part of her plan, part of her ascent. She never would have guessed all those years ago that she would soften for the boy, not just his status. Loving him was a lucky accident.

"But you *are* a senator's son" was all she could bring herself to say, a lump in her throat.

"I know." He swallowed. "But what if I wasn't?"

"If you weren't." Ingrid caught his eye, searching for something she didn't want to see.

Honest desperation looked back. "Please, Ingrid. I need to know. You would still marry me if I gave all this up, right?"

She chewed her bottom lip, stalled in a place between lies. "Of course." She slung her legs over the edge of the fence, hoping the trellis would be stronger than her conviction.

"You would?" Linden murmured.

"Yes," she whispered. A cool breeze caught her dress as she began to descend, and then she dropped, stone scraping her knee as she landed inexpertly. She rose on shaky legs and ran. By the time she reached Gwendolyn's office suite, she was windswept and weak. She'd fallen at least ten feet and escaped with only a few bruises.

She'd fallen much further for Linden, of course, but she'd yet to land, and she wasn't sure she'd survive it in the end.

CHAPTER TWENTY-THREE

The office was dark and still. The quiet inside clashed with the uproar in the streets, where panic and sirens filled the air. Not even the howl of the wind followed Ingrid across the threshold, the sound of the door closing behind her a distant, faded click.

Ingrid took a hesitant step inside, feeling as though she were somehow intruding, the space thick and slow like it was moving to a different clock. Her heart was beating too fast.

Where were the others? Her ribs gripped her like shackles, and her breath shattered inside her, making carnage of her lungs. She wanted to fall, to clutch at the ground and tear up the floor until she found her friends, but her knees were locked, her jaw was clenched, her mind was stuck on a single, horrible thought.

Who else died?

Their names ran through her mind, a repeating list, over and over.

What if Gwendolyn didn't make it? They would be nothing without her—no candidate, no campaign—but she was more than all that. Gwendolyn had said it the first time they met—Ingrid wasn't no one. She'd never been treated like that by anyone so immediately. To everyone else, her worth was something to prove.

But Gwendolyn had seen inherent value in her without knowing her at all.

Birdie, Clarence, and Faye too had become something she held close to her chest. Ingrid could barely imagine what the office would be like without any one of them as part of the team. And Alex. Alex, who'd seen the potential Senator Holt had ignored, who'd watched her fall apart in the orphanage and never thought her weak. It was a painful thing to know how precious that kind of friendship was and how willing she'd been to let it slip away.

And for what? For the love of a boy who could not be himself in the world where she wanted him, and she could not be herself in the world where he wanted her.

She could do nothing now except wait for them all to come through the door. She wouldn't leave until they were all accounted for, all safe, all alive. She found the silhouette of a chaise longue against the wall and let herself fall back against it with a heavy sigh.

"Ingrid?"

Familiar fingers twined with hers, and she glimpsed Alex curled into a ball on the floor against the foot of the chaise before he engulfed her in an embrace. He clutched her with trembling hands, his heart a hammer against her chest. She held him just as close, collapsing into his grip until they were but a single form, enmeshed in each other's grasp.

"You're alive," she murmured into his shoulder.

"You're a mess."

She broke against his words, something between a laugh and a sob escaping her lips. "Thanks. What with facing my own mortality, my appearance was really top priority tonight." She glanced at her dress, a tear in the fragile fabric where her knees had scraped the ground, the hem dirty and frayed, but she didn't care. It seemed an impossibility that she, Ingrid Ellis, would have let something so terrible befall her best gown, but she was no longer the same girl she'd been when she'd donned it.

Alex tugged the hair at the nape of her neck and said with a note of levity in his voice, "It's important to still be stylish even when everything is literally burning."

"The others?" Ingrid asked, hoping his cavalier attitude meant what she thought it did.

"Faye and Clarence got out with me," he said into her hair. "I don't know about Gwendolyn and Birdie."

"They have to be okay," Ingrid murmured. "We can't go on without them."

"No, we can't."

They sat in the quiet for a few moments, holding each other. Ingrid's heart rate slowed and her breath came easier. Alex's fingers rested on her spine. Somewhere on the fringes of her mind, Ingrid knew she should pull away now; the appropriate amount of time had passed for such an embrace and any longer would be an imposition. But she didn't want to let go.

She didn't want a lot of things. She didn't want to report back to Senator Holt, she didn't want to spy on Team Meyers, she didn't want to lie to Alex, and she didn't want to wake up the next morning to find out who among their number had died.

"Gerald Cork is dead," Ingrid said finally, unable to keep the words in any longer.

"What?" Alex pulled back.

"I saw it happen. They just——" Words failed her. Instead, she gestured with her hands rather pathetically and let her gaze wander. "Burned him."

Alex's grip on her shoulders tightened. "That didn't happen to Birdie. It can't, okay?"

Ingrid's eyes found his face, and she winced. "We don't know that."

"No, no. I'd know. I'd feel it."

Ingrid wondered what it would be like to hold someone so close to her heart as though they were her own body, to know they were alive because so was she. "What do you think will happen now that he's dead?"

"They'll replace him," Alex croaked. "That's how they work. They're all expendable."

Ingrid took hold of his shoulders too, looking him in the eyes. "Birdie's not."

Alex sniffed, catching a single tear with his palm. "None of us are. That's the difference between us and them."

"It's not the only one." Ingrid reached to wipe beneath his eyes, but Alex caught her hand with both of his and gently guided it away.

"How did you escape?" he asked, lowering his eyes.

"Linden," she replied without thinking. And there it was, the reason she had to do what she didn't want. Because no matter how many things she didn't want to do, they were all in service of a larger purpose, the biggest want of them all.

A frown wrinkled Alex's brow. "Linden? But I thought—"

Ingrid covered her face, afraid that even in the dark she might give herself away. "After I lost you, there was a rebel." She shook her head, leaning back against the chaise and curling her knees up against herself involuntarily as she remembered the look in the rebel's eyes behind his mask. "I think he would have killed me, but Linden pulled me out."

223

"He saved you," Alex said, nodding. "That's not nothing."

"No." The word shook through her. "It's not."

"You miss him."

Ingrid froze, the truth of it more cutting than any of the scrapes on her knees. How could she miss someone she hadn't lost? But lost, he was. If all her time with the Meyers campaign had taught her anything, it was how far they'd both strayed from the path. Linden didn't even want the same things she did anymore, and Ingrid had begun to fear that she wasn't the only one resting behind the comfort of a disguise in their relationship.

"I do." The words rang hollow, like it was them, not her, who felt empty.

"It's okay, you know." Alex's hand slid around her shoulder and squeezed gently. "To miss him, I mean."

Ingrid nodded and let her hands fall away from her face. She was tired of hiding, of holding it all back, of lying to everyone. But most of all, she was tired of lying to herself. "Is it, though? Is it okay?"

"I mean, he is a Holt." Alex scrunched up his nose. "But your questionable taste aside, I think letting yourself miss him is good. It means even though it's over, it wasn't all bad. It means at least you got something out of it along the way."

"Isn't that a little cynical? It makes it all feel so transactional." The word left her lips a hypocrisy fully formed, for hadn't she treated the relationship as exactly that? Linden was a means to an end, a step on her stairway to status. No matter that she'd loved him in the end, no matter that maybe she'd loved him all along, it had always been about so much more than love.

"Sorry," she said, waving a hand to dismiss the matter. "I don't know what I'm saying. We're quite seriously waiting to see if our friends survived a horrible attack, and here I am going on about this as if it matters."

"It does matter." Alex's voice was quiet but steady. "It all matters. You matter."

Ingrid's voice caught in her throat, words she couldn't say stuck unsaid.

"Things like this, they happen to people, they happen to *us*, and if we can't sit back and take stock of our lives, of our relationships, of our mark on others and theirs on us . . . well, if we can't do that now, when can we?" He leaned back, his eyes focused on a point in the distance. "There's a lot out there that will hurt us, so I don't think it's cynical at all. I think it's beautiful if you can reflect on those things and try to hold on to the parts that were good, the parts that make you who you are. And maybe it can help you heal and move forward."

Ingrid nodded and tried to grasp on to a memory—any memory—that felt warm and light and full of joy. She wandered through the archive of her and Linden's relationship. She rushed past the discomfort of meeting his father, of public eyes on them as he kissed her in the snow, of the dinner he'd planned for them when all she'd wanted was his support. She lingered on the spark between them when they were alone, when he wasn't asking her for more of herself than she could give, when everything was slow and sensory and solitary. She thought of the moment he'd asked her to marry him, and of the weight she'd carried on her shoulders, across her chest, around her throat ever since.

What did forward look like if not a cage?

"What if I can't move forward?" The question was gone before she could decide to ask it.

Alex shrugged. "You can. Maybe not in the way you think, but you can. Forward is always an option, even when you've fallen down."

"Sometimes I feel like forward isn't really a direction at all." Ingrid's legs slid back to the floor, and her eyes found a spot on the far wall without really seeing it. "It feels like I'm just going in circles, trying to take even a single step, and I keep finding myself back where I started. I feel like I can't even breathe unless I'm running, but I never get anywhere."

Alex let out a long breath, a whistle against his teeth. "That's familiar."

"It's like, I know I can be happy if I can just get . . . *something*. But what if I never get it? What if I keep chasing it and making myself miserable all for nothing? Is it even worth it?"

"Maybe," Alex said slowly. "I think so, when it's what you really want." He leaned back, his elbows propped against the chaise as his eyes flicked to the ceiling. "There was something I wanted for a long time, something a lot of people told me wouldn't be worth the trouble. I was never rich—not even halfway rich. It was going to take years of work to earn enough money so I could have it. And I did it. I worked hard. I worked harder than anyone I know. And in the end, it still wasn't enough. Eventually Birdie came along and, well, she and Gwendolyn understood and helped me, so in the end, I was just . . . lucky."

"Did it make you happy, though, when you could finally have it?"

A smile spread out across Alex's lips, unfettered joy in his rosy-brown cheeks. "It did."

"And you don't regret all the years you were unhappy?"

Alex sighed, slow and quiet. "There was nothing in the world that could have stopped me from chasing it. Maybe I would've worked my whole life and never got where I am now, but maybe I would have, and to me that's worth it."

"What was it?"

Alex paused for a fraction of a moment; then he collected himself, exhaling heavily. "Maybe someday I'll tell you."

Ingrid puzzled over him, narrowing her eyes. What would someone like Alex want so badly? Maybe it was this job, maybe it was Gwendolyn's charity, or maybe it wasn't hers to guess. Maybe it was his, all his, and she had no right to ask. "Fair enough."

"So do you want it?" he asked.

"Want what?"

"Whatever it is you're chasing. Do you want it enough to keep going?"

Ingrid bit her lip, her thoughts cascading like twin waterfalls around a stone. She wanted so hungrily, so terribly. She wanted so much and so acutely she'd forgotten what it was like to do anything else. She wanted Linden Holt, and she wanted to *be* like Linden Holt. But where did one end and the other begin? Were they one and the same? Were they even what she wanted, or were they only part of a plan that would never work?

"I don't know," she said. "Sometimes I think it's the only thing that matters, and sometimes I think I got tunnel vision and I *made* it the only thing that matters." She couldn't bring herself to say it out loud, but the longer she spent with Alex and the Meyers campaign, the more she found other things that mattered too.

Alex nodded sagely. "That's okay. Just think about it. Maybe you'll know tomorrow."

That there could be another day, another chance to try again, seemed impossible. Everything felt so urgent, so present, like if she didn't decide something tonight, she never would. "What if Linden's my only shot? What if I . . . what if I missed it?"

"What do you think you missed?"

Ingrid didn't know the answer. Or maybe she knew too many. He was her shot at power, he was her shot at magic, he was her shot at status. But instead of all those, she said in a quiet, shaky voice, "Love."

Alex bit down hard, his jaw jutting strangely to the side as he surveyed her. "Why do you think you missed it?"

And Ingrid came undone, her stomach curling in a spasm, her lungs faltering, her sight clouding. "I—because I—" But she couldn't find the words.

"Was he . . . ?" Alex hesitated. "Had you been in love before him?"

Ingrid shook her head.

"Well, how do you know it won't happen again?"

"It took so long the first time, I just wonder if maybe he's it. He's all I get," she said.

Alex tilted his head, kind eyes searching, but he said nothing, leaving her the silence to fill.

"Falling in love wasn't easy for me. I just have never felt that immediate romantic attraction. It took such a long time to finally feel it with Linden, and I've never really been sure what's love and what's power." Ingrid swallowed hard. When she'd first recognized her feelings as love, she'd felt no happiness, only dread. Even after Linden had asked her to marry him, she'd felt only a slow burning in the pit of her stomach, like she was constantly being branded from the inside. Love had never made her happy, only careful, only bruised, only confused. "I don't think I really loved him until . . . well, until I started thinking I might lose him."

"Weren't you together for a long time?" Alex asked.

"Three years." Though it felt like longer. They'd slipped into romance so seamlessly, it was difficult to tell the difference between before and after.

"That's a long time to be with someone you don't love."

"It's not that I don't . . . that I didn't . . ." Ingrid pressed the heel of her hand against her sternum to release the tightness in her chest, but it stayed stubbornly put. "Love is a lot more than just love when you're with someone like Linden Holt. It was never just me and him. It was me, and him, and his family, and his legacy."

Alex nodded sagely. "I get that. Status and money bring a lot into a relationship and you can never really be sure how much of the dynamic is about power. When someone has so much more than you, it's hard to feel like enough."

Ingrid's throat closed around the feeling, unshed tears gathering behind her eyes. "Yeah" was all she managed to choke out.

"So is that what happened between you two?"

She shook her head instinctively, then paused. It was difficult to honestly examine something Alex thought was over when, in truth, it was all still happening. She'd not left Linden; Linden hadn't left her. They were still together, just separated by something intangible but fiercely real.

"Linden's father never thought I was good enough," she said, as much truth to her words as she could manage before she injected a lie. "I suppose I just got tired of hearing it, tired of feeling it." But as she said it, Ingrid realized it wasn't a lie. Their problems were still problems. Just because she hadn't acted on them yet didn't mean she couldn't talk about them.

"Wow. Imagine what it would feel like to be that wrong," Alex said, shaking his head. "And people think he should be president."

"It wasn't only his father. It was . . . everyone." Courage

swelled in her lungs, giving strength to her voice. "The papers, our classmates, even Linden. Everyone has an opinion about what a relationship should look like, what romance is supposed to feel like, and not only who can love whom, but *how*."

"That's none of their business," Alex grumbled.

Ingrid shrugged. "I don't know. Maybe it just isn't for me. Even Linden sometimes—" She swallowed her words. They were too present, too real. She'd almost slipped. Instead, she said, "I don't know if I like the way love is supposed to feel. I don't know if I like love at all." She'd never thought of it in such certain terms before, but as soon as she said it, it felt true. It felt true, and it felt light, and it felt like the first deep breath she'd taken in years.

Alex placed a hand on her elbow and turned her to face him. For a moment, Ingrid thought he might lean in and kiss her. For a moment, she thought she might let him. But then he clasped her hands between his and squeezed.

"You don't have to fall in love in order to love. You don't have to fall in love to *be* loved. Nowhere is it written in stone that you must love in only one way, only one person, only one time. You haven't missed your shot at love, because love isn't just one thing. Maybe what you had with Linden was one kind of love, but there are others. Love is family, love is friends, love is caring whether the people in your life survive a rebel attack. Love is love, Ingrid."

"Love is love," she repeated, blinking away tears she hadn't known would come. Warmth spread through her, and her awareness of her limbs—every toe and every finger—exploded like flare. It was as if she'd left her body outside in the cold and it had only just caught up to her.

"It was a surgery," Alex said after a moment, taking his hands back.

"What?"

"The thing I wanted. It was surgery—for my chest." His hand floated to his sternum. "For me, it wasn't really enough to change my name and my pronouns. I know that's not how it is for everyone, but the longer I thought about it the more I wanted it."

"Oh. I didn't know," Ingrid said quietly.

"Course not. I didn't tell you." Alex rolled his lip between his teeth. "But it was really important to me—*is* really important to me. When I told people at first, a lot of them didn't really understand. They didn't want to change how they looked at me, so it was just easier for them not to look at all. I thought I had to perform identity for them, sitting evenly between two boxes in order to fit expectations, but that's not what identity should be about."

Ingrid nodded. "Right. It should be about you."

"I sat on that dream for a long time. It's expensive and it's surgery, so not only did it mean raising an astronomical amount of money, but it meant I couldn't work for a while after." He shook his head, curls falling across his forehead. "And there's a whole other layer to it when you're not a girl, and you're not a boy, and not everyone understands why you'd want to change your body, and it's just . . ." He trailed off and looked at the ceiling again.

"It's yours to understand, though, right? They want to conceptualize it before they consent to it, but it's not theirs to decide, it's not theirs to own."

"Yeah," Alex said, his voice half a whisper, half a crackle. "That part doesn't change, you know."

"Change?"

"Getting what I wanted didn't suddenly make people respect me or like me. But I realized it's a lot more important that I respect and like myself. And that means being around people who *do* respect and like me. I can choose who to call my family because this change isn't about them; it's about me."

She felt it like a burst of flare in the night sky, the desire to be his chosen family. "I like you," she whispered.

Alex let out a laugh like a bark. "I know you like me, silly. That's why I told you. Because I want you to like me for who I am and I want you to respect me too."

"What pronouns should I use?" Ingrid asked.

"I'm fine with *he* and *him*," Alex said quickly, but then he paused and tilted his head. "But actually, I'd like it if you would avoid calling me a man, or a boy, or Mr. Castille."

"If I ever use an honorific for you, assume I've hit my head." She tried a smile.

Alex returned it. "On the contrary, I will simply assume you've finally recognized my superiority."

They laughed, their elbows knocking. Ingrid didn't mind his touch. She didn't mind much about him at all, actually. Being with Alex was comfortable the way few of her relationships were. She never felt like he was going to cast her aside or ask her to be more than she could be, but still she knew he wouldn't let her be less than she was. He was there, and he was real, and he was honest.

So she would be honest too. "I thought . . ." She cracked a shy smile. "I thought for a second earlier that you were going to kiss me."

Alex raised an eyebrow. "Why would I do that?"

"I don't know." She shrugged. "In my experience, it's an awfully effective way to shut someone up when they're rambling on."

Disgust crisscrossed his brow. "Is that what Linden used to do?"

Ingrid blushed, though the color didn't show in the dark. "No, he was the one doing most of the rambling."

"Well," Alex said, shaking his head. "I won't kiss you."

232

"Why not?" The question slipped out before she could stop it.

"Because I think you need to be heard a lot more than you need to be kissed. Rambling on isn't so bad, and I'd rather listen to you talk right now than anything else in the world."

"Not even political broadcast radio?"

"Not even political broadcast radio."

Relief traced a stencil of her limbs, and like an ambush, exhaustion crept up on her and then descended all at once.

A gentle blanket of silence fell around them. It didn't hunger; it didn't ache. It was comfort and ease. In it, Ingrid curled into the crook of Alex's arm, and the last thought she had before she let sleep claim her was if love was family and friendship and caring if someone died in a rebel attack, then maybe it was the word for what she felt for Alex.

CHAPTER TWENTY-FOUR

Ingrid woke to a faceful of Charlotte Terry.

"You're alive!" The other girl swept her into an embrace that was more tackle than hug, repeating herself over and over until the words bled together into nonsense.

"Alive, yes; awake, no," Ingrid said through a mouthful of Charlotte's hair. "Ow. Charlotte, you're squeezing me."

"Mm-hmm." Charlotte loosened her grip.

"Okay," Alex said after a minute. "I'm going to get us some coffee . . . and maybe a new spine." He rubbed his neck and glared at the chaise.

Charlotte pulled back to look at Ingrid once Alex had crossed to the other side of the room, where an exhausted Clarence had already begun boiling water. Charlotte looked about how Ingrid felt, deep circles beneath her eyes, a crease along the side of her face as though she'd fallen asleep on a magazine, and faint tear stains tracking through the previous night's makeup.

"We're in a fight," Charlotte proclaimed.

"You and Alex?"

"No, you and me, silly. Who's Alex?" She whirled around to

get a better look at the stranger in question. "That's Alex?"

"Alex Castille. He's the one who recruited me for the Meyers campaign." Ingrid frowned. "How did you even get in here?"

"I wasn't the only one worried about you. You didn't come home last night."

"Sorry. I fell asleep here." Ingrid glanced back at the chaise where she and Alex had slept the night before. At the time, it had seemed the only logical thing to do. Going home had never even crossed her mind.

Returning to the office had felt more like home anyway.

"Lucky you." Charlotte sniffed. "I didn't sleep a wink last night, not that you asked." She let go, at long last, and turned away. "I stayed up waiting for you. I thought . . . I thought you might have died."

"I'm sorry." Ingrid reached to touch her friend's shoulder, but Charlotte shrugged her away.

"Normally I'd be furious with you, but we have more important matters to discuss." She sniffed and set her jaw, turning back to fix Ingrid with an incinerating stare. "Who—and I mean *who*— is Alex Castille and why did I find you with him"—she gestured to the chaise—"canoodling?"

"We were not *canoodling*!"

"*Please*. If there is something you aren't telling me, tell it. You know how I hate not to know things."

"There's nothing to know." Ingrid ducked her head, trying to hide her uncertainty. She remembered the night before, feeling like maybe Alex would kiss her. But he hadn't, and she was glad. It was the easiest way she knew how to express intimacy, and she'd almost fallen into habit instead of saying what she meant. But what *had* she meant?

"Tell me, tell me, tell me." Charlotte narrowed her eyes in scrutiny. "You're a single girl now. It's not as though I'd be one to judge."

Charlotte's attention to the matter irked her far more than anything else. It was just like with the press, always clamoring for the best shot, the best headline, the best way to twist Ingrid's life into a picture-perfect image they could use to sell papers.

"Really, it's nothing," Ingrid said more firmly than she'd meant to. Her eyes wandered to where Alex bent over three mugs, steam rising from the coffeepot around his face like smoke, and her heart thundered with the injustice of her words. She'd felt so empty when she thought he might have died, and so full when she knew he hadn't. That wasn't nothing.

It was something. Something. *Something.*

Whatever it was, it felt immersive but not consuming, captivating but not captivity. It was simple and sturdy but significant, like the silhouette of something bigger and grander that she couldn't see. It was not to be compared to whatever she had with Linden; it wasn't romantic, it wasn't twisted by power and magic. It was respect, it was mentorship, it was friendship. Charlotte, who desired platonic relationships above all, would surely understand.

"We're friends," Ingrid said, a smile coming unbidden to her lips.

Charlotte grinned back and prodded her in the ribs. "Look at you, making friends instead of enemies."

"Hey, I don't make that many enemies."

"You could make more." Charlotte fixed her with a withering glare. "I hear the Holt campaign isn't so pleased with your change in allegiance. If I wasn't your friend first and a reporter second, I'd write about it."

Ingrid shuddered. "Remind me never to get on your bad side."

Charlotte scrunched her face. "Ingrid Gertrude Ellis, you will have to try harder than not dying in a rebel attack to make an enemy of me."

Alex mouthed the word *Gertrude*.

"Speaking of enemies, Gerald Cork died last night." Clarence joined them with his own mug of coffee. "Birdie's in a state. Gwendolyn told her to take the day off."

Charlotte's eyes went wide. "That's big news. I'd better get to the office. It will be all hands." She squeezed Ingrid's arm, and she was gone.

Once the door was shut again, Alex contorted his face and asked, "When was the last time Birdie took a day off?"

"One would assume during infancy," Clarence replied.

"You're not funny." The coarse tenor of Birdie Collins wafted in from the cold. She was flanked by Faye and Gwendolyn, each wearing matching expressions of concern. "But you are correct."

Clarence exchanged a masked look with Alex that Ingrid knew she wasn't meant to understand. They all had this shorthand, this history. They knew one another in a way Ingrid had never known anyone, not even herself. It should have made her feel distant—that's how it always was to be an outsider—but instead it made her feel like there was something more to be had, something more to earn, like she would not leave this place alone.

Gwendolyn led Birdie across the room to the chaise Ingrid and Alex had just vacated.

"I'm not ill," Birdie said in protest, but let Gwendolyn tuck her against the chair and cover her with a blanket.

"She's not *ill*," Faye said quietly, bending to whisper to the rest of them. "Just very rattled. She seems to have taken Gerald Cork's passing personally."

"Course it's personal," Birdie barked from her perch. "We scrapped for some thirty-odd years. It was all building to this—the fight of our careers—and he has the gall to go and die in the middle of it. What's the point of winning if I don't get to beat him?"

"I think this means you *did* beat him, love." Gwendolyn handed her a steaming mug and smoothed her flyaways.

It was as tender a moment as could be, to see this monument of a woman care for Birdie in such a way. It felt private, like it shouldn't be observed by outsiders. If the roles were reversed and Linden was patting Ingrid's hair and serving her tea in front of them all, Ingrid would swat him away. But Birdie didn't. She leaned into the touch, like it was part of her. Like Gwendolyn was part of her. That kind of comfort felt impossibly far away.

Or impossibly close.

Alex palmed her forearm lightly and gave her a questioning look. *Are you all right?* he seemed to ask. She remembered the way his gentle touch had grounded her so when she'd lost herself at the orphanage and how his hand in hers had made the President's Ball more bearable. If he gave her coffee and brushed back her hair, would she recoil? The answer rocked her, but not like a violent sea, more like being pushed on a swing. *No.*

It was *something*.

"We still have to win," Birdie grumbled against the lip of her mug. "And the worst of it is, his death will only give them more momentum. Now they can point to a face and say, 'The rebels will kill your campaign manager.'"

"Well, most people don't have campaign managers, so that's all right," said Faye, a hesitant smile pulling at her lips.

"This rebellion is really going to be what decides the election, isn't it?" Ingrid asked gravely. She thought of the charts she and Alex had made over the last few weeks with all the many issues Candesce was facing and realized with a pang that none of Gwendolyn's positions on flare equity, the out-of-control reliance on Flare Force, or even her promises to expand industrial flare research would end up mattering at all.

Everyone nodded.

"If not for this, we'd be beating them two to one in every poll." Clarence shook his head. "It's almost as if they engineered it to benefit him."

"Don't say that." Gwendolyn's voice was chiding. "A man is dead, Clarence. Have a little respect."

"Even the Holts aren't stupid enough to get their front man killed on purpose." Birdie tucked her legs beneath her. "They lost a leader."

But as the rest of the team got to work, Ingrid couldn't help but think they'd lost a leader but they gained a martyr, and that was a lot more valuable.

Louise was waiting for her outside Ainsley Academy.

"Oy!" she called with a quirked lip, leaning out from behind one of the perfectly manicured hedges lining the school's front entrance. Instead of the ruins of someone else's wardrobe, she wore a large coat over a blue pinstripe button-down, baggy gray pants, and a pair of tight suspenders to hold them up. With a newsie cap worn jauntily askew, she was almost unrecognizable from the girl Ingrid had sprung from prison only a week ago.

Ingrid stared at her for a minute, paused mid-step. She'd forgotten to expect her. She'd forgotten about her altogether. What with the party and the rebel attack, Ingrid had barely spared a thought for Louise in over twenty-four hours. She'd no idea what the other girl had been up to at all, for that matter.

"Any progress?" she asked, moving into the shadows with Louise. She'd last seen Louise to sneak her into the Ainsley Academy library. Ingrid didn't really understand what Louise was looking for, but the other girl's growing stack of notes at least were promising and she'd left with a large stack of texts. "The books I gave you—"

"Were boring, just like the rest of them." Louise let her eyelids fall as though she were asleep.

"So have you learned anything at all, or am I just wasting my time?" Ingrid asked, a bite to her words.

"Oh, you're definitely wasting your time, but not on this. While you were off doing whatever it is you fancy folks do, I was actually accomplishing something." She snapped her suspenders and grinned. "Get a load of this." From her coat pocket she withdrew her thick notebook and thrust it toward Ingrid.

On the page was a sketch of complicated machinery with notations and measurements Ingrid didn't understand. It looked like some kind of boxy coffeemaker or other kitchen appliance she might find in a magazine for home decor. "What is it?"

"It's a miniature distiller." Louise flipped the page to show more detailed drawings. "Those books weren't completely useless. After I got through the self-congratulatory forwards and the condescending chapters about flare distribution, and the gasconading—"

"Okay, okay, I get it." Ingrid waved her on. "Was there a single thing in the books that helped at all?"

"There were some good pictures."

"Do you have to—"

"Yes." Louise crossed her arms and settled back on her heels. "I think I absolutely do." She gave Ingrid an appraising look before moving on. "I'm not joking, though. The pictures were good. Especially the up-close shots of the technology they use in the distilleries. I could even see some of the numbers on valves and such."

"And this is important?" Ingrid asked.

"We need this first." Louise tapped the notebook in her hand. "It has to be easy for everyone to make flare in their own homes without relying on massive distilleries. It has to be something everyone can access, and it has to be cheap to produce."

"Yes, I know. If the rich control the distilleries, they control magic."

"Thanks to this little contraption, they won't." Louise grinned. "This one is going to be pocket-sized!"

"So where do we start once you have a working distiller?" Ingrid asked.

"Next up I'll do some work with that flare sample you gave me." Louise flipped to a new page in her notebook. "Of course, I know the ingredients already—ethyl decadienoate, vanillin, traces of copper and iron—"

"I don't need a chemistry lesson."

Louise wrinkled her nose. "Oh, you think so? I bet I can make a better batch of flicker than you in half the time."

"It's not a competition."

"Ah, but shouldn't it be?"

Ingrid rolled her eyes. "Fine, you win. You're better at chemistry than me."

"Sweet, sweet victory." Louise held her fist to her chest.

"Speaking of sweet, what's your plan to make flare this time instead of flicker?"

Louise lowered her arm. "Look, flicker's not just some

alternative someone cooked up in their kitchen one day on purpose, you know. It came from the same sort of mission we're on now. We're not the first ones to try to make flare. Flicker's as close as they could get without any of the fancy tools the flare distilleries have. Basically, we know what the end product should be made of, we know the ingredients, but without knowing either the chemical makeup of the original raw magic or the distilling process, I won't be able to re-create it. I need at least two of the three parts to the equation in order to get this right, and I only have one. At the end of the day, we're probably not going to make flare. It'll still be flicker, but if I can figure out how to get it more refined, we might land a lot closer to the target."

"What do you mean, more refined?" Ingrid had tasted plenty of flicker, and it had never occurred to her to think of it as less refined except perhaps in the societal sense.

"You know when snow's got little pine needles and dirt in it?" Louise screwed up her face. "It's still just frozen water, but it's not as pure as clean water. You can boil it down and shake the contaminants loose, but it still won't be as clean."

"What does that have to do with flare?"

"Well, we're going to boil it and see if we can't purify it." She tapped her notebook. "Using this distiller, I can mimic the actual techniques used in flare factories. It's not like flare comes out of the ground completely refined, so it's possible we just need to play around with evaporation techniques until we find the right balance."

"What exactly is the refinement process?"

"You've tasted flare." Louise raised a brow in acknowledgment of their shared experience, fire coursing through their veins as hot as anger as they'd fought. "Burns, doesn't it?" Louise's voice went flat. "And then it's gone."

Ingrid nodded, something solid and cold in her throat. They'd both held magic in their mouths that night, but only Ingrid had truly wielded it. She'd stolen it from Louise, stolen it to save her life. And when it was all gone, there was an emptiness left behind. Ingrid saw in Louise's gold-and-brown-peppered eyes that she'd felt it too.

"Just like an object in motion stays in motion, magic in use wants to stay in use." Louise's voice returned to its normal, present quality. "When we use flicker, it's gone after the first burn. It doesn't get more powerful because it gets used up before it gets a chance. But flare gets distilled first—they evaporate it and re-condense it to burn off the impurities."

Ingrid felt her brain jostling with every nod of her head. "So you're saying when you evaporate flare, that gives it a head start."

"Exactly. It essentially teaches flare how to burn." Louise nodded, a spark in her gaze. "If we can find the right balance that will burn off the contaminants and activate the magic without burning it all up, that will keep the magic happy, so to speak."

"You talk about it like it's sentient," Ingrid muttered.

"May as well be." Louise shrugged. "It's enough of a mystery, as far as compounds go. Not worth ruling that out."

Ingrid laughed hollowly. "This is going to change everything, isn't it?" She'd known all along it would, but before she'd only thought of it in the abstract. They weren't just going door-to-door to hand out flare like charity. They were going to make flare. They were going to tear down the system that upheld the hierarchy. They were going to force Candesce to change instead of letting it continue to wreck them.

"Sure is," Louise said with a grin. "When I'm done here, you'll be able to blow up the capital if the fancy strikes you."

Ingrid winced. "Maybe let's not joke about that."

"Suit yourself. But I don't think you'll find a more worthy use for it."

It seemed impossible that this same girl had thrown fire at her not so long ago. Maybe Senator Holt had been right all along and Louise *was* dangerous. Maybe Ingrid had made a terrible mistake bailing her out. And maybe Louise had donned her own mask last night, doing her best to burn down the capital just like she said.

"Do the words *Everybody burns* mean anything to you?" Ingrid asked before she could stop herself.

"That's the slogan on all those posters. They've been in the flicker clubs for ages."

"Right, but does it mean anything else to you?" Ingrid asked. "You said it right before you attacked us."

Louise shrugged. "Seemed dramatic, so I said it. So what?"

"Nothing. No reason." Ingrid stepped out from the shadow of the hedge. "I trust you."

But Ingrid knew the irony for what it was. Louise wasn't the liar; Ingrid was.

CHAPTER TWENTY-FIVE

The capital ushered in the first blossoms of the year as the day of the election approached. Two weeks had passed since the attack on the President's Ball, with two more weeks remaining until they all learned the fate of the nation. But nature waited for no one, not even the future president, and spring was thoroughly upon them. Trees lining the streets sent a flurry of petals to the ground, covering the earth with a blanket of pink as though it wanted them to forget the bloody, burning night they'd spent there only days ago. It made the city look like winter, but it smelled like spring.

Ingrid, whose sinuses appreciated this change about as much as Gwendolyn Meyers appreciated President Morris endorsing Senator Holt, spent most of the following week indoors. It was just as well; with the date of the election on the horizon, they had more to do than ever before. Faye and Clarence were writing speeches faster than Gwendolyn could give them, and Birdie was an orb of stress, traveling from room to room like a tornado.

The numbers were so close, *too* close. Every one of Ingrid's waking moments was spent preparing talking points for the meetings Gwendolyn was taking with each senator between campaign events. To win, she would have to court the vote of every resident of the capital, including each member of the legislative body.

"What is this supposed to be?" Alex flung a piece of paper at her. "You can't go waxing poetic about wealth inequity to Senator Verden right after promising Senator Leopold we'll soften our policies." He pointed to their upcoming schedule of meetings, indicating the two senators they were meeting that afternoon. "If it gets out we're flip-flopping, we'll lose them both."

"We shouldn't promise Senator Leopold we'll soften our policies." Ingrid tilted back her chair, a challenge in her gaze. "He's not going to vote for us anyway, and we'd be lying."

"We have to give him something." Alex leaned against the table, a grumble in his very bones.

"The candidate has always held this position. I don't know why you want to change it at the eleventh hour. Everyone already knows what she thinks. Senator Leopold may not be smarter than that, but the voters certainly are."

"We have to change our strategy with the senators, or we'll lose this election." Alex threw his hands in the air. "The vote's going to be too close. The Senate vote will almost certainly be the deciding factor."

"We've never been for the Senator Leopolds of the world. We should care less about what the other senators think if we start promising more than we plan to deliver, and we should worry about the people who matter—the voters. If we betray them now, it won't even matter what the senators think, and all our maneuvering will be for naught."

Alex groaned. "Two months ago you'd have argued the exact opposite."

"Two months ago I would have been wrong."

"I know! That's what kills me. When did that happen? When

246

did you become all moral-compassy and righteous? Have we finally converted you from your residual Holt mentality?"

Pushing down the discomfort in her belly, Ingrid cocked an eyebrow. "Would you prefer I go back to being incompetent?"

Alex's face fell, the undercurrent of mirth that always accompanied their disputes evaporating. "You were never incompetent. Insufferable, though . . ."

"There's a compliment in there somewhere, I'm sure."

"Don't look too hard for it." He grinned.

She grinned back, despite the guilt rising like a tide inside her.

"What do you two lovebirds have to be happy about?" Birdie barked at them as she set a stack of papers on the center table. "Stop smiling. Smiling makes me queasy."

It made Ingrid queasy too—not the smiling so much, but the word *lovebirds*. She scratched her forearms, returning her gaze to her notes. It wasn't that she couldn't imagine herself with Alex. As far as her options were concerned, Alex was far from a poor one. Still, Ingrid couldn't shake the unpleasantness. It was familiar. It was intimate. It was expectation.

And still the idea of Linden weighed heavily on her shoulders. He was everything to her, or at least he had been. Now she had so much more than him. To go from being his to Alex's felt wrong. It didn't feel like moving forward. It felt like standing still while the rest of the world moved around her, or like running in place and expecting things to change. But at the end of it all, she would still be trapped, and she would still be tired.

Alex was not her escape route. He was more than that. He was more than the lover Birdie and Charlotte and everyone else seemed to want him to be to her. He was more than a possibility. He was more than a maybe someday. He was a right now, and he was a friend.

That too was love.

Ingrid's fist balled around the page, crumpling the paper between her fingers.

"Whoa, Ingrid. Don't just throw it away." Alex reached for her hand, his fingertips grazing her knuckles.

Ingrid jerked back and stood. "I'm going to . . ." She trailed off, her feet carrying her toward the door. "Go," she finished, letting the speech fall into the wastebasket as she went.

The anonymity of the capital's streets gave her back her breath one step at a time, despite the pollen. She kicked flurries of blossoms into the air, watching the petals languish and fall to the ground like snow. Crocuses cracked the frozen ground with white-and-purple petals, and a songbird serenaded the welcome change in the weather. It was almost too picturesque to be pleasant.

By the time Ingrid reached her room back at Ainsley Academy, she felt better, if not a little silly. Her departure had been dramatic, to say the least, and over what? A little teasing? But it hadn't felt like teasing in the moment. It had felt like judgment. Even among friends, expectation still reigned supreme.

It was what it was, and Ingrid could do little to change it. She would take a few minutes to collect herself now before going back. There was more work to be done, and the work was more important than her feelings, whatever they were.

Ingrid came to a stop outside her room, bending to unlock the door, but her key only grazed the handle before she dropped to the floor. There in the crack between the door and the ground was a small gray stone with three white chalk marks on the back.

Something in her stomach fluttered to life and died all at once. Three marks meant Linden would be in their special meeting place at three. Ingrid jumped to her feet and made a dash for the stairs, letting the stone fall back to the floor.

She wanted to feel excitement in her veins, but instead dread beat a rhythm against her skin. Last she'd seen Linden, he'd practically told her he didn't want the life they'd planned. Maybe it would be soothing to let him embrace her, to feel the calm of his arms around her. But even the thought of it felt spoiled somehow. His love, however true in his eyes, didn't feel true anymore. She'd found so much more to herself over the past few months than she could have imagined, more to herself than he knew. Would he still love who she'd become? He'd asked his own mirrored question the night of the rebel attack. Would his answer be as uncertain as hers had been?

"Linden?" she whispered against the old wood door as she turned the doorknob.

But it wasn't Linden who waited inside for her. There, in the plush armchair in the corner, sat an intruder.

"Good of you to come, Miss Ellis."

CHAPTER TWENTY-SIX

Senator Holt rose to his feet, filling a space that wasn't his. Though he was tall and imposing even in wide-open spaces, here his power felt even more all-consuming.

"I've been wanting a word with you," he said through tight lips.

"Senator!" Ingrid closed the door behind her. "I wasn't expecting you."

This room, which had always been a comfort, always been her secret to share with Linden, was suddenly no longer hers. Uncertainty cobwebbed the air, making Ingrid's skin prickle. These walls and the little space between them were never meant for observation. It was her respite from the world, but the world had finally come calling, and it was time to answer.

"Yes, you were expecting *Linden*." Senator Holt sneered. "I thought it best I meet with you directly, since my son has been distracted. It doesn't seem he's particularly dedicated to the campaign."

Ingrid swallowed a retort, remembering Linden's words on the terrace. He *was* distracted. Linden's face flashed through her mind, the gentle wobble of his chin, the bags beneath his eyes, the crease in his forehead. She'd rarely seen him in such a state, not even during their exams. He was grappling with something far more complex than she could understand, and it seemed a miscalculation to label him *undedicated*.

"Of course," Senator Holt continued, "he's not the only one." He raised a single gray eyebrow. The accusation in his eyes was as unexpected as it was unwelcome.

Ingrid's breath caught as he surveyed her. Slowly, oh so slowly, understanding crashed around her. "Me?" Her voice came small and subdued. She straightened her shoulders and adopted an indignant tone. "Whatever do you mean?"

"It would serve us both well to put aside pretense."

"Then please," she said, gesturing to the space between them, "let us put it aside."

Finally, Senator Holt exhaled long and slow and said, "The time has come for you to earn my trust. I'll admit, when you first proposed this arrangement to me, I wanted you to lose. I was *certain* you'd lose. You are only a child after all."

Ingrid balled her fists.

Senator Holt looked her up and down, seeming to measure her worth in those moments of silence. "This election will be much too close. Let it never be said that I was too arrogant as to ignore an asset, even if she's lacking."

Ingrid held her breath. Every syllable he spoke drew closer to the words she'd hoped to one day hear, but now faced with the prospect, she wasn't sure she wanted them anymore. Senator Holt's respect had once been the only thing she'd wanted. Now, earning it felt less like success and more like a trap—perhaps of her own making.

"You're an astute girl, Ingrid. Tell me, what are my chances of winning this election?"

Ingrid swallowed. She'd done this exercise with Alex only yesterday. "Not bad. Not good."

"Exactly. I don't know where I stand, but I do know where I'm strong. I know the public agrees with my response to the rebel attacks—I know they see me as a protector and as an aggressive force willing to stand up for everyone's safety. What I don't know are my opponent's weaknesses. That was supposed to be your job."

Ingrid opened her mouth, unsure if she planned to defend the candidate or betray her. In Ingrid's eyes, of course, Gwendolyn had no weaknesses. But it was not Ingrid's eyes that mattered. "Her weaknesses are much the same as your strengths. I thought I made that clear in the messages I passed through Linden."

"Those are not the weaknesses I mean." Senator Holt shifted, an ominous look in his eye. "I don't want you to tell me what my political advisers can already surmise just by looking at polling data. I want you to tell me what they can't. I want you to find her vulnerability, and then I want you to exploit it until Gwendolyn Meyers is nothing more than a stain on my sidewalk."

Ingrid's insides itched as he stared at her, his gaze making her want to shrivel into ash.

"Can I rely on you? Or are you simply a leech?"

Insults danced on her tongue, but she wouldn't make an enemy of this man. Not yet. Not unless she had to.

"Give me some time." Her heart raced. What could she give him that he didn't already have? What could she give him that wouldn't wreck her newfound campaign family? "I'll deliver."

"You'd better." Senator Holt took up his hat—a black bowler—from the armchair and returned it to his head. "You don't have very long. Election day is only a week away, and I'm running out of flare." He swept past her, knocking her shoulder with his own. "Oh, and Ingrid," he said, pausing with his hand on the doorknob, "if you fail, our little arrangement is over. The Holts don't have room for any deadweight."

With that, he was gone, leaving Ingrid to the mercy of her own false promises.

Ingrid dragged her feet across the threshold of her bedroom and fell face-first into her pillow. She'd intended to return to the office, but her encounter with Senator Holt had taken every ounce of drive she had. She could shoulder whatever teasing they threw her way, but Ingrid didn't think she could look her friends in the eye just yet with the senator's words hanging over her.

"Ingrid Helen Ellis."

Ingrid pushed herself up on her elbows to see Charlotte perched at the vanity. She held her hand in the air, the chalk-marked stone pinched between her thumb and forefinger.

"Have something to share with the class?"

Ingrid opened her mouth to speak, but no lie came to her lips. She could think of nothing to say when her head pounded so terribly with the senator's ultimatum.

"Don't think for a second you can get out of explaining this." Charlotte balled her fist around the stone and strode across the room to kneel beside Ingrid's bed. "You were with Linden again, weren't you?"

No, Charlotte, I've just come back from a private meeting with Senator Holt.

Ingrid groaned and let herself fall back into her pillow. Perhaps letting Charlotte believe this lie was better than the truth.

"You sly thing!" The bed shifted as Charlotte's weight settled against the mattress. "I won't pretend I'm not terribly furious with you for not telling me, but this makes a lot of sense."

"It does?" Ingrid said into her pillow.

"Well, you were very touchy when I suggested you and Alex might have an amorous connection. I assumed it was because you've never been particularly comfortable about other people's commentary on your love life. Really, I was sure there was *something* between you two. I suppose I was right. I just never in a thousand years thought that something was Linden."

Ingrid rolled over on her side, letting her hair fall across her eyes, with no care for how the pillow squashed her cheek. "It's not. He's not *between us*. That is to say there's nothing between us. Nothing."

"The evidence points very much to the contrary." Charlotte held up the stone. "When did this start up again?"

Ingrid bit her lip. She wanted nothing more than to spill it all, to tell Charlotte that it never ended in the first place—that it might still. Lying to Charlotte felt like a fragile thing, like she walked a narrow road between vulnerability and safety. But Charlotte wasn't just her friend; she was the press too. Nothing Ingrid said was entirely safe. "We're off the record, right?"

"Naturally." Charlotte scooted closer. "You don't have anything to fear from me, remember? Besides, I'm working on a new story— getting pretty close to something, as it happens."

"Oh?" Ingrid asked, hoping to deflect the conversation onto safer territory.

Charlotte eyed her carefully. "I don't want to worry you too much, but I suppose you should be told—that girl who attacked the speakeasy is out on bail."

"Louise?" The name slipped out before Ingrid could stop herself.

"Someone bailed her out about a week before the President's Ball. I haven't managed to get any more information, but my money's on the rebels. The timeline's too suspicious to be a coincidence. I think if I can track down the guard on duty and get a real paper trail, I might be sitting on the story of the year." She rubbed her hands together mischievously. "Since my last article turned out to be so horribly wrong, I really need something good."

"I liked your last article!" Ingrid exclaimed, a note of offense in her voice. Charlotte was a good writer. It was simply rotten luck her thesis had been so quickly proven wrong by the attack at the President's Ball.

"You're the only one," she grumbled. "But if I can find this Louise girl, I think she might lead me to the rebels."

Ingrid's heart drummed a rapid rhythm in her chest, and her hand closed around a fistful of fabric. "Oh, I don't know about that. Louise didn't seem the rebel type to me."

"What do you mean, not the rebel type? She has rebel written all over her." Charlotte shot her a befuddled look. "Don't you understand? If the rebels bailed her out, there will be a real connection. She might have even been part of the attack on President's Ball herself. I'll be able to find out *something* about their operation, and then—who knows? Maybe it will lead to bringing them down once and for all."

Ingrid took shallow breaths, afraid to let herself move. What if Charlotte was right? Maybe Louise *didn't* seem the rebel type, but Ingrid didn't really know what the rebel type was. She wouldn't know a rebel if she saw one on the street. Louise could just as easily be a liar as Ingrid, and Ingrid had told enough lies for the both of them in recent days. But Ingrid needed to believe Louise was telling the truth more than she needed to know the actual truth, so she said, "She was just a flicker chemist before. Honestly, I don't think she has rebel ties."

"Well, I think she does." Charlotte frowned and settled herself against Ingrid's pillows. "She attacked a senator. She attacked *you*."

"She was just a scared girl out for revenge. I'm the one who fought her. I should know."

"It wasn't cheap to bail her out. That's big, rebel or not. You said so yourself—she was a flicker chemist. Don't you think if a family member had that kind of money she wouldn't have been slumming it? Something's off, and I'm going to find out what."

"I really don't think there's a story." Ingrid swallowed with difficulty. Charlotte's logic didn't hold any water, to Ingrid's relief, but rather than point to rebel ties, it pointed back to Ingrid herself. She didn't need Charlotte messing about with that. "Be careful, Charlotte. You shouldn't mess around with the rebels. They're actually dangerous. This story's not worth putting yourself at risk."

"I can handle myself. They've got bigger fish to fry than a lowly intern—like your presidential candidate. You're in a lot more danger than me." She chuckled. "Besides, I've thought of a perfect headline: *Rebaillion*."

Ingrid cringed. She would have to revisit this topic later when she had something more to wave Charlotte off the scent.

"Well, you've finally done it," Ingrid said.

"Done what?"

She cast a pitying glance at Charlotte. "That is a truly *terrible* pun, which I think makes you a real journalist."

"Oh no, I've become one of them. I swore this wasn't going to happen!" She groaned and dragged her hands down her face.

"It's okay; there's still time." Ingrid spoke in a low voice, as if they were conducting a covert operation, and grabbed Charlotte by both shoulders. "We can rehabilitate you, but you'll have to put a stop to all wordplay right this instant."

Charlotte laughed and shoved Ingrid off her. "Well, this journalist is going to get back to the hard-hitting questions."

Ingrid groaned.

"You didn't think you'd distracted me, did you? Tell me, when did you start seeing Linden again?"

"The night of the President's Ball," Ingrid said, mapping the falsehood in her mind so she might at least remember it. "But it's complicated."

Charlotte pursed her lips. "I'll say. We've found ourself in a veritable love triangle, haven't we?" She flicked the tip of Ingrid's nose with her finger.

Ingrid's skin crawled, and she shivered involuntarily. "Some kind of triangle, at least," she muttered.

Charlotte slid down onto the bed so she could look Ingrid in the eye. "You don't like that word, do you?"

"What word?"

"Love. You never use it. I don't think I've ever heard you say it."

Ingrid flopped onto her back. The ceiling was a kinder conversation partner.

"Do you love Linden?" Charlotte asked.

Ingrid's throat felt heavy, like words could never rise to the surface, forever submerged in the murky marsh of her lungs, so she just nodded.

Charlotte caught Ingrid's hand in hers and squeezed. "Does it feel good? To be in love with Linden, I mean."

It felt like flying, and it felt like falling. It felt like laughter, like twinkling flicker lights. It felt like velvet upholstery against bare skin. But it also felt like money and magic and manipulation. It felt like burning, like blistering, like the opposite of breathing.

"I don't know," Ingrid said finally after far too much silence. "I don't know if it feels good." She remembered what she'd said to Alex that night, and the words came to her lips as naturally as they had before. "I don't know if I like how it feels. Or maybe I just don't like how it's *supposed* to feel. I don't want to feel like I might die if I don't see him, and I don't want to feel like I might die if I do."

"That's what it feels like?" Charlotte asked, her voice small, her words tight. "Like dying?"

"It feels like a lot of things."

"And what about Alex? What does that feel like?"

Ingrid sat up. "I'm not in love with Alex. It's not like that with us. I don't know how else I can explain it. He's not—I'm not—we're—" How could she explain something that felt as big as romance but resembled nothing Ingrid had ever been told was romantic? How could she explain that she was *with* Linden, and it didn't make what she had with Alex worth less? How could she explain that none of it felt as big as the knot she'd tied herself in to get what she wanted only to find she didn't know what she wanted after all?

Charlotte cleared her throat. "I don't want any kind of partnership—romantic, platonic, physical, what have you. None of it appeals to me. It's not for me, and I know that. But I also know you don't have to be in love with someone to choose to be with them, and I know you can be in love with someone and choose not to be."

"I know," Ingrid said, her voice small.

"Do you?" Charlotte's brown eyes were almost sad as they

258

searched Ingrid's face. "Because sometimes I think you're holding on to someone else's choices instead of your own." She swung her feet off the bed and made for the door, pausing on the threshold before she backtracked to toss the chalk-marked stone onto the vanity table. It landed with a dull thunk.

It was the same sound, Ingrid thought, her bruised and tired heart would make if it broke.

CHAPTER TWENTY-SEVEN

Alex met Ingrid in front of Ainsley Academy the next morning with a fresh cup of coffee and a brow furrowed so intently Ingrid feared he might burst. "I need to talk to you," he said as she fastened her coat.

Ingrid's stomach turned over, empty and aching already. "Look, about yesterday. I'm sorry for leaving early. It's just I—"

"That's what I wanted to talk to you about." He gestured her toward a stone bench off to the side.

"What's going on? Did I do something?" Ingrid asked, but she already knew the answer. She'd certainly done something. She'd done a lot of somethings.

Alex pressed a warm mug into her hands. "Actually, I think *I* might have done something."

Ingrid couldn't help herself. "You?" She clutched at pearls she wasn't wearing. "Alex Castille? Done something? What a world— quick, alert the media."

"Ingrid, take this seriously for a minute, please."

"Okay." Ingrid slowed herself. "You're scaring me."

Alex sat rigid, his back pressed firmly against the bench, staring forward at the street. "The other day, Birdie made a comment—a completely inappropriate comment—about us being, you know, *together.*"

"Oh yeah, I mean, that's—"

"Would you let me get this out? I want to apologize."

"For what? That's not your fault." Maybe it was his fault. Maybe it was her fault. Maybe it was no one's fault at all.

Alex turned to catch her eye. "You've been avoiding me, and I think it made you uncomfortable. It made *me* uncomfortable anyway."

Ingrid shrugged, the motion so exaggerated she spilled a bit of her coffee on her shoes.

"We work together. I'm your . . . mentor. It's not appropriate for anything to . . . for Birdie to insinuate . . ." He trailed off and shook his head, starting again. "That night of the rebel attack—"

"Nothing happened," Ingrid said quickly.

Alex fixed her with a narrow stare. "We were both there, Ingrid. That wasn't *nothing.*"

Somehow on his lips the words felt bigger. She wasn't the only one who'd felt . . . whatever it was.

"Well, it wasn't *something,*" Ingrid said finally. "Not that kind of something anyway."

Alex nodded. "Right, exactly. It was a lot of things, but it wasn't that. And I just want to clarify a few things. Make sure we're in line and everything is aboveboard."

"And you thought this conversation was best had *before* coffee?" Ingrid asked, indicating her woefully still-full cup.

Alex ignored her. "You said you thought I was going to kiss you."

"Oh." Ingrid stared at the heat curling up from her coffee.

261

Every instinct in her body told her to look at him, to see if maybe, *maybe*, that's exactly what he was going to do. The question burned against her lungs like flare. *Would it feel the same?*

Linden was the only person she'd kissed, but she'd kissed him long before she'd loved him, and she knew the difference. How would it feel to kiss Alex? She knew it somewhere in her body, even if it wasn't her mind, that she loved Alex in one way or another. There was a scientific curiosity to it. It wasn't a deep longing or desperation. She didn't want to kiss Alex like she wanted to kiss Linden or drink flare or wear the Holt name like a badge of honor. She wanted to kiss Alex like she wanted to learn political theory or puzzle through Louise's flare theories. She just wanted to know if it would be something, or if it would be *something*.

But when she finally looked up, there was no answer in Alex's eyes. Instead, there was a gentle quiet, a stillness and a solemnness that shook her from her musings.

"I'm not going to kiss you," he said, just as he had that night.

"I know." Ingrid's shoulders climbed higher. "It would be inappropriate now, of course. We work together. But I suppose someday if the fancy struck you—"

"It won't." Alex sliced through the air with his hand as though physically halting the idea in midair.

"Okay." Ingrid tucked her chin. "If I promise I understand, will you promise to talk about something else? I love to be rejected first thing in the morning as much as the next girl, I'm sure, but . . ." She trailed off as his expression turned pained.

"No, that's not it. That's not what I mean at all." He cradled his face in his hands, rocking his head back. "What I mean is, the fancy won't ever strike me—and not because of anything to do with you. I just mean—ugh!" He made eye contact with her through the slits of his fingers. "This is harder to say than I thought it would be."

Ingrid wanted to prod him a bit more, tease him for making such a terrible show of rejecting her when she'd never meant to offer herself up at all, but there was a look in his eye she recognized: fear. He'd listened to her as she spilled her soul to him without poking fun. She could offer him the same.

Alex took a deep breath and said, "Kissing isn't something I like to do. I don't like any of it, really. The physicality part of relationships has never appealed to me, and I just don't see that changing ever."

"Okay," Ingrid said. "That's fine, Alex. It's like you said, you don't have to love in only one way. If that's not part of the equation for you, that's fine. You don't have to fit a certain model to exist, and a relationship can be defined by the people in it." She paused, feeling the warmth of her own words, the affirmation in them that made her feel whole and wanted the way nothing else ever did. But then the weight of her words crashed around her, and she hurried to add, "Not that—not that this is any kind of—not that we're—"

Alex nodded vigorously. "Yeah, not that there's anything to . . ." He gestured between them with his hands, a nervous, frenzied bridge connecting them. "Boundaries are important."

Ingrid grabbed his hands and squeezed. She had her answer— he wasn't going to kiss her, and in that answer, she found a sort of relief. It started in her fingers where their hands touched and spread through the rest of her. Alex wasn't going to ask for more than she could give, just as she'd never ask for more than he could. They understood each other, and within that realization was a singular kind of joy Ingrid had never truly felt before.

She dropped his hand, and the calm fled her bones. Her stomach churned an angry sea, but the truth was there, waiting to be spoken. Alex was her friend. For that matter, so too were Faye and Clarence. Ingrid even felt affection for their grumpy campaign manager these days. She didn't want to leave them, and though telling them she was a spy might alter their relationship forever, continuing to lie felt worse.

"I have to tell you something," Ingrid blurted, but before she could continue, a head wearing a newsie cap and toothy smile popped between them.

"I hate to interrupt what looks to be a riveting conversation . . . Actually, no, I love that for me," said Louise.

Ingrid's mouth dropped open, speechless for a moment. She'd been about to spill one secret to Alex when another had come barreling into their conversation uninvited.

"Louise, I wasn't expecting—I mean I didn't— This really isn't the time," she stammered.

"Isn't it fun when things don't go your way?" Louise smiled, her pointed features sharpening in mirth. "I've been trying to get a word with you since yesterday, but you were nowhere to be found. You know who I did find, though? That awful senator—what's his name? The one running for president. Had to hide under the stairs to avoid him."

"Alex Castille," Alex said, hand extended awkwardly over the bench. "Ingrid, your friend is an utter delight."

"Hear that, Ingrid?" Louise took his hand and shook it. "I'm a delight."

"Is this a nightmare?" Ingrid muttered under her breath, and pinched her forearm, disappointed to find that it hurt a lot. "Did you want something?"

"As a matter of fact, I did." Louise leaned in closer. "I have a pretty . . . important update, if you know what I mean."

"What does she mean?" Alex, who'd leaned in along with Louise, blinked at her from only a few inches away.

Ingrid let out a long breath. "Okay, okay. I suppose I was going to have to tell you eventually." She looked up and down the long pathway leading from the school to the street, but found no one within earshot. "Louise here is helping me with our little flare shortage problem."

Alex retracted his head as though he were a turtle, staring at her from under furrowed brows. "Ingrid, you can't—you of all people should know you can't just *steal* flare. You know what happened to your father."

"We're not stealing it." Louise shot him a piercing look. "We're making it."

Alex opened and closed his mouth several times, but no sound came out.

Ingrid stepped in to cover the awkward silence with an explanation. "When you said the free-flare program was shutting down, it got me thinking—"

"Oh, danger alert," Louise interjected.

"It got me thinking," Ingrid said more firmly. "If we can make things like rubber and glass with chemistry, why not flare?"

"Why not flare?" Alex spluttered.

"Why not flare?" Louise repeated. "Seriously, why not?"

"Well, it's impossible, for a start. Don't you think someone would've done it by now if they could?"

Louise stared him down, her gaze unwavering. "No."

Alex ran his fingers through his hair. And then he did it again. "Because anyone with the resources wouldn't want to destabilize the very structure that keeps them in power."

"If you're done having a conversation with yourself . . ." Louise began.

"It's not actually possible, is it?" Alex asked, turning from Ingrid to Louise and back to Ingrid.

"Do you want to stand out in the cold wondering, or would you like to actually find out?"

"Not out here. Anyone could see us." Ingrid glanced out toward the street where Flare Force patrols passed by every few minutes. Heightened security had been announced immediately after the attack at the President's Ball, but somehow it made Ingrid feel even less safe. She put a hand on Louise's shoulder and turned her back toward the school. "Follow me."

She led them inside, her lungs tightening with each step. In a few moments, they might actually do the impossible. Ingrid could hardly breathe for anticipation as she ushered them into the supply closet usually reserved for her and Linden. Its special quality had already been sullied by Senator Holt's surprise visit yesterday, and it was the only place on campus Ingrid knew they wouldn't be disturbed.

"All right, what have you got?" Ingrid asked.

Louise paused for a moment in the doorway, tapping her fingers on the doorframe as she took in the small room. She looked like she might make a snide comment of some kind, but then she stepped inside and let the door swing shut behind her.

"First three batches are ready for testing. What do you say?"

Ingrid wrinkled her nose. "You expect us to test them?"

"Of course. Not like we have much of a choice." Louise withdrew three vials from the inside pocket of her coat. "Do you trust me?"

"Not in the slightest," Ingrid said, but she held out a hand anyway.

Alex grunted as he took his vial, holding it at arm's length. "You sure about this?"

Louise unstoppered the last vial and said, "Nope," before downing it.

It took a moment for the mystery liquid to take effect. Louise pinched her nose and made a face before unleashing an almighty belch of silver and gold sparks. They danced in the air for two seconds, maybe three, before dissolving.

"Looked like flicker," Ingrid said.

"That's because it was." Louise stuck out her tongue. "Only drier. Think I overevaporated this batch."

"Okay, my turn." Alex uncorked his vial and took a hesitant sniff. "Here goes nothing." He took a small sip and immediately spat it back out. He opened his mouth to speak, but all that came out was a sound like *haaaah* as he waved his hands in front of his face, fanning his tongue.

"Verdict: not great?" Louise asked.

"Hot!" Alex managed to say through his tongue.

"Well, it's flare. It's not going to be cold." But Ingrid eyed her own vial with suspicion. "You're not trying to poison us, are you?"

"Scorch it! I should've thought of that." Louise crossed her eyes. "If I wanted to poison you, you'd already be dead. I don't have the patience for a long con."

Ingrid swallowed a lump in her throat. Louise hadn't meant it as a jab, but it felt like one just the same. Who was Ingrid to question Louise's trustworthiness when she herself had been planning to betray them all along? It was time to put that behind her and find out what trust tasted like.

It didn't taste like much of anything, Ingrid discovered as she emptied the contents of her vial into her mouth. She'd almost always had flare cut with something else, like cider or champagne, but familiar bitter notes burned into her tongue and left behind a fruity aftertaste.

"How do you feel?" Alex asked, peering at her from beneath nervous eyebrows.

"A little warm." Ingrid rolled her tongue against her teeth.

Louise slapped a notebook down on the table and began to write.

"And tingly too. Write that down."

"Tingly? Really?" Louise raised an eyebrow. "Can't you be more specific?"

"I don't think it's working." But Ingrid felt it almost as soon as the words left her mouth, and she took a step back, then another, hitting the wall. It was as if a little wick in her chest had lit up, a flame pulsing in time with her heartbeat. She closed her eyes and listened for the telltale whisper of magic.

And there it was, the snicker of fire. When other people used magic, she could hear it too, quieter, crueler, like it was laughing at her for having none of her own. But this fire, it laughed with her, like together they were in on the joke.

"Are you all right?" Alex asked.

But Ingrid couldn't find the words. She couldn't say anything at all. All she could do was raise her hands before her and let them burn. Blue fire shot up from her palms, twin flames casting an eerie glow across the room. The magic hissed and sputtered before going out.

"Did that just happen?" Alex looked from Ingrid to Louise and back again. "Am I having a fever dream, or is Ingrid actually on fire?"

"Coloration's wrong." Louise bent over her notebook and wrote something down.

"I was on fire," Ingrid whispered in the wake of the flames. But it hadn't felt like burning; it felt like thriving. It had felt like magic.

"Is there any left? I want to try!" Alex took the vial from her with a grin on his face. Little flames erupted from the ends of his fingertips a few moments later, and he wiggled them like he was a delighted infant discovering the versatility of their phalanges for the first time. Then the fire went out, and he pouted most impressively.

Louise laughed as Alex tried to empty the already-empty vial into his mouth. "I can make more. Lots more."

"Good." Alex nodded vigorously, then turned to Ingrid. "We have to show the others too. This could change everything. I hope you know how much this matters."

"Oh, I know," Louise said, and snatched the empty vial back. "Come on. We'll whip up some more, and then you can do whatever you like with it."

"No, no, that leaves too many options open," Alex began, but as they exited the supply closet and began their slow descent toward the first floor, Alex stopped dead in his tracks.

Ingrid stumbled into him, but before she could utter a single rebuke, she saw who impeded their progress.

On the steps below stood Birdie, her hair blown back and out like it was permanently fixed there by the wind. Her fists were clenched around a copy of that morning's paper, and her eyes were fire.

"Where is she, Ellis? Where is the rebel girl you've been hiding?"

CHAPTER TWENTY-EIGHT

"Where is she?" Birdie growled. "Don't play games with me."

"What are you talking about?" Alex asked, stepping between them with a hand outstretched.

"Story broke this morning." Birdie pointed to the front page of the *Candesce Courant* in her hand.

"What story?" Ingrid leaned forward to get a glimpse over Alex's shoulder.

"You tell me, Ellis." Birdie crossed her arms as Alex, followed by Ingrid and Louise, shuffled down to the landing.

Alex took ahold of the paper and scanned quickly, his eyes flicking back and forth. "They're saying we might not just be rebel sympathizers, but the rebels themselves."

"And that's my fault because . . ." Ingrid tried again to get a better look, but Birdie stepped forward to block her.

"Is this the girl?" Birdie asked, pointing at Louise.

"The who?" Ingrid's heart beat into the shallow of her throat.

A sneer spread across Birdie's face, slow and sinister. "You'd best think hard, because you bailed that rebel girl out of jail, and now you're going to put her back."

Alex whipped around to look at Louise. "You're a rebel?"

"She's not," Ingrid said quietly, but there was no confidence behind her voice.

Louise looked like she was ready to bolt, but Birdie was blocking the only exit.

"You know about her too?" Birdie snapped her eyes toward Alex. "Please tell me you're joking."

Alex raised his hands in surrender. "I just met her this morning. I didn't know she was a rebel, and I didn't know *you bailed her out of jail*." He said the last words through his teeth, glaring at Ingrid. "I can't believe you didn't tell me."

"I can't imagine why I didn't tell you." Ingrid widened her eyes. "It's almost like I thought you'd judge her unfairly."

"She's a rebel, Ingrid. I think we're judging her pretty fairly."

Louise cleared her throat and stepped forward. "Maybe let her speak for herself."

"Believe me when I say this: You do not want to involve yourself in this discussion." Birdie's cheeks went concave as she clenched her jaw.

"Why's that?" Louise stepped forward, a glint of a challenge in her eyes. "Seems I'm already involved. If you're going to talk *about* me, might as well talk *to* me."

Birdie's eyes swept over Louise, seeming to take in the little details of her defiance: the slightly crooked cap, her thumbs hooked around her suspenders, her weight sent back over her left foot as if to say *I'm staying right here*.

Alex turned panicked eyes on Ingrid. "She's a convict—a rebel! What were you thinking?"

"I'm not a convict. I haven't been convicted of anything yet," Louise shot back.

Ingrid set her jaw. "I don't see why this is such a big deal. It's not like I *broke* her out of jail. What I did was legal."

"Maybe it was legal, but it was also incredibly stupid." Birdie leaned against the railing, eyes narrowed. "Or perhaps it was all part of your plan."

"Plan?" Ingrid repeated. "No, I just wanted her help to make flare. When Alex said the free-flare program was canceled, I thought we could get it started again if she could only—"

"Make flare?" Birdie laughed harshly.

"I know it sounds wild, but I saw it with my own eyes, Birdie. They actually did it." Alex stepped forward but immediately retreated as Birdie's gaze flicked to him.

"A likely cover story."

"It's the truth," grumbled Louise.

"But not the whole truth." Birdie paced back and forth along the landing. "Tell me, if you were tasked with bringing down the Meyers campaign, what weaknesses would you exploit?"

"Well, I guess—"

"Not you, Alex. I want to hear it from her." She pointed at Ingrid.

Ingrid tried to swallow, but a lump in her throat made her cough instead. "I—I suppose it would have to be something about the rebellion and security."

"Exactly. And what better way to ruin us than to tie us directly to a suspected rebel? Senator Holt's already coming at us for being too soft on this issue, so it plays into what he's been saying all along, and it has the added bonus of making us look like we were behind the attack on the senator himself."

"I didn't mean to," Ingrid tried to say, but it came out small and croaky. "I didn't want to hurt the campaign."

Birdie stopped her pacing directly in front of Ingrid and sneered. "Didn't you?"

Ingrid blinked at her. "No?"

Birdie plucked the paper from Alex's hand like an apple from a tree and let it unfurl between them. "Is that you?"

A picture was nestled beneath the headline. Ingrid almost didn't recognize herself. It felt like a lifetime ago that she was standing on a crowded train platform with Linden's arms around her, a hundred camera flashes glancing off the snow. She felt so far away from that girl who cared so much what the press thought, what the *Holts* thought.

"You weren't just on the Holt campaign staff, were you?" Birdie asked, her voice gravel.

"No," Ingrid replied hollowly.

"But you and Linden broke up." Alex's voice sounded far away. "You said you weren't together anymore."

"You knew about them?" Birdie roared. "You knew, and you recruited her anyway?"

"I don't see what the problem is—"

"She's a spy," Louise said quietly.

Everyone turned to look at Louise.

"I thought it was only coincidence when I saw Senator Holt yesterday. I thought I was just imagining things when you took us to that same room I saw him leaving. But this—this makes sense. You did it because you still belong to them. Because you still think you deserve better than us. But let me tell you, it doesn't matter who you marry or who you wreck in order to get what you want. You'll never be better than me." She pushed past them

274

and made for the door. "I'm out," she said. "I hope you burn."

The door clicked closed behind her.

"Alex, I—" Ingrid began.

"Is it true?" He stared intently at the window, looking out into the street.

Ingrid reached for his arm, but he flinched out of her grasp. "I wanted to tell you—I tried to this morning before Louise, but I—"

"It *is* true. You used me. You used Louise. You used all of us." Alex turned away and put his head in his hands. "I thought you were better than this."

"Look, I didn't orchestrate this. I didn't think anyone would go digging, and I certainly didn't think they'd find anything. And maybe I joined the campaign to spy on you originally, but I realized I don't want to work for Senator Holt. I thought I needed his approval to get what I wanted, but I don't want that anymore. I just want to fight for what's right. I want to help the people who need it. Senator Holt was never going to do any of those things, and you all were. Don't you understand? I changed my mind. And I'm not trying to ruin your campaign."

"It's not about *trying*," Birdie grumbled.

"Enough." A clear voice rang out from behind them.

Ingrid turned to see Gwendolyn Meyers standing in the doorway to Ainsley Academy in a pale green silk blouse and carrying a white blazer over her arm. Her eyes were unreadable, her posture a blueprint of neutrality.

"I've heard enough," she said more quietly. "Get back to work." She nodded to Birdie, who gestured to Alex to follow in retreat.

Alex shot Ingrid a look full of pain. His eyes were cloudy and his cheeks red.

Ingrid took a step forward, but Gwendolyn blocked her path.

"Not you, Ingrid."

Ingrid looked up into the candidate's face, searching for an ounce of compassion, a splash of understanding. She found none.

"You're fired."

A lot of things had gone wrong in Ingrid's life for which she didn't know who to blame; this wasn't one of them. Blazing anger carried her up the stairs to her room. Behind the door, she found Charlotte pacing back and forth, her brow wrinkled, arms held tight to her sides.

"What happened to off the record?" Ingrid spat.

Charlotte's eyes turned on her, pleading etched into her pores. "Ingrid, I never meant for this to happen."

"Sure, you didn't."

"I had no idea you were involved at all until it was too late. I promise, I didn't sell you out on purpose."

"But you still sold me out." Ingrid scoffed and made for the vanity. She couldn't bring herself to look Charlotte in the eye, and it was easier to say her piece with a mirror filtering Charlotte's image. "I told you to drop it. I told you to leave the story alone. Why couldn't you just listen, for once in your life?"

"If you'd told me *why*—"

"You'd, what, not have told your bosses exactly what I said?" She slammed her hand down on the vanity, a few pieces of jewelry jumping at the force. "How'd you figure it out anyway?"

Ingrid watched her friend's reflection lift her fist and unfurl her fingers to reveal a familiar ring. A sapphire winked under the flare lights, and Ingrid's stomach twisted painfully.

"I thought at first it meant the Holts had done it. You and Linden, you broke up, so I assumed you'd given back the ring." She set the sapphire on the vanity with a click. "But the pawnshop said it was a girl who brought it in. I knew then it had to be you. You never really broke up, did you?"

Ingrid covered the ring with her hand. "No," she whispered.

"So, why?" Charlotte came around the side of the vanity, kneeling and leaning on her elbows. "Did you want to implicate the Meyers campaign or something?"

It's what she should have done from the beginning. If she'd been focused on her goal, if she hadn't let herself get drawn in by Alex's intelligence and Frances's plight and Gwendolyn's goodness, if she'd just stuck to the plan, she'd have everything she wanted. If she'd never let them all worm their way into her heart, she never would have faltered. But she had, and somehow she couldn't bring herself to regret it.

"That's what they think," Ingrid muttered. "I can't believe you'd let them print this."

"Why? It's the truth, isn't it? You bailed a suspected rebel out of jail."

This is too important, she meant to say.

"I'm too important," she said.

Charlotte rose to her feet, a grimace on her face. "Maybe it wouldn't be newsworthy if you weren't so *important*. Scorch it, Ingrid! What did you think was going to happen?"

Ingrid glared at Charlotte with as much animosity as she could muster. "You got me fired."

Charlotte rapped her knuckles on the vanity table and shook

her head. "I'm sorry I couldn't give you more of a warning about this, and I'm sorry I couldn't stop it from going to print, but Ingrid, I didn't get you fired. You got yourself fired."

And with that, she was gone, leaving Ingrid with nothing but a cold ring she didn't want.

CHAPTER TWENTY-NINE

Ingrid Ellis had no plan.

She had nothing left to fight for, and nothing left to fight with. Everyone she cared about was back in Gwendolyn's office, and they'd all decided she was too much of a liability. There was no one left to care.

But that wasn't true. There was still one person who loved her, though whether or not he'd want to help was uncertain. After all, she hadn't treated him very well as of late.

There was only one way to find out, so she turned her feet north and found her way to the last place in the world she wanted to be.

"Good morning, Miss Ellis. What a pleasant surprise to see you again," Officer Scott greeted her as she made the trek down the long hall to his receiving desk.

"I'm here to see my father," Ingrid said, the words sticking on her tongue. "Please," she added. It hadn't yet been a full month since she'd visited, and Officer Scott could easily turn her away.

Officer Scott eyed her with a soft gaze, searching but not prying. Perhaps it was something in her dispirited appearance or the waver in her voice when she'd said *please*, but he came out from behind the desk and said, "Of course. I'll take you back."

Ingrid settled herself in the visiting room to wait, finding a familiar routine in the understanding glance she shared with Officer Scott, the table she chose to sit at, the way she hooked her toes around the chair leg. She couldn't decide whether to be comforted or disturbed by how easily she fell into the habit of it all.

For seven years, Ingrid had gone through the motions, molding melancholy onto her bones like muscle. She'd grown taller and bolder, if not wiser, but here in the prison, nothing seemed to change. It was as if this world behind bars dissolved into nothing the moment she departed, leaving behind only a low ache in her chest and a weight around her neck.

Though Oscar Ellis had never been particularly sturdy before, either in physique or in character, Ingrid found it was she who crumbled as he came around the corner. For a moment, Ingrid was ten years old again, seeing her father after his incarceration for the first time, feeling that lonesome, lost longing, digesting the prospect of an unknowable future.

But this was not the first time. She'd lost count. Still, she longed for a time when her father still looked like her father and she still looked like herself, and the prison they stood in was just a backdrop to a moment in their family history, not a fixture.

"Papa," she said quietly, the word slipping through her lips like a coin through a hole in her pocket.

Her father smiled, a kind and honest thing. "It's good to see your face." He sat across the table from her, reaching up to touch his own cheek.

Her hand snaked up to mirror him, sliding back down only

when his did, feeling the ghost of a touch never exchanged when it was gone.

"I'm sorry," Ingrid began, biting her lip. "I'm sorry for what I said before."

"I understand," he said. "This isn't easy—for you, for me, for *us*. None of this is easy, and none of it is good."

"I know, but I shouldn't—I shouldn't be so angry. You didn't try to hurt me. I should forgive you."

"You should do what you feel you need to do, Ingrid. Nothing more." Her father peered at her through eyes unhindered by the kind of resentment she held in her stomach, in her chest, in her jaw. "I'm not going anywhere. If you need to be angry, be angry. I'll still be here. And when you need to forgive me, I'll be here too."

"How do you do that?" Ingrid asked.

"Do what, Dewdrop?"

Her emotions turned concave at the nickname. All that time she'd spent waiting for him—as sure as morning dew—now it was he who was always waiting for her. As he stared at her with soft green eyes not unlike her own, she wondered if he understood she'd put a wall between them to protect herself. It hurt too much to love him, so she'd found a way to hate him too. Maybe that was more painful anyway.

"Wait for me." Her voice was as small as the feeling was large. Her chest felt brittle and breakable under the weight of her breath. "How do you just wait for me to forgive you?"

He peered at her with tired eyes. "There's not much else I can do from behind bars."

"You could fight for me. You could try to make me. You could—"

"Try to make you?" He raised his eyebrows. "You are a force of nature, Ingrid. I couldn't even make you eat your greens when you were little. How am I supposed to change your entire perception of me?"

"You could at least try," she murmured.

"Would that really change anything? You have a life to live, and I have time to serve. It doesn't matter that I did what I did to try to give us a better life when what I gave us was a life apart. I hope someday you'll understand it, Dewdrop, but forgive? That isn't something I can try to make you do. You have to decide to do it on your own."

"And what if I never do?"

Ingrid could have sworn she saw him flinch.

"Then that's your decision." He exhaled long and slow. "I haven't been a big part of your life in a long time. I won't ask for a place in your world, Ingrid. If you want me there, you can invite me."

"You left me in that orphanage with nothing." She slammed her palm onto the table, shaking the surface beneath them. "This life I have? I had to get it on my own."

"You deserved better." His gaze fell to his clasped hands before him.

Ingrid's stomach clenched. "I deserved a father."

He nodded solemnly. "I know you're angry with me."

Ingrid rose from the table, standing without meaning to. "I am! I'm so angry!" She threw her hands up and kicked the chair back so she could pace. "I'm angry you stole flare, I'm angry you put our family on the line, and I'm angry you got caught." She stopped and let her hands fall. "But mostly I'm angry that Candesce forced you to make that choice."

"I wish I could have made a different one."

"Aren't you angry too?" she asked, slipping back into her chair. "Aren't you angry that in this nation a father has to choose between taking care of his family or working an honest job? Aren't you angry that no one has enough flare to get by? That no one has enough flare to make any kind of change? Aren't you just so angry?"

"I've had a lot of time in here alone to be angry, Ingrid. Angry doesn't make the time pass faster. Angry doesn't make the bars melt away. Angry doesn't bring your daughter back to see you sooner."

Ingrid swallowed, hot guilt rising in her throat. "I'm sorry," she said simply. She didn't know how to elaborate, but he didn't seem to need her to.

"I'm sorry too," he said.

They sat there in the wake of their apologies, neither speaking nor moving, barely breathing.

Finally, Ingrid said, "So you just wait? When you want someone to forgive you, there's nothing you can do about it?"

Oscar tilted his head. "There's nothing you can do to make them forgive you, but there's plenty you can do to be the kind of person who deserves that forgiveness." He glanced around and added, "Even in a place like this."

"What do you mean?" Ingrid leaned forward. "What do you mean, be the kind of person who deserves it?"

Closing his eyes, Oscar sighed and cradled his chin between his fingers. "Whoever you've hurt, they see something in you that has the capacity to keep hurting them. That doesn't just go away. You have to decide if you can change, and then you have to do it for yourself, not for them."

"For myself." Ingrid nodded slowly. "I can do that."

"Good." The hint of a smile fell across his face. "That's my girl."

"I'm not your girl!" The words came out sharper than she meant them. "I'm *my* girl," she said more softly. "I've been on my own so long I don't know how to be part of something anymore." She put her head in her hands. "And I think I may have lost my chance to try."

"I know," her father said. "I know. I took that away from us. I broke our family, and I'm sorry."

Ingrid looked up and caught his eye, a sad, sweet olive. "No, you didn't. You didn't break us. This country did." She gripped the table, knuckles white. "And I'm going to break it right back."

Her father's gaze turned sharp. "Ingrid, be careful."

"I've been careful long enough," she growled.

Her father inclined his head, letting his eyes fall to her rigid hands. "I love you, Dewdrop." He pressed his hand to his lips and brought it to his cheek.

Ingrid mirrored him, but she barely felt her own touch. Instead, she felt in herself a thousand fires, small and steady like candle flames, ready to build into something bigger, something brighter, something that would rage until there was nothing left to burn.

When Ingrid knocked on the brown door with peeling paint and the rusted number three on the outside, she expected to be met with hostility, so she was ready when Louise tried to punch her in the face.

"I come in peace!" Ingrid said, bobbing out of the way and holding her hands up in surrender.

"Sure you do. And I'm the next secretary of flare." She hopped out onto the stoop, readying another punch. "How'd you find me?"

Ingrid held up a small scrap of paper with Louise's home address printed in the corner. She'd found the wrinkled page of notes in her pocket from a page Louise had torn from her notebook weeks ago.

"Hear me out at least, will you?" Ingrid asked. "I have a lot to apologize for, and I'd love to get that finished with before you break my nose."

Louise paused mid-swing. "And I can break your nose after?"

"If you don't like what I have to say, you can break whatever you like."

Louise narrowed her eyes, then lowered her fist. "Okay. Say what you came to say."

Ingrid took a deep breath. "I wanted to say that I'm sorry for lying to you. I didn't really know what I wanted when I bailed you out, and I thought it would be easier to let you believe I was cut off from the Holts than tell the truth."

"Which is?" Louise jutted out her chin and crossed her arms.

"The truth?" Ingrid chewed her lip. "The truth is, I wanted to do something good. I thought I had to wait until I had the kind of power they have to enact change, but that's not true. That's what you—and Alex, and Gwendolyn, and everyone—taught me. I don't have to be like them to be powerful. I don't have to be powerful at all."

Louise didn't move but for the slow tapping of her foot against concrete. "And?"

"And I wasn't ready to let go of what I thought they could give me just yet. That was obviously a mistake."

"Obviously." *Tap tap tap*. "So?"

"So what?" Ingrid asked.

"What are you gonna do about it?" *Tap tap tap*.

"That's why I'm here—I need your help."

"With what?" Louise's face was blank, her eyes cold, but she'd stopped tapping her foot.

Ingrid's lips twitched into a smile, and she said her four favorite words. "I have a plan."

CHAPTER THIRTY

The Holt residence in the capital was smaller compared with their estate in Alorden, but it more than made up for its size with a modern design. White wood paneling stood stark against the gray skies, and a chimney puffed smoke into the air above dark slate-gray shingles. Casement windows were closed against the spring chill, but Ingrid could see dark blue curtains just inside that would billow with a warm wind in summer.

She imagined, for a moment, what it would be like to live behind those walls. If she were a Holt, this would be her home. She could be one of those women with money in their hands and magic on their tongues. She could let the past burn and in the ashes be reborn. But nothing they could give her would make her happy. She knew that now.

Senator Holt's valet let her in when she knocked. She remembered his stern demeanor from the train and the subtle superiority he'd held in his shoulders when she'd been sent away to fetch the senator's tea.

"The senator said we might expect you at one point or another this week," he said, guiding her down the hall. "I thought you wouldn't show, but who am I to argue?"

It was impossibly odd that Senator Holt had confided anything so secret as their arrangement with his employee. Then again, he was the senator's personal manservant. If Ingrid had learned anything from her precarious position somewhere between the classes, it was that the upper class ignored the lower class as if it were a practiced art. To the senator, his valet was as much a fixture in the home as the fireplace, and to the senator, the valet had about as much brains as the fireplace as well. The Holts were just rich enough to be stupid enough to speak freely around the servants, forgetting they were more than a uniform but people as well.

He led her down the hall to the door at the end and knocked. "It's Miss Ellis, sir."

"Come in."

The senator's voice came bored and bruising. He didn't look up from his desk as she entered. The valet returned a moment later, placing a tea tray in the middle of the desk with settings for two, before he shut the door behind him. She was alone with the senator now, the only sound between them the scratch of the senator's pen against paper.

"Senator Holt," Ingrid began, fingering the paper in her pocket. Louise had needed less convincing than she'd expected and handed over the formula for flare with more trust in her eyes than Ingrid deserved.

"Miss Ellis," the senator replied, finally looking up from his paper, expectant. "What do you want?"

What did she want? She wanted so many things, they'd fill the room and then some. But mostly, she wanted to watch him burn. *Patience, Ellis*, she reminded herself.

"I've brought you what you asked for," she said, sitting across from him.

288

He tapped his pen against the oak desk. "I've already heard about your little fiasco with the rebel girl who attacked me. That could have been clever, you know, if only you'd thought to consult me first."

"I—I know," Ingrid stammered. "I had something else in mind, though."

"Truly, if we'd coordinated, I could have exposed her before the papers got wind of it. If there's one thing you must learn in this business, Miss Ellis, it's when to play your hand. You waited too long. Now the Meyers campaign has the time and the platform to recover from what could have been a true body blow. They've cut off the infected tissue, so to speak, and they'll live to fight another day." He gestured to her with his pen. "You're tainted now, I'm afraid, and they'll never let you back into their confidence."

He wasn't wrong, and he wasn't right, and it was all too tangled and confusing. It was best to forget what she'd already done and instead focus on what she was about to do.

"Then it's a good thing *that* wasn't my silver bullet, isn't it?" Ingrid swallowed a mouthful of tea, letting the bitter peppermint nip her tongue.

Senator Holt grunted. "I doubt it will much matter at this point, but go on."

Ingrid pulled the formula from her pocket and held it before her. "This is a formula for artificial flare."

Senator Holt stood abruptly, reaching across the desk to take the paper from her. "This is . . ." He ran a hand through his graying hair. "This could be very useful."

"I thought so." Ingrid tried her best to keep the smugness from her voice. Just as Senator Holt had said, she had to know when to play her hand, and the time had come to play the first real round.

"Now, what to do with it, is the question." Senator Holt stood up and began to pace behind his desk. "Revealing the Meyers campaign's discovery would be one option. It might work, but it would be so messy. It might be enough to ruin her chances, but if there's no actual election fraud, people will talk, and then there will always be questions about who was rightfully elected and so on. Besides, it would mean sharing this formula with the world, and I can't begin to imagine the ramifications. All exports would cease, of course. The value of our land would diminish. Candesce would no longer be special."

Ingrid tightened her jaw to stop herself from saying what she was thinking, that it was not Candesce that would no longer be special, but Senator Holt and all his magic-rich friends.

"You mentioned you were running out of flare." Ingrid forced herself to slow down so as not to appear too eager. "So make some."

"Indeed. This *will* be useful." He shook the paper.

"If the Meyers campaign is planning to use such underhanded tactics, you may as well level the playing field," she said—too quickly, too confidently. "Right?" she added, injecting her voice with an uncertain wobble not her own.

Senator Holt didn't look up. "You can go now, Miss Ellis."

But Ingrid didn't move. She'd done what she'd intended, passing this grenade of information to her target and hoping he'd light the fuse. But she couldn't leave yet. She couldn't appear satisfied—it would surely tip him off to her duplicity—but more than that, she had to know if she was right.

"What about our agreement?"

Senator Holt looked up from the formula slowly, as though his eyes moved through heavy molasses. "Like I said, you're tainted. I cannot allow you to join my family."

It took everything in her not to roll her eyes. "I fulfilled my promise. Now fulfill yours."

She knew he wouldn't. She didn't even hope he would.

Senator Holt sneered. "I don't think I will."

"You promised," Ingrid snarled. She thought he might react this way. She didn't even care so much—the girl who'd wanted a marriage with Linden was long lost to her—but she'd thought somehow at the end of all this, Senator Holt might find it in himself to respect her just a little.

"I don't recall any promise. If only there was a witness or some documentation of the event." He laughed bitterly. "I was never going to give you what you wanted, Miss Ellis. Linden is too precious to give to you. He is more valuable than you will ever be, and I won't waste his potential on you."

Ingrid clenched her fists, her jaw, her very core. "Thanks for nothing."

She'd bear no more of the senator's condescension. She'd thought she'd have to summon false anger to sell her play, but she found it was very, very real. This man had wrecked so many pieces of her life; she wanted to wreck some of his.

"Actually," she said, reaching for his teacup and taking a sip, "thanks for the tea." Then she let the cup fall and shatter on the desk.

Ingrid had never wanted to leave so desperately. If she'd had any flare in her bloodstream, she might have torched the place on her way out. As she departed, she imagined her feet were coals, her breath was fire. Their house was made of wood, and if anger were magic, she'd burn it all to the ground.

"Ingrid?"

The voice came before his touch. Linden's fingers grazed her shoulder, but where calm usually rooted in her chest when he was near, rage burned too bright.

Ingrid didn't know how fragile a breath could be until she tried to inhale and it came, rattling and rioting, into her lungs. "Linden," she croaked.

"What are you—what are you doing here?" he asked, and took a step forward. "Are you all right?"

"I'm sick of being asked if I'm all right." Ingrid threw her hands in the air.

Linden reached for her, drawing her from the hall. She caught sight of a simple walnut-finished headboard and stark white linens before she was engulfed by Linden's arms. She let him hold her for a minute, waiting for her pulse to slow, her anger to ebb, but it never did. It pounded in her veins, threatening to burst from her chest.

"I haven't been all right in years." She ripped herself from his grasp and whirled to face the opposite wall. There, she found bare shelves and a writing desk boasting only a few pens and a briefcase.

Linden rested his knuckles in the small of her back. "You will be, though. I'm here with you."

"With the way things are going, I highly doubt that."

Linden circled her so they stood face-to-face. "I won't let any harm come to you." He pressed his thumb to the inside of her wrist, and almost immediately she felt the quakes in her stomach settling.

She took a breath, and then another, and another, letting his touch soothe her nausea the way it had time and time again. It did not matter in that moment that harm had already come, that nothing could be the way they'd hoped, that even if it could, Ingrid wasn't sure she would hope for it anyway. He was there, and so was she, and that wasn't nothing.

"Whose room is this?" she asked finally.

"Mine," he said. "Not that I've ever lived in it much. I always stayed at Ainsley during school, and we went home to the Alorden estate for most of the holidays." He glanced over at the empty shelves, his eyes sweeping over the room one bland detail at a time. "There's not much in here that really feels like mine, to be honest." Then his eyes landed on her and a smile came to his lips.

Except you.

The words went unsaid, but Ingrid felt them at the center of her spirit, not as the balm he meant them to be but as the knife they were.

"Your father won't let me marry you," she whispered.

Linden shook his head. "He will. You'll see. He'll change his mind."

"He won't. He said—well, he said some things. We'll leave it at that."

"There's nothing he could say that would keep me from you."

Ingrid sighed, her head falling forward onto her chest. "I brought him the intelligence he needed. It wasn't enough. Nothing will ever be enough, Linden. Don't you see that? He was never going to give me a chance. I'm not good enough for your family; I'm not good enough for *you*."

Linden stood, lifting her chin with his fingers. "Let me be the judge of that," he said, and leaned in to kiss her.

Ingrid turned away, letting his lips collide with the side of her jaw. "You don't understand."

"He doesn't control me. I don't need his permission to do what I want. And, Ingrid"—he turned her to face him—"there's nothing in the world I want more than you."

Ingrid crumpled against his chest, burying her face in the apex of his shoulder and collarbone. He smelled like vanilla and pine and dreams she couldn't have anymore. Even if it were possible, Ingrid couldn't say it back. There were a dozen things she wanted more than him.

"We don't need him," Linden was saying as he rubbed slow circles against her spine with the heel of his palm. "I told you, I don't care about this life. I don't care about his permission, I don't care about his world where reputation matters more than respect. I don't want to grow up to be like him, and I'm afraid if I stay there'll be nothing else for me."

Ingrid tensed under his touch. This was a dangerous line of conversation. It led toward uncertainty; it led toward undoing.

"I'm serious." Linden pulled back to look her in the eye, seeming to mistake her discomfort as disbelief. "Let's leave all this behind. I don't want it—the politics, the spotlight, the society—and it doesn't seem to want us either. Why stay?"

"Because"—Ingrid stepped out of his grasp—"this is what we are; this is what we know. This world is all there is."

"It doesn't have to be."

Ingrid choked on the words as they came pouring out, as though she'd held them back a thousand years. "It does, and it is. You don't see it because it's already yours, but for me—for me this is it. This is all I've thought of since I came to Ainsley. This is what I've studied for. This is the finish line. If I don't beat it, it beats me."

Linden cocked his head, his amber eyes gentle against her hostile tongue. "It's not a flare fight, Ingrid. You don't have to prove anything to me. I know you're everything and more. You're the best thing I've ever known. Who cares who else knows it?"

She grimaced. He'd said exactly the opposite the night of their engagement. What she wouldn't have given for him to have felt then what he felt now. But it was too late.

Linden wasn't finished. He trailed his fingers across her collarbone, painting the map of a future on her skin. "We can leave, and maybe we should. Politics makes cannibals of us all, with the constant climb, the never-ceasing gears. This world wants us to devour each other in the race, and I'm not sure it's worth it. While we throw punches, the world keeps turning, the world keeps living without us."

"No, it doesn't." Ingrid pushed her palms against his chest to keep him at arm's length. She needed distance to get through this. "The world keeps *dying*. Do you even know what the world is like outside your bubble? Do you know what it is to live a normal life in Candesce?"

"No," Linden said quietly. "But with you by my side, we can weather anything."

"Could you weather a one-room flat where you wait for your only family to return from his work each night, hoping there will be something to eat when he does, hoping it will be before dark? Could you weather a cold orphanage bed with no blanket, and no heat because no one cares to provide a flare furnace for children like you? Could you weather returning to the capital jail once a month to see the ghost of a father who loves you more than you can let yourself love him?"

Linden kissed her knuckles. "Anything for you."

"All I want is to be like you, Linden. I want to know power the way I know poverty. I want to know privilege the way I know purpose."

"And I want peace. You understand that, don't you? I want to live without the shadow of my father, without the shadow of this nation. I want to be nothing to the press but an old story, and I want to live my life in comfort with you, out of sight. I want to rest my eyes at night and know I can rest my mind too."

Ingrid never wanted to rest. She wanted to work until her bones ached. She wanted to climb as high as she could, then build a ladder so she could climb higher. She never wanted to stop; she never wanted to sleep. She wanted to want and she wanted to reach, and if he didn't, she would carry on alone.

"Then maybe you should leave," she said quietly.

"We. Maybe *we* should leave."

Ingrid let her hands drop. "No, I mean you. You should have the life you want."

"What about you?"

Ingrid shrugged, turning to look out the window. The street below was quiet, the sun setting on more than just the horizon of their city. Flare lamps lit up below them in the dusk, tiny pinpricks of light mapping the world she knew. "You asked me if I would still love you without the politics, without the power."

Linden came to stand behind her, his presence a permeating warmth, though he didn't touch her. "You said you would."

She gripped the window ledge painfully as the words formed on her tongue. A tear fell from her cheek to her bone-white knuckles.

"I lied," she whispered.

She'd known it all along. Before, she'd thought the lie was that she'd love him without his power, without his status. She wanted those more than she wanted him, she knew that now, but what she wanted more than all the magic and money in the world was Linden the way she'd imagined him. She'd wanted a Linden who cared what happened to the world, who'd fight for what was right, who'd help her rise so she could fight for those things too. Maybe she hadn't wanted that all along, but she did now. She wanted him to be someone he wasn't, just as she knew he wanted her too.

"You——" Linden choked out the word, but he couldn't finish.

When she turned to face him, he held both hands to his throat as though the words were stuck, but his eyes told her all she needed to know. "I lied," she said again. "Because I loved you then, and I love you now, but I can't keep loving you like this when it hurts more than it helps, when it means I have to break myself into pieces, hide myself away. Our love isn't good for us, because we aren't us when we're together. I try to be the girl I think you want, and you love her. I love the boy who was his father's son, only better. But you aren't him, and I'm not her. Somehow we've tricked ourselves into thinking this is love."

Linden let out a small sound somewhere between a gasp and groan. His hands trailed down his sternum and came to rest above his heart. The pain in his eyes was excruciating, but Ingrid soldiered on, knowing if she didn't say it now, she could very well find herself in obscurity living out a life by his side, never saying it at all.

"But I love more than what we could be," Ingrid continued. "I love this work, I love Candesce, and more than anything I love all the things I could do. I want to make change, I want to make waves, I want to make history. It hurts to see someone like you, who was given so much just by merit of being born, not want to use that position to do the same."

"I'll stay," Linden said, his words small and sterile. "I'll do whatever it takes. I'll be whatever you want me to be."

She strode the three steps it took to reach him and brought her hand gently to the crook of his neck. "Linden," she said softly, leaning in and letting her lips fall against his cheek. "I want you to be yourself." She kissed one cheek, then the other; then finally she closed her eyes and touched her lips to his, soft and final like a last, tired breath.

She was gone before he opened his eyes, tears dotting her cheeks. But as she stepped out into the street, the wind brushed them away, and she breathed in the night air. It smelled like freedom.

CHAPTER THIRTY-ONE

Ingrid spent the next few days gathering her courage. Though she'd mustered a great deal of bravery already, she had one last battle to fight against the toughest opponent of them all: her own pride.

She slept not a wink the night before, curled tightly on the cushion of her supply closet armchair, but she found a new kind of energy the morning of the election as her boots hit the stairs and she climbed toward the dormitories. She'd not been back since she'd fought with Charlotte, and still, it did not truly feel like home. She raised her hand to knock before realizing it was her own room and she could come and go as she pleased. She didn't need Charlotte's permission.

But she did need Charlotte's help.

The door swung open, and Charlotte leapt back at the sight of her, Ingrid's fist still poised to knock.

"Ingrid? What are you—"

Ingrid lowered her hand and cast her eyes to the floor. "Can I—can I come in?"

Charlotte stepped aside and gestured for her to enter, but Ingrid couldn't seem to make her feet move.

"Well?" Charlotte asked. "Are you coming or going? I have somewhere to be, and—"

"I'm sorry," Ingrid blurted.

Charlotte blinked at her. "You're sorry?" Her jaw relaxed, and she backed up.

"I am." Ingrid leaned against the doorframe, still not sure how to make herself cross over into the room that was not hers and was not Charlotte's but was somewhere in the realm of shared. "I said a lot of things I regret. I can't say I didn't mean them, but I do regret them. I know you didn't sabotage me on purpose, and I know I should have trusted that you'd value our friendship over a story. It turns out, I'm not very good at trust. I don't give it easily, and I'm not worthy of it most times. I want to do better, if—if you'll give me another chance."

"Ingrid Irene Ellis, did you just apologize to me?"

"Did I do a bad job? I can try again—"

Charlotte engulfed her in an embrace. "You did fine."

Ingrid stood rigid in the circle of Charlotte's arms; then she melted, letting all her exhaustion and relief pour into her grip. The last time she'd been held, it had been by arms she'd rejected, arms she didn't deserve, arms she'd broken. Embracing Linden had felt like falling, but this felt like standing up.

"I don't have a middle name," Ingrid murmured against Charlotte's shoulder.

"What's that?"

"A middle name—I don't have one."

Charlotte pulled back, her expression pinched. "You *don't have one*? And you let me keep guessing all this time?"

Ingrid's lips quirked into a smile. "Do you still forgive me?"

"I don't know. This is a big betrayal."

Ingrid let out a long breath.

"I'm kidding, Ingrid. You know that, right?"

Ingrid laughed, but it was half-hearted, the weight of what she had to say next lying low in her lungs. "I know. But there's something bigger—something *a lot* bigger I have to tell you."

"Okay . . ."

"And this time, we're on the record."

The capitol building was a sight to behold. Its architecture suggested thorns, gray iron rising from the street in spires. Ingrid had learned in class that it had been designed originally to mimic the shape of an open hand, five fingers to represent the five districts forming gentle towers around a central hall where the public could meet with their officials, representing the capital. They had never finished construction, however, so only the shell of the concept survived, starkly imprinted against the sky.

"Are you ready?" Charlotte asked, nudging her in the ribs and gesturing toward the building before them.

Charlotte, with all the tact of a bulldozer, had marched Ingrid into the *Candesce Courant*'s offices and demanded an additional press pass to the Senate election. She'd said less than a dozen words to her editor before she had another pass for Ingrid.

As they approached, Ingrid caught sight of Gwendolyn Meyers at the top of the stairs. Dressed in a vibrant blue suit, she stood out against the dark backdrop. Ingrid's eyes snapped from her face to her shoulders to her toes, taking stock. The candidate looked confident, her feet pointed forward, frame square, chin held high.

Perhaps subconsciously, Ingrid had styled herself after Gwendolyn that morning, sporting her own suit of green velvet over a pressed white blouse. Despite herself, it made Ingrid feel more confident somehow, like she was ready to take on the world, or at least the Candesce Senate.

Surrounding the candidate, Ingrid caught sight of familiar faces. So many people she'd worked with and come to know as fiercely loyal and hardworking. Her heart snagged as her gaze fell on Alex, the person she'd hurt the most.

"They'll forgive you," Charlotte murmured.

"Maybe."

"They will! Just give it time."

But Ingrid wasn't there for forgiveness. Like her father said, it was never a guarantee, and it pained her far too much to hope. She would not expect a warm welcome from the people she'd betrayed. All she dared to want was to reveal the truth and get a little justice.

Ingrid watched as Gwendolyn finished with the reporters and made her way toward the entrance. Alex shuffled papers, handing what Ingrid knew were new sets of remarks to different staffers. Even in the last hours of the campaign, he was busy. She longed for that feeling, for the rush of adrenaline that came with the pressure. She longed for the other feeling too—the one that came from being near Alex's inspired calm that made her believe everything would be all right and that she had the power to make it so.

Alex paused on the top step and looked over his shoulder.

She froze. Had he seen her? Would he stop her? Did she want him to?

But then he continued on, jogging to catch up with the others, and they all funneled into the capitol, disappearing from sight.

"What if I'm wrong?" Ingrid whispered.

"You better not be!" Charlotte grabbed hold of her arm and tugged her forward.

"Why, because you have a story hinging on it?"

"No, because more than anything, I want to see Senator Holt break the law and not get away with it." And with that, Charlotte pulled her out of the sun.

The capitol was unimpressive from the inside. The dappled marble floor and stark white walls were a disappointment compared with the exterior, but Ingrid could barely be bothered to care, for in their path was a steadfast Alex, feet planted, jaw set.

"What are you doing here?" he asked.

"We're allowed to go where we please," Charlotte said, waving her press badge around like a weapon.

"I'm not talking to you."

"Well, that's uncalled for. I never did anything to you."

Alex blinked hard. "Not like that—I'm still *talking* to you; I'm just not *talking* to you."

"That sure clears things up," Charlotte grumbled.

Alex turned his attention back to Ingrid. "If Birdie sees you, she'll have a conniption."

"Then she'd best not see me." Ingrid tried to keep her voice light, but inside her heart beat too fast, jumping into her throat as she spoke.

"Go home, Ingrid. You shouldn't be here—maybe after the election things will be different, but for right now, they're all still angry."

Ingrid tried not to flinch. "And you?"

Alex turned his brown eyes up to the ceiling, avoiding her gaze. "Yeah, me too." He chewed his lip. "I'm angry, Ingrid. I'm angrier than I've been in a long time. You took our trust and you threw it in the trash, and you didn't even do it for a good reason. I thought you were better than that and I thought you were smarter than that."

Ingrid gritted her teeth. "Sorry I turned out to be such a disappointment."

"Then don't be one." His gaze fell back to hers, a quiet stillness in their depths. "Listen, I thought you were better and smarter, and I don't think I was wrong. I *hope* not, at least. I want to look back on this someday and be glad you were a part of it."

It was as though her mouth was full of gravel. She couldn't form the words to thank him. He hadn't forgiven her, but maybe he wanted to. And that was almost better. Somehow, Ingrid had stopped living for the future over the last few days. All her life, she'd planned with one eye on the horizon, but lately she'd only been able to process a day at a time. To imagine any further felt extravagant, presumptive. Alex had just reminded her there was more to life than the present, and though it's where they were now, it wasn't where they had to stay.

"Then let me stay," Ingrid murmured. "I want to fix this."

Alex shook his head. "You've already done enough. You don't have to fix this."

"I do," Ingrid said solemnly. "I'll do whatever it takes. I don't care what—I'll do it."

"You don't have to wreck yourself, Ingrid. You just have to stop wrecking us." Alex touched her arm for the briefest of seconds and sighed. "Don't make me regret this." And then he was gone, back with the rest of the Meyers group.

"Come on." Charlotte beckoned her forward.

Together, they entered the Senate chambers.

It was a grand, ovular hall with temporary raised seating

around the edges. The senators were gathered in the center along with President Morris, and near the edge of the pack, Ingrid saw Gwendolyn Meyers and the rest of her staff.

They looked nervous. They looked happy.

On the opposite side of the hall, Ingrid caught sight of the Holt delegation. Senator Holt stood front and center with his new campaign manager at his right hand—a man Ingrid didn't care to know. Linden was nowhere in sight. For a moment, she thought the senator saw her and she froze. His eyes, even from so far away, pierced her through the middle. It was as if he could sense how much she didn't belong. Then his gaze moved on, as though she'd never been there at all.

Ingrid sat back in her chair in the press section beside Charlotte as the other seats around her began to fill with reporters, and she let out a long, quiet breath. It would all begin soon, and then it would happen, and then it would be over. If not Alex, Ingrid thought perhaps it would be she who found herself submerged in regret by the end of this. But what was done was done, and she would simply have to wait it out and see if she drowned.

CHAPTER THIRTY-TWO

To Ingrid, voting was akin to legend. She'd heard tell of voters with barrels full of magic, pouring their fortunes into a candidate's coffers. Ingrid could scarcely imagine having so much flare, and even then she could not imagine simply giving it away.

It seemed such an impractical format, to let go of so much magic all in the hopes their choice would somehow help them earn more. Her civics teacher had said it was like taxes, but with an incentive—the more they gave, the more likely their chosen candidate was to win. And when Ingrid had proclaimed it made no sense, he'd sent her to the dean's office. Now she knew it didn't need to make sense; it just had to be complicated enough that it made the rich feel important.

Faced now as she was with the spectacle of it all, *important* seemed exactly the word for it. Or, perhaps more aptly, *self*-important. There was an extraordinary amount of pomp and circumstance as each member of the Senate marched across the floor to take their seat.

The current tally, represented by two massive glass jugs at the end of the hall, was nearly even, showing the combined votes from Alorden, West Cendium, East Cendium, Excandridge, Cintilmore, and most of the capital. They looked like glimmering decanters, but instead of wine, they held the proportional representation of magical votes cast. Gwendolyn's was slightly fuller, but Ingrid wasn't foolish enough to feel hope just yet. The senators and the candidates themselves had yet to vote.

Ingrid waited with bated breath as the wide doors shuttered to a close and silence fell over the room.

President Morris took to his feet, a weary crease threaded across his brow. The last time Ingrid had seen him, fire had rained from the sky and rebels had crashed through the crowd. Somehow, he felt smaller now. Perhaps it was the impending events that cast a shadow over him. They were, after all, about to choose his successor. Ingrid wondered, though it was his own decision to retire, if he didn't resent the both of them just a bit.

"Welcome, all," he said, his voice steadier than his feet. "The time has come to choose a new leader. Though I have served Candesce with as much grace as I could manage, it is with the utmost respect that I now turn to candidates Meyers and Holt. To you, I say, you are our future; may you earn our favor." He gestured to the open floor and sat back down.

Ingrid leaned forward. The reporter in front of her was blessedly short, so she had a clear view of the space below as Gwendolyn and Senator Holt both made their way to the center. They shook hands, and Ingrid silently cursed their position, as she couldn't see the details of the exchange. What she wouldn't have given to see their faces, to read their lips, to look for signs of distress in their fingers. But the moment was over almost before it had begun.

Craning her neck, Ingrid saw Birdie stand and pass Gwendolyn a small bottle of flare. Gwendolyn squeezed the other woman's shoulder, only to be swatted away unceremoniously.

She glanced at Senator Holt, who stood in low conversation with his new campaign manager. A vial passed between them as well, and Ingrid's heart hammered against her chest.

"Are they going to fight?" Ingrid whispered, leaning toward Charlotte.

"Of course not," Charlotte scoffed. "They outlawed that practice fifty years ago."

"Right." Ingrid recalled reading about the elections of old where presidential candidates would duel for the office. Now they simply performed for the spectacle of it, one last chance to leave an impression on the surrounding audience.

Aside from the debate, Ingrid had never seen Gwendolyn use flare, and what a shame it was. The moment the magic touched her lips, light began to stream from her fingertips. Weightless and frothy, like the foam on a cappuccino, her magic took to the air around her, circling and swirling into hoops. Golden clouds were born above her head, light streaming through them like rays of sun.

Then she began to sing.

It was no song in particular. No lyrics, just bare melody. Ingrid gripped the back of the seat in front of her as the song washed over the crowd. It was full and bright, no hint of a waver. As she sang, the light she created with her flare swirled around her, faster and faster, more and more. It darkened and churned, a stormy night sky. As she hit a crescendo, her magic vanished in a flash. Then golden fire burst from her mouth and expelled toward the ceiling, swooping up toward the dome. The ball of light slowed and tumbled, unfurling sparkling wings. The enormous bird surveyed the Senate with a steady gaze, then burst into a hundred stars.

Ingrid brought her hands together once before she realized no one was clapping. Perhaps applause was not customary, but it seemed a shame when Gwendolyn had exhibited such artistry. It was a joy to see destructive magic used in a beautiful way. Ingrid had nearly forgotten it was fire at its core.

"Wow," said a reporter a few rows down.

Another murmured to no one in particular, it seemed, "Never seen anything like that before."

Ingrid wished, not for the first time, that she was seated below with the rest of her friends. She wanted a chance to ask Alex what was normal in these situations. How had they come to decide this would be Gwendolyn's display? Surely much conversation had gone into choosing the exact song she ought to sing and the right set of flare techniques. If Ingrid had to guess, she thought it likely that most candidates for president displayed force rather than artistry. But she still wished she could ask, if only to hear Alex's answer.

Senator Holt still had his turn to show his own skill, a moment Ingrid hoped would end with his total defamation.

Senator Holt stepped forward with the confidence of a winner. He shot an ill-disguised sneer in Gwendolyn's direction as he moved past her. He lifted the vial up as if toasting the room; then he downed the contents in one swallow.

Ingrid's heart beat an uncomfortable rhythm against her throat. She leaned forward, watching, waiting. Any moment now, it would be clear to everyone something was terribly wrong.

Only, nothing went wrong. Senator Holt punched his fist into the air and a torrent of orange flame burst upward. Fire lingered above them; then with exaggerated force, he shaped it into a cone, spinning like a dancer's skirts around Senator Holt. For a moment, he disappeared completely, consumed by magic. Then his boot appeared, followed by the rest of him, as he stepped through the fire, unscathed, unscarred, not a speck of ash on him.

The fire dissolved into smoke, and Ingrid's last hope went with it.

"No," she whispered against the silence, but no one seemed to notice except Charlotte, who nudged her repeatedly. Ingrid ignored her, following the senator with her gaze. He crossed over to an intern positioned by the flare-filled decanters to point out his barrels of flare. The page counted, bouncing the tip of her pencil at each barrel in turn and jotting down a number. He must have tested the flare beforehand. He knew the coloration was off, so of course he wouldn't use it for something so important as the demonstration. But the barrels—his voting flare—no one would test those until it was far too late to determine *who* had cheated.

Ingrid shot to her feet. "Stop!"

"This is highly irregular." President Morris rose to his feet, his eyes trained on Ingrid.

Ingrid swallowed. She glanced down at Alex, who sat with his head in his hands. "I have reason to believe the senator's flare is impure."

A whisper broke out across the crowd, as if it were one voice sweeping through the room.

"Impure?" the president asked. "How do you mean?"

"It isn't real flare. It's been artificially created."

The president cocked his head and said, "Do you mean to tell me his flare has been tampered with?"

"No," Ingrid said as clearly and loudly as possible. "I don't mean his flare was tampered with. I mean he deliberately solicited and utilized a formula for artificial flare so he could create enough to win the election."

The crowd dissolved into uproar, as though a wildfire had set their chairs alight. Senators stood, shouting at one another unintelligibly. Others simply rose with the rest of the crowd, staring openmouthed at Senator Holt or at Ingrid herself.

Finally, the president calmed them with wild hand gestures, managing to bring most of them back to a seated position. "I'm sorry to say, Miss . . . What is your name?"

"It doesn't matter," Ingrid replied, an edge to her voice.

"Ellis. Her name's Ellis." Senator Holt's words rang out like an accusation, for that was what they were. A name was never just a name, and Senator Holt knew exactly how to weaponize hers. "You might know her as the daughter of Oscar Ellis, convicted some seven years ago for flare theft."

Some members of the Senate nodded knowingly. Others looked on in confusion.

"You'll forgive me, I hope, if I don't take her accusations seriously."

The president fixed her with a searching look. "Come down here, Miss Ellis," he said, curiosity in his tone.

Ingrid had half a mind to refuse. If they were only going to discredit her for the name she happened to share with her father, she didn't want to give them the satisfaction. She could leave this hall with her head held high, without letting them put her on trial for something her father had done. But this was no longer about such trivial things as dignity.

Descending the stairs took what felt like an eon, but when she finally came to stand before the president, he met her on the floor. He looked her in the eye like an equal and said, "I don't care who your father is, Miss Ellis. You've levied an accusation at one of our presidential candidates, and I will not proceed without investigating your claims."

Ingrid's chest bloomed with hope. Now all he had to do was

311

order Holt to use some of the flare bottled up in barrels, and his campaign would be over.

But the president wasn't done. "However, before we continue down this particular road, I'd like to ask a few questions. Artificial flare would be a significant scientific advancement, and none, to my knowledge, has been registered with the government. Is it even possible?"

"It is," Ingrid said through a lump in her throat. "I saw the formula with my own eyes, and I believe it's the one Senator Holt used."

"And why would you imagine that?" the president asked.

"Ingrid." Alex whispered her name, but it carried in the silence.

She looked back at him and remembered his words from before. *You don't have to wreck yourself, Ingrid. You just have to stop wrecking us.* Maybe he was right. Maybe she didn't have to throw herself in front of the proverbial train in order to regain their trust, but maybe she had to do it to win them the election. It wouldn't really be self-sacrifice if it was all for her anyway.

Turning to face the president, Ingrid steadied herself and said, "Because I gave it to him, sir."

"You . . . gave it to him . . ." the president repeated. "Walden, is this true?"

"Of course not!" Senator Holt said dismissively. "She's the daughter of a criminal. Do you really think I'd take political advice from her?"

"Your son certainly didn't seem to have a problem associating with her. It's a valid question," someone grumbled from the risers.

Senator Holt shook his head. "My son's indiscretions have nothing to do with this. I cannot believe you would take some girl's word over mine."

Ingrid narrowed her eyes. "If you're so confident, Senator, why don't you prove your innocence?"

"This is outlandish! Totally unprecedented!"

The president raised his hand between them, effectively silencing their disagreement. "If it's so outlandish, then you should have no trouble proving it." He turned to Ingrid. "And how might he prove it to your satisfaction, Miss Ellis?"

Ingrid bit her lip. "If he's telling the truth, the flare in those barrels should be completely normal. If he's not . . . well . . . the flames will be blue."

"Well, then." The president gestured to the barrels behind Senator Holt. "If you would."

Senator Holt didn't move a muscle. He fixed Ingrid with a vile stare, as though he could somehow incinerate her with his gaze alone. But he'd need flare for that. Her eyes flicked to the barrels behind him, and as if his own thoughts mirrored hers, he let out a heavy breath and retreated.

There was a general bustling from that side of the room as they hastened to remove the barrel lid. With the help of a metal lever, they pried the lid free, and Senator Holt dipped his now empty vial into the liquid within.

Ingrid's heart beat a bruise against her chest as he raised the flare to his lips and drank. For a moment, nothing happened. Then he raised a hand, and orange fire erupted into the air above them, full and bright, the heat of the flame washing over them all.

Everyone stared at Ingrid. Ingrid stared at the senator. The senator brushed his hands together and turned to the president. "Satisfied?"

"Miss Ellis?" President Morris asked with tempered exasperation.

Ingrid swallowed. Sweat pooled in the palms of her hands, and the back of her neck felt overheated, long after the senator's flame had disappeared.

"There are still more barrels, sir," she said quietly, pointing behind the senator to the line of barrels—at least a dozen. She was certain he'd cheated; they'd just not yet found the artificial product. The senator wasn't a stupid man. He wouldn't have filled all twelve barrels with it. He'd have mixed them in among genuine magic.

The senator didn't wait for the president's pronouncement. He simply turned on his heel and repeated the procedure with the second barrel with the same result.

"I can do this all day," he said sharply.

Ingrid watched with a slowly deflating heart as the senator drank and used the flare in each barrel with the same effects. There was no sign of blue fire. The senator had told the truth. The magic was real.

"I think that's enough," the president said, punctuating his words carefully. "This has been a waste of time. Frankly, I question whether or not you had any reason for this but to cast doubt on the senator. I'll have no further interference on this matter. Kindly remove yourself." He turned away, motioning in the air with his left hand.

Before Ingrid had time to process what he'd said, she was grabbed by both elbows and forced toward the door by two Flare Force officers. Her heart sank as far as it could go, as if she'd crushed it beneath her own boots with each step. She'd sought to discredit him, and instead it was she who'd been discredited.

She'd gambled, and she'd lost.

One of the Flare Force officers shouldered open the door and pushed her through, sending her back into the hall.

She was met by a wall of white masks. The Shadow of the Flame stood resolute and ready, violence in their eyes and fire in their hands.

But something was wrong; something was different.

Their fire was a blinding, brilliant blue.

CHAPTER THIRTY-THREE

Ingrid stared into the face of rebellion. The Shadow of the Flame stared back.

The two Flare Force officers at her sides jumped in front of her to block the attackers. From behind them, Ingrid could hear the crackle and snap of flame, so close, so hot.

"Warn them!" one of the soldiers said through gritted teeth.

Ingrid took off at a run back through the doors. "Run!" she screamed into the stillness. "They're attacking! The Shadow of the Flame is here!"

For a moment, no one moved. They all stared at her like she spoke another language, like she was playing some elaborate prank on them all.

Then, with a roar unlike anything Ingrid had ever heard, the doors burst open, and blue fire poured inside, a rumbling, fiery wave.

Panic built up in her throat, suffocating like smoke. And then there was *real* smoke billowing up from every corner, filling the air, blocking her path. She forged on, swiping at the air to see. She had to find the other door. She had to get out. Stumbling forward, Ingrid looked for a telltale flash of Gwendolyn's satin or the distinctive curl of Alex's hair. They had to be there somewhere, and Ingrid would not leave without them. In that moment, it didn't matter whether they would ever deign to call her a friend again. She just needed them to be safe. She just needed them to live.

Alex had said love was love, and love was caring whether the people in her life survived a rebel attack. She needed them to live because she needed them to know she cared, she needed them to know, no matter how messy and imperfect she was, that she loved them—all of them.

"Alex!" she yelled into the chaos. Pandemonium had spread out across the room, politicians and reporters alike all pressed together in a mass exodus, funneling like ants through the single exit on the opposite wall. "Charlotte? Birdie?" she cried out, cycling through their names one by one until her voice grew hoarse. She let herself be pushed toward the door, no longer struggling against the current, until she was outside, back in the courtyard where she'd stopped Alex before.

Stumbling over her own feet, she quickly sidestepped the flow of people and scanned the crowd. She found them standing in a corner at the edge of the stairs. They stood in a circle, bent low in conversation. Gwendolyn held Birdie's hand tightly in her own, no sign of protest from the campaign manager, whose face was ghostly white.

Alex gripped the small vial of flare Gwendolyn had used and cupped Clarence's shoulder with the other. The others pooled together in a tightly tangled knot of disbelief.

Ingrid tried to read their energy. Would she be welcome there? She cast her eyes around for Charlotte, but before she could find her, the others spotted her. Birdie waved her over, an unreadable expression on her face.

"You're okay," Ingrid said upon her approach. "I'm so glad you're all okay."

"Thank you, Ingrid," Gwendolyn said stiffly.

Ingrid felt the gratitude grate against her insides. No matter if Gwendolyn was genuine, Ingrid couldn't accept it. She'd done more harm than good to the campaign, and since she couldn't find it in herself to move past it, she doubted any of them could.

"There are still people inside," Alex said through clenched teeth.

Ingrid looked back at the building as the stream of people slowed and then stopped. "Charlotte?" she asked quietly. "Has anyone seen Charlotte?"

"Your friend?" Alex shook his head. "I think she's still inside."

"They'll find her, Ingrid," Faye murmured. "Flare Force will save her."

"No, they won't." Alex gritted his teeth. "They'll prioritize capturing the rebels over saving innocents. They're not looking for survivors; they're looking for a fight."

Alex's words were all it took to send Ingrid into motion. She snatched the bottle of flare from his hand and said, "Then I'll have to do it myself."

She charged for the door, uncorking the vial as she went. When the magic hit her blood, it was like the rest of the world melted away in the heat.

A flame reached down her throat to take root in her belly. It twined through her, making familiar marks against her insides, a slow burn, reminding her it was in charge. But Ingrid didn't have time to let fire rule the day. She would not let magic hold her back. She closed her eyes and leaned against the wall, listening for the snap, crackle, pop of roaring fire as it filled her from the inside out. And then she followed its path down her tongue, draping her mind around it like coiling threads until they were one.

She wasn't just full of fire; she *was* fire. She would walk among rebels, she would find Charlotte, and she would burn everyone else in her way, even if she had to burn along with them.

Gathering herself, Ingrid focused on the image of flame appearing in her hands, willing it to become true. Warmth filled her hand, but it was not the familiar touch of flame that found her now. It was Alex.

"You can't go alone," he said into her ear.

When she opened her eyes, Ingrid did not expect to see him standing before her, certain she had imagined it, but there he was, his brow resolute, his gaze a riot of emotion. From her other hand, he took the vial and downed the rest, before pulling her forward. Fire pooled between their interlocked fingers. Alex held tight to her, even when flame burst out from their skin. Ingrid's grip was just as firm, afraid to let go in case he vanished like smoke.

"Ready?" Alex asked as they approached the main door to the Senate chambers.

Ingrid nodded once. She didn't think she could speak, certain that it would be fire, not words, on her tongue.

He waited a beat, breathing in and out. Her heart beat furiously in her chest, in her arms, in her wrists. With the same sudden desperation that she needed to save Charlotte, she needed to tell Alex—

He pushed the door open and led her into the inferno.

Blue and orange fire warred like different factions of the same family. They both burned bright, leaving charred wreckage in their wake. Through the smoke and bursts of colorful flare, Ingrid could see bodies moving, more shadow than human as they navigated around one another. She couldn't tell which was rebel and which was officer but for the color of their fire.

She looked to Alex, following his line of sight toward what remained of the risers.

"I don't see her," she said. She could barely hear herself, the rush of fire in her blood too loud in her ears.

Alex shook his head. "Take the left. I'll go right. Check under the seats."

He let go, leaving her suddenly cold, even though sweat had begun to bead on her forehead, the heat of magic blistering the very air around them.

He gave her a final look that said all too plainly, *Stay out of trouble*, as though they weren't both neck deep in it already. The unpredictable nature of trouble made her feel more alive than all the safety and certainty a plan could promise anyway. Still, Ingrid did her best to travel unnoticed through the haze of smoke. Her skill with flare was all instinct and no training. If she found herself in a fight, she'd be surely outmatched.

Creeping along the edge of the hall, which looked more and more like an arena with each passing moment, she fixed her gaze low. If Charlotte were still there, she'd be hiding.

If she were still alive.

Ingrid shook herself of the thought. It wasn't worth considering now. Dread would only slow her down. Instead, she mounted the stairs, praying they were still intact and would hold her weight, and made her way down each row, checking the ground for bodies—alive or dead.

A layer of ash covered the floor, and Ingrid tried not to think too hard about what—or who—they'd been originally as it crunched beneath her feet. A reporter, who looked to have suffered a blow to the head rather than any magic-inflicted injuries, lay on the floor in the seventh row from the top. Ingrid checked for a pulse but found none. Perhaps it was for the best, for when she removed her hand, she found the skin of his wrist burned, a layer of flame softly flowing from her hand.

Spend it or it will spend you.

Ingrid shuddered but stood to continue her search all the same. She tried to focus, but with each row she cleared, Ingrid's vision clouded. Her skin felt clammy, and little bits of magic leaked from her fingertips, showering flame down on the floor in her wake. She knew what was coming, and there were only two outcomes: She could let the fire consume her, or she could use it. Magic climbed in her, building to a fever. It was overwhelming, overflowing. A single coherent thought passed through her mind—that perhaps she should have waited to drink the flare until she knew she needed it—before she hit the floor.

Woozy and more than a little bruised, Ingrid let go of a burst of flame. Fire lurched from her fingers and leapt from skin to air with the freedom of a falling star. It jumped from her hands, a dance more than a blast. She sighed, relief flooding through her with the same torrential energy as magic, and she turned on her side. Wide brown eyes stared back at her from under the chairs, unblinking.

Ingrid's heart skipped. It was Charlotte.

"Get out of here!" Charlotte mimed pushing her away.

Forget skipping, Ingrid's heart did a full somersault. "You're alive," she breathed.

"It's not safe."

Ingrid glared. "You're telling me? What are you doing here? They'll kill you if they find you!"

"Someone has to tell this story."

"You can't tell it if you're dead."

Before Charlotte could reply, a jet of blue flame came arcing down at them from above. Without thinking, Ingrid rolled out of the way, crashing straight into Charlotte and toppling them both into the row of chairs before them.

"The blue looks so peaceful," Charlotte whispered. "*Looks* being the operative word, I guess."

"Blue . . ." Ingrid stopped breathing as the pieces began to fall into place. Senator Holt's flare was supposed to be blue, but instead, the rebels had come in with azure fire blazing from their hands. Could it be?

A rebel, dressed in what had surely once been a white mask before the fighting began, loomed over them, hands brimming with magic.

Ingrid leapt to her feet and squared off against him, heart hammering faster than she'd thought possible.

"I don't want to fight you," Ingrid said. "I just want to take my friend and leave."

"Get out of here," he growled.

Ingrid raised her hands to fight.

The rebel sent a jet of blue fire at her. It sped past her right side, so close she could feel its heat. She clapped her hand over her ear, feeling a distinct lack of hair along the side of her head.

"Okay, maybe I *do* want to fight you," she said, throwing a handful of fire at him.

They carried on, volleying magic back and forth, but they were both running low on magic, and their battle was little more than a highly dangerous game of dodgeball. At long last, Ingrid tried to send another jet of fire at the rebel, but nothing happened. Her hands were empty, and they were cold. She was out of flare, and she was out of time.

The rebel grinned beneath his mask, mustache twitching. "I win," he said in a gruff, familiar voice. "Now leave."

"I know you," she said quietly. It felt surreal that in this moment of life or death she cared more about the puzzle of his identity than escaping, but she'd seen him before. She'd seen him at the President's Ball, and she'd seen him again . . . but where?

Blue fire pooled in his hands, readying as much as he had left to engulf her. Ingrid tensed her shoulders and bent her knees. Maybe she could still escape this unscathed. With all the might she had left, she sprang into a run. The rebel followed, his magic still growing. She braced for impact, ready to accept her fiery end if it meant saving Charlotte. If she had her wits about her, Charlotte would take this opportunity to flee, ensuring Ingrid's sacrifice wasn't in vain.

As it turned out, Charlotte did not have her wits about her. She extracted herself from her hiding place, grabbed hold of a chair, and wrenched it from the floorboards with ease. Then she swung high and she swung hard.

The rebel froze; his magic faded along with his consciousness.

"Go! Get out of here!" Ingrid cried.

"Not even a *thank you*?" Charlotte gave her a disgruntled look.

"Now isn't the time." Ingrid grabbed ahold of her arm and pulled. "Come on."

Ingrid started toward the exit but tripped over the rebel in her path. Pausing, she bent down to get a better look.

"You found her!" Alex gasped, jogging over to join them, but he too paused, his enthusiasm fading as he leaned over Ingrid to look down at the rebel. "What's wrong?"

Ingrid couldn't put her finger on what, exactly, it was, but a certainty boiled in her stomach. It was a solid, heavy thing, the wrongness that rose in her as she reached out to remove the rebel's mask. Before her was the wrinkled complexion and waxy mustache of a solid memory. "I know him," she whispered.

"From where?" Alex asked.

"I—I don't—" But Ingrid's mind worked faster than her words, piecing it all together. She removed what remained of his mask to reveal the superior brow and crisp mustache of the senator's valet. The pieces fell into place—his presence in the garden right before the attack at the President's Ball, on the train from West Cendium before it exploded. He'd always been there. But he wasn't the architect of the rebellion.

"It's Holt," she said. "It's all been Holt. This man is his servant." She looked up, almost too overwhelmed by the realization to say it aloud. "The flare formula I gave Holt was supposed to turn the magic blue. And his flare was fine before because it was actually flare. He didn't need more for the election; he needed more for the rebels, because . . . because . . ."

Charlotte and Alex stared at her in disbelief, their mouths open, their eyes wide and unfocused. She could hardly believe what she was saying herself, but even so, she thought they'd have more to say about the matter.

"Come on," she said. "He's the one who's supplying the rebels. He's not cheating in the election so much as he is committing treason in an attempt to, I don't know, destabilize Candesce? Force the election to focus on this?"

"Ingrid, I—" Alex began.

Ingrid cut him off. "Don't you see? He's behind it all."

"And he's behind you too," said a voice she knew, deep and drizzled with the false sweetness of political seasoning.

She blinked, seeing now that Charlotte and Alex were not staring *at* her but *past* her. Turning slowly, Ingrid saw him, a towering figure, bathed in flame. He held orange in one hand, blue in the other, and in the duality of light, smoke swirling against the walls, understanding curling around her heart, Ingrid saw Senator Holt for what he truly was: a monster.

CHAPTER THIRTY-FOUR

"Run!"

Charlotte and Alex didn't need telling twice. The dampened thud of their feet against the ashy floor was the only sound as Ingrid stared down her adversary.

"Ingrid? Come on!" Alex shouted over his shoulder.

Ingrid didn't move. Her feet felt like lead, like roots, like claws. Maybe she couldn't run. Maybe she didn't want to. Part of her had always known it would come to this. Her and Senator Holt, a fight on their fingertips. Of course, she'd thought they would be arguing over Linden, not over the moral compass of Candesce, and she'd thought they would duel with words, not magic.

Out of the corner of her eye, she saw Alex and Charlotte duck out through a side door. She had to hope they understood she had no plans to follow, that she would occupy him as long as she could while they fetched help.

Ingrid squared her shoulders. "You've gone too far."

"I'll go further," Senator Holt said.

The room had grown still, and much of the smoke had cleared. The dead piled up around the edges like sandbags awaiting a flood. Some wore white masks, others wore uniforms, and at least as many were neither rebel nor soldier, simply in the wrong place at the wrong time.

A few feet away, movement caught her eye. Ingrid turned to see a rebel pushing himself up on his forearms, groaning as he tried to stand.

Senator Holt sent a jet of orange fire at him and it hit the man squarely in his mask, consuming it and his face beneath. He wobbled before crumpling to the ground once more, silent and still.

"No one will stop me."

Ingrid stared at the body, mouth agape. "But he was one of yours—and you killed him?"

The senator shrugged, readjusting the magic in his hands. Each flame burned a little brighter, a little higher, for a moment, a technique Ingrid recognized from her own attempt to burn off the excess earlier. "I don't need any witnesses."

"So you're killing everyone who sees you for what you are, no matter who they fight for?" Ingrid grimaced. "Is that why you let them kill Gerald Cork?"

A sneer uncoiled on his face. "Cork was weak willed. He couldn't stomach the tactics of a winner, so he had to go."

"You could choose to be a merciful man."

The senator laughed, a cold and heartless sound, as though he'd only heard of laughter by rough description. "Mercy is not the man; it is the tool. These souls are more use to me dead, as are you." He held out a hand, and a tornado of flame spiraled toward her.

Blue and orange fire curled around her body, licking at her clothes, at her hair, at her skin. At first, she felt nothing; then heat took hold and didn't let go. She whirled about, hands dancing, trying to extinguish a flame far larger than her palm. There was nowhere to run, and there was nothing to do, except fall to the fire and burn.

Ingrid's body hit the floor, and she realized with a sudden heaviness that it was where she ought to be. Fire stung her eyes, blistered her palms and forearms, burned her skirt with unmatched hunger, but it was the heat in her lungs that overpowered her— soft and creeping—then it took root deep inside her, closing a fiery fist around her beating heart.

And that's when she heard it, a soft whisper of magic inside her. Or was it outside her? It beat a rhythm against the floor, against her skin, against her mind. All she had to do was open her mouth and let it inside. With her eyes closed, she drank, and she tasted the sharp flavor of hope.

Ingrid's eyes snapped open, and the fire outside her seemed to cool in contrast to the one raging inside. The flare she'd drunk earlier had expired long ago, but now she felt the strong grip of magic pulsing along with her rapid heartbeat. Flare awakened inside and out. She glanced down at herself to find the fire had stopped devouring her clothes. Instead, it had begun siphoning away from a small puddle on the floor to gather in her palms. A barrel stood mere feet away, a large crack in its side, spilling flare onto the floor in just the right place.

Ingrid stood up and walked through the fire and into the clear air beyond in mimicry of the senator's display before the Senate.

His expression turned to mild surprise at the sight of her, an underwhelming reaction if ever she'd seen one, but now was not the time for vanity.

"You were wrong," she said, now actively drawing power from the well in her center.

"About what?"

"You keep doing these terrible things—inciting a rebellion to win this election, killing innocent and guilty people alike because you think you get to pass judgment, hoarding your wealth as though you alone are exempt from the pitfalls of greed—and you think you can because you're untouchable. You think no one will stop you, but you're wrong."

"Who will stop me, little girl?" he spat, the fire in his hands nothing to the inferno behind his eyes.

Ingrid slid her stance apart, weight on the balls of her feet. "I will."

She didn't wait. She struck first, sending a fistful of orange fire toward him. He ducked, but she tried again, bobbing and weaving around him as she did, trying to make no discernible pattern with her movements. It would do her no good if he could predict where she'd go. She needed to stay fast and keep him distracted. The longer they fought, the better her chances of survival.

"Is that all you've got?" he asked as he dodged another ball of fire—orange this time.

"I'm just getting started." But it wasn't true. As she moved about the Senate hall, dashing along the rows of burned chairs and ducking behind a roughly charred podium, her breath came uneven and stabbing pain tormented her right side. She was not used to such intensive physical activity. The magic inside her began to wane as well. She'd hurled almost everything she had at him, and he'd dodged all her attacks. Now she had only one or two more balls of fire left before she'd run out of magic.

Casting her gaze about for another source of magic, Ingrid's eyes fell on the barrels of flare. Some were empty, undoubtedly used in the fight; others were cracked or broken. The nearest barrel was only a few yards away. She just had to get to the spill zone before he tried to immolate her again. She sprinted, leaping over rubble and bodies on her way. *Almost there.*

She felt the fire before she saw it. A massive column of orange flame sprang up before her, stopping her path. The senator must have worked out the same logic. She turned quickly to go back the other way, but another wall, this one of blue fire, trapped her there. Two fires, two colors, two ways she could not run.

No one was coming to save her, not Alex and Charlotte, not Flare Force reinforcements. So she faced the senator head-on, waiting to catch fire.

The echo of Senator Holt's boots as they clicked against the floor filled the quiet. He took a drink from a vial of flare hanging around his neck, too long, too much. It was enough flare to turn her to ash and then some.

"Are you going to kill me?" Ingrid asked, surprised to find no fear lurking beneath her tongue. She did not feel brave either, but such was the way of it when she'd already outrun death before. A part of her felt she'd been living on borrowed time since her father left. Of course, Senator Holt would probably say she'd *stolen* that time.

"Yes." Senator Holt narrowed his eyes. "But first, I want to know how you did that. How did you make magic without any flare?"

"Maybe I'm just better at this than you." Ingrid shrugged, stalling. The little magic she still held in her veins was beginning to twist and curdle inside her. Soon, it would turn on her too. She had to use it, but what use was a fight when Senator Holt held all the power and she held none?

The senator scoffed. "You, who have had no training? I don't think so. You've learned some trick or other. I've been at this much longer than you, but even I can't make magic out of nothing."

"You get used to making something from nothing when you're born to it, even if all you can make is hope."

She took a step forward, then another, and another, letting her magic leak slowly toward the ground and across the floor. The senator's expression grew wary the closer she came, sweat beading on his brow. His breaths became more labored from the flare building in his body.

Ingrid stopped a few yards away. She didn't need to get any closer, not now that she could hear the pulse of the flare in his veins, pounding a rampant rhythm of adrenaline. She closed her eyes and spread her arms wide, as though to welcome death by his hand, to embrace her fiery end.

"The good news is, you get to be right about me, Senator Holt," she said as slowly as she could, winding her flare around his, the way she had with Louise back at the speakeasy.

"Right about you?"

"I am my father's daughter." She grinned, letting her smile spread wide and wicked across her face. Her fingers tingled with the warmth, and she opened her eyes on hands full of bright fire. One orange. One blue. Both hers.

Senator Holt raised his hands to ignite her, but realization dawned on him rather too late. She watched as his eyes traveled to his hands, where only a trickle of flare remained.

"Thief!" he spat, and uncorked another vial of flare, downing it in one gulp. Then he swallowed another, and another.

"Thief," she agreed. Then she pulled the flare taut, revealing the strings of magic she'd pulled from him. Ingrid had followed the call of magic from her veins to his and made what was not hers bend to her will. Magic was disloyal, she'd found, and though she'd first employed the technique out of a desperate need to save

331

Linden—and Louise too—this time, she did it to save only herself.

"How are you doing this?" Senator Holt asked through a clenched jaw. Pain lanced through his eyes as she unraveled his magic. "That's mine!"

"Have I impressed you yet, Senator?" she spat. It had been so long ago she'd sat in that hospital room, craving nothing but his acknowledgment. Now all she wanted from him was his silence.

"Is that what this is about?" he asked, an edge to his voice. "You still want my approval?"

She shook her head, beginning to feel dizzy from the heat of all the magic she'd taken. "It is you who should be seeking my approval. I may not be able to vote, but what is a vote worth, really? I don't need to vote to ruin you now." The words felt crisp and burned, like they'd languished too long over hot flames.

"Give it back, little girl." He scoffed. "You can't kill me with my own flare."

"I could," she said, but her voice wobbled.

He sneered. "Is that really what you want to do?"

With a twisted cinch of her stomach, she knew the answer. *Yes.* She wanted to watch him burn. She wanted to see his skin melt from his face as he screamed, his bones turn to ash on the ground, his life leave his body like a wisp of smoke. She wanted to watch him die.

But she didn't want to kill him.

"No," she whispered.

His smile twisted. "I knew you didn't have it in you. That's the difference between you and me. You *want* power; I simply take it."

"That's not the difference." She let her hands fall, as if in defeat. "You may take power, you may take flare, but you want to keep it all for yourself."

332

Senator Holt laughed. "And you don't?"

"I don't, Senator. I'm willing to share." And she let go, allowing all the magic in her body to siphon back into his.

For a single moment, his eyes burned triumph. Then they just burned.

A dozen Flare Force officers flooded inside, their hands lit with orange fire, but their flames didn't hold a candle to the senator's inferno.

Energy rocketed from him, a shock wave of light and heat. It knocked Ingrid off her feet, her body sliding back along the floor, collecting bruises as she went. Her head knocked against the president's podium. She felt a trickle of blood easing down her face, but she barely noticed the pain.

She scrambled to sit up, her gaze falling on the senator in the center of the room. He howled as bright light shone through him as though he were transparent, as though he were the sun itself. And then he was only a man, falling to the ground and splintering into a cloud of dust.

CHAPTER THIRTY-FIVE

Prison was not so small a place as Ingrid had thought. From the outside looking in, visiting once a month, she'd seen only a sliver of what lay beyond the iron bars. She imagined, apart from her visits, her father's life must be terribly dull. He sat in his cell, pondering his crimes, his mistakes, his memories, for hours and hours until she returned.

But she was wrong.

Ingrid arrived not at all on schedule after she'd debriefed a room full of terribly important people, as Officer Scott was eager to tell her. Despite her chains, he treated her still with an odd civility that felt wrong, somehow. It was as though he were talking to a version of her that no longer existed, treating her like the girl she'd assembled for his benefit over the years rather than the girl she was, raw and wretched in the aftermath of battle.

He'd taken her to her cell, so like a bellhop she would have tipped him, had she any coin. But then she was alone, and her cell was no penthouse suite. It was a small space, barely room enough for a cot. She sat in the center of the old mattress and found herself looking out rather than in. She felt so minuscule in the wake of what had brought her here, and she shivered.

She stared down at her palms. How long had it been since she'd held fire in her hands? Since she'd let a man's greed kill him? Since she'd unapologetically survived? She almost couldn't remember, like it had happened to someone else.

But it had happened to her, or she'd happened to it.

Either way, here she was, behind bars. It was where people went when they'd done wrong. But *wrong* was a faraway word, reserved for people who committed crimes, who cheated in elections, who lied to their friends and betrayed them. She'd done wrong before, and she'd felt the wounds it left on her heart. But this . . . this didn't feel wrong. This felt right.

At least twice, a guard came to fetch her and led her to the cafeteria at mealtimes, but Ingrid didn't remember eating. She passed through the days—how many, she couldn't be sure—in a haze. She might have slept, but it was difficult to tell the difference when consciousness didn't feel like being awake. She couldn't tell if she moved through the world too slowly or if the world moved too quickly around her. Either way, they were out of sync, and Ingrid wasn't sure she didn't prefer it this way.

Finally, Ingrid woke with a firm sense of presence and a hunger in her belly. It was as if for the last few days she'd been concussed—and perhaps she had been. She could remember her fight with the senator in only muddled detail, and the pain she felt through her entire body was strangely dulled.

Keen to be taken to breakfast, Ingrid tripped over her boots on the way to the door. They were a size too large, as they'd none that fit her, and she'd been permitted no laces to tighten them. Peering out between the bars, Ingrid swept her gaze up and down the hallway. A block of cement stood opposite her cell, but she could see out of the corner of her eye that other such cells lined her side of the hall.

"Hello?" she said tentatively.

"Finally, she speaks!" a voice replied.

Ingrid could see dark brown curls peeping through the bars of the cell next to her.

"Who's that?" she asked.

"None of your business."

Ingrid's insides seemed to shrink, and her hands felt weak as they gripped the bars. There were others. She'd known there were, of course. They'd all been there at mealtimes, and she'd sensed if not seen them leave their cells with guards to be taken to their labor. But Ingrid had not truly processed what it meant to be inside these walls with others.

"Did any of you know a girl named Louise?" Maybe she'd be able to earn some goodwill with these people if they knew she was friendly with one of their own. "She was here a few months before she got out on bail."

"If you want to kill her, I won't be helping you find her."

"I don't want to kill her," Ingrid said in a rush.

"You'd say that even if you did."

"Pay Agnes here no mind, child," another voice chimed in. "She's had murder on the brain since she killed her husband near ten years ago."

"You'd have killed him too, given the chance." The woman called Agnes scoffed loudly. "As if you didn't stab your own kin, Dot."

"Yes, but I didn't kill him."

"What difference does that make?"

"About a decade off my sentence."

For the first time since she'd faced fire and won, Ingrid felt the cold tendrils of fear wrap around her wrists. How long would she stay here? She had no money for a legal defense. Maybe it didn't matter. Her version of events was the truth, but lies seemed to hold more power in Candesce. No one would listen to the word of a school-aged girl with a convict father over the unimpeachable honor of a senator, whether or not he was dead. The reality of her circumstances thundered against her chest, echoing down the hall like boots on concrete.

"Who's this?" Agnes asked before Ingrid could come up with a reply.

"Fancy man for you, dearie?"

It took Ingrid a moment to realize they were talking to her, the sound of her panic far louder than their voices.

"Ingrid."

She rubbed at her eyes, willing her pulse to calm. Her throat was too dry; her ears rang with the sound of a friend calling her name, a painful, piteous hallucination.

"Ingrid. Ingrid!"

Ingrid looked up.

There before her was an unexpected but not altogether unwelcome sight.

"Linden?" Ingrid was mere inches from him, though they were separated by bars. "Are you . . . here? How is that possible?" She looked past him for a sign of Officer Scott, but he wasn't there.

"He sure is, dear," said Dot.

"You'd best marry him if he's asking. It's slim pickings in here," Agnes added.

"I'm not asking," Linden said quietly. "I swear. That's not why I've come."

Ingrid barely heard them. It was as though the rest of the world had melted away, and a loud humming had filled the space it used to occupy.

"Why *are* you here?" she asked, fearing for a moment that he'd come to tell her she would stay there forever, that he thought her a liar and a thief like her father, that the rebellion was all her, and other such lies. Would they kill her? Surely not without a trial.

Linden cut her spiraling short with an answer. "I've come to bring you home." He blinked, a frown creasing his face. "Or rather wherever you'd like to call home. I realize that isn't with me anymore, of course. But you understand what I mean."

"Not in the slightest." Ingrid tried to laugh, but it came out wobbly. "Do you mean I'm free to leave?"

"You will be in a minute. The front guard went to get the key—odd fellow. I thought he'd have me wait by the door, but he let me come through. Said you'd likely want to see me, though I didn't think that was right, and I tried to tell him so, but he just—"

"Linden." Ingrid cut through his words, letting her fingers reach through the bars as far as they would go. "I'll always want to see you." She smiled sadly, knowing the words were true but in a different way than they might have been once before. He was not the warmth in her cheeks or the heavy rush in her chest, he was not an embrace to come home to or even a person she really knew, but he was Linden, and she didn't think there would come a time when she didn't feel just a little joy to see his face.

The tips of his fingers reached for hers, and they touched, ever so briefly. Then they both let their hands fall, a shared agreement that this was not the way of them anymore.

Ingrid cleared her throat. "I thought you were leaving."

"I thought so too." He swallowed, casting his gaze to his feet. "I didn't even make it to the train station before I turned around. I couldn't—not when I knew—I couldn't let him do what he was doing."

Ingrid snapped to attention. "What do you mean? You knew?"

Linden shrugged a shoulder. "Not exactly. I suspected not all was aboveboard, but I also didn't want to see it. I wanted everything to be easy and everything that wasn't to be someone else's problem. But that's it, isn't it? That's what you were trying to tell me. That *someone else* is you—or people like you. It's always someone, and for better or worse, people listen when I speak. I may not want to run for office or live my life in the public eye, but that doesn't mean I can't still do . . . *something*."

Ingrid's chest swelled, a slow inflation as she made room in her heart for this new version of an old boy. "I'm glad," she whispered, and she found it was an understatement.

"I wanted to run away from the problems my father caused instead of dealing with them, and the fact of the matter is, it's not better to run, just easier. Many things have been made easier for me, I know, just by virtue of my birth. It may not be in my blood to fight, but it's in yours, and you showed me how." He took a deep breath, as though preparing for a rigorous climb. "I don't have so many passions as you. I haven't had many things worth fighting for, but I think I finally found something I care about enough to really do the work."

"What's that?" Ingrid asked, her breath tight in her chest, unsure if she wanted to know the answer.

"Me," he said in a heavy exhale. "It's like you said, I wasn't being myself with you. I was trying to be some version of myself I wasn't, and it was killing me—it was killing you too. We don't deserve that; *I* don't deserve that. I deserve a chance to be who I am and grow into that person. I never could have done that in the shadow of my father."

Ingrid winced. "I can't honestly say I'm exactly sorry about that."

"I wouldn't ask you to be."

"Are you—how are you coping?" Ingrid asked. She couldn't feign sorrow over Senator Holt's death, but the pang she felt at the thought of Linden alone was almost more than she could stand. She'd left their romance behind, but she was glad to find she could still care about him.

"I'm a little numb, to be honest. I wish . . . Well, I wish a lot of things. I loved my father, but I don't think I liked him very much. That's a terrible thing to say, but it's the truth."

"I don't think it's terrible."

"Thanks." Linden wrung his hands. "I think it will be some time yet before I believe that too. I'll be moving back to Alorden for a while after everything is squared away with the inquiry."

"The inquiry?"

"I told the Senate what I knew, and I think it helped. They still have a lot more questions about the reach of Father's activities and the Shadow of the Flame, but I can only tell them so much. Really, Victor's the one who's helped the most."

"Victor?"

"My father's valet. He confessed it all, told them how the senator hired impostors to act like the Shadow of the Flame. He had it in his head the only way to beat Gwendolyn Meyers was to make those with the most voting power fear the people she wanted to champion. Worst of all, he wasn't even wrong. If not for your interference, I think most of the Senate would have voted for him."

Ingrid blinked rapidly, trying to keep up with Linden's words. "Does that mean they believe me?"

Linden grinned. "You, Ingrid Ellis, are no longer under suspicion of treason. A few senators are actually calling you something of a hero, but I think they were predisposed to think so, as they were already my father's political enemies."

"I'm not a hero," Ingrid grumbled.

"Well"—Linden quirked a lip as he stepped out of the way to let Officer Scott unlock her door—"you're *my* hero."

"Please," Office Scott said, rolling his eyes. "Don't give her an ego. She was just becoming tolerable."

Ingrid and Linden left together, pausing for her to collect her things. She hadn't had much on her when she'd arrived. Her dress had been mostly destroyed, so even though her prison clothes were hardly the most fashionable, they were altogether more whole. She did take her shoes back, covered in ash as they were. They fit better, and she relished the feel of walking with a bit of a lift on her heel again.

"Ready?" Linden asked.

"One last thing," she said, pausing just shy of the exit. "When we walk through those doors, I want us to be ourselves. No more confusion about who we are to each other or to everyone else." She held out her hand, offering the ring he'd given her. It was the only one of her personal effects not impacted by fire in one way or another. "I want to make a promise."

"A promise? What are we, twelve?" The laughter died in his throat as his eyes landed on the ring. "Ingrid, I—"

"I want to promise that even though we're over, we're also just beginning."

Linden cocked his head. "You mean, like, we can be friends?"

"I'd really like that, if we could be. I know we don't really know each other anymore, but I also feel like you know me best of anyone. I don't want to lose that."

"So we get to know each other." Linden nodded. "We don't

just end this and go our separate ways. We end it and . . . and we let something else take its place."

"Exactly."

"And you want that?"

"I really do," Ingrid said.

Linden took the ring and wrinkled his nose. "Friends, then."

"Friends," Ingrid agreed.

With a pang, she realized in this moment that Linden might be the only friend she had. None of her Meyers campaign colleagues had come to see her, so she'd no idea the status of those relationships. They might still hate her, for all she knew. But even so, Ingrid wished she could introduce them to Linden—Linden as he was now. They might detest one another, but it would have brought her joy to see what was left of the Holts become part of the Meyers team.

Linden led her down a narrow hall and back out into the entryway. There, as if somehow the universe had heard her, stood Alex and Charlotte, with Louise a surly shadow in their wake.

It was with torrential verbiage that Alex berated Officer Scott, whose brows had become singular in his frustration.

"We demand at once that you acquiesce to our request. We have every legal right to see her, and if you do not allow us through, I will have no choice but to—"

"Goodness," Ingrid said. "Don't threaten the poor man. He's only doing his job."

Officer Scott crossed his arms. "If you'd only let me finish, I was trying to tell you she was on her way out."

No one but Ingrid seemed to hear him, as she was engulfed immediately by Charlotte's arms.

"You're okay," she squealed. "I was trying to tell them, you

342

know, that you'd need medical care after—and they just kept brushing me off like I didn't matter, and— Oh! You must have heard! Gwendolyn Meyers is the president-elect. Obviously, she won by default, but the Senate affirmed her election anyway. Only a few senators abstained, and I think they'll be facing tough reelection campaigns as a result and—"

"Let her breathe, Charlotte," Alex said, peeling Charlotte off.

As Charlotte relinquished her grip, Ingrid searched Alex's eyes—looking for forgiveness or blame, just a hint of honesty in his gaze—but he wasn't looking at her. She followed the line of his sight, and her stomach curled in on itself.

"Ah, right." Ingrid cleared her throat. "Everyone, this is Linden. He, um . . ."

"Linden Holt," Alex said coldly. "Yes, we know who he is."

"You're not still with him, Ingrid," Charlotte muttered in a low but easily discernible voice.

"No, not anymore," Ingrid said loud enough for everyone to hear. "But you shouldn't hold that against him."

"Which? That he's not your beau anymore or that you were together in the first place?" Alex asked, an edge to his voice.

"Take your pick." Linden gave them all a little bow.

"He is not my mistakes," Ingrid added. "We still have a long fight to go, and now we're all on the same side, I hope you'll give him a chance to show you he's actually a very good person—better than me, at any rate."

"Is that supposed to be impressive?" Louise sneered at them both. "You set a very low bar."

"Ah, yes." Linden scuffed his boot against the floor. "It's not exactly *good* to see you but, I—uh—I'm terribly sorry for—"

"It sure is *something* to see you." Louise sniffed. "I promise not to light you on fire if you promise to stop being the worst."

Linden nodded. "I'll certainly do my best."

Alex linked up with Ingrid on one side, and Charlotte took the other. "We missed you."

"Come on," Charlotte said, pulling her to the door. "Come home."

And though she didn't say it aloud, Ingrid felt, sandwiched between Charlotte and Alex, she was already there.

CHAPTER THIRTY-SIX

Ingrid had never been one for procrastination, but as the weeks followed her miraculous ascent into notoriety, she found there were no longer enough hours in the day to accomplish all she wanted. Her time was filled with interviews with the press and depositions with lawyers. The case against the deceased Senator Holt was proceeding swimmingly, which was more than could be said for the case of asking her friends for forgiveness.

At long last, Ingrid scheduled herself a meeting with the former Meyers campaign staff, now current transition team, so she couldn't keep putting it off. It was a strange thing to return to the Meyers office as a guest rather than staff, but it was nice all the same. She wanted to see everyone again, even if they didn't want to see her. When she arrived, however, only one person was there.

Gwendolyn Meyers, dressed in a cream satin blouse and a rose capelet, sat alone at the long table in the center of the room, sipping from a pink patterned teacup. A matching cup and saucer rested in front of the chair beside her.

"Ingrid. Good of you to come," she said, standing when she caught sight of Ingrid.

Good didn't quite seem the word for it, but Ingrid wasn't about to argue. "Thank you for agreeing to see me."

Gwendolyn gestured for her to sit.

Ingrid sat.

Silence made a fist between them.

"I'm sorry," Ingrid blurted finally.

"Whatever for?" Gwendolyn raised her eyebrows over the top of her cup.

"You're joking, right?"

Gwendolyn set her cup back in its saucer. "If you're going to apologize, at least do it right. Where's the specificity?"

"I'm sorry for . . . everything, really. For lying to you, for risking your campaign to bail out Louise, and for any complications my actions after the fact caused you. I know I betrayed your trust, and I know that's not an easy thing to forgive. I'm doing my best now to be better than before. It might take a while, but I'll get there."

"You aren't going to pretend like you planned it all along? Defaming your former mentor in front of the entire Senate is no small thing to attempt." Gwendolyn eyed her, a softness to her gaze. "I won't pretend I wasn't impressed when you stood up in the Senate chambers to call him out. Impressed, and a little proud."

Ingrid tried not to smile but knew she must be glowing as bright as Senator Holt had just before he died. "I wish I could claim it was my intention all along, but I stumbled my way through it. If that article had never been printed and you never fired me, I can't be sure I wouldn't have betrayed you in the end. I hate that it took losing all this to realize how much it meant to me." She gestured at the room around them. But it wasn't the room. It was the people. They were her family, and she'd been ready to toss them aside.

"I can't offer you your job back, Ingrid." Gwendolyn reached for her hand atop the table and squeezed. "But I do forgive you."

"Thank you," Ingrid said quietly. "It's more than I deserve." She made to stand, but Gwendolyn didn't let go of her hand.

"I can't offer you your job back, because it doesn't exist anymore." She smiled kindly, gesturing for her to sit down again. "So let's talk about your future instead."

"My future?" Ingrid asked, returning to her seat.

"What is it you'd like to do."

Ingrid was reminded heavily of their first meeting on the train. Gwendolyn had asked her what she wanted, and Ingrid hadn't had a single clue. She felt much the same now as she cast about for an appropriate answer and landed on the inappropriate one instead. "Take a nap, maybe."

Gwendolyn chuckled. "You and me both."

"I think I'd like to continue with school. Get a law degree like you did."

"And what will you do with that law degree once you have it?"

"I don't know." Ingrid shrugged. "Is there any point in thinking that far ahead? A lot of things can change between now and then."

"That doesn't sound like the Ingrid I know."

"I don't think that girl exists anymore." Ingrid let a shockingly painful breath rattle through her. "I think we'll both have to get to know her all over again."

Understanding threaded its way through Gwendolyn's gaze. "Then let's ask a different question. What do you *want* to do?"

"With my law degree?" Ingrid asked with a dread-soaked voice. "I guess I *want* to find a way to change the world."

"So what do you want to do a year from now that will help to change the world?"

"I don't know, maybe something to do with your free-flare program," Ingrid said, thinking of Frances and the hollow shell of the orphanage. Frances deserved more than Ingrid had given her since she left, and so did the children who lived there now. "I'd like to see elections divorced from flare entirely, and a future where everyone can vote no matter how rich they are. Maybe I'll do something about that."

"And what do you want to do a week from now?"

"I want to visit my old home." The words came faster now. "I want to bring them Louise's formula for flare."

Gwendolyn smiled, a twinkle in her eye. "And what about tomorrow, Ingrid?"

Ingrid had an answer for that too, but it scared her so much more than any of the uncertainty.

Ingrid couldn't sleep that night. She knew what she had to do in order to move beyond this strange state of in between—housed just after knowing who she was, but before she was ready to be her. Now she was ready to step into her own shoes and walk into the world authentically as herself, unashamed of where she'd come from and not knowing where she'd go. But she had one last question to ask, and she couldn't be the one to answer. For that, she needed Alex.

She crept out of bed and made her way to the former Meyers campaign office well before the sun rose. If she couldn't get any rest, she could at least get a head start on coffee before Alex arrived at the office. Ingrid let herself in, not bothering to light the lamps, as her eyes were already adjusted to the dark. Before long, the sweet smell of hot coffee filled the air, and she was well on her way to a productive morning. She poured herself a cup and made her way around the large center table toward the desk on the opposite wall that was now hers once again.

"What are you doing?"

Ingrid yelped and dropped her mug, spilling coffee down her front.

A shadowed form rose from the chaise and moved toward her into the soft moonlight spilling in from the window. A very disgruntled-looking Alex stood before her, sleep beneath his eyes.

"It's the middle of the night, Ingrid. Why aren't you asleep?"

"Why aren't you?" Ingrid shot back, spluttering.

"I was *trying*!" He gestured to the chaise, blankets heaped in a pile at the end.

"Yes, well, I was—I was—" Ingrid struggled to craft a retort. Instead, she stomped across the room to light one of the lamps. There was no point arguing in the dark. She regretted it almost immediately, as the coffee stain down her blouse was much more prominent than it had been in the dark. "I was nervous."

Alex put his head in his hands. "So you decided the best thing for your anxiety was a jolt of caffeine?" He sighed and stumbled over to a chair. "At least make some for me too."

Ingrid nodded a bit too much, then busied herself with the kettle. When she was done, she did her best to carry both mugs to the center table without shaking, though she did slosh a bit of coffee over the side onto her hand. The skin smarted terribly, but she'd been burned far worse in recent memory.

Alex lifted the mug to his lips, and, as though his speech was activated by the taste of coffee itself, he said, "Wait, why are you nervous?"

Ingrid's cheeks burned, and she shook her head. "It's not—I—no reason at all, I just—"

Alex reached for her shoulder and looked her squarely in the eyes. "It is too early in the morning for obfuscation." Then he shook himself a little and added, "And also for the word *obfuscation*."

"Sorry, it's just that I have so much to say."

Alex sipped his coffee, surveying her over his mug.

She mimicked him.

"So," he said pointedly.

"Yeah."

"You said you had lots to say?"

"Right."

"Ingrid, I swear, if you woke me up just to stare into space . . ."

"Sorry!" Ingrid set her mug down. "Sorry."

"You don't have to apologize, just—" He gestured for her to get on with it.

"That's it—that's the first thing anyway. I know I did a lot of bad things for a lot of bad reasons, and I think I hurt you."

"Course you did." Alex shrugged. "We've been over this, though. I know you're sorry. I don't need you to do some sort of formal apology."

Ingrid let out a long breath, shaking her head. There was a pain to his acceptance. It felt rushed and contrived, like he was using it to hold her at a distance. "I don't know how to say this exactly, but I mean it differently than that. I know there's the fact that I betrayed the team, and I own up to that, but there's something more. I betrayed *you*, and that's not the same. It's separate. I don't want to act like it's not."

Alex tensed, and she knew she'd hit the heart of it.

"You invested in me, Alex. You saw something in me from the

beginning, and you bet on me. You taught me what you knew, and I used that against you. That wasn't fair, and it wasn't okay. I don't want you to think I don't know that this is personal."

Alex stood and walked around the table, trailing his hand along the wood. "Course it's personal."

Ingrid rose as well and tried to catch his eye. She needed to see what he was feeling, but he wouldn't look at her. If he wouldn't say it, she would. "It's personal because you mean something to me, Alex. You mean something, and it's a different something than everyone else."

Alex froze, still turned away with his hand touching the table like a waypoint. "How do you mean?" His voice was low and crackly.

Ingrid made her way around the table until she was only a few feet away. "I don't know," she whispered. "But you do. It's not . . . I don't know how to define it. But I think you know what I mean, because I think I mean something to you too."

He didn't turn around, but neither did he deny it, so she carried on.

"Alex, I don't know what I'm saying, but I'm going to say it and hope you understand it better than I do. You make me feel like I can do anything, and you make me feel like I *should*. You don't just make me want to be better; you make me feel like I'm already better. It's like you see some part of me other people don't, and you know exactly how to bring that out in me. Working with you has taught me so much about the kinds of things I care about and how to care about them in a meaningful way, and I think what I mean is that you're one of those things. I care about you, and I want that to be meaningful."

He turned around then, his brows furrowed, a frown bone deep in his face. "You mean you want to be friends. Ingrid, I—"

"No, well, yes. I want to be friends. Being friends with you is one of my favorite things." A smile snuck onto her face. "But I want to be something else too."

"What's that?" he asked, a hollow echo to his voice as though it came from deep within him, equal parts fear and hope.

Ingrid took his hand between both of hers and looked him in the eye. "I want to know you'll be there to tell me when I'm wrong just as often as you tell me I'm right. I want to learn enough to teach you as much as you teach me." She gestured to their desks against the wall. "And I don't want to sit side by side while we both work on our own lives in solitude. I want to work on both together, like they're one project."

"You mean—"

"I mean, I love you, Alex Castille. And I love you in a way I didn't know I could. It isn't like with Linden—it isn't romantic, it isn't physical, but it's still so much, so, *so* much." Overcome with the feeling, and afraid she'd said it all wrong, Ingrid tried to step back, but Alex held her fast, his hand gripping hers tight.

"You—you love me."

"You told me once love didn't have to be just one thing," Ingrid said, her eyes flicking to the chaise where they'd once talked in the dark and he'd told her that love was love and she'd believed him. "And I just thought . . . I thought you should know."

Alex stepped toward her and took her chin in his hands. He met her gaze with smiling brown eyes. "Yes, but now that I know, what shall I do with this knowledge?" He lifted his hand, fingers grouped together, toward the sky. "For knowledge is power, and you have made me powerfu—"

"Alex!"

"Right. Sorry." He returned his gaze to hers and grinned. "I love you too." He wrapped his arms around her and drew her close.

She leaned in, letting her eyes fall closed as he rested his chin on her head.

"So," Alex said after a time. "What would you call this . . . ? You're not my girl. I hate that kind of language anyway, and I swear if you call me your *beau* I will chuck you out the window."

"I promise, I won't." Ingrid smiled against his shoulder. "What do you think of . . . partner?"

"Partner," Alex repeated, nodding against the top of her head. "I like it."

"Partners, it is." Ingrid pulled back, sporting a grin brighter than the sunrise making its way over the skyline.

"Shall we?" Alex gestured toward their twin desks in the corner.

Hand in hand, they crossed the room to begin their work together.

EPILOGUE

On the morning of inauguration, Ingrid and the rest of the staff—a smiley bunch, much to Ingrid's surprise, considering it was Birdie who'd hired most of them—gathered together in the campaign's capital office, which they'd soon be giving up in favor of more prestigious property. Someone had poured a round of celebratory flare, passing it around in crystal champagne flutes.

Ingrid longed to be among them.

"Can't we go inside now?" Ingrid whined.

"Not yet!" Alex looped his arm through hers and grinned. "There's a surprise coming, and I don't want you to miss it."

"Meanwhile, we're missing *that*." Ingrid pointed inside just as the crowd erupted with cheers.

"Not important." Alex shrugged.

"How do you know? We can't even hear what they're saying."

Alex considered. "Well, not as important as *this*."

Ingrid narrowed her eyes. "Seriously, Alex."

"Seriously!" He pointed toward the street, an enormous grin on his face.

There, making his way up the street, was the echo of a man she knew. She'd forgotten, somehow, in the years that sundered them, how tall her father could be when he stood upright. It was as though prison had weighed his shoulder down, forcing him to be smaller than he was, but now, dressed in what was clearly a brand-new suit, he looked a man she did not entirely know.

"Papa!" The word broke from her, cracked and wounded.

He smiled, the lines around his eyes creasing.

She ran to him, unable to restrain herself, but as she drew close, she slowed and stopped. They'd not been together without a table between them in seven years. Their interactions had all been overseen by rules and an officer, not free to say what they pleased or touch without reprimand. Now there was no one to tell them what not to do. Only air, only time, stood between them.

Arms shaking, Ingrid reached for him, slowly at first. Unsure how to do it after seven years of mirroring affection. She drew her arms back. What if he didn't want her to touch him? What if he wasn't ready? It didn't matter how ready she was to fall into his embrace if he wasn't ready to catch her.

Instead, Ingrid raised her hands and wrapped them around herself, hesitantly catching his eye. She hoped he understood.

"No, Dewdrop," he said. "Not anymore." And he took her in his arms like it was habit, like it was natural, like he'd never forgotten what it was to want to hold her.

She tried not to crumble in his grasp, but she was unused to his touch. For a moment, she was ten years old again, so small and so young. Then she'd thought her papa was everything. He was the world and the world was him. She'd known nothing of what lay beyond until he'd been snatched from her, and then she'd filled in the place where he'd been to make herself feel whole again. Now she knew he was not the world, but she knew too that he was part of hers, and she never wanted to lose him again.

"When did you get so big?" he whispered into her hair.

Ingrid smiled and pulled back a little, finding the voice on her tongue belonged to the girl she'd been before he'd left. "I've always been big, Papa. You were just bigger."

He laughed and ruffled her hair, measuring the top of her head against his frame.

"The judge agreed to parole him early, thanks to Clarence's expert lawyering," Alex said, descending a few steps.

Shortly after Ingrid had been released from prison, Alex had cajoled the more sympathetic members of the Meyers campaign into taking on Ingrid's father's case. He'd said something about precedent and good behavior, and she'd completely stopped listening by the time he started rambling about prison as a penalty for being poor. She'd been too full of gratitude to really hear him, or at least that was the excuse she'd given.

"This is Alex." Ingrid gestured to him with her head, afraid if she let go of her father he would vanish.

"We've met, actually. Alex was good enough to get me this suit. Said I deserved to wear something new my first day back in the world." Her father grinned, pointing out the neatly creased pants and the slim tie he wore. "He said you're something of a fashion expert, so it was extra important, since all my old clothes would be out of style. I've never had anything this nice before, you know."

"Would you like a drink, Mr. Ellis?" Alex asked, pointing inside at a tray full of champagne flutes.

"Oscar, please!" He clapped Alex on the shoulder, then leaned in to whisper in Ingrid's ear, "That partner of yours is a good one. I like him," before making his way inside.

"Good surprise?" Alex asked.

All Ingrid could do was nod, tears threatening to break free.

"There you two are!" Charlotte's head popped around the doorway. "Come on, you'll miss the toast!"

The *Candesce Courant* had offered Charlotte a staff writer position and a front-page spot for her exclusive "Inside the Inauguration" piece. Nearly every paper in Candesce wanted her after her article on the "Holt meltdown," as she'd called it. "Better than *A Season for Treason*," she'd tell anyone who so much as looked at her funny.

"I thought we already missed it," Ingrid said, leading the way inside.

"Not *our* toast." Charlotte handed them each a glass. "Wait, we're missing one. Louise!" She waved at the other girl, who had her head bent deep in conversation with none other than Birdie.

With considerable effort, Charlotte dragged Louise away, and Birdie rejoined the others on their way out the door, muttering under her breath, "Weirdos."

"I thought she hated you," Alex said.

Louise just shrugged. "We have a lot in common."

"Like what, being impossible?" Ingrid made a face.

"Like finding your questions annoying."

"Oh, come on!" Charlotte huffed. "Can't you give it a rest? It's toast time!"

They all raised their glasses and waited for someone to say something toast worthy.

"Charlotte," Ingrid said after a few moments. "Did you gather us for a toast and then not actually have a toast planned?"

"I'm not a speechwriter!" She threw her hand in the air.

Ingrid shook her head, laughing, then turned to Alex, who'd been promoted as part of the transition. "Well, then, speechwriter?"

Alex looked stricken. "I didn't prepare anything. If I'd known,

I could have—can you give me a few minutes? Oh no, I don't have a pen."

Ingrid sighed and turned back to the group, looking at them each in turn, the faces of friendship. What could she say that would mean everything she felt? What could she say that would not take hours upon hours to craft into a perfect sound bite?

Finally, she raised her glass and said simply, "To us."

They all laughed, but they raised their glasses and repeated after her.

Ingrid drank, letting magic run through her for the first time since she'd faced Holt. Her friends pulled her forward after the rest of the bigger and better Team Meyers on their way to usher in a new president, and Ingrid set her glass down on the porch, leaving it nearly full. Magic made her feel tired and tormented. It was a shadow of a flame dancing to the hypnotic rhythm of money, and Ingrid didn't need it to feel powerful. Not anymore.

As she made her way outside and down the street, Ingrid felt the flare leave her body, little golden stars shooting from her fingertips. And as it did, she felt no less powerful, because power wasn't about who she could tear down in a ruin of flame. It was about who she could lift up, and she didn't need magic to do that.

She took Alex and Charlotte by the hand and, with an aggrieved Louise tailing them, broke into a run, laughter on their breath, hope in their chests. The flutter in her veins was a little bit friendship, a little bit family, and a little bit future, and she knew this feeling was more powerful than any magic.

ACKNOWLEDGMENTS

I wrote and revised the majority of this book during a year of isolation, but I was never alone. I am endlessly grateful for the support of my community, my publishing team, and my readers.

First, to my incredible agent, Saba Sulaiman, who saw the potential for this book from just a single-sentence pitch. I would never have admitted it at the time, but I secretly hoped you'd like this idea the most. Thank you for saying yes even before this idea felt real.

This book would not be what it is today without the brilliant guidance of my editor, Orlando Dos Reis. Thank you for somehow always knowing what I'm trying to do, even when I don't. Thank you also to Jacey and Yaffa Jaskoll for the *beautiful* cover. I am so lucky! And to my fabulous team at Scholastic, including Janell Harris, Jackie Hornberger, Priscilla Eakeley, Jessica White, Zachary Brown, and Elisabeth Ferrari.

Eternal thanks to Linsey Miller, whose mentorship and friendship were instrumental in the writing of this book; Jenny Howe, whose enthusiasm for this project from the very beginning has meant the world to me; Emily Lloyd-Jones, I would not have written this book without your encouragement so many moons ago;

Rachel Griffin, without whom this book would lack my favorite Alex moment—you are a guiding light in this book-writing storm; and Kalyn Josephson, whose camaraderie and kindness got me to the finish line. You're all stars. To my early readers, Sarah Harrington, Emily Grey, Kat Hillis—thank you for your insight and most importantly for scolding me when I needed it. And thank you to Kieron Scullington and Idris Grey for your invaluable feedback.

To my relentlessly cool friends, I love you all: Faye, April, Mandy, Dante, Stephen, and Lance. Claire, this one's for you. Thank you for always pushing me to question things in ways that make me grow, and thank you for growing along with me. Thank you to Elizabeth, who heard me talk about this book more than probably anyone else, and to Colleen, who lived through this entire process with me. What a time it has been. Thank you to my parents, who, unlike many of the parents in my books, absolutely rock. Your example as successful creatives keeps me going.

And thank you most especially to Tess, who is perfect, and Jane, who is *purr*fect.

ABOUT THE AUTHOR

Author photo by Lens of Lakhani

Rosiee Thor began her career as a storyteller by demanding to tell her mother bedtime stories instead of the other way around. She spent her childhood reading by flashlight in the closet until she came out as queer. She lives in Oregon with a dog, a cat, and an abundance of plants. She is the author of the young adult novel *Tarnished Are the Stars*.